The Earl of Monquefort stood patiently and waited for an opening in the conversation.

"Miss Wentworth, I do hope you remember me," he began.

Olivia was quick to respond. "Of course we do, Lord Monquefort."

"Please, let me introduce you to a friend of mine who is most anxious to make your acquaintance."

Olivia's eyes shifted away from the earl to take in the gentleman standing next to him. The sight of the darkly handsome Marquis of Traverston shocked her speechless.

The marquis took Olivia's hand and held on to it for just a little longer than polite society would dictate as proper, before smiling into her pale blue eyes and making his own introduction.

"Your husband, I believe."

Olivia's famed cool gaze gave out with a vengeance. Without a word she crumpled slowly to the floor.

Dear Reader,

Every year at this time, the editors at Harlequin Historicals have the unique opportunity of introducing our readers to four brand-new authors in our annual March Madness Promotion. These titles were chosen from among hundreds of manuscripts from unpublished authors, and we would like to take this time to thank all of the talented authors who made the effort to submit their projects to Harlequin Historicals for review.

Among this year's choices for the month is a Regency novel by Susan Schonberg, *The Phoenix of Love,* the story of a reformed rake and a society ice princess who must come to terms with their marriage of convenience, overcome their tortured pasts and defeat their present enemies before they are free to love. *The Wicked Truth* by Lyn Stone was a second-place finisher in the 1995 Maggie Awards. It's the story of a woman with a ruined reputation and a straitlaced physician who join forces to discover a murderer in Victorian England.

The two remaining titles for the month are *Heart of the Dragon* by Sharon Schulze, the medieval tale of a young woman searching for her identity with the help of a fierce warrior, and *Emily's Captain* by Shari Anton, a story about a heroine whose father sends a dashing Union spy to get her safely out of Georgia against her wishes.

Whatever your taste in reading, we hope you'll find a story written just for you between the covers of a Harlequin Historical.

Sincerely,

Tracy Farrell
Senior Editor

Please address questions and book requests to:
Harlequin Reader Service
U.S.: 3010 Walden Ave., P.O. Box 1325, Buffalo, NY 14269
Canadian: P.O. Box 609, Fort Erie, Ont. L2A 5X3

The Phoenix of Love

Susan Schonberg

Harlequin Books

TORONTO • NEW YORK • LONDON
AMSTERDAM • PARIS • SYDNEY • HAMBURG
STOCKHOLM • ATHENS • TOKYO • MILAN
MADRID • WARSAW • BUDAPEST • AUCKLAND

ISBN 0-373-28955-3

THE PHOENIX OF LOVE

SUSAN SCHONBERG

As a ninth-grade English project, Susan Schonberg rewrote *Romeo and Juliet* as a spoof (for which she received an A). From that time forward, she knew she wanted to write novels—specifically romance, which has always been her favorite category. Her professional writing career begins with this book, *The Phoenix of Love*. When Susan is not writing, she works alongside her husband, Stan, as a financial analyst for the Clorox Company in the San Francisco Bay area.

To the Riley women—Sue, Meghan and Erin—
for always knowing that this would be published.

Chapter One

Norwood Park, Surrey 1808

"Dammit, man!" exclaimed the marquis. "You must be mistaken!"

John Richard Markston, the fourth Marquis of Traverston, paced the worn carpet of his library floor. One hand moved distractedly through his raven black hair, standing the none-too-clean strands up and then immediately smoothing them down again. His gray eyes, colored at the moment like some dark forbidding sky before a storm, looked about him with a restlessness that betrayed his inner feelings all too well.

He felt trapped.

The marquis had once been a handsome man. There were few who could contradict that. But the dandies and bits of muslin he had once taken as companions back in his younger days would be hard-pressed to recognize him now. It wasn't just the blue-black shadow across his jaw and neck, silent testimony to his recent self-neglect, but the rest of his appearance, as well. Proud shoulders now slightly stooped over with hunger, tattered clothing that hadn't been patched in years and the black shadows under his eyes all spoke of years spent in self-destruction.

The solicitor, Mr. Babcock, was at first incredulous to think that the bitter man pacing in front of him was really the marquis. He had come to know the marquis's maternal grandfather rather well over the last few years of that gentleman's life, and it shocked the lawyer to finally make the acquaintance of the notorious grandson. Of course, he had heard stories about Traverston, but he hadn't realized how little they were exaggerated until he saw the man for himself.

Looking around the library now, Mr. Babcock thought that the room showed about as much abuse as the nobleman himself. The solicitor guessed that it had been months since the fireplace had been used, and probably much longer since it had been swept. The furniture, what few moth-eaten remains of it there were, looked every second of its age. Indeed, Mr. Babcock would not have attempted to seat himself in this room, even if he had been asked, which he had not, for fear of inflicting undue hardship on his carefully groomed person.

The small portly man measured his reply to the marquis before finally giving it in as soothing a tone as possible. He did not want to agitate his client any more than he was already. There was no telling what the madman was capable of. Not too many years ago, hadn't there been some tale about the marquis in connection with a young girl who had gone missing? He shuddered and forced himself to go on.

"Be assured, my lord," he responded in a bland, colorless tone of voice as he took off his spectacles and gave them a thorough rub with his handkerchief. He took his time cleaning the lenses before replacing them on his nose. "There is no mistake. Your grandfather's will clearly states that you are to inherit five hundred thousand pounds upon his death, provided that you are married."

The solicitor put his arms behind his back, unconsciously spreading both feet out slightly in order to look more authoritative. "In the event that his death finds you unmarried..." he paused, wrinkling his nose at the marquis's surroundings in order to indicate that he gathered this was the case "...then you have exactly two weeks to remedy the situation before the entire fortune goes to your cousin, David Hamilton."

Traverston's look was thunderous. A more perceptive man would have immediately left the room after delivering such a speech, but sadly, Mr. Babcock was not noted for his powers of observation. Therefore it was a great shock for the solicitor to find himself lifted some foot above the ground with his feet dangling in the air and the marquis's enraged visage just inches from his own.

"My good sir," Traverston muttered between clenched teeth. "I suspect that you have failed to look for *some alternative*, some loophole," he said, emphasizing the last words with a little shake, "in as complete a manner as possible. Might I suggest," he growled, indicating that it was not really a suggestion, "you do so now."

Believing he need make his request no clearer, the marquis dropped the solicitor. With a speed incredible for one of his ungainly bodily proportions, Mr. Babcock raced to the other end of the room. Belatedly comprehending his error, he attempted to straighten his clothes and his dignity while keeping a wary eye on his aggressor.

"My lord," he cooed even as he smoothed his person, "I fail to understand." At the marquis's intensified frown, Mr. Babcock began to sputter, all of his lawyerly aplomb completely forgotten. "I mean...forgive me, my lord, it's just that with this hovel, I thought you would be happy to..."

Mr. Babcock broke off, his hands held out in front of him to ward off the marquis's impending attack as the nobleman began to stalk him. But Traverston stopped just short of his quaking visitor.

"My dear Mr. Babcock," Traverston growled, "it is not your job to understand my motives." His eyes seemed to shoot plumes of fire straight through the heart of the man cowering before him. "I pray you remember that in the future!"

Mr. Babcock gulped audibly. "Yes, my lord."

Turning his back on the lawyer, Traverston walked over to the fireplace. It was an action Mr. Babcock divined was born of habit as there was no heat to be gained there now. Lost in thought, Traverston took his time before addressing the solicitor again. When he finally did, all trace of his former antipathy was gone, leaving in its wake what appeared to be a hint of the former cool and regal marquis.

His shoulders back and his manner direct, Traverston said, "Return here at eight o'clock tomorrow morning. I will expect a full report on your progress at that time."

"Yes, my lord," groveled Mr. Babcock. He turned around and headed for the door, his host making no effort to show him out. Still he hesitated before opening the great double doors that would take him to the hall and ultimately out of the accursed house. Turning around to face the marquis once more, he opened his mouth in a final inquiry. Then, remembering what had happened the last time he had dared to question matters, he thought better of what he was about to say and immediately returned to the doors in order to resume his previous course out of the house. Two minutes later, the solicitor started to breathe easier as a hired post chaise drove him away from Norwood Park.

As Traverston listened to the clip of the retreating horses' hooves, he sank into the only usable armchair left in the library and acknowledged the weariness he was feeling. At eight and twenty, he knew he was too young to feel this tired, but he was exhausted all the same.

He closed his eyes and leaned his head back against the cracking red leather upholstery, trying to wipe his mind clean of all thought. He clenched his hands and released them, willing the tension his solicitor's visit had caused to leave his body. He took several deep breaths. He thought of blankness and dark, empty fields. He rolled his shoulders and settled more deeply into the chair.

It wasn't working. His body still felt like a tightly coiled spring. Without opening his eyes, he fumbled for the decanter of brandy he always kept handy by the chair. Keeping his eyelids closed, he poured himself a glass of the fiery cheap liquid, miraculously not spilling a drop. He winced in pleasured pain with the first gulp, his muscles relaxing just a fraction. With another two swigs, he emptied the glass, his free hand automatically reaching for the decanter.

Four glasses was the absolute minimum required for Traverston to reach the mind-numbing state he was seeking at the moment. Unsurprisingly he had plenty of time for reflection until he got there.

After several more hearty swigs from the grimy glass, Traverston cracked open his eyes and glanced around the room. With something akin to surprise, he noticed for the first time in several years what had happened to his surroundings.

The library was filthy. Cobwebs hung from the top of the bookcases to the corners of the ceiling. Dust a quarter of an inch thick covered most surfaces up out of the marquis's immediate reach, and it only thinned to an eighth of an inch further down. The rug was torn and smeared with something that looked like lard, and the mirror over the fireplace was so tarnished, it was impossible to get a clear look at what it reflected. Great threadbare and rotting husks of velvet hung at odd angles from the tall windows on the far side of the room.

In short, the library was a disaster area.

No doubt Mr. Babcock had been horrified at the room's condition when the marquis had led him here. For some reason that thought pleased Traverston, and he smiled a little even as he took another drink.

Slowly he got up from the chair and poured himself another glass. Without consciously meaning to, he walked over to his only remaining possessions of any value, the books lining the walls of the room. Despite all of his other attempts to strip the house over the years, the marquis was unwilling to part with his books. Books, as well as drinking brandy from a glass, were the only remnants of a gentleman's life that he had allowed himself to keep. He didn't even own a horse anymore.

Tiredly his eyes sought a place of rest among the busy shelves, and so he began browsing through the titles. Poetry he mentally shrugged off without even pausing to absorb the titles. Shakespeare flickered into the corner of his vision and then immediately skittered out again. And then he was there. Among the great literary titles he saw a small collection of books. His eyes absorbed fairy-tale titles and, without meaning to, Traverston began to reflect on his childhood.

No one could have called his early days happy, but before his mother died, there had been some good times. His fingers wandered over the leather book covers, stopping on the gold stamped title of *Robinson Crusoe*. Just for a moment, Traverston could feel the gentle touch of his mother's hand on his brow and he closed his eyes, lingering over the remembered sensation. Frowning, concentrating, he cast his mind back...and—ah! It was there—her soft, delicate voice, reading to him by the last light of sunset.

Physically shaking his head clear of such thoughts, the

marquis dragged his limbs back to the decanter and poured himself another drink. Hoping to break his suddenly maudlin mood, he walked over to one of the long windows and pulled back its dusty drape, the tattered soft material long since faded from its original forest green. The action scattered a few spiderwebs and created a dust cloud, but the marquis stood his ground. He felt desperately in need of some sunlight.

Staring through the filthy panes, Traverston felt numbed by the sight of the mansion's grounds. For some reason he didn't understand, the grass outside the window was waist high and the garden overgrown with weeds. Directly outside the window, a rosebush seemed determined to choke out all available sunlight defiantly filtering through the leaves.

With another shake of his head, Traverston's memory came back. Of course. He himself had neglected these grounds for years. Why was the sight of them now such a shock?

As he stared down into his brandy glass, he wondered how he had let himself come to such a pass. He had been bent on self-destruction, it was true. But was this sorry state really what he had planned so many years ago?

With a sudden movement so quick it surprised him, Traverston pulled back his arm and threw his glass across the room. The glass exploded into a thousand shards in the fireplace. No! In his mind the thought was so loud, so sudden, it was almost as if someone had shouted the word.

A few seconds later, Traverston realized that he had indeed spoken aloud. *No.* This was no answer. Killing himself and destroying his family's estate and heritage had seemed the perfect solution to his problems five years ago, but now Traverston knew he couldn't finish what he had started. Who could in light of this second chance at life?

The marquis laughed aloud, the bitter sound ceasing on a curse. "Damn you, you bastard!" he shouted to the empty room. "Why couldn't you have left me alone?"

Gateland Manor, as the house was optimistically called by its occupants, was a shambling estate that marched alongside the Marquis of Traverston's own home, Norwood Park. Locally the saying went that the two houses were like two generations of humanity—parent and child—where the fruit had fallen not far from the tree. Norwood Park was the run-down father, while Gateland Manor was the shabby, good-for-nothing offspring.

Riding up on a borrowed nag to the front door of the smaller house now, Traverston was pleased to note that the rumors were true. Gateland Manor appeared to be in no better condition than his own estate. Peeling white paint decorated the once pristine columns on the Queen Anne–styled home. The red brick walls, while engaging from a distance with their aged and mellow beauty, were covered almost completely with ivy, and where the bricks could be seen at all, they were crumbling and falling apart.

Traverston smiled to himself. The state of the house's interior, if it were anything at all like the exterior, would bode well for him. The marquis needed Gateland Manor's owner to be in dire need of funds if he was going to win his objective this day.

The door of the manor was answered by an old man so bent over with arthritis that he could hardly look up into the face of the visitor. The ancient's appearance was neat but threadbare, his black and gold livery was antiquated. But even so, the servant appeared to take great pride in the uniform.

When no greeting seemed to be forthcoming from this relic of humanity, Traverston took it upon himself to take the initiative. "If you would be so kind, my good man," he commanded, adjusting his tone to a shout, "please inform Mr. Wentworth that the Marquis of Traverston would like an interview with him."

It was a few moments before the man replied. When he did, the sound was so much like a groan, Traverston didn't have a clue as to his reply. It was only when he saw the old man shuffle away, leaving the door open behind him, that he decided it would be best to follow.

After what seemed to Traverston an interminable amount of time, the butler finally led him to a huge pair of double doors. It was another few moments before the marquis realized that he was expected to open the doors, the servant not having the required strength to do so.

As it turned out, the doors led into the manor's library. This surprised Traverston as he had thought he would be shown into a parlor to await his host. Then realizing that, like Norwood Park, the library was probably the best room in the house, the marquis made his way over to the fireplace, silently gloating over the fact that Mr. Wentworth's penury was indeed as bad as his own.

The library doors closed with a loud boom, alerting Traverston to the fact that he had been left alone. Using this opportunity to thoroughly study his surroundings, the marquis looked over his host's library. What he saw there only confirmed his earlier suspicion that Wentworth was operating on a constrained budget.

The room, while large, was almost devoid of furniture. A few battered-looking but comfortable armchairs adorned the room, along with three tables and one sofa. Books were scattered throughout the many shelves on the walls, and the marquis noted with mild interest that Wentworth owned almost as many of them as he did. Apparently the man had some scholarly inclinations.

The one clear advantage Gateland Manor did have over Norwood Park, however, was its relative cleanliness. Here, unlike in his ancestral home, there were no cobwebs of astronomical dimensions hanging from the ceiling, nor was there a blanket of dust coating everything within sight. In addition, there was a small but cheery fire roaring away in the tidy fireplace at one end of the room.

Resisting the urge to grind his teeth at the unfavorable comparison his own home made with the manor house, Traverston was just about to stride to the fire to warm his chilled bones when the doors opened behind him to admit his host. Mr. Wentworth, a middle-aged man of somewhat portly dimensions, hesitated only slightly before stepping into the room. He took his time closing the doors behind him, much as if he were collecting his thoughts. When he turned to face the marquis, his countenance was unexpectedly grim.

Wentworth studied Traverston as he hesitated again. Finally he walked over to the peer with his hand stretched out before him. "My lord, this is a surprise." He shook the marquis's hand gravely before continuing. "It has been a long time since this house has been *honored* by your presence."

The meaning of the slight stress Wentworth put on the word *honor* was not lost on Traverston. He had no doubt that a neighbor as close as Wentworth would have heard of his less than honorable escapades over the past several years. But the marquis decided to ignore the slight, at least to all outward appearances. He smiled a smile that did not reach his eyes and replied with passing civility, "A long time indeed."

Wentworth studied his guest carefully, weighing the advisability of having a private conversation with a man whose reputation did not bear close scrutiny. Finally he made up his mind. "Pray be seated, my lord."

"Thank you, but I prefer to stand."

After one final piercing stare, Wentworth shrugged his shoulders and walked over to a bellpull in the corner of the room. He yanked the rope several times before turning around and walking back toward his guest. Settling his bulk comfortably in one of the armchairs he had indicated earlier, Wentworth waited for the marquis to explain his presence.

Misinterpreting Traverston's continued silence, Wentworth finally spoke. "I'm afraid it takes old Bentley awhile to answer my summons. If he even hears it at all, that is. Past retirement age, you know," he apologized with an embarrassed air. "He would do better at home, but I haven't got the blunt to pension him off."

Traverston was momentarily taken aback. He hadn't expected his neighbor to be as open as he was about his lack of funds, but there it was. Wentworth's confession gave him the perfect opening, if he were but to seize the opportunity.

Before Traverston could form a suitable reply, however, the servant Wentworth had identified as Bentley opened the library doors. The decanter of brandy and two glasses he carried on the tarnished silver tray seemed to weigh him down and slow his pace even more than before. He made his shuffling way across the room, set the tray down on the table near his master, poured out two glasses of brandy for the gentlemen, handed the glasses around and made his pathetic trek back across the room. The whole process took about five minutes, but watching him, the marquis was sure it had taken twice as long.

With the servant's delay, Traverston had time to make up his mind on how best to obtain his host's cooperation. He could, if he were that sort of man, couch his offer in all sorts of flowery terms and euphemisms. Or, if he were the gambling sort, he could lie to Wentworth and say that he had fallen in love with his daughter after seeing her from a distance one day. That approach, however, was decidedly risky. Not only did he not have the least notion as to what his host's daughter looked like, but he doubted that anyone would believe for a moment that the marquis was the kind of man to fall in love, let alone from a distance. He dismissed that option almost immediately. In the end, he decided that there was really only one choice. He would have to be truthful, at least partially so, and pray that Wentworth's greed would overcome any sense of responsibility or feeling of affection he might have for his daughter.

With the doors once again secure, Traverston went neck or nothing to the point. "How would you like to be able to pension 'old Bentley' off, Mr. Wentworth?"

Wentworth's eyes grew twice in size. "I b-beg your pardon?" he stuttered. "What did you say?"

Holding his impatience in check, Traverston repeated his question once more. "I said, how would you like to be able to pension off your retainer? As well as any other antique examples of humanity that might be lurking around your residence? I haven't seen any others, but surely there are one or two."

Wentworth blinked several times, appearing for all the world like a confused owl. Warily he sat more erect in his chair, a spot of color appearing on both cheeks. "My lord," he responded through stiff lips, "I must ask that you explain yourself."

In a fit of agitation now that the moment was upon him, Traverston took a sip from his glass, hoping to stall for time. Fleetingly, somewhere in the back of his brain, he decided that the refreshment was much better than his own swill he kept at home. Without realizing he was doing so, Traverston began pacing the room. So much rested on Wentworth's acceptance of his proposal. What if he didn't accept it? Should he then go solicit all of the neighborhood farmers for their daughters? Pretty soon word would get around of Traverston's mission, and if doors weren't slammed in his face, then he would be the laughingstock of the town. No, he must succeed the first time. This time.

In midstride, he ceased his pacing. Setting his glass down on a nearby table, he came forward to stand in front of his host. He grasped his hands behind his back, spread his legs into a wide stance and squarely eyed the man seated before him. Bluntly he came to the point. "Sir, I would ask for the hand of your daughter in marriage."

Silence. For long seconds, Wentworth's eyes slowly bulged from his head. Alarmed, the marquis rushed forward to pound his host on the back, but Wentworth managed to wave him away before he could get started. Still it was a moment before Wentworth could find the breath to gasp, "My lord, you must be joking!"

The marquis was quick to fortify his position. He leaned down into his face so that he could look the other straight in the eye as he replied with deadly earnestness, "I assure you, my good sir, I am not."

Wentworth had just managed to summon the trace of a smile at his guest's perceived joke when the marquis's answer managed to wipe it clean off his face. As the horrifying truth set in that his visitor really did mean what he said, the color in Wentworth's face leeched out of him by degrees. After what seemed to both men an interminable amount of time, Wentworth made a feeble attempt to brush the marquis aside. Traverston, perceiving his host's need for some kind of action, stepped back and allowed the man to face his opponent on his feet.

Gaining his feet allowed Wentworth some measure of his old confidence, and he gathered enough bruised dignity to face the marquis squarely. "I fail to see how this cannot be a leveler, my lord," he responded with scorn. "Olivia is but ten years old."

"I beg your pardon, sir," Traverston apologized, genuinely confused. "I could have sworn that your daughter was at least eighteen by now."

As comprehension dawned on Wentworth, his hostility faded away. "Ah," he breathed softly, "that explains it then." Walking away from the marquis to look out one of the library windows, Wentworth continued speaking with his back turned to his guest, as if his words were more for himself than the marquis. "Of course, being out of local society for so long you could not have known." He reached up to scratch his jaw through his graying beard.

"Margaret," he said, turning back around, "whom I presume you meant to ask for, died in a riding accident not three years ago." He walked over to the brandy decanter and topped off his glass before continuing. "She tried to take an old nag over a jump. The horse balked and threw her over the fence, snapping her neck on impact." He stopped and stared down into the glass before continuing. "It was my fault, really. I was never very good about restraining her wilder impulses. And I never should have allowed her to take out Fancy that day." His final words were almost lost in his glass. "She was a bonny lass."

As Wentworth became oblivious to the passing minutes, Traverston used the brief interlude in the conversation to think. The daughter he had planned to marry was dead. So what now? But didn't Wentworth say he had another?

Waiting an appropriate interval before speaking, Traverston interrupted with all the delicacy he could muster. "My apologies for bringing up, however inadvertently, a topic which is evidently very painful for you." He took a deep breath before continuing. "But my petition remains as it stood a few minutes ago. I ask for the hand of your daughter in marriage."

"What?" exclaimed Wentworth, immediately shaken from his reverie. "What manner of devil is it that compels you to offer for a ten-year-old chit?"

"I pray you, sir," offered the marquis quietly, "hear me out." He indicated the chair Wentworth had so recently vacated.

When his host was seated, Traverston began his explanation. "I understand your confusion, and the truth is I have to be honest with you and say that before this very instant I never in my life thought to be proposing for the hand of a young girl."

Wentworth's snort was answer enough to this statement.

Holding his hand out to indicate he be allowed to continue, Traverston waited until his host was ready to listen. "Still," he said, "I need a wife. And I am prepared to do what I must in order to secure one."

Wentworth couldn't hide his amusement. "My lord, with all due respect, I doubt that there is any way you can compel me to hand over my daughter to you."

Traverston mentally wrestled with his anger. He deserved this, he reminded himself. Wentworth had every right to laugh. The fact that it was at his expense cut him to the quick, but the affront was of little import at the moment. "Please," supplicated the marquis, his impatience just barely under control, "allow me to finish."

When Wentworth did not respond, Traverston continued. "Five years ago," he began, "my life became intolerable." He looked straight into his host's eyes. "Without going into too much detail, let's just say that I took every chance available to degrade myself, my name and that of my family's. It became my dearest wish to die, but not before I had a chance to bring everything and everybody associated with the name of Traverston down with me."

Here he paused, and as his host had done earlier, the marquis walked over to the window and looked out. He stopped only for a few seconds, however. Traverston had a mission to accomplish—he had to get this man to agree to his wishes—and he couldn't afford to be absorbed in self-pity now. Facing Wentworth again he said, "But now all that has changed."

Wentworth had not looked at his neighbor closely before this moment, but now as the marquis walked over to join him, he studied the man thoroughly.

His face and body were evidence enough of the hard living the marquis had testified to. Lines, where there shouldn't be any for years, already showed on his face. Bags under his eyes, unkempt hair—the inventory went on. Wentworth was amazed that he hadn't noticed these things earlier. Traverston's proud bearing must have disguised those characteristics from him earlier, he thought.

The nobleman leaned down into Wentworth's face, unconsciously giving the man a closer look at his dissipation. "But just when I thought I had hit bottom, when I thought there was no reason to go on, when I thought I could drink myself to death and no one would look twice at my demise, I find that I cannot." He looked angry, yet somehow faintly elated. "From the depths of his muddy grave, my grandfather has seen to curse me.

"Oh, not many men would call it a curse, but I do. You see, Wentworth, my grandfather somehow knew how hard this was for me. He knew I was a weakling."

Traverston was speaking so forcefully, Wentworth had to exercise an inordinate amount of self-control not to cringe back from him. Inexorably Traverston continued, grinding and clenching his words together in an effort to force them out. "My grandfather, damn his soul for all eternity, knew that I could never run through two fortunes." He laughed, backing away from Wentworth. "He knew I didn't have the strength."

Traverston wiped his forehead on the sleeve of his coat, suddenly weary. He dropped his body into the armchair across from Wentworth, the action giving the impression that he didn't have the strength to keep standing.

"He's making me marry to get the money, though," he finished tiredly.

Bemused, Wentworth gazed in puzzled silence at his guest. Before he could help himself he asked, "Then, why bother getting married at all, my lord?"

As if he had unleashed a tornado, Traverston immediately hurled himself out of the chair again, his face a study of livid rage. He practically shouted, "Because that bastard half brother of mine will get the fortune if I don't!"

But as quickly as it had come, his anger vanished. Realizing he had shocked his host, Traverston added more calmly, "And that, you see, my good sir, would be unacceptable." As nonchalantly as he could, he passed a hand through his hair, pushing the strands back into place. He looked away from his host, mentally cursing his lack of self-control.

"My lord," answered Wentworth as softly and with as much entreaty as he could muster, "As much as I may pity your situation, and as much as I may be inclined to help you, you must realize that I cannot give you my daughter."

Traverston, still looking away, answered in a deceptively neutral tone, "But you see, sir, I cannot go to anyone else for help. My reputation is such that no social butterfly, even given a title and fortune as a lure, would be inclined to have me. Even if she were so inclined, the fact that I must wed within two weeks would be such a shocking proposal that I could never gain her agreement. So you see," he finished, turning sharp eyes on Wentworth, "I must have Olivia."

"My lord, you must see that the very argument you use to preclude yourself from a *ton* bride applies doubly so to my daughter. By your own admission, you are a danger—to yourself and everyone else around you. Olivia is but ten years old. Given these facts, how could I possibly entrust her to you?''

The marquis had known what Wentworth's answer would be, but now he was ready. The trap was laid and all he had to do was draw the net in.

Carefully the marquis responded, ''While it is true that I had originally meant to ask for Margaret's hand, sir, I now see that an offer for your second daughter, Olivia, would really work out much better for the both of us.''

''I am afraid I do not follow you.''

''I have need of a wife immediately, that is true.'' Holding his index finger up, he added, ''But only on paper. If your daughter is but ten years old, then I will gladly wait until she turns eighteen to collect her and make her my wife in something other than name. I confess, the thought of taking a leg shackle at this point in my life has little appeal. But I know that I will need one a few years down the road, for an heir if nothing else.

''I will marry Olivia now, but until she is eighteen you may keep her and raise her as you see fit. During her eighteenth year, I will come for her myself, and you will be safe in the knowledge that you have secured for her a husband with both title and fortune. Who knows,'' he added with a flat smile, ''I may even be dead by then, and then she would be a wealthy peeress indeed.''

Without giving Wentworth a chance to reply, the Marquis of Traverston quickly added, ''Of course, I would expect to pay you handsomely for raising my wife in a fashion befitting her station in life.'' He paused for dramatic effect. ''And to reimburse you for the future loss of your daughter.''

The room was quiet. Wentworth was vaguely aware of the kind of sounds existing somewhere in the countryside. Like a clock ticking away the minutes, those soft sounds—of wind blowing and leaves stirring, as well as a multitude of other quiet, unidentifiable noises—accompanied his thoughts as he vainly sought to fight against the insidiousness of Traverston's proposal.

On the one hand, Traverston's request was unthinkable. If he agreed to such an outlandish plan, he would be no better than a white slaver. In fact, he thought, he might be something worse. For he would be selling his own daughter.

But it wasn't so simple. Although he rarely admitted it in public, he was strapped for cash. The manor house had already been mortgaged twice, and he had racked up such a pile of tradesmen's bills that he wasn't sure he would ever have the ready to pay for them all. Wentworth realized he was not a very good administrator, and the current state of his finances was a more than adequate testimony to how bad he really was.

As though the question were dragged from his lips, Wentworth stared at his clenched hands and asked quietly, "How much recompense?"

"Thirty thousand pounds!" Traverston announced in ringing tones.

Wentworth gasped involuntarily. The things he could do with that money were almost beyond thought. It was a fortune, more money than he could have hoped for in his wildest dreams.

And yet, it was a traitorous thought. He couldn't sell his daughter, no matter how high the price. She would have no say in the matter of her marriage if he agreed to the marquis's request. No opportunity for choice at all.

But would he really be selling her when the money would actually benefit Olivia? In the present state of matters, he could barely afford to educate her, much less clothe and feed her. How much worse would the situation get over time? Worse yet, what would happen in seven years when she became of marriageable age and there was no dowry for her? That would preclude her from making a choice as surely as arranging the affair now.

But would she understand? Would Olivia know he made this pact because he wanted her to be happy? Or was the money such an incentive he was justifying the means to the wealth? Wentworth could barely stand to think about such things.

With Traverston, she would have a husband of vast means. His impending fortune must be great indeed for him to offer such a large sum as her bridal portion. He doubted that under ordinary circumstances, even were she to blossom into a great beauty, she would receive half as much.

But would she be happy? Could wealth and a title make up for being married to a rake, a blackguard, in fact?

Traverston watched his host struggle internally with these issues, but he was not moved. He was confident as to what the outcome would be. What it must be.

Wisely the marquis held his tongue until Wentworth turned to him, his eyes clouded with remorse and sadness at the result of his internal battle.

"You win, my lord," he said, but his voice was not congratulatory. His shoulders had become stooped, as if the weight of the world now rested on them. He sighed deeply, sadly and with defeat, and he couldn't look the marquis in the eye as he determined his daughter's fate. "When will you wish the ceremony to take place?"

Traverston's eyes fairly glittered. "Tonight," he said firmly.

Chapter Two

"Impossible!" The effrontery of the marquis stunned Wentworth. To come into his house with his insulting offer was bad enough, but now to add insult to injury, Traverston actually wanted him to sacrifice Olivia immediately.

"Impossible!" he shouted again.

"I beg to differ, my good sir," replied the marquis, all calm, cool efficiency now that he had what he wanted. He reached for the glass he had set down long ago and took a long, satisfying pull. "You've already agreed to my bargain. What difference can it make *when* the actual ceremony takes place?"

Traverston studied his neighbor through slitted eyes, his fear and impatience effectively hidden behind a mask of contempt. "You wouldn't want to go back on your word now."

The marquis's words hit home, as he knew they would. His blow to Wentworth's honor stung the man, and his host fell for the simple trap with comical willingness.

"Of course not!" he blustered with bruised dignity. After a brief period of tugging at his waistcoat, as if that action would help him to straighten his spine, Wentworth continued in a calmer tone. "It's just that it is so soon.

I hadn't expected..." His faltering tongue trailed off, unequal to the occasion. He dropped his gaze and returned to staring at his glass. "And what, if I may inquire," he asked softly, all of the righteous indignation taken from his sails, "hour would you be expecting us?"

The marquis gave Wentworth's dejected form a small and mocking bow. "Ten o'clock, if you please." His sardonic imitation of his host's politeness echoed hollowly around the room. "At Norwood Park. I have a private chapel there. I think you'll agree with me that this is one ceremony that is better conducted without a large audience."

The short nod Wentworth gave Traverston was almost lost on his guest, it was so brief. Wentworth sat lost in thought for a long time, oblivious to the silent, amused contemplation of the marquis. And in the end, it was up to Traverston to show himself the way out, for his host was not up to the courtesy.

Finally, just as Traverston was opening the door, a brief flicker of hope flitted across Wentworth's brain. He sat up in his chair suddenly and, like a desperate man hanging over the edge of hell, he flung his question out with all of his strength.

"You have a license, I presume?"

The abject misery on his neighbor's face almost caused the marquis to relent. What was he doing after all? His life was over, finished. He had no more claim to Olivia, a pure and sweet innocent child, than had the devil. And yet, here he was, demanding her to be sacrificed, willing her to a life of suffering and misery as his bride. Hadn't he caused enough harm for one lifetime? Did he really need to do this?

But then the old resolve returned. This was a choice Wentworth had made, after all. He could justify his avarice any way he wanted to, but it was still plain and simple greed that motivated him in the end. If Traverston was a blackguard, then Wentworth was a traitor. Let him live with the consequences of his own actions and be damned for them, he decided.

Again Traverston gave his neighbor a mocking little bow, then laughed unpleasantly as he noticed his host's reaction to his silent affirmation.

At the new insult, Wentworth grew both angry and remorseful, and without realizing it, he shrank further into his shell. Grasping his brandy glass with both hands, he hunched over it, seeking some warmth from the bowl as the front door to the house slammed shut, announcing the departure of the marquis. Black hatred and resentment welled up in him, directed both at himself and at the perceived source of his misery.

Ye Gods! he wailed internally. What had he done? He should have known that Traverston would not have come to Gateland Manor without a license. The marquis had expected to win, the damn villain, he thought miserably, and he had let him have his daughter without so much as a fight. For the first time since his encounter with the nobleman that day, Wentworth truly began to despair.

The approaching footsteps were bold and swift. They didn't belong to anyone she knew, but Olivia could guess at whose they were. Calmly, knowing that she had plenty of time, she reached down to stroke the small kitten once more before holding out a tiny morsel for the ball of fluff to consume. Above the contented purring noises made by the cat, Olivia heard the footsteps hesitate, and she was surprised. He hadn't struck her as the kind of man to be unsure of himself.

All at once he was there beside her. She turned her head to look at him, curious, but not overly so. As when she had witnessed his arrival earlier, she felt guided by an unknown force, and she moved her head and limbs as though she were merely following the actions written for her in a play.

As she turned her head to face him, Traverston was momentarily taken aback. What he had expected, he did not know, but it was not this silent child-woman before him. Her skin was like porcelain, a soft creamy white, except on her cheeks where the wind had kissed them a soft rose. Her hair, as blue-black as the edge of night, was lush with luster and health as it hung down her back. But her most exceptional feature, the one that made him stop breathing just for a moment, were her eyes. Olivia had eyes of a blue so pale they seemed as translucent as ice, and about as forthcoming.

When she spoke, her voice was low and clear, yet with a girlish quality at odds with her serene and mature appearance. "You've been to see my father," she said, and she watched his reaction with unblinking eyes.

The feeling of unreality for Olivia intensified with his answer. "Yes," she heard him respond, and she knew without question that was all he was going to say. Distantly, as if she had no more control over herself than an automaton, she evaluated him.

His clothes were worn, but they were those of a gentleman. But it wasn't his clothes that interested her, so she dismissed them with hardly another thought. His hair, like her own, was black, but it was the dead black of charred wood, not the vibrant shade of night like hers. It was wild, untamed hair, coarse and difficult to train, and too long in places, as though he had tried to trim it himself without the use of a looking glass. But even this feature had no prolonged interest for her. What Olivia really needed to study, what she had to understand, she knew, deep inside her, was his face.

It was a hard face. The line of his jaw was much too strong, his chin too pronounced. His eyebrows were live things, crouched beneath a creased forehead too tall and noble to speak of mercy. His nose, full and proudly Roman, was not the nose of a man known for his kindness and generosity.

But, she thought, there was more to him than that.

The lines of his chin and the hollows in his cheeks were more the result of hunger than anything else. She could tell because she had seen that look before on beggar children in the street. He was tall, very tall, but his jacket flapped loosely with space that had once been filled with muscle.

As for the bags under his eyes, she knew they were due to a combination of sleeplessness and drink. Her father, on rare occasions, looked like that when he had had a particularly rough night of carousing in town. And the wrinkles on his brow, and the intimidating way his eyebrows drew together, those could be fixed if he were but to smile.

That, of course, was the heart of the question. Could this man be brought to smile?

And so it was that Olivia finally sought the one part of him that would tell her the answers. She looked into his eyes. Dark, dark eyes, she thought. Exceedingly dark; they were stormy eyes, full of horrible promises. Eyes that had seen too much from a mind that had done too much. Eyes that were full of terrible secrets that could haunt you in the night.

Eyes that begged for help.

And then, without realizing it, Olivia answered their silent plea. "If you want," she said slowly, offering him the only thing she had to give at the moment, "you can pet her if you like." And she held up the small ball of fur for his scrutiny.

A shudder ran through the marquis. It gripped him so strongly that, for a moment, Olivia thought he would surely fall. But then, just when she knew he would turn away, the tremor passed, and he slowly sank down to the ground beside her. Then, tentatively, as though he were afraid the small animal might bite him, he reached out one hand and began to pet its tiny head.

"Maddie," exclaimed Olivia that afternoon as she grabbed a jam tart and popped it into her mouth, "did you see the pirate?"

"Now, love," shushed the young girl's nursemaid tenderly, "you know there are no such thing as pirates." She held up an admonishing finger to her charge. "And how many times have I told you not to talk with your mouth full? And what do you mean by not washing your hands after playing with that filthy kitten?"

Olivia, not the least bit abashed by this chastisement, tried to hold on to her nanny's attention. "But there are! I saw one here today! He even played with Isis!"

Maddie, having glimpsed the marquis herself earlier, knew full well whom Olivia meant. But she didn't believe in giving in to flights of fancy, and she told Olivia as much.

"Olivia!" chided Maddie just as she was about to retort. "I told you not to talk with your mouth full. Now no more talk of pirates, child. I mean it!"

Olivia, left to her own thoughts as she munched her tart, reflected that it was a pity her nursemaid couldn't have been with her to see the pirate. But her father had seen him, and he would surely understand her reference. After all, he certainly did look like a pirate. Even if he hadn't exactly acted like one.

As always when she thought of her father, a smile began creeping its way up her face. Papa had promised to teach her about the ancient Greeks tonight, and she loved his lessons on Greek mythology. Maybe when he was done, they could talk about the pirate, and she could find out why he had come....

After dinner, much the same as before dinner, Olivia

was alone. Wandering now through the empty house, she stopped suddenly as she heard voices raised in anger. She immediately recognized her father's voice, but the other one was unfamiliar to her.

Softly tiptoeing around the corner, Olivia made her way gradually to the door of her father's study. The door was open a crack, and without feeling the least remorse for her actions, she peeked through the opening.

Her father was in what her nurse would have called a "heated discussion" with a local tradesman. After racking her brain, Olivia remembered having seen this man make deliveries of wine and brandy to their house. It wasn't an unusual conversation for her father to be having, thought Olivia morosely. She'd overheard several of its kind in the recent past.

As Olivia moved quietly away from the door and went upstairs to the bedroom, she grew increasingly unhappy. She was an intelligent child, and she knew that her father didn't have much money. Ever since she could remember, Maddie had emphasized to Olivia the importance of practicing economies. But no matter what lengths Maddie and she went to in order to cut expenses from their daily budget, it never seemed to be enough.

Olivia sat down on her bed, her chin in her hand. She didn't know what she could do to help her father pay the bills, but she was determined to try. Perhaps she and Maddie could expand the kitchen garden out back? She'd have to think about it.

Wentworth had long ago done away with the age-old custom of children eating their meals upstairs. It wasn't really out of any noble sentiment that he ignored that form of etiquette—just the opposite, in fact. If the truth be known, Wentworth simply got lonely.

At supper Wentworth seemed inclined to be more melancholy than at any other time of the day. Perhaps it was the candlelight. Perhaps it was the empty expanse of table and the encroaching shadows. Who knew? In any case, before Margaret's death, he liked to have his children with him at supper to keep him company. After his first daughter died, he grew almost fanatical about having Olivia there.

Wentworth's melancholy tonight was so palpable that Olivia could barely eat. Sometimes she chattered brightly in order to shake her father from his blue studies, but tonight Olivia's attempts had met with dismal failure. Her father spoke in monosyllables throughout the indifferently cooked meal, speaking only when spoken to, and often not even then. It didn't take much, thought Olivia, to see that he was preoccupied with his own thoughts.

After a time, Olivia could stand the oppressive atmosphere no longer. Without realizing what had put her father into such a depressed mood, she asked in an unusually loud voice, "Who was that man today, Papa?"

Wentworth's head snapped up from where he had been studiously examining a chip on his plate. The eyes of his innocent young daughter speared him in his seat like a pin in a butterfly, and for a second all he felt was agony. If Olivia had slapped him in the face and called him a devil, he could not imagine how she could have struck him with a deeper sense of guilt.

Gazing at her in a kind of shock, Wentworth vainly attempted not to think about Olivia's resemblance to his now long-dead wife. Silently he cursed the impulse that possessed him in a moment of madness to name his second child after his wife. His beloved's creamy white skin, lush dark hair, firm chin and high cheekbones were replicated on the smaller version before him. Worst of all, though, were Olivia's eyes. His dead wife's eyes stared back at him from across the table, and tonight, in his own mind, they were full of accusation.

Tiny wrinkles formed on Olivia's brow as she realized

that something was dreadfully wrong with her father. He looked angry, upset and terrified. Worse, she thought, her father looked possessed.

Trying desperately to bring him back to the here and now, Olivia asked her question again, enunciating each word slowly and carefully.

"Papa. Who was that man?"

Wentworth, dropping his eyes before the interrogative stare of his daughter, attempted to take a bite of the boiled beef on his plate. But the dry meat stuck in his throat, choking him. Recovering quickly from his coughing fit, he got up from the table and threw his napkin onto his plate. The next second, he strode from the room without saying a word.

The long shadows, with their ominous shapes creeping across the room, were the only response to Olivia's unanswered question.

A few hours after Olivia had finally drifted off to sleep, she was gently awakened by Maddie. The woman's voice was soothing and calm. Although indistinct at first, the sound finally became words in Olivia's consciousness.

"Here now, my love," cooed the nurse. "I know you're tired, poor wee thing, but we've got to get you ready for a trip."

Olivia sat up in her bed slowly, stretching and rubbing her eyes. She blinked sleepily, trying to clear the cobwebs from her mind. After a moment, she was able to focus her eyes on her nanny.

"A trip?" she asked uncomprehendingly.

Maddie turned away from Olivia and returned the covers the little girl had tossed about in her sleep to the end of the bed. The old woman had her doubts about this strange trip in the middle of the night, but she kept them to herself.

"Indeed, yes," she replied in as cheerful a manner as

she could manage. "You and your father are going to Norwood Park."

Olivia stared blankly at her nurse, the words not making any sense to her. Where was Norwood Park? What was it? Finally comprehension dawned.

Olivia's eyes went round with fear. She had seen the park, and not so very long ago. Occasionally Olivia was able to slip away from Gateland Manor unattended, and on one of her more recent forays, she had glimpsed the house through the woods. The thought of going to that spooky old mansion, with all of its encroaching weeds and darkened windows, did nothing to assuage her fear.

"Now, now, my poppet," soothed Maddie, gently patting her charge's hand. "'Tis nothing to be worried about, I'm sure. You mustn't believe all those Banbury tales about the place being haunted, for I'm sure it simply isn't true."

In point of fact, Olivia was so isolated at Gateland Manor that she had never heard this particular rumor about the house, but she didn't think that now was the appropriate time to bring up that fact. Maddie would just be upset if she found out Olivia had never heard the story before now.

Maddie made a dismissive gesture as she continued. "Besides, the master is going with you, and you know he would never put you in harm's way."

Olivia digested this bit of wisdom from her nurse and concluded that what she said was true. Her papa would never let anything happen to her.

"And look, Olivia. He brought you this."

Maddie's voice broke into the girl's reverie, and she looked up to see her nanny holding the most beautiful dress she had ever seen. The material was pale blue and trimmed with navy ribbons. Around the neck and cuffs was delicately scalloped lace, and it felt rich to the touch of Olivia's tiny fingers. When she put it on, the dress reached to the middle of her calves. Maddie had given her a pair of white stockings to complete the ensemble, and to Olivia, the effect was enchanting.

"Oh, Nanny!" cried Olivia, spinning around in circles in front of the peer glass. "Is it really just for me?"

Maddie laughed softly, her eyes gleaming with pride. "Yes, my dear," she answered fondly, "it really is for you."

When Olivia came down the main staircase thirty minutes later, Wentworth's breath caught in his throat. Never had he seen such a perfect-looking angel! The dress, with its contrasting shades of blue, was the perfect setting to show off his daughter's unusual eyes and creamy skin. Her dark heavy hair, held back from her face with a navy ribbon bought specifically to match the dress, swayed gently against her back as she descended the staircase.

"You look just like your mother, child," he whispered as she approached him.

And then it hit him. The vision struck so hard, it was just like a physical blow. Wentworth staggered back, his hands out before him in a plea of supplication and remorse. "No, my dear," he pleaded as the ephemeral form of his former wife floated down to him, her eyes ablaze with righteous anger. "It's not what you think! I did it for you! I did it for you!" He cringed as the dress he had just given her burst into flames around her form, consuming everything within its reach but leaving her fragile figure unscathed. He closed his eyes and moaned piteously until he felt the frantic tugging on his greatcoat.

"Papa!" Olivia cried, her eyes wide with alarm. "Are you all right?"

Silently he stared at her, his eyes uncomprehending. Then, with just the barest hesitation, his expression changed. His lids closed halfway over orbs that were crafty and furtive. He straightened his back, took hold of his daughter's arm and scrutinized her appearance carefully.

Yes, he thought. This was going to be just as he planned. That dress made his beautiful sweet daughter look just like Persephone, the goddess of spring. The marquis ought to appreciate her sweet innocence, he chortled internally.

At the thought of Olivia's impending marriage, Wentworth's mercurial mood turned instantly black, and he scowled at his daughter. He was glad she looked so lovely and innocent. Just let Traverston see the beautiful creature whose life he was about to destroy. Just let him see what his black hand was about to corrupt. By God, he vowed, he would see the marquis in hell for this! Quickly he yanked his daughter with him toward the door and the carriage, before he could lose his newfound sense of purpose.

Although Norwood Park was really quite close to the manor, the carriage ride in the hired post chaise took over fifteen minutes. For Olivia, the minutes dragged by. Far from being reassuring, her father's presence in the coach was an added torment. His actions today had been so strange that Olivia didn't know what to think.

When they finally did arrive, Olivia was stunned by the spectacle that met her eyes. She had expected the house to be a forbidding sight, but instead the building and its surroundings were serenely beautiful. In the autumn moonlight, Norwood Park was enchanting. A silvery lake, illuminated by the brilliant moon, reflected a hauntingly mellow vision of the grounds around the water. A great oak arched majestically over the edge of one shore, hinting to the observer of quiet summer nights long past.

The house itself was a marvel, as well. Great blocks of gray stone formed the exterior, suggestive of chivalrous times and knights in shining armor. And best of all, every single window was brightly lit with candles, welcoming Olivia to the ethereal home. By the time the carriage stopped, she was breathless with wonder and excitement.

If her father had expected her enthusiasm to die down once she was inside the dusty tomb of a house, he was sadly disappointed. Although the interior of the home was sagging and tired, Olivia saw only what the mansion must have been like once long ago, and she wandered the halls behind her father in a daze.

Olivia's attention became riveted on her immediate surroundings when she realized that the butler had taken them a long way into the house. The guest parlor, she rationalized, should have been located much closer to the great hall she and her father had just come through. They were no longer in the main wing of the house, and she wondered where the servant might be taking them.

Olivia was more than a little relieved when the servant finally stopped before a door. As the man stepped back in order to let them pass through the opening, she could see he had led them to a chapel.

Wentworth, not being overly religious, had taken Olivia to church but rarely, and usually then only on special occasions. So it was that now Olivia racked her brains trying to remember what religious holiday today might be. But she could think of nothing.

Puzzled, Olivia looked up at her father for an explanation, but his face was as closed and shuttered as it had been all day. He was as silent as the grave.

The butler slipped away, his footsteps making no more noise on the worn carpeting than those of a ghost. Father and daughter were alone. Following some inner instinct, Olivia wandered a few steps into the room, gazing around in awe at the ceiling and walls. The chapel was a beautiful example of Gothic architecture, with high pointed arches, an intricately ribbed ceiling and delicate stained glass windows. Lost in the pleasure of the moment, she started toward a small statue set in one wall, but before she could walk more than a few steps, a sudden tug on her arm brought her up short. Still silent, Wentworth pulled her back to his side and began to march her down the aisle between the pews.

It was then that Olivia noticed what she had failed to see upon entering the chapel. She and her father were not actually alone. Facing the pair was what appeared to be a minister. At least his vestments proclaimed him to be a religious man, but she was unfamiliar with his particular costume.

A second man was facing toward the minister and so had his back to Olivia, but she recognized him all the same. He was her pirate.

His dark green velvet coat fit his broad shoulders perfectly while his black pantaloons showed off every lean muscle in his thighs. Although Olivia didn't know much about gentlemen's clothing, surely, she thought, these were the sort of clothes only a pirate would wear!

When they reached the front of the chapel, Wentworth nudged his daughter forward just a bit. The action brought her parallel to the pirate, and she was able to take her second close-up look at his face.

What she saw there made her want to gasp. She stared at him unabashedly. Why had she not noticed what must have been so obvious before? He was, she decided without any hesitation, a handsome man. His gray eyes, so dark and unusual in color, stared straight ahead, looking at neither the minister nor at her. His nose, a perfect aquiline in profile, sat between prominently chiseled cheekbones. Olivia thought he had a noble brow. His forehead was tall and square without being too large, and it carried his raven black hair without pretension.

But the expression she had noted earlier on him was

still there. He had a solemn, unhappy look to him, she thought. Oh, he wasn't crying or anything like that— grown men didn't cry, after all—it was just that he looked so...so determined. And intense. And more than a little scary.

Olivia gave a start. The whole time she had been staring at the man she called her pirate, the one who looked like a minister had been speaking. She had been so engrossed in studying the man next to her, she had completely failed to take in the rest of her surroundings. Guiltily she tried to concentrate on his words now. She blinked a time or two before she gave up trying to follow the lofty language. She had never been fond of religious talk, anyway.

As the odd ceremony continued, a frown began to form on Olivia's delicate brow. What did this evening mean, and why was everyone acting so strangely? She tried to puzzle the clues out, glancing back at her father as she did. But from his glassy eyes, she guessed she would get no help from that quarter.

With another guilty twinge, Olivia brought her attention back to the front of the room. The minister had stopped speaking and was staring at her with an intensity that was somehow frightening. Had she missed a response? Gads, that would be awful. He would think she didn't know the first thing about religion. Usually when there was a silence like this, it meant a response of some kind was in order. Muttering the only religious phrase she knew, Olivia quietly avowed, "Amen."

As the silence stretched on, Traverston began to collect that the chit standing next to him had no idea what was going on. Her ridiculous response to the question only confirmed his suspicions. Wentworth must not have told his daughter a thing. His already low opinion of his neighbor dropped another inch. The cad probably hadn't even mentioned that she had a speaking role in tonight's little drama, he thought disgustedly.

For the first time in that strange, unearthly night, the tall stranger looked down at Olivia. His eyes, smoky with a depth that seemed to penetrate her to her very soul, smiled gently into hers. Carefully taking one of her small hands into his own, he spoke.

"You have only to say 'I do,' and your father will take you home and tuck you into your nice warm bed. You'd like that, wouldn't you, Olivia?"

His deep voice, soothing and gentle to her ears, lulled Olivia into a kind of trance. Acting without conscious thought, she nodded as she opened her mouth and softly repeated, "I do."

Traverston rewarded the child with a smile and turned to face the minister, her hand still firmly held in his own. Olivia glanced back at her father, but he looked as though he had been turned to stone. His eyes never left the marquis's back.

The ceremony ended quickly. Before leaving the room, the minister signed a piece of paper and handed both pen and paper to the marquis. With quick efficiency, he scrawled his name and title across the page. Next he handed both over to Olivia whom he instructed to do likewise. Finally, Wentworth also signed the page, his handwriting barely legible.

Without saying a word to his host, Wentworth grabbed his daughter by the hand and began pulling her down the aisle at a rapid pace. Olivia looked back over her shoulder to see if the pirate was following her, but he simply stood near the alter and watched them go.

As the pair reached the hallway, Olivia managed to tug herself free from her father. Frustrated and tired, she demanded, "Papa, what was that all about?"

Wentworth did not bother to answer her, but simply regained his grip on his daughter and resumed dragging her toward the great hall. He had one thought and one thought only—to get out of the house as quickly as possible.

Stumbling behind him, Olivia was just about to descend the stairs leading down to their hired carriage when a voice from behind brought them up short. Wentworth took one look at Olivia and ungently pushed her in the direction of the coach. "Get in the carriage," he commanded. His tone brooked no argument.

The Marquis of Traverston's tall, lean frame appeared in the giant entrance of his home. "Ah, there you are, Wentworth." His smile was sardonic, triumphant. Without giving the least hint he was aware of his guest's discomfort, he paused to take an object out of his coat pocket before continuing. "'Tis a trifle big for her now, but I will expect it to be on her finger when I come for her eight years from now."

Slowly Wentworth opened the box the marquis had handed him. Inside, a magnificent diamond and sapphire ring rested on a bed of velvet. When Wentworth failed to make a response, Traverston added cuttingly, "The ring was entailed with the estate. It was one of the few things I wasn't allowed to hock in this crumbling heap. Otherwise, you can be sure, she would have received nothing from me."

Without a word, Wentworth snapped the box shut and stuffed it into his coat pocket. Traverston noted the speed with which his guest raced down the stairs was most unbecoming to a gentleman. Pleased with Wentworth's reaction, the marquis smiled. His new father-in-law had acted as though he were being chased by all the devils in hell. Good, he nodded to himself complacently. It would be nice to have some company when he got there.

Chapter Three

Olivia sat before the solicitor, her hands folded neatly in her lap. Her black bombazine dress trimmed with the faintest smattering of lace, more appropriate on a widow of advanced years than on a young miss still very much in the schoolroom, loudly proclaimed to all and sundry her state of mourning.

It wasn't that she was pretentious, thought the middle-aged gentleman sitting across his desk from her. Olivia just genuinely seemed to have preferred that particular style of gown above all others. He should know: his wife had helped her choose it. Still she looked neat and tidy. He studied her openly from his vantage point.

Olivia was a beautiful child, of that there could be no doubt. But her beauty lacked something. Mr. Potts's frown deepened as he tried to ponder what that missing element might be. Then he had it. She lacked fire. Olivia was simply not a spirited child. Oh, no. And she was not your typical twelve-year-old, either.

Mr. Potts continued his analysis of the girl, careful to keep his scrutiny away from his visitor's eyes. Olivia's icy blue eyes unnerved her solicitor. Whatever thoughts she might have had on the matter at hand were carefully locked away behind those cool eyes. They absorbed everything around them and gave absolutely nothing back.

The rest of her face, while equally noncommittal, was much less disturbing to him. He studied her finely chiseled features and then frowned. She might as well have been a wall for all the information her attitude gave away to him.

Nervously Mr. Potts cleared his throat. He had thought this interview would be rather simple, really. Just give the chit the get-go and be done with it. Faced with her impenetrable silence, however, he wasn't sure the task would be as easy as he had first imagined. He cleared his throat again, loosening his cravat with one finger. No, this wasn't going to be easy. If only she wouldn't stare at him so!

Thankfully, Olivia was getting rather impatient with her lawyer. She decided to have pity on him, if only to get the conversation moving. "You found a place for me to go." Her voice, although still childish in pitch, sounded strangely grown-up. She didn't phrase the sentence as a question. She simply stated what she knew to be true.

Mr. Potts jumped for the olive branch with startling quickness. "Yes!" he said in a relieved voice. Belatedly regaining some of his composure, he sat back in his chair pretending an ease he didn't feel. "Yes," he repeated more calmly.

In his element now that the topic had been broached, the solicitor pushed his spectacles to the bridge of his nose and looked condescendingly down at the girl before him. In the space of a few heartbeats, he managed to go from his impersonation of a nervous Nellie to that of a schoolmarm.

"As you know, my dear," began the man somewhat fatuously, "it has been well over a month now since your poor father died." Here he took the time to give Olivia a sympathetic look. "And you have borne your bereavement well. Nay! Better than well. You have been exemplary in your conduct."

He paused and glanced at her meaningfully.

If Mr. Potts had expected Olivia to be flattered by his words, he was sadly disappointed. In truth, she thought him a pompous old windbag and an insufferable bore. But rather than voice these opinions out loud, she kept silent. Her expression gave away none of her thoughts.

Again Mr. Potts cleared his throat, trying to regain his earlier equanimity. After glancing briefly at Olivia over the top of his spectacles, he continued his speech. "But now the time has come for you to leave your humble abode and go on with your life. Yes." He nodded like a silly ass. "That's it exactly."

Olivia's heart skipped a beat at his words. Oh, she knew that the inevitable must happen, but did it have to happen right now? Stoically she kept her external appearance of composure, though on the inside she was seething.

This conversation could only be taking place if her solicitor had found someone willing to act as her guardian. Who was this person and what did they want with her? Didn't she do a good job of taking care of the manor? Maddie had died, it was true, but she got along just fine, thank you. Besides, she preferred to be alone. Olivia longed to say the words, but she knew they were futile.

Instead she inquired, "Where am I to go?"

Mr. Potts, relieved that Olivia appeared to be taking all of this so well, gave an audible sigh of relief. "Your grandmother, Lady Raleigh, the Dowager Duchess of Stonebridge, has kindly offered to have mercy on you. Even though she disowned your mother some twenty years ago, it appears as though now she is willing to forgive past grievances and take you in. You are sensible of the honor she does you, I am sure.''

The silence stretched on. Outside, the falling snow deadened all of the street noises, leaving the solicitor no hope of a distraction. He waited in vain for Olivia to agree with him. Then he took a deep breath and sighed. He should have known, he grumbled to himself, pushing his spectacles upright once more. Olivia could never be expected to do what she was supposed to. She was a very strange child.

"Lady Raleigh is waiting for you at the Three Crowns even as we speak." As Olivia's eyes widened slightly at the pronouncement, Mr. Potts gave a humorless smile. Finally he had gotten some kind of reaction out of her. With relish he continued. "Yes, it was all somewhat of a surprise, actually. One minute Mrs. Potts and I were quietly having our dinner, and the next minute there she was, pounding on our front door." He muttered almost to himself, "Never thought for a moment she'd answer the letter in person."

Olivia's brain had almost ceased to function upon mention of her grandmother's name. Surely she could not be going with her? It was beyond all thought!

And yet, who else did Olivia have? All of her immediate family was deceased, and all of her father's family, as well. That just left her mother's relatives.

But Lady Raleigh! Olivia's father had never been able to mention the Duke and Duchess of Stonebridge without turning purple. He had been enraged at the way they had treated him and his poor darling wife. Why on earth did they want Olivia now?

Her eyes came back into focus and met with the solicitor's. With anger she noted that he was pleased by her discomfort. She chastised herself severely. She hadn't hidden her feelings well enough again, and now he was gloating—gloating just as her father had done every time she let her guard slip. Well, it wouldn't happen again. She had had enough derision. She had vowed to take charge of her life, and she was going to do it. She'd never be at anyone else's mercy again. No one would ever be able to use her emotions against her again. She wouldn't let them.

Like a slate being wiped clean, Olivia's face lost all trace of visible expression. She had her composure firmly in hand once again. Neutrally she repeated Mr. Potts's earlier declaration, "She is waiting for me now?"

Disconcerted with her abruptness, Mr. Potts replied a little harshly, "Yes, at the Three Crowns, as I said." He relented a little as he reminded himself Olivia was only a child. This whole experience was probably a great shock to her. He paused before adding more kindly, "Shall I escort you there?"

The child-woman speared him with her icicle eyes. Was he trying to manipulate her again? But no, that thought was too uncharitable. Mr. Potts was a fool, it was true, but he was not unnecessarily cruel. Still she would keep him on a short rein. Expressionlessly Olivia made her reply. "Thank you, Mr. Potts."

After accepting his offer as escort, Olivia and Mr. Potts arrived at the Three Crowns some half an hour later. The snow on the ground crunched beneath their feet as they walked toward the door. Stopping a few feet away from the entrance, Olivia turned around and faced her solicitor. With a dignity unusual for one so young, she offered him her hand.

"Thank you so much for escorting me, Mr. Potts. You have been a tremendous help."

Astonished, Mr. Potts stared at the young girl before him. He couldn't quite comprehend that he was actually being dismissed by a chit half his size. Before he could make a suitable reply, however, Olivia reached down, grabbed his hand with her own, pumped it up and down a few times, and turned and walked through the door.

Somewhat uncertainly, Mr. Potts stared at the door that had closed with a solid thud behind Olivia's retreating back. Finally, as if doubting the whole encounter, he shrugged his shoulders and began walking back to the carriage. He collected that this was one meeting where Olivia preferred not to have an observer. For once in his life, his assumption where Olivia was concerned was correct.

Once inside the establishment, the innkeeper's wife immediately spied Olivia and rushed over to her. She was a big woman, and her sheer girth was enough to intimidate the young girl, although Olivia was careful not to show it.

"Well, little lovey!" she exclaimed, beaming. "You must be the little girl who must meet her granny!" She squeezed both of the girl's shoulders in a friendly way, emphasizing her own excitement at the occasion.

Olivia thought this had to be the worst misinterpretation of the situation she had ever heard, but she wisely kept that opinion to herself.

Momentarily confused, the woman looked about them, still firmly grasping Olivia. "But where's the little whatnot, deary?" she asked in her great booming voice. "Blimey if he didn't tell me directly that you were both coming and that I should be preparing some refreshment. I don't be understanding it at all. He shoulda come with you!"

Olivia stepped back a pace, inadvertently taking the large woman with her as her grasp on Olivia's person held firm. "Mr. Potts was unavoidably detained," she responded with quiet authority. "I have come here by myself."

"Gone for a nip to stoke the fires, has he?" The innkeeper's wife gave Olivia a searching glance. After a moment, she shrugged. "Well, it ain't no never mind. The old lady's been waiting for you." She indicated somewhere behind her with the flick of her massive head. Then she maneuvered herself behind Olivia, taking hold of her shoulders from behind. "Just 'round here, love," she directed from the back, pushing Olivia toward the door of a private parlor.

The giantess nudged the door open with her shoulder. Inside, the room was surprisingly warm and cozy. A cheerful fire burned brightly in the grate, and the room was well lit with tapers.

In the center of the room sat Lady Raleigh. Her back was inches from the carved wood of an elegant Hepplewhite chair that she had no doubt brought with her, and her spine was as straight as a ramrod. Next to her elbow rested an untouched glass of water on an otherwise empty side table. Adorning the room was a comfortable-looking sofa, several armchairs and a pier table of cherry wood. But Olivia had eyes only for her grandmother.

She was even more striking in person than Olivia had imagined. Lady Raleigh, her back to the fireplace, stared across the room at her only remaining grandchild with eyes almost as pale as Olivia's. Her gray velvet dress, capped with a gathering of lace high at the throat, only seemed to emphasize the unusual color of her eyes. Added to that, Lady Raleigh's white hair and pale skin, combined with the profusion of pearls she wore about her arms and neck, made her look almost colorless.

She had a birdlike quality, thought Olivia. If she had any weight on her bones at all, she could have been a pigeon. As it was, however, her thinness undermined the comparison. For all her stern expression, she really looked to be a thin, frail old woman. That thought was oddly comforting to the girl.

Olivia had been so mesmerized by her grandmother's

appearance, she was somewhat startled when the apparition before her actually spoke.

"Leave us," she commanded the woman behind Olivia in an imperious voice that only trembled slightly with old age.

The innkeeper's wife abruptly let go of Olivia and bowed her way out the door, taking Olivia's cape with her. Olivia thought it rather mean of her to leave a child all alone with the strange lady before her. But she managed to hold her ground anyway.

A few seconds brought about Lady Raleigh's next words to her grandchild. In a surprisingly gentle voice, she asked, "Are you going to stand there all day, child, or are you going to come over here where I can get a better look at you?"

Obediently Olivia went to stand before her grandmother. Lady Raleigh took her time in examining Olivia. She reached out a hand and firmly grasped one of Olivia's own, pulling the girl toward her. Squinting slightly, she studied Olivia from head to toe. Finally she spoke again.

"Who dressed you, child," she asked with a genuine expression of mystification, "that you look older than I?"

Olivia thought this remark so highly amusing that she bestowed on her grandmother a smile. Or at least she thought it was a smile. In reality her eyes grew only a little warmer, and the corners of her mouth curled upward hardly at all.

She answered the question frankly. "I chose it."

Lady Raleigh nodded thoughtfully. "I see."

In point of fact, she did not see, but she had no immediate concerns about that now. Given time, she and Olivia would get on quite famously, she was sure of that, despite the fact she had known the child for only a few minutes. The girl held her shoulders back proudly, and she did not wince or whine like other little girls. That was a good sign. Lady Raleigh didn't like whiners.

The old woman beckoned the girl to sit down in a chair across from her. Waiting until Olivia had seated herself, she began her quizzing. "What have you heard about me?" she demanded.

Olivia looked at her elder with candor. "Not much."

"What exactly does that mean...not much?"

Again her lips hinted at a smile. "Not much good."

Lady Raleigh leaned forward in her seat, trying to get a good look at Olivia. As if she thought she could startle a confession out of her, she barked, "What do you think of me?"

Olivia's expression turned ever so slightly wary. But her eyes were still cool. "I'm not sure."

"Well," replied her grandmother, leaning back a little in her chair after she had completed her own examination, "I shall be honest with you. You are not what I expected."

Lady Raleigh waited for a reaction. She didn't get one. Nonplussed, she continued. "No, whatever monstrosity I had expected Edgar to raise, you certainly are not it." Her look was approving. "You act very poised, Olivia, just like a young lady. You impress me."

Olivia couldn't break her gaze from her grandmother's. Her eyes were positively mesmerizing. Was this what it was like to be on the other side of her stare? Unsure, she replied, "Thank you."

At that moment, a knock on the door announced the arrival of a visitor. The innkeeper's wife, having regained her earlier blustery manner, came into the room like a ship under full sail. Setting the refreshments out, she kept up a constant stream of chatter, not once noticing that her conversation was completely one-sided.

For Olivia, the interruption was an opportunity to reflect on her own impressions. She decided that Lady Raleigh was not what she had expected, either. From her father's countless tirades, she had expected her grandmother to be a veritable dragoness. Oh, she had a bark... Olivia could see that, but she doubted the frail body before her had much of a bite. She narrowed her eyes a little as her thoughts steamed onward, but it was the only change in expression she allowed herself. At least until she got a good look at the spread laid out by the landlady.

With the woman gone and the food before them, Lady Raleigh was about to continue her conversation when she noticed Olivia's expression. The child was not as good at hiding her feelings as she thought she was, Lady Raleigh noticed. The stare Olivia was giving the hot, buttered scones was practically burning a hole in the table.

In truth, Olivia was very smitten with the idea of biting into one of the scones. It had been so long since she had had anything like them. Looking hungrily at the treats before her, Olivia had to use all of her willpower not to reach out and snatch one.

Lady Raleigh's words broke into her thoughts. "Go ahead, girl," she offered kindly. "Take one while they are still hot."

Olivia started to reach for a scone and then abruptly remembered her manners. "Wouldn't you care for a scone, Grandmama?" she asked with all of the graciousness of a grown hostess.

Lady Raleigh, pleased at both her granddaughter's polite behavior and her new name, shook her head. "I believe I'll wait," she replied.

While Olivia finished her scone and sat eyeing another one, Lady Raleigh continued their discussion. "Do you miss your father, Olivia?" she asked in a clipped voice.

Unsure of how to answer such a question, Olivia took a moment to think about it as she finished chewing her food. She regarded her grandmother seriously. "I accept my loss."

"That's a rather grown-up attitude for someone as young as you," the lady replied.

Olivia shrugged her shoulders delicately. Her grandmother had meant no offense by the comment and none was taken. Still she wasn't sure how to respond to her. For the moment, she decided not to try.

Lady Raleigh continued. "I do not pretend to have had any affection for Edgar, Olivia. He stole my daughter away from me and her rightful heritage and I cannot forgive him for that." She added almost as an afterthought. "I can't forgive her, either."

Olivia regarded her grandparent gravely. In a quiet voice, she told her, "Papa blamed you for Mama's death."

Instead of snorting in disgust as Olivia was sure her relative would do, Lady Raleigh sat still, as if stunned by this bit of information. But after a moment she regained some of her composure and replied with an indication of uneasiness, "I do not doubt that my daughter and I caused each other grief during our respective lifetimes, but I can hardly be held accountable for her death. Your father never did want to see anything for what it really was. That's one reason, although it is hardly the only one, my husband and I disapproved of the match."

Olivia's eyebrows quirked together in puzzlement. "One reason?"

"Yes." Lady Raleigh's own eyebrows drew together in a frown. "Olivia—your mother, that is—was engaged to an earl when she ran off with your father. The wedding papers were all but signed. We had no choice but to cut her." She gazed at Olivia with brutal frankness. "She was a fool and she should have known better."

Olivia took her time thinking this over. Up until now she had only her father's version of the story. It was interesting to hear another version of an event that had caused so many people bitterness and pain. Still she felt somewhat unaffected by the whole affair—as if the story were an entertaining bit of gossip about someone else's family.

Without warning, Lady Raleigh changed the topic. "You will be coming to London to live with me." Her voice brooked no argument. "My husband died some years ago, leaving me a widow. The estate in Sussex went to my nephew, a pompous young man whom I detest, but he was kind enough to let me live in the dowager house, if I so chose. I detest the country, however, and live year-round in London instead. I have a house on Wimpole Street. It's not overly large, you understand, but more than adequate for the pair of us." She looked at Olivia expectantly.

Not wishing to offend her grandmother, she replied, "I'm sure it is quite nice."

Lady Raleigh gave her a brisk, decisive nod. "Very well. We will leave in three days' time. Although I doubt you have much to pack, I'll need to stay at least that long to make sure all of Edgar's affairs are in order. God knows, there are probably a hundred debts to pay off.

"I shall stay here at the inn until we leave for town. I won't stay at your father's house—you understand I cannot. Edgar would turn over in his grave if I did, and my husband would rise from his in outrage. You may come and visit me here as often as you like in the meantime.

"Mrs. Potts has graciously offered to oversee your packing for me. I'm sure she is already waiting for you at the house even as we speak. My coachman will drive you back."

As she seemed dismissed, Olivia got up uncertainly from her seat. Subdued, she walked across the parlor to the door. Before she opened it, however, she turned around to face her grandmother. Politely she waited to be acknowledged.

"Well?" queried the lady, her imperial bearing once again very much in evidence.

"Do you..." began Olivia hesitantly. She searched for the right words. If she asked this question, then she would be opening herself up to attack. This strange woman before her would know her vulnerable spot. She'd know how to wound her in the future.

And yet how could she not ask it? She couldn't very well leave Isis behind. An argument over the Siamese would be a terrible way to start her new relationship with her grandmother.

She almost bit back the words. But, no, she had to ask. Finally she opened her mouth again. Her eyes grew unconsciously wistful as she phrased the question. Such an awful lot of her future depended on the answer she would receive. "Do you...like cats?" She waited silently, building up her defenses against the rejection that was sure to come.

Again Lady Raleigh spied the little girl hiding behind the grown-up facade. With a conviction that would have surprised many of her cronies back in London, she declared soundly, "I adore them."

Chapter Four

London, 1816

"Olivia!"

With painful slowness, Olivia brought her vision back into focus on the oil painting in front of her. The gay foursome, frolicking in the great Italian outdoors, danced across her eyes, the delicate brushstrokes of their picnic spread not quite becoming clear fast enough.

Knowing she had slipped back into her memories as easily as she had slid into her chemise this morning, Olivia strove for the center of calm that would help her retain her composure. There, she had it. But she hadn't yet responded to the call of her name. Mortified but determined not to show it, she dropped her gaze to the slight form of her grandmother across the room, only to see the old woman perched precariously on the edge of a Georgian armchair covered in maroon-and-gold-striped upholstery.

"You haven't heard a word I've said for the last five minutes." The look Lady Raleigh gave her was stern, but there was a worried frown that creased her brow, and her lips were white with fright.

Olivia was instantly contrite. "I'm sorry, Grandmama.

I've been losing my concentration a lot lately. I guess I'm just tired,'' she dissembled.

The dowager stared intently at her relative, knowing full well she was being put off with a half-truth. But she decided not to make an issue out of it. "Marie," said Lady Raleigh, loudly addressing the seamstress on her knees who was pinning the hem of Olivia's gown, "Olivia is exhausted. And to be frank about it, so am I. It looks as if we shall have to fit her ball gown at another time. Say, tomorrow at four?"

"*Oui, madame.*" The petite French seamstress immediately got to her feet and began helping Olivia out of the dress. In moments, all trace of the afternoon's fitting session were gone, and the two ladies were left alone in the charmingly decorated room.

Lady Raleigh got up from the chair and walked over to the bellpull. Her steps came slower now that she found it necessary to walk with a cane.

"We shall have our tea in here today, I think," she said as she turned around to face her granddaughter.

"That would be lovely," Olivia responded without the kind of tonal inflection needed to make the statement ring true. Immediately she went back to her contemplation of the painting.

But instead of reaching up and pulling on the rope, Lady Raleigh merely rested her hand on the velvet cord and frowned at her charge. It tore at the old woman's heart to think that to Olivia, her life was a normal one. Even after all these years in her grandmother's loving company, she had never seen the girl feel anything. Not really. She had never seen her look unhappy or sad. She had never appeared angry or disgruntled. She never looked frustrated or upset. Her face, as beautiful as it was, seemed to be carved from marble, for her features never moved with expression.

But more than any other expression, Lady Raleigh

wanted to see Olivia smile. Underneath it all, she knew that her granddaughter was suffering. The masque she played for the world was the way Olivia hid pain so deep it seemed impossible to heal. Of that, Lady Raleigh was sure. But she so desperately wanted to see her smile. She wanted so much for her granddaughter to be happy.

A few times, the old woman remembered with hope, a few times she had seen something lingering at the corners of Olivia's mouth. Sometimes, when her guard was down, she would smile just a tiny bit, a ghost of something that could be much grander, much more impressive, if she were but to try.

But that was the problem. Lady Raleigh knew that now. Olivia had no heart to try. Whatever feelings the girl had were locked away deep inside her heart, behind walls so high and thorny the old woman had little hope of ever seeing them in her lifetime.

Yet, she knew they were there. She knew because she also knew that Olivia was fond of her aged relative. It showed in her gestures and in her voice. Sometimes her voice would grow soft and wistful, even while her face kept its expressionless lines. But only on occasion. It was actually very rare.

Lady Raleigh knew that her granddaughter responded to intimacy by stepping back, by avoiding the situation like a colt shying from its handler. It was as though Olivia distanced herself from any contact with other human beings that would put her on any footing other than that of a distant acquaintance. Even with her grandmother.

And she so needed that contact, thought Lady Raleigh as she gazed with fond sadness at the beautiful young woman across the room. Olivia desperately needed someone to tear her away from those silent, damning thoughts—the ones that ate at her and kept her from her grandmother's company, even while she was in the same room.

"What do you think of your gown, dear?" inquired the dowager loudly, hoping to break Olivia from the new trance that had gripped her young charge.

Olivia turned her head to look at her grandmother. Her eyes, even though they were focused on her relative, seemed to look through her. "It's lovely, of course."

Lady Raleigh nodded vigorously. "And so it is. There can be no doubt about that. And you will look lovely in it, my girl," she announced in ringing tones, and she hit her cane on the ground for emphasis.

Slowly Olivia dropped her gaze from her grandmother's, and she searched distractedly for the embroidery she had left near her seat. Finding it, she picked at the tiny threads with abstracted movements of her hands, all the while a single crease deepening on her forehead.

Olivia's response to compliments always mystified Lady Raleigh. Any other girl her age would be overjoyed to have Olivia's looks, and make no bones about it. Her lovely dark hair, straight yet richly imbued with body, made her skin look incredibly pure and creamy. And those eyes! God help any man who could look into those exquisitely unnerving blue eyes twice and not be intrigued.

In addition to all of this, Olivia was statuesque and perfectly proportioned. No one could accuse her of being too thin or too heavy, or too anything, except maybe too beautiful.

But Olivia was not any other girl, as she knew all too well. Among other things, she was not interested in her appearance. She refused to pick out her own gowns, but had her grandmother choose them for her. Whenever the topic of fashion was brought up, she never participated in any of the discussions.

But even more peculiar was her reaction to compliments. Even the vaguest reference to her beauty sent Olivia off in another direction. It was as if she found the whole thought of her appearance an anathema to her existence.

Lady Raleigh had tried to get her granddaughter used to the idea of being complimented, but so far she had failed miserably. She worried about what would happen when Olivia was asked for her hand in marriage. How would she react then?

Time would tell, thought the dowager grimly.

After the servant arrived with the tea things, Olivia set herself to the task of pouring out the steaming liquid. Keeping her hands busy helped her to think, and she needed to think right now.

Her grandmother didn't mean to be unkind, she knew, but she wished she wouldn't waste so much time thinking about her granddaughter's appearance. Olivia didn't want to be attractive. Beauty just called attention to itself, and she did not wish to be noticed. When she was young, being noticed had only brought her trouble, and she did not want more of that kind of attention. She didn't feel equal to it. Not even after all these years of practicing self-defense.

Like a trigger, her desire to forget the past only brought the memories on more strongly. Immediately her surroundings faded, and she was cast back into her childhood.

The manor house had grown dark and murky. Maddie was too old to do the cleaning, and even if she did not suffer so severely from arthritis, her father would not have let anyone diligently clean the house anyway. He had professed a liking for the tumbledown feel of the house with its dark and musty corners. He had called it scholarly, although where he had gotten that notion from, Olivia had no idea.

Their visitors had dwindled down to nothing. Except for the occasional tradesman, no one came to Gateland

Manor except the postman, and even he showed up infrequently. Olivia didn't know who was in the neighborhood anymore because she was not allowed to wander out of the house to find out. Even the grounds surrounding the house were forbidden to her. She had to sneak outside while her father was drunk in order to get any fresh air.

The wrinkles on Olivia's fair brow grew more pronounced as she thought for the hundredth time about those last few years of her father's life. As an adult, she could look back at them and calmly rationalize that her father was sick. He had suffered some debilitating illness, and he didn't want anyone to see him. But what always puzzled her was why he didn't want anyone to see her.

In his most debauched states, when Olivia had been unable to avoid him, he had spouted something about her being as good as dead. His beautiful child, he would cry, was dead, just like her mother. Then, seeing past Olivia into some other life, he would drag himself to his knees and beg her, his Olivia, to forgive him for killing her. He hadn't wanted to do it, he had said. He had just wanted her to be happy.

At other times, Wentworth would simply rage at her. He had called her names that Olivia had never heard, and had ranted that she had sold herself to the devil. Olivia had covered her ears to the abuse, but she could always hear it. Sometimes the hate echoed in her head for hours on end, and there would be no one else around to dispute the perceived truth of his words.

Perhaps Olivia could have dealt with the abuse had she felt she had not been the cause of his sickness. Just to look at her seemed to drive her father further over the edge. And when he remembered how much she looked like her mother, he was always worse.

Desperate to protect herself, Olivia had tried to wall

off her feelings for her father. She tried not to pursue his love. She tried not to want to make him happy.

But at times, when Wentworth seemed more lucid than others, he would hold out his arms and beg Olivia to forgive him for saying the things that he had. He loved her, he would say, because she was his last remaining bonny lass. And couldn't she see her way to being patient with him just a little while longer? Olivia had cried and promised that she would. And then the cycle would start again.

A heavy weight fell slowly inside Olivia, oppressing her. Diligently she struggled against its strength, fighting for control. Her father's sickness was not her fault. She had not caused it. She had to believe that. Otherwise she couldn't live with the truth.

With a soft thud, a furry white body landed in her lap. More by rote than by conscious thought, Olivia's hand began to stroke the fur. Slowly, painfully, the black memories receded. Then, after a million years, as she fought down dread and remorse, the object she was holding became familiar. "Isis," she murmured, her hand fondling the cat's head, smoothing the softly shadowed black ears. The vitality of the other voice brought reality back with a crash.

"That cat is terribly spoiled, Olivia."

With feigned calmness, Olivia looked up at her grandmother. How long had she been lost in her past? Minutes? Seconds? With relief, she saw that Lady Raleigh's face was filled with mild reproach, not concern. Good, it couldn't have been too long, then. She picked up the Siamese cat and held it to her face, looking into its eyes. *Only you know how close I came to losing everything, Isis,* she thought. *You were the only one that was there.*

"Yes, I know."

Gently she placed the cat on the floor and picked up

the teapot. More assured, Olivia started to pour the hot fluid into the little delicate china cups.

Her lips were a lush shade of red. She looked closer. Green cat's eyes; large and seductively slanted with kohl. Platinum blond hair framed a perfectly flawless complexion. One small mole sat strategically near those full, red, pouting lips.

Lady Beatrice Chisolm scrutinized the face looking back at her in the mirror carefully. It was a beautiful face, she knew. She glanced down at the full figure carefully accented by the flimsy negligee. She took another mental inventory. Firm torso, long silky legs, magnolia petal skin. Beatrice meticulously counted up her assets. Her eyes flew back up to her face, and she smiled at her own reflection. This would be the night, she decided. She had never looked better.

The door behind Beatrice opened soundlessly, and the Marquis of Traverston emerged from the bedroom beyond. He crossed the intervening space between them, silently admiring his mistress's form in the diaphanous gown, just as he was meant to do.

The high-heeled mules encasing her tiny feet hid more of her body than did the rest of her ensemble, Traverston thought sardonically. He treated himself to a long look at her sumptuous perfection as he finished tying his cravat.

"Don't say you have to go now, my love," purred the countess in her most seductive voice. "I've just ordered us a light supper." She pouted her full lips with a practiced ease. It would take a stronger man than him to leave her now. She was sure of it. "You can't just leave me to eat all by myself." She placed a long slender finger on her lips, playfully nipping the end of it with her perfect white teeth. Then she pushed the digit more fully in her mouth, looking at the marquis through her lashes as she did. She couldn't quite keep the triumphant smile from teasing her pursed lips.

Traverston knew this game better than she did. His response was ruthless. Turning away from her, he replied, "I'm sure you will manage."

With another pretty pout, she picked up her hairbrush and began to stroke her gleaming yellow hair. The movement of her arms gave Traverston tantalizing flashes of her almost naked breasts, and he smiled to himself at the obvious ploy even while consciously resisting his body's reaction to her.

"It would be a shame if I had to send it back," she finished with a seductive glance at him from the mirror.

Despite himself, the marquis was intrigued. She seemed more resistant to the idea of his leaving than usual. They did have a good time together, true, but he sensed something more to her machinations than just another romp under the covers. What could she have planned? He smiled inwardly. She was too obvious by half. For that reason alone he was planning on giving her the congé tonight. It would be amusing to toy with her first, though. He wanted to see what petty scheme she might try on him now.

Reaching over her to take the brush from her hand, his arm rubbed against her. He could see the excitement his touch caused her through the peer glass. Her rosy nipples had grown hard, and she squirmed with anticipation as he examined the silver setting thoughtfully. Finally he pulled a chair close to hers and sat with his knees touching her back. With slow, ponderous strokes, he ran the horsehair bristles over her head.

Beatrice closed her eyes and gave in willingly to the seduction. She made little moaning noises with every stroke of the brush.

Traverston bent his head forward and began nibbling on her neck. She had a lovely neck, he had to admit. Her creamy skin, soft and appealing over the graceful arch, was incredibly enticing.

But that wasn't all. He inhaled deeply. Her perfume was the kind that invaded a man's nostrils. He took another whiff, its strong, heady scent yet another invitation to remain.

Beatrice purred like a cat and reached back over her head to grab his shoulder. She angled her body back to get more of his lovemaking, turning her head to receive his lips with her own.

After the first long, deep kiss, she murmured against his neck, "Oh, Trav. We're so good together."

It had finally come. He was a little disappointed that the game hadn't lasted longer. The chase had an intrigue of its own which he rather enjoyed. But then he pushed that thought back. Beatrice was no school miss, and he would have to be careful around her. Whatever she had in mind, she had been a long time in planning it. She must be impatient to have done with it, though, to have brought up the subject before he had a chance to take her back to bed.

Traverston pulled back a little to look into her face. Her eyes were still closed, her lashes long and dark against the skin. As she reveled in the luxurious feel of a woman who was being admired, she purred contentedly. She kept her eyes closed and pretended to be unaware of his scrutiny.

After a short while, she pulled him by the shoulder and back up against her lips. She licked his mouth, inviting his tongue to mingle with her own. His mouth opened obligingly, and she daringly explored the upper reaches of his mouth with a slow, heavy and suggestive movement of her tongue. He was quick to capture her lips more fully with his own, and briefly he let himself enjoy the honeyed taste of her mouth as he waited for her to continue with the verbal portion of her assault.

"I'm so lonely without you, my love," she murmured against his lips, her voice husky with passion. "All those long nights without you, when we must pretend indifference to the rest of the world. And so—" she kissed him more deeply before continuing "—I've been thinking...why don't we make our liaison one of a more permanent nature?"

Beatrice was so absorbed with her own desire, it took her a moment to notice that the marquis had sat back in his chair, distancing himself from her. Piqued when she no longer felt his touch after a while, she opened her eyes. The space above her was empty.

In confusion, she turned around on her stool to look at him. Traverston's cold expression took her by surprise. Reflexively she grasped the transparent material of her negligee more closely around her neck for protection.

The marquis waited a moment before answering her question, his smile tolerantly amused. "You shouldn't think, Beatrice, it's not a chore that you're accustomed to."

She pouted her lips more fully. "You don't have to be rude, Trav," she sulked. "I don't see that it's such a bad idea."

He laughed outright then. Her ire rose as she realized he found the thought genuinely comical.

"Do you know why we will never marry, Beatrice?" he asked her. Then he immediately answered his own question. "No, you wouldn't. You don't see the things you don't want to, love, and that's why you've completely missed your target this time."

"What do you mean?" She had a slightly desperate edge to her voice, and Traverston understood that she was just beginning to realize that she was not going to win this particular battle.

"We're lovers, my dear. That's all. Nothing more. And in about—" he glanced at his pocket watch "—five minutes, we won't even be that anymore." He stood up and brusquely dug through his coat to find the long slender box he was seeking.

When he had located it, he brought the gray velvet case over to her where she sat before the mirror, and held it out to her. "Here. This is it."

Tentatively she took it from him, her expression confused. "I don't understand, Trav. Haven't you enjoyed my company these last six months?"

"Immensely, my dear. But it's time I moved along."

She opened the box and glanced briefly at the stunning diamond bracelet that lay glittering on its soft bed of velvet. Then her wide, staring eyes locked with his again. "But why leave if you like us being together? I don't understand."

Traverston realized she was genuinely upset when the diamonds failed to hold her interest for more than a few seconds. He sighed and pulled over the chair he had recently vacated. As he seated himself, he explained. "It's very simple, really. Let me see if I can put it plainly for you." His mouth quirked up at the corner. "You're too predictable."

The lady was indignant. "I don't know what you mean." Immediately Beatrice cursed herself. She hadn't meant to sound so shrewish.

Traverston laughed. It wasn't a pleasant sound.

"Come, come, Beatrice," he mocked. "What did you expect me to do? Fall down at your pretty little dimpled feet and beg you to be my bride?" He laughed again, shaking his head. "Surely you know me better than that by now."

Beatrice looked vexed. "You don't have to make it sound like such a ridiculous idea," she said tartly. "After all, you must have an heir one day, and then who are you going to marry?" She sneered. "Some little missish girl out of the schoolroom?" She laughed a sound almost as unpleasant as the marquis's. "No, you are right, Trav," she agreed. "I do know you. You'd never marry some milk-faced puling little brat."

In the span of a heartbeat, her manner changed. Once again she was soft and seductive. She stood up and melted into Traverston's arms as if she had every right to be there.

Lowering her eyelashes, she looked up at him through their silken length, the action making her appear more felinelike than ever. "But you could marry me. I'm a countess, and eminently respectable. I even have a small fortune of my own...not that you would need it." Her voice grew softer. "Wouldn't you like to be married to me, Trav?" she purred, her hands stroking his body. "Don't you like it when we're together?"

Abruptly he stood up, inadvertently dumping the countess on the floor. He stalked away a few paces before he snapped around to face her again. The lines and planes of his face were harsh, and his expression was one of contempt.

"Do you know, Beatrice? I find that I grow more tired of you every day. That's why you got the bracelet instead of a ring." He laughed when he saw her expression. "Oh, please. Don't play the wounded lover with me." Abruptly he moved to where he had dropped his coat and pulled it on, his movements hard and rigid with anger. "You know the rules of the game as well as I do, and I've let you step around them once too often."

She gasped in outrage, but he cut her off before she could make a reply. "This liaison has gone on far too long." He smiled coldly at her. "It's been a pleasure making your acquaintance, my dear."

As she struggled to get up off the floor and retain her dignity, he let out his final parting shot as he was opening the door. "Oh, and Beatrice," Traverston added almost as an afterthought, "I'm already married."

The door slammed shut on her outburst.

It should have been a magical scene. It was not.

The green-marble and gold ballroom was filled to capacity with the wealthy and the beautiful, but the sight filled the marquis with disgust. The hot, airless ballroom was permeated with the sweet pungent odor of exotic perfumes overlaid with the acrid smell of unwashed bodies. The combination made Traverston wish that he had gone anywhere but to this gathering tonight. Still, for some reason he could not name even to himself, he stayed.

He lounged negligently against a fluted Corinthian column and casually watched the crowd through narrowed eyes. In silence, he cursed the misguided sentiment that led him to accept the invitation to this particular ball. If only Beatrice hadn't chosen last night to spring her little surprise on him, he might have been at the opera tonight with her instead.

But no, he corrected himself. Regardless of what her intentions had been, he would have had done with her yesterday. To think otherwise was plain and simple folly.

He grunted in disgust. He must be getting old to be thinking such maudlin thoughts. Absently he retrained his wandering mind onto the whirling couples below him.

Traverston did not normally attend social functions of the ton. This came as a great relief to most of the hostesses of the upper ten thousand. As a wealthy bachelor with an important title, the marquis's presence in London could hardly be ignored, so the ladies sent him their engraved invitations edged with gold. But they usually prayed fervently that he would not come. On one thing the gossipmongers were all in agreement: the Marquis of Traverston was a most disturbing man.

Usually it was in Traverston's best interests to oblige the dragonesses that dictated the whims and fancies of society. He didn't, after all, think much of their frivolous parties and gay gatherings. But tonight, he hadn't been in the mood to oblige them. In fact, he had gone out of his way to get the vicious rumor mill started tonight. Already he had ruined one gentleman's reputation over cards, and if he had anything to say about it, he would terrorize the sweet young debutantes later this evening just for fun.

"What? Lord Traverston?" A jovial voice bombarded his eardrum, disturbing his solitary reverie. "Bit of a surprise to find you here, old chap."

Reluctantly Traverston acknowledged the existence of Sir John Whetmore, a distant acquaintance of his from the club, with a barely perceptible nod.

The gentleman stared good-naturedly at Traverston, mistaking the peer's lack of civility for an inability to recognize him. He took the marquis's hand and moved it up and down several times like a water pump. "Don't you remember me?" inquired the gentleman with too much jocularity. "Sir John Whetmore," he supplied helpfully.

Traverston remained where he was, slouched against the pillar. "What brings you to this insufferable crush, Whetmore?" inquired the marquis languidly.

"Oh, tush-tush!" pronounced the intruder with a booming laugh. "You've got too much town bronze, my lord! This party is simply ripping. Never had such a fine time." Whetmore grasped the edge of his waistband as if to emphasize his own complacency with the affair. "After all, 'tis a great success for Lady Eddington, don't you know."

When Lord Traverston failed to look impressed at this piece of information, Whetmore added significantly, "She's my niece, don't you know."

"Ah," said the marquis knowingly as he pushed himself upright off the column. He had definitely had enough of this pompous little man. He executed the smallest of bows to his fellow club member. "Then I must apologize, sir. Of course her ball is a smashing success."

Traverston excused himself from Whetmore's presence, keeping his exit just a cut above a snub. If there was one thing he was not in the mood for, he thought grimly as he stalked away from his former perch above the main floor, it was issuing mealymouthed phrases to placate some overblown tulip of the gentry.

The marquis fought his way down the short staircase and forward through the crowd, heading in the general direction of the refreshments at the far side of the room. He didn't make it more than a couple of feet, though, before he was stopped dead in his tracks.

The object that prevented his continued passage through the crowd was perhaps seventy-five feet away from him across the room. In addition to that, there were at least two dozen people between him and her, including several whirling couples. But she stopped him all the same.

She was absolutely dazzling. Unlike most of the debutantes tonight, who looked insipid or even silly in white, this woman was magnificent. Even from a distance Traverston could see that she was unaffected by the oppressive heat and noise of the room. She looked calm, cool and pretty, and the crowd seemed to part for her automatically as she made her stately way through the masses.

"She's fantastic, isn't she?"

The voice in Traverston's ear was so close to his own sentiment that he didn't realize at first that someone was actually speaking to him. Still somewhat distracted, the marquis turned slowly toward the source of the rhetorical question, his eyes only reluctantly leaving the vision behind.

When Traverston identified the speaker, his reply was

smooth and even. "Monquefort. I've no idea how you managed to find me in this squeeze, but I'm grateful. This gathering has become intolerable."

The gentleman Traverston addressed was almost as devastatingly handsome as the marquis himself. Almost, but not quite.

Like the marquis, Lord Buxley, the Earl of Monquefort, was tall with broad shoulders and well-formed legs that needed no padding to look good in the formfitting clothes currently in fashion. But his slim, perfectly proportioned physique was where the similarity stopped.

Where the marquis was dark and mysterious, the earl was open and friendly. His smile was famous with the ladies, or perhaps infamous, as the dowagers would say. Women of every age seemed to gravitate to his blond good looks and careless charm, almost against their will.

For the *ton*, it was the mystery of the decade as to why the two men were friends, for they were almost as dissimilar in temperament as they were in looks. Indeed, it is doubtful that even Traverston or the earl could have said why they were friends. But neither one ever doubted the fact.

Tonight, as always, Monquefort had chosen his clothes with impeccable taste. His blue bath coat fit his shoulders without a wrinkle; his buff-colored pantaloons were snug and firm. The cravat around his throat was intricately tied in the style known as "the waterfall", and the shine on his Hessian boots made all the dandies present groan with envy.

In comparison with the earl, the marquis was almost casual about his clothing. To be sure, he chose his outfits with the same care as the earl, patronizing only the finest tailors for his raiment. But, unlike Monquefort, once Traverston put on his clothes he forgot about them, never pausing even once during the day to examine his appearance.

As a consequence, the marquis had a certain masculine laissez-faire quality to him—an aura most members of the *ton* perceived but were never quite able to put their fingers on. His raven black hair, too long to be called stylish, only added to his rakish good looks.

All signs of dissipation, so evident eight years ago, were almost completely erased from the marquis's appearance. All that remained of the hard living he had subjected his body to back in his younger days were the lines etched around the sides of his mouth, and the hard glint in his chilling gray eyes. They gave him a hard, implacable look. Many members of society had remarked that Traverston looked like a man who had fought with the devil...and won.

Monquefort's reply to his friend was amused. "Excruciating, indeed, my lord." His next comment caught the marquis off guard. "I see you have noticed the Ice Queen."

Traverston's raised eyebrow was the only prod Monquefort needed to burst out laughing at his friend's expense. "Come now, man," he exclaimed. "Don't try and tell me you didn't notice her. I saw you gaping."

"Really, Monquefort," purred the marquis warningly, "your attempt at levity fails to amuse me. If you really want to amuse yourself, I suggest you seek your pleasures elsewhere. I'm not in the mood to entertain you tonight."

With his usual lack of respect for proprieties, the earl plowed ahead with his observations. "But that's why you like me, Trav," replied the man. "I'm such an amusing fellow. Besides, you know part of my charm is my disarming honesty," he smirked.

"Cut line, Alex," demanded the marquis with none of his usual tolerance for the young nobleman's witty banter. "You've obviously got something you want to say. Come out with it!"

Monquefort blinked at the marquis in mock confusion,

his hands held up in a gesture of innocence. "I just wanted to give you the information you are looking for. What more could a friend offer than that?"

Though the silence emanating from Traverston was palpable, the earl managed to retain his easy smile even in the face of this unencouraging response. But he didn't have to wait long for the marquis's reply.

"And what," he growled softly, "is it, pray tell, that I want to know?"

Monquefort's smile was triumphant. "But her name, of course," he replied equally quietly.

In the face of the marquis's black frown, the earl wisely decided not to tease his friend any longer. "The lady in question is Miss Olivia Wentworth." When this tidbit of information failed to lighten the expression on Traverston's face, Monquefort cautiously added, "Miss Wentworth is the granddaughter of the Duke of Stonebridge."

In point of fact, the marquis did not react to Monquefort's news for the simple reason that he was stunned. It was a full five seconds before Traverston whipped around to seek out the vision in white again.

There she was, just ten feet away from where he had spotted her originally. The young lady was deep in conversation with one of British society's queens, Lady Jersey. Any other girl in her slippers would be quaking in fear, noted the marquis, but Olivia was not.

Olivia's height and posture gave her a regal appearance, and she somehow managed to make Lady Jersey, an animated person with a powerful presence in her own right, look small and bland by comparison.

Her perfectly shaped head was blessed with the classical features found only on Greek statues. That, and her long, graceful, swanlike neck, made Olivia look like a goddess who had stepped down from the heavens to temporarily grace a gathering of mortals. Her white gown of gossamer-thin silk, draped in folds over a petticoat of pale blue satin, only heightened this illusion. And her hair! He had never seen such a glorious pile of rich dark hair on any other woman.

The heat didn't touch her, Traverston noticed as he felt the sweat trickle down his own brow. She was a spot of calm in a tempestuous sea of humanity. She was as cool as...as cool as ice. The Ice Queen. Wasn't that what Monquefort had called her? Somehow the name seemed fitting. And not altogether appealing.

Traverston turned back to his friend. His hand shot out and he grabbed the earl's upper arm in a viselike grip. Ignoring the other man's outcry, Traverston propelled him backward through the crowds until they reached the far corner of the ballroom. The immediate area was cluttered with potted plants, providing the men with some measure of privacy.

"What the devil..." sputtered Monquefort, but Traverston quickly cut him off.

"What do you know of her?" demanded the marquis, shaking Monquefort's upper arm for emphasis.

Monquefort, startled at his friend's unusual behavior, looked astounded. "What the devil has gotten into you, Trav?" queried the earl.

Traverston removed his hand from Monquefort and partially turned away from him in an effort to gain control over himself. Without meaning to, he automatically searched for Olivia. She was still with Lady Jersey. After the briefest of moments, he turned back.

"What do you know of her?" repeated Traverston again, only slightly more calm than before.

Monquefort eyed his friend warily before answering. "Very little, actually. Mostly what I've just said." He hastily continued when the marquis started to become angry again. "She's just come out...made her debut about a month or two ago. It took her awhile to do it, seeing as how her grandmother was sick last season. Apparently she had no one else to see to the task. She doesn't seem to care for men, leastwise not the young ones." He racked his brains for something else to say. Traverston's look grew grimmer until the earl quickly added, "Flattery turns her off. Doesn't seem to be any way to get a reaction out of her. That's why she's called the Ice Queen." He stopped and eyed the marquis with trepidation.

Traverston's eyes seemed to ignite with an inner fire as he listened to the words trip off Monquefort's tongue. His face took on the lines of decisiveness as his friend finished his litany. "Introduce me to her," he commanded.

"Hell and damnation, Traverston!" exclaimed the earl belligerently. "I can't do that. I've not even properly made her acquaintance myself!"

Traverston was remorseless, however, and he gripped Monquefort's arm tightly, leaning into his face for emphasis. "Introduce me to her," he said slowly, enunciating each word carefully.

The look Monquefort gave the marquis was penetrating, and what he saw there must have convinced him that he could not refuse his friend's request, because the next thing he knew, he was leading Traverston over to where the beautiful Ice Queen herself was standing.

A minute or so passed before Olivia and her grandmother noticed the presence of the two men standing to their left. Thoughtfully, both ladies graciously turned enough in their direction in order that the men could politely "do the pretty" without undue hardship on their part.

The Earl of Monquefort stood patiently waiting for an opening in the ladies' conversation, but a painful pinch reminded him of the marquis's urgency. He kicked himself mentally as he butted in. "Lady Raleigh, Miss Wentworth, I do hope you remember me," began the earl with no little embarrassment.

Olivia was the first to respond to the handsome peer's polite intrusion. She graciously inclined her head. "Of course we do, Lord Monquefort. We met at the Seftons' masque."

The earl's relief was almost palpable. "You are quite gracious to remember, Miss Wentworth. But please, allow me to introduce you to a friend of mine who is most anxious to make your acquaintance."

Olivia's eyes shifted away from the earl to take in the gentleman standing next to him. She was totally unprepared for the sight of the darkly handsome marquis. Traverston's sudden appearance at her side shocked her speechless.

By this time, the marquis's control had returned to him. Bowing over Olivia's hand and brushing her fingers with his lips, he allowed himself to make eye contact with her. He was momentarily taken aback by their unusual color. They were such an unusual shade of blue he didn't see how he could have forgotten them.

He held her hand for just a little longer than polite society would dictate as proper before righting himself again. He smiled into those pale, pale eyes and made his own introduction.

"Your husband, I believe."

At Traverston's words, Olivia's famed expressionless cool gave out with a vengeance. Without a word she crumpled slowly to the floor, her body having no more firmness to it than that of a rag doll.

Chapter Five

As Olivia's grandmother let out an exclamation of horror, Traverston picked up his wife's still form and carried her swiftly from the room. With luck, he found an unoccupied salon a few doors down from the ballroom. Carefully he deposited his bundle on a red velvet sofa.

Within moments, Lady Raleigh and the earl came hurrying into the room, each demanding an explanation.

With a calm that astonished the earl, given his friend's intensity earlier in the evening, Traverston swiftly walked to the entrance of the salon and closed the door, effectively blocking out the startled onlookers. He turned back to face the pair, his expression a mask.

"Is this young woman really Olivia Wentworth?" he demanded, his harshness at odds with the delicate way he had treated his wife. His question cut through Lady Raleigh's impending tirade.

"Of course she is," she replied with outrage. "Why should you doubt it? And what on earth possessed you to say such an incredible thing to my granddaughter?" The dowager duchess's demands were every bit as compelling as the marquis's in tone and temper.

Traverston sneered slightly as he replied, "I doubt it, because the last time I left my *wife*," he said, emphasizing the last word, "she was safely ensconced at Gateland Manor." The marquis's hostile glare beat down on the small wrinkled form of Olivia's grandmother as he waited for her reply.

Before his very eyes, Lady Raleigh seemed to gain height and stature. She drew herself up to meet the marquis's challenge. "My lord," she began grandly, imperiously, "I believe we should discuss this in private."

Turning briefly toward the earl, who had witnessed the past five minutes in stunned silence, Lady Raleigh supplicated in a very different tone of voice, "My lord, I kindly ask that you watch over my granddaughter. I don't want her to wake up in here alone." He had nodded his head, for once unable to move his normally quick tongue, and the old woman marched out of the room without sparing a single glance for the marquis. It was obvious that she expected the marquis to follow.

Amazingly he did. It was evident to the marquis that Lady Raleigh was familiar with the house, because she unerringly led him to the Eddingtons' massive library. After a quick glance around the dimly lit room, she beckoned the marquis in and shut the door.

With a grim smile she turned and faced her opponent. "I doubt the tabbies will be able to make anything of my being cloistered in here with you. I'm at least twice your age." Then, as if it had only been an illusion, her smile disappeared. "We must talk."

Traverston responded with a slight nod and waited for her to continue.

"My lord," began Lady Raleigh, only to falter. The fact of the matter was she didn't know what to say. Her magnificent diamond tiara and necklace sparkled in the candlelight as she began to agitatedly pace across the carpet. In all her long years, she had never had to deal with a situation like this. The simple fact of the matter was that the Dowager Duchess of Stonebridge was at a loss.

Watching her evident confusion, the marquis felt a trace of pity for the old lady. But almost immediately he squelched the emotion. She should be uncomfortable, he reasoned. This muddy state of affairs rested on her head. How dare she bring his wife into society without notifying him first?

At length, Lady Raleigh began again. "My lord," she addressed him, her voice stronger and with more authority than before, "my granddaughter has lived with me for the past six years, and I never once heard her mention your name." She stared at the marquis triumphantly, as though she had finally hit upon the heart of the problem.

Traverston was silent, his eyes mere slits as he studied her. Did this woman really expect him to believe that she knew nothing at all about his marriage to Olivia? It was impossible! Unthinkable!

And then his conscience nagged at him. Or was it?

Casting his mind back to the scene in his family chapel so long ago, the scene he had tried so carefully not to remember, Traverston realized it might indeed be possible.

After all, what proof did he have that Wentworth had informed his daughter of her married status? What mention had he heard made of the arrangement in front of Olivia? A smile almost flashed across his face as he remembered a young girl solemnly declaring "amen" to the question of matrimony. She hadn't even realized she had a leading role in the wedding ceremony, the poor chit.

But she was hardly a chit now. His loins became warm at the thought of the regal beauty lying close by. No, she was a woman, and a highly desirable one at that. He couldn't quite grasp the enormity of having such a stunning morsel as his wife. For that matter, he couldn't quite grasp the reality of having a wife at all, much less one that looked like Olivia.

As the marquis mused on these matters, his reply was almost inaudible. "I imagine that is because she never knew my name."

Lady Raleigh stared at the marquis, her mouth forming a surprised O. His was an unanticipated response. "But...but that is absurd!" she sputtered.

At the dowager's outrage, he snapped out of his reverie. "What? Not knowing her own husband's name? I couldn't agree with you more." His words were angry, clipped. "I imagine her father never told her of my presence at all. I doubt Olivia even knew she was married." Suddenly he looked intense, murderous, and he stalked closer to Lady Raleigh. "Where is her father now?" he demanded.

Despite her best efforts to keep calm, a quiver of fear ran through Lady Raleigh's breast. What rumors had she heard of this man? Something about a black and tainted past? What crimes to her person would he be capable of committing?

Pulling the pieces of her dignity around her like a cloak, Lady Raleigh replied as fervently as she could, "He's dead, thank heaven!"

When the marquis made no move to back away from her, she explained, "He died when Olivia was twelve years old. After that, she came to live with me. She has no other family." Lady Raleigh tried to still her quaking knees as she stared bravely into the marquis's fearsome visage.

Traverston's features were so still that his face might have been etched from stone. "Then it would appear, madam, I was correct. Olivia was never informed of our marriage." He backed away as quickly as he had stalked her.

As Lady Raleigh's courage began to seep back into

her bones, she confronted the marquis with the obvious question. "But how could Olivia go through a marriage ceremony and not realize what was happening?"

One corner of his mouth twitched up in a slightly mocking smile and he replied enigmatically, "You had to have been there."

Both parties were silent. Lady Raleigh was appalled by the marquis's words. Desperately, grasping at any straw to extricate her granddaughter from this horrible mess, she jumped on the dim possibility looming in the back of her mind. "I don't suppose your lordship could produce proof of this wedding?"

The sound the grim man made sounded very much like a snort. "I don't happen to have the papers with me right at this moment, my lady," he remarked with ill-concealed and bitter amusement, "but it wouldn't take more than a minute to locate them at my solicitor's. Hardly enough time to postpone the inevitable, I should think, from your point of view. Still, I'd be happy to send him round with them on the morrow. I wouldn't want you to harbor any doubts."

Lady Raleigh drew herself upright at this insult, but she remained quiet and without a response. After a moment, she decided to try a different tack with the highly volatile marquis.

"My lord," she began uncertainly, still trying to gauge his temperament, "You must have married Olivia when she was very young." She waited, expecting him to deny that fact.

Traverston turned away from her. He placed one hand on the fireplace mantel and stared into the flames. Finally he answered.

"Yes. At the time I had no choice."

"No choice? And that was why you have ignored her all these years? Didn't you think to inquire how she was doing? Didn't you have any plans to remove her from Gateland Manor?''

He took his time in answering, his gaze coming up to meet hers reluctantly. ''I had at one time, if you must know. The fact of the matter is I lost track.''

She was flabbergasted by his bald confession. ''Lost track? You lost track of the fact you had a wife? My lord, I cannot believe that you love her!''

He would not be shamed into looking away.

''No.''

Lady Raleigh licked her lips as a sudden thought occurred to her. ''Does this wedding, perhaps,'' she asked tentatively, ''have anything to do with a certain thirty thousand pounds?''

Again he paused before answering. ''Yes.''

''I thought so.'' Her voice was stronger. ''Then it is yours again, my lord. Just leave Olivia alone.'' She walked to him and stood barely a foot away. As he didn't turn around, she addressed her words to his back. ''I am wealthy in my own right. What I have will pass directly to Olivia. She doesn't need your money. It's never been touched.

''I don't know what happened between you and my son-in-law so long ago, my lord, and I don't want to know. I simply want my granddaughter to be happy.

''It is obvious to me that you do not want her. So please, I beg of you, leave this house and never speak of this matter again to anyone. The money will be returned to you tomorrow.''

Slowly he turned around to face the old woman. His look was chilling.

''I don't think so.''

''But why not? You've already expressed your disinterest in her by ignoring her for the last six years—maybe longer, I don't know. You just admitted you've never even attempted to communicate with her. Nothing was found in my son-in-law's papers that even hinted at your existence. Until you showed up proclaiming yourself this evening, the money's origin was just one more mystery surrounding Edgar's death. You can't pretend otherwise." Lady Raleigh's pitch rose with her mounting distress.

"Indeed. I don't deny it."

"Then why do you trouble yourself over Olivia? You don't even know her. Surely it would be best for all of us to carry on as before, with no need for you to take Olivia home as your wife? We will find a way to quietly dissolve the marriage with no one the wiser. Then you can choose any woman to be your wife, if you are still determined to have one."

Traverston's eyes burned brightly as he responded. "My dear lady," he muttered, "I find being married very convenient right now. Pray disabuse yourself of any grand notions you might have about saving Olivia from some terrible fate. It won't happen."

He paused calculatingly. "You see, there is a certain woman I wish to discourage. It wouldn't do at all for her to find out that I'm available, especially when I've taken pains to inform her to the contrary."

"My lord," she pleaded. "Even if you are determined to have Olivia, you must not tell anyone that you are currently her husband!"

Lord Traverston quirked an eyebrow in response. It was a disdainful expression meant to belittle her. "Are you forgetting she and the Earl of Monquefort already know?"

But Lady Raleigh would not back down.

"That doesn't matter. Olivia would never say anything, and I know you could control the earl's tongue. You must not tell anyone else. It would be simply disastrous if it became generally known that you are married to each other. Imagine how it would be batted about when the tabbies found out that after years of marriage, you had to be introduced to each other at a ball!'' Lady Raleigh pounded one fist into her other hand for emphasis. "It would be scandalous!"

Traverston's eyes hardened and they gleamed with a martial light as he addressed the old woman before him. He designed his next words to cut her to the quick. "Maybe you have not heard, my dear lady, but I don't care a great deal about scandals."

But Lady Raleigh was instantly skeptical. She gave the marquis a hard look before saying, "That may have been true at one point in your life, my lord, but it is not true now. Lady Eddington does not invite just anyone to her parties.

"Oh, I know you're still a rakehell and that half the *ton* trembles when you appear, but you're no wastrel. Your manners and appearance are the envy of no few bucks of English society. Your honor is renowned—most of it gained on the dueling field—or so I have been told. You care about your reputation now."

Lord Traverston's reply was vehement. "I assure you I don't care a fig for all of those virtues you have just rambled off. I've lived my life before without honor or virtue. What makes you think I will not choose to do so again?" His eyes sparked red-hot anger, and Lady Raleigh felt her knees start to turn soft.

Olivia, she thought to herself bracingly. This is for Olivia. "All right," she retorted just as angrily. "Maybe you don't care a whit for your life, but I care for Olivia's. If you insist on being her husband now, then you will ruin her, and that I will not allow. I have lost one daughter in this lifetime to poor actions and poor choices, and I will not lose a second."

The marquis's reaction was cool, smothering and disdainful. "I don't see that you have any choice."

His opponent's eyes flashed. "No, you're right, my

lord. I don't have any choice. But I do know that if you take Olivia away from me right now, take her away as your wife, your mother will never forgive you."

Traverston stood stock-still with surprise, not believing what he had just heard. Then quickly, he wiped the shock from his face. "What do you mean by that, old woman?" he rasped from between clenched teeth.

Lady Raleigh's face grew keen. "Oh, yes. Didn't you know?" she asked, knowing full well that he did not. "Your mother is still alive...and doing quite nicely, I might add."

The marquis eyed her warily, his temporary shock giving away to anger. "You're wrong, old woman. My mother died over a score of years ago, defamed and dishonored when the ship she and her lover were on went down in the Mediterranean."

"Oh, I'm sure that is what your father told you—what he wanted you to believe—but it couldn't be further from the truth. She's very much alive and living in Italy. She and I have been correspondents through all of these years." Lady Raleigh glanced at him speculatively, weighing her next words carefully. "We were very close in school, you see."

Traverston's expression became shuttered. There was no way Lady Raleigh could tell what he was thinking. "Very clever," he said evenly, and he gave her a mocking bow. "Very clever, my lady. But your news doesn't matter now. It might have mattered a great deal at one time, but not now. Your surprise announcement changes nothing."

"My lord," responded the dowager, trying one last appeal. She placed her hand on his arm. "If you will not wait to claim Olivia for any other reason, then do so merely because I ask." She looked into his eyes, her own misting. "Have pity on an old woman, for I am old, just as you have taken pains to point out to me tonight. Have pity on an old woman who has just found her granddaughter, and is now about to lose her. I fear her sudden absence from my life would be too much for me. I'd be all alone again, just like after the duke died. I need time to adjust to the idea of Olivia's marriage. Please, I beg of you, give us one last month together.''

The marquis looked down on the woman begging him for mercy and for the first time in as long as he could remember, he felt the stirrings of some softer emotion. Lady Raleigh's plea tugged at his heart and melted its stubborn core just a little. Without volition, he sighed. He brought one hand up to rub at the grit in his eyes, the action more telling than his next words. With resignation he asked, ''What do you suggest we do?''

Lady Raleigh closed her eyes briefly in thankfulness. Her prayers had been answered. She had won her reprieve.

When she opened them again, they were clear and decisive. ''You must court her like you would any young girl you would consider marrying.''

Traverston's laugh was sharp. ''But my dear lady,'' he replied sarcastically, ''I am not contemplating marriage with any young girl.''

''No,'' she agreed with a hint of contempt, ''you've already wed one.''

The light of amusement left his face as quickly as it had come. ''You do not know the circumstances surrounding that decision,'' he growled. ''And no,'' he added, before she had a chance to interrupt, ''I do not care to share them with you.''

Lady Raleigh was piqued, but she chose to ignore the slight. ''You will court her,'' she said, verbally challenging him to defy her, ''so that society can get used to the idea of your relationship. In a month's time, you will depart London for your estate, taking Olivia with you. I will put it about that you were married by special license, with my approval, of course. Neither you nor Olivia were interested in a large societal wedding.''

Heavily, as if he were pondering the proposal, Traverston walked over to one of the bookshelves. But there was nothing to think about, really. It was a good plan. But he didn't mind making her squirm a bit while she waited for his response.

It wouldn't hurt him to wait a month to take possession of the beautiful Miss Wentworth. He had, after all, waited eight years already, at times almost forgetting her existence. But not any longer.

He smiled at the thought. The Ice Queen. What a perfect foil for his tempestuous self. It would be amusing to see if he could arouse in her the more passionate feelings inherent in human nature. He would set himself the task of melting this oh-so-chilly Ice Queen.

"Your plan is fine," he finally announced, his back still to her.

When Traverston finally turned around to face the dowager again, his grin made her heart begin beating fearfully once again.

Monquefort studied the features of the beautiful woman reclined on the sofa before him. God, she was exquisite! In sleep she was even more attractive than before. Probably because when she was unconscious, she lost all trace of her haughty coldness. She looked as harmless and innocent as a little girl, he thought.

Monquefort mentally brought himself up short. What was he thinking? Why, he hardly knew this girl! And yet, amazingly enough, he recognized in himself a strong desire to protect her.

As if his thoughts were enough to wake her, Olivia's eyes flew open and she bolted upright. He laid a gently restraining hand on her. She gripped it hard and looked up into his face with anxiety.

"Who was he?" she asked, her eyes wide with fear.

Monquefort looked at her questioningly. Then, realizing her anxiety must have been caused by the marquis, he smoothly disengaged one of her slim, graceful hands and placed it in his own. He patted it reassuringly.

"His name is John Markston, and he is the fourth Marquis of Traverston," he replied simply.

Olivia turned quickly to look at the door. It was closed and they were alone. Relieved, she slumped back against the cushions and closed her eyes. Thank God, he wasn't here.

Still holding her hand, Monquefort attempted to soothe her. "He isn't a bad bloke, you know. I mean," he interrupted himself hastily, "I have no idea what all that hubbub was about, so I couldn't begin to defend him even if I wanted to, but, in general, I mean, he isn't bad." The earl stopped speaking when he realized he was blathering on nonsensically like a schoolboy in short pants.

But already Olivia's mind had drifted away from her present surroundings. She was remembering the only other time she had seen Lord Traverston since that strange day so long ago at Norwood Park. She had nearly blacked out then, too.

One day when Olivia was sixteen, Lady Raleigh had asked her granddaughter to accompany her to the shops, thinking that the two ladies could obtain some ribbon to refurbish some of their older bonnets. Olivia, who was only too happy to comply with her grandmother's wishes, went along with her willingly.

The women had just stepped from the carriage and onto the pavement when Olivia saw him. He and a companion, a lush red-haired vixen with beautiful green eyes, were in the process of crossing the street.

Olivia inhaled sharply at the sight of him. Without her knowledge, her hands became numb and she dropped her reticule. Her mouth dropped open and she stood quite still, staring at the couple crossing the street. Her mind went blank with shock, and the only thing Olivia was aware of was an incredible searing pain in the middle of her heart.

He had lied to her. Her father had lied.

Olivia had awakened the morning after the strange ceremony at Norwood Park and rushed downstairs in her nightgown to question her father about the events of the previous evening. But her father was inexplicably angry at her questions. He had insisted that he didn't know what Olivia was talking about. He told her that she had dreamed the stranger up. He argued with her, adamant that there had never been any journey the night before, never any visitor to Gateland Manor the day before. He did not know what she was talking about. The more Olivia insisted she hadn't invented the pirate, the more furious Wentworth became.

Her father told her she was delirious. He told her that if she didn't stop talking about her crazy fantasies, that he would lock her up. He became blue in the face, spitting rage at her. Olivia was forbidden to ask any more questions.

After that, Olivia had run upstairs to be comforted by her old nursemaid. But Maddie wouldn't talk. She became closemouthed and frightened every time Olivia brought the topic up, even casually.

Deep in her heart of hearts Olivia knew that she hadn't imagined her pirate. And there he was! As large as life, walking across the street with his paramour. Wentworth had almost convinced Olivia that the mysterious man from Norwood Park was a fiction of her imagination.

Almost, but not quite.

Traverston was even more handsome than she had remembered. Granted, she had been only ten years old when they first met...if you could even call their few brief meetings an acquaintanceship. But he had been uppermost in her mind almost every day since the first.

Olivia had suffered horribly since she had seen the marquis that day on her way to the shops. Her father's perfidy burned its way through her heart. She didn't understand why her father had despised her so much, or why he should have lied to her. She didn't know what had happened to the loving, caring man she remembered from her early childhood when her sister was still alive. To Olivia, in her simple mind's eye, one day Wentworth had been a loving father, and the next day he was a cold, hard-hearted man.

She really didn't know what had changed his attitude toward her, but secretly, somewhere in the back of her brain, she knew it was her fault. After all, hadn't he reiterated a hundred times that he couldn't stand the sight of her? Wasn't she the cause of all his distress?

Olivia squeezed her eyes tightly shut as she tried to push away the memories flooding through her. She wouldn't cry. She would not. She hadn't cried since she was twelve, and she wasn't about to start now. Instead, she took deep calming breaths, concentrating only on moving the air into and out of her lungs.

Slowly she opened her eyes. She was calmer now; she could cope. Belatedly she realized that she had captured Monquefort's hand again and that it was gripped tightly in her own. His fingers were bloodless from her clasp.

Quickly she released him, giving him an abashed look. "I beg of you to forgive me, my lord," she whispered with embarrassment. "I did not mean to hurt you."

The earl's smile was gentle and refreshing. "Miss Wentworth, I hope you don't get all stiff and formal on me again. The pleasure of holding your hand was well worth a few pins and needles of pain." He laughed at her look of horror. "I'm teasing you, my girl. You look as if you are in need of it."

Olivia, momentarily taken aback by the warmth in his voice, allowed herself a little smile. "You are very kind, my lord. I'm sure I can never repay you for your thoughtfulness."

His look was friendly without being licentious. It was a new experience for Olivia. She had never before held a conversation with a man who didn't try to leer at her and pay her painful compliments. When he spoke again, his simple request took her by surprise.

"Of course you can. By calling me Alex."

"Alex." She tried the name out gingerly. Then with a tentative almost-smile that wavered at the corners of her mouth, she held out her hand. "Please, call me Olivia."

Monquefort's smile grew bigger as he took hold of her proffered hand. "Olivia," he repeated dutifully.

The earl's next words were interrupted by the entrance of Lady Raleigh. Olivia immediately noted the anxiety on her face and felt a stab of guilt for causing it. The dowager was quick to hurry to her granddaughter's side.

"Olivia, my love," she asked with a worried frown, "are you all right?" She tightly gripped the hand Monquefort had so recently released.

Olivia patted her grandmother's hand with her free one. "I'm perfectly fine now, Grandmama. I can't imagine why I fainted." She grimaced at her audience, blithely ignoring the truth for the moment. "I really must learn to eat more at dinner before trying anything as strenuous as dancing."

Lady Raleigh glanced back at the earl with anxiety. She knew Olivia was putting on a brave front for his sake. "My dear, you must be more careful. I'm going to take you home right away. I think perhaps we have been doing too many late nights. You need your rest."

Olivia sat up on the sofa, bracing herself on the cushions for support as she stood up. "Of course you are right, my lady," responded the earl as he, too, gallantly played along with the charade. He assisted Olivia to her feet. "A good night's sleep will be just the ticket. I am sure tomorrow she will feel more the thing."

Olivia turned to the man beside her and held out her hand. Then, with unusual feeling, she showed her gratitude. "Lord Monquefort, thank you for your kind assistance. I hope that the next time I faint I find as gallant a knight as you to come to my rescue."

He smiled into her eyes. "I hope for my own sake that I am that knight." He bent over her hand and kissed it.

Forgetting her manners, Lady Raleigh frowned at the earl's pretty speech and hurried Olivia out the door.

Once in their coach, Lady Raleigh was at once both anxious and reluctant to broach the topic of the night's events. It all seemed like such a hopeless muddle to her. How was she ever going to be able to hand over her granddaughter to that…that…man? He was a cruel, desperate person. It was beyond comprehension. She didn't need to stretch her imagination to believe that Olivia would have a hard time dealing with the mercurial marquis.

The strained silence continued all the way home. The quiet house on Wimpole Street seemed like a haven to both women as the coach came to a stop. As soon as the coachman opened the carriage door, Olivia got out of the vehicle and hurried up the main staircase. She made no effort to keep pace with her grandmother. That would be asking too much from her right now. She had to be alone.

An hour after their return from the Eddingtons' ball, Olivia was still sitting in front of the mirror brushing her hair. She had thought that the normal activity of preparing for bed would help soothe her troubled mind, but it had not. Absently she looked down at her legs and saw Isis rubbing up against them. "Not now, Isis," she said tiredly. "I'm in no condition to comfort you, my pet." In a fit of pique, the cat stalked off toward the window seat. Jumping up with lightning quickness, it settled itself comfortably on the pillow there.

Olivia was not surprised when the knock on her door came a few minutes later. As her grandmother stepped through the door, her ball gown still clinging to her ancient form, Olivia finally stopped her distracted brushing. She set it down and turned to face her guardian.

"It's true, isn't it." Olivia's voice was dead, devoid of emotion.

Lady Raleigh stopped her advance into the room, her face a picture of sadness and pity. "Oh, my dear." The old woman's voice shook with unshed tears.

Olivia turned away and stared at her hands clasped in her lap. Neither said anything for a moment. When Olivia finally looked up again, her eyes were wide and clear. No hint of moisture lingered in their depths.

"I'm going to him," she said firmly. "Tomorrow."

Lady Raleigh immediately became galvanized. "Oh, no, Olivia! You mustn't do anything of the sort!" She rushed to her grandchild, placing herself in front of her as if she could stop her with physical force.

"Why not?" Olivia said with the barest hint of anger, her grandmother's reaction confusing her. "He's my husband, isn't he? If that is the case, then I should be with him."

"Olivia, Olivia!" wailed her grandmother. "You aren't thinking clearly. It's the shock. You can't go running off hurly-burly to some man who claims to be your husband! He hasn't even shown us any proof!" She took a shuddering intake of breath, letting it out in a sob.

"I don't understand what's happened in the last few hours. I never knew that you had a husband. You never mentioned anything like it! Now you tell me that you're going to leave me at a moment's notice for some blackguard who's never even had the decency to write!" She stopped suddenly, looking reproachfully at her grandchild as a new thought hit her. "You haven't been keeping a secret correspondence with him, have you, Olivia?"

Olivia's gaze softened as she looked at her grandmother, all the determination of a few moments ago gone. "Oh, Grandmama. Of course not. I haven't even set eyes on him since I was ten." It was a lie, but a small one. She couldn't possibly explain about that day in front of the shops.

Lady Raleigh was immediately belligerent again. "Then why must you leave me all of a sudden?" she demanded, wiping at her eyes. "And for what? Is he more important to you than I am?"

Olivia's sigh was heartfelt. "Don't be silly. No one is more important than you. I must go because he is my husband." That explained everything, didn't it? She dropped back into the chair and leaned her head into her hand, her elbow resting on the table.

A second silence descended on the room, broken only occasionally by the soft sounds of Lady Raleigh wringing her handkerchief. The seconds ticked away like hours as Olivia pondered what to do. Her grandmother was right. She couldn't just leave her. The shock would be too great for her heart. Indeed, it would be too great for both of them. Olivia felt lost and helpless as she tried to school her thoughts.

Finally she broke the silence. "You spoke to him, didn't you?"

Lady Raleigh's response was dragged from her lips. "Yes."

"What did he say?"

She paused, searching for the words. "He said he wanted you to come to him right away." She interrupted Olivia before she could reply. "But he agreed to wait a month."

Olivia expelled her breath, only just then acknowledging that she had been holding it. "Why did he agree to wait?"

Lady Raleigh temporized. "He realized there would be a scandal if you went to him now."

"Yes." Olivia absorbed the explanation, not judging it. She looked up at her grandmother, her familiar gaze now strangely unnerving to the old woman. "What do we do now?"

Lady Raleigh got up and began pacing the floor. "We act out a part in a play," she explained. She hesitated, thought some more, then resumed her walk. "Lord Traverston will be your suitor. He will take you out to balls, parties, plays, musicals, the opera. You will be his betrothed. A month from now, you will be married quietly by special license. He will then take you to his estate in Surrey."

"Norwood Park," breathed Olivia, her eyes unseeing.

Lady Raleigh glanced sharply at her. "Yes, Norwood Park." She faltered. It was all happening too soon, too fast. She should have had time to get acquainted with her granddaughter's suitors. She should have had time to direct the courting to her satisfaction. She should have had a chance to get used to the idea of Olivia's absence. Nothing was going as it ought to have.

As the situation fully dawned on Lady Raleigh, she stopped pacing and eyed her young relation wearily. Did she have any idea what was happening to her? She didn't seem to really know. Her actions were too cool, too measured. Her shoulders drooping forward, Lady Raleigh finished off quietly by announcing, "He's coming to take you driving in the park tomorrow."

Olivia looked back at her grandmother, her eyes glittering like topaz in the dim candlelight. Her face was as still as a funeral mask. "You don't like the marquis, do you?"

The old woman hesitated, not sure what she should say. Finally she replied, not quite able to control the tremor in her voice. "He frightens me."

Chapter Six

The sound of the front door knocker reverberated through Olivia's head like a gunshot. Normally she hardly noticed it at all, but today the sound was terribly loud. Perhaps it was because she had been listening for it all too intently the whole afternoon, half dreading, half longing for the pounding that would herald the arrival of her new husband.

No, not new husband, she corrected herself. Far from it. That was what was so difficult to believe. For eight years she had been married to a man she didn't know. Eight very long and incomprehensible years.

The door to the salon opened, shattering her private thoughts. With a solemnity that seemed to fit the occasion perfectly, the butler intoned, "The Marquis of Traverston, to see you, Lady Raleigh, Miss Wentworth." He bowed and made way for the visitor.

Lady Raleigh got up from her seat by the window where she had been making a halfhearted attempt at her needlepoint. She made her stately way over to their guest as Olivia dropped the book she had long since ceased reading. As her grandmother came to a stop in front of him, Olivia stood up from the fainting couch where she had been sitting. Lady Raleigh extended her hand to the marquis after only the briefest of pauses.

"My lord. Welcome to our home."

He took the lady's hand in his own and executed a half bow over it with unexpected courtesy. "Lady Raleigh, your servant." He turned to Olivia. "Lady Traverston."

Olivia's eyes narrowed a fraction at the pointed thrust of his words. So, she reflected, he was determined to make this difficult, was he? She moved toward the door, careful to keep a wary distance between herself and her lord. Purposely she did not acknowledge his greeting. "My lord," she announced smoothly, "we weren't expecting you so soon." That wasn't true, but she wanted to make him sweat a few minutes. He didn't have to know that both she and Lady Raleigh had been hopelessly useless this past hour, waiting for him to turn up at the door. His insufferable smugness should be taken down a peg or two. "I need to run upstairs and collect a few things. I'll return in a few moments." She exited gracefully out the door and raced up the stairs before either Traverston or her grandmother could suggest sending for a maid.

Once upstairs, Olivia rushed to her silver-framed cheval glass, anxious that no sign of her inner tumult should be apparent on her face. It wasn't. Thankfully she moved away from the glass and took a few calming breaths. She closed her eyes. It was ridiculous the effect this man had on her. She didn't even know him, after all.

An insidious thought told her she would soon enough. She was his wife, and she doubted the marquis was the kind of man to be married in name only. Not when it ceased to be convenient, as it apparently had.

She pulled on her pelisse and bonnet with bloodless fingers, issuing calming words to herself all the while. She would be all right. She had to be.

Olivia's progress down the main staircase was measured and regal. Traverston stared up at her appreciatively, thinking how incomprehensible it was that this creature was now his. But her first words shattered his momentary complacency.

"My father said you didn't exist."

Olivia was just as amazed at her own temerity as the marquis. She hadn't known what she was going to say to him until the words had actually come out.

His eyes narrowed as she came toward him. "Perhaps he was correct," he replied repressively.

She eyed him coldly and with only the barest hint of civility. "What do you mean by that?"

"I mean that evil creatures aren't supposed to exist in the real world, are they? They are just figments of overactive adolescent imaginations."

She drew level with him, uncomfortably noting as she did that he was almost half a head taller than she, and she was by no means a short woman. But her thoughts did not show on her face as she turned expressionlessly flat eyes on him. "Do you mean to frighten me?" The lift of her eyebrow conveyed her disdain at such an attempt.

His eyes burned their way through hers. It was as though he could see what everyone else had failed to notice. There was a woman hiding behind those tremendous eyes. "If you're not, you're a fool."

Olivia dismissed his words without even deigning to give him a response. She turned on her heel and strolled through the open door. Over her shoulder she called, "Lovely day for a drive, isn't it?"

He grabbed her arm and spun her around just as she reached the carriage. Involuntarily she gasped at the sudden violence of his actions. Dark, bitter eyes met hers as she brought her imperious gaze up to clash with his.

"You think this is a game, don't you? You think you can ignore me the same way you do everyone else in this

world, don't you?'' He squeezed her arm for emphasis.
''Well, I won't let you. Let me tell you right now, Olivia,
I won't be ignored. You may play cold and hard to reach
with everyone else, but I won't settle for that. I won't
rest until I make you feel what it is like to be human,
what it means to be real.'' His breath was warm and
compelling on her face, and her eyes widened in alarm
at his impassioned speech. ''I won't know peace until
you feel remorse, anger, hurt, pain. Wake up, Olivia! This
is no dream you can just drift your way through anymore.''

She almost fell down when he released her. The action
was almost more violent than when he had grabbed her.

Her head was spinning. He frightened her, all right,
but not for the reason he probably imagined. How could
she be so easily read? Did he suspect that there was really
something there after all? He must have! How could he
know what she was feeling, what she had been trying to
hide so hard all these years from the rest of the world?
How could he threaten to let loose the torrent of emotions
she had locked away in her heart? The ones she knew
could destroy her?

He is bluffing, she thought. He may think that he
knows me, but he does not. How could he? They hadn't
even met. Not really. They'd only spoken a few, mysterious words to each other.

She determined then that he would never know her,
not even if she had to die first in order to protect her
identity. Her soul in the hands of a man like that would
kill her anyway.

But deep inside her, she knew her fate had been determined long ago. Just as she knew, although she was
unable to admit it, that she knew the marquis, too. If he
had the secret to her existence, then she had his, as well.

As Olivia worked to regain her equanimity, Traverston
had already ascended into the carriage. He didn't bother

to help her into the high perch phaeton, a vehicle no female in skirts could get into without assistance. His decision to ignore her had been deliberate. He wanted to humiliate her.

God help her, she groaned inwardly. She was married to this man.

Her face an emotionless mask, Olivia summoned a footman to help her into the carriage. She would give this man no reason for triumph. As far as he was concerned, his insult meant nothing to her. He was beneath notice. He was smaller than a bug under her shoe.

Ten minutes out on the road and Olivia knew Traverston had begun his assault on her senses in earnest. The phaeton took turn after turn at dangerously high speeds. She started to count the number of times the wheels came off the ground and gave up after five. Her knuckles were white as they gripped the edge of her seat. Her bonnet had blown off her head and hung down her back by its ties. The wind threatened to pull it completely off her head every few seconds, but she was too afraid to take her hands from their holds.

Instead of heading toward Hyde Park where she had originally thought they were going, the marquis drove toward a part of town she was unfamiliar with, taking every possible opportunity along the way to show off his prowess with the reins. He glanced surreptitiously at his wife, not believing he would see a hint of fear, but hoping just the same. As he surmised, to all outward appearances, except for the bonnet, of course, she seemed calm. For a moment, he wasn't even sure her mind was with him in the carriage. Then he caught a glimpse of her death grip on the vehicle's seat.

So, the little minx can be frightened after all. The knowledge was particularly gratifying, and he whipped his horses further into a frenzy.

Olivia's only encouragement during this drive from

hell was the knowledge that Traverston wouldn't really want to kill her. That would take all the fun out of breaking her will later on, and she was sure that was what he wanted to do. She was a horse to him, something to be controlled and tamed. Her resolve grew firm at the realization. Suppressing all conscious thought, she held on tightly until the carriage finally pulled to a stop in front of a seedy-looking establishment.

Releasing her hands from the grips as nonchalantly as she could, she looked over at the marquis, her eyes frigidly questioning.

He smiled unpleasantly. "I thought after the ride you could use some refreshment."

Her gaze drifted over to the inn. She looked at the shabby exterior and the none-too-clean individuals patronizing the place. Out of the corner of her eye, she caught a glimpse of a scantily clad woman in one of the upper windows. Just then, a bawdy laugh followed by some rude comments drifted out from the open door and into the courtyard. She turned back to the marquis, her face a marble shield except for her eyes. They were flat and angry. "I will not go in there."

"No?" he asked in a conversational tone. "And why not?"

Ice, ice, ice, read her eyes. "My lord, you may think it is amusing to tease me, to abuse me, but I have my limits. I know what kind of place that is. I know what it would mean to my reputation to be seen there."

"Really?" His look was one of sardonic amusement. "And what kind of a place is it, pray tell?"

Her eyes spoke of impossibly high snowcapped mountains. "A brothel."

He laughed, a full-bodied sound issuing from the depths of his chest. Suddenly his eyes grew equally cold. "And what do you know of brothels?"

"You have no right to subject me to an inquisition."

Suddenly her soft voice carried a surprising amount of venom. "Do you think to humiliate me by my ignorance? Or are you disappointed I'm a little more worldly-wise than the average young miss? I may not know everything about the kind of dissipated life you seem to enjoy, but I know enough to know that I will not go in there." Inspired, she asked in a different tone, "Why are you testing me, my lord?"

He was taken off balance by her perceptive change of conversation. To hide his surprise, he slapped the reins on the horses' backs, sending them on their way again. As if the issue were of no importance to him, he replied, "To see what manner of woman my wife is, perhaps." He offered no further explanation.

Surprisingly the pace the marquis set for the journey home was comparatively sedate. Apparently he had some little feeling for the welfare of his horses, thought Olivia. She assumed it wasn't on her behalf that he made the trip back to her grandmother's house more slowly. She kept quiet and let him attend to his own thoughts, just as she was attending to hers.

Drawing up in front of the house on Wimpole Street, the marquis finally deigned to look at Olivia again. He kept his seat, not bothering to get out and assist her down. "We'll go driving again tomorrow at the same time." It was not a request.

"I don't think so, my lord." She jumped down from the phaeton nimbly, not waiting for the footman to come forward to help her again. She would show him at every opportunity that she could well take care of herself.

He lifted an eyebrow in response. He was not used to having his commands questioned.

She continued, looking up at him from the ground. "If you want me to go out with you tomorrow, Lord Traverston, then bring me a horse. I much prefer sallying forth on a mount under my own control."

"I see." He grinned like a snarl at the challenge. "To-morrow at five, then, my lady."

Before Olivia could give in to the urge to grab his horsewhip and treat him to a little of his own medicine, the carriage pulled away. Anger burned in her heart when she caught the full-throated laugh of its only occupant drifting back to her on the wind.

The chestnut gelding snorted and reared up off the ground. Olivia raised dispassionate eyes from her examination of the restless beast to the mocking gaze of the marquis.

"You wanted to ride, I believe." His tone was insolent, intolerable.

At least he had provided a sidesaddle, she consoled herself. She walked slowly toward the bucking animal, schooling her own writhing fear. Holding her hand out firmly in front of her, she moved slowly toward the horse's nose. After a moment, her hand was upon his head, smoothing his brow. To her surprise, the horse quieted down a bit.

Traverston dismounted his own magnificent stallion, its coat a creamy, milky shade of white. While Olivia watched in amazement, he came around to her side and wordlessly offered his assistance. After eyeing him doubtfully, she accepted his offer.

He put his hands on her waist. Then he lifted her. Somehow his hands got under the short-cropped jacket of her riding habit. They were warm through the thin fabric of her lawn shirt, and the sensation sent a shiver down her spine. As he tossed her up into the saddle, she cursed herself mentally for such a reaction to a man who had gone out of his way to be unpleasant to her. She only hoped he hadn't felt her reaction.

He had. But he was more amazed at his own. Olivia was beautiful, but he had bedded beautiful women before.

He had never, however, been so aroused by an accidental touch as innocent as this had been. He could only think that it had been too long since he had been with a woman. He'd have to rectify the situation soon.

As Olivia waited for the marquis to regain his mount, she gripped the reins of her horse and focused all of her energies on controlling it. She had to let the creature know that she meant business. Traverston had intentionally chosen a steed for her that would challenge her abilities as a horsewoman. And if she failed that challenge, then she would wind up either looking ridiculous or dead. She shivered again, but this time for a very different reason.

Within moments, Traverston had mounted his own horse and they headed off toward Hyde Park. As Traverston had undoubtedly predicted, Olivia's younger male horse was antagonized by his stallion. The creature had already attempted countless bolts. It was only Olivia's talent as an outstanding horsewoman that had kept her in her saddle thus far.

Traverston didn't wish her any real harm. He was prepared to come to her rescue at the least hint the horse was too much for her. Despite his attempts to repress the thought, he was really quite disappointed that it looked as if he wouldn't have to ride to her rescue. The thought of Olivia's gratitude, and all the ways he could make her show it, warmed his blood. But she seemed to have the situation well in hand.

The park was incredibly beautiful this afternoon. Olivia was enjoying the challenge of keeping her horse under control, and she truly longed for the excuse to run him in the long open stretches of grass in front of her. But that would be unthinkable. No one, absolutely no one, rode a horse at a pace exceeding a trot during the fashionable hour in Hyde Park.

"Do you know, my lord," announced Olivia as they

trailed behind some carriages on their way around the public green, "I find your attempts to unsettle me a little amusing, really."

"Oh?"

Her mouth quirked with humor at his disgruntled tone. "Yes. I don't remember the last time I was so diverted."

"If it is diversion you're after," he replied, spotting Lady Chisolm and her companion, David Hamilton, riding toward them at a determined pace, "I think you're about to get it."

"Trav!" The honeyed music of Lady Chisolm's voice was audible from a fair distance. Several heads turned in her direction at the call, just as they had been meant to do. Languidly the couple on horseback approached the marquis and his companion. "How absolutely astounding to run into you here!" She smiled wickedly as she and her companion closed with the couple. "I had no idea that you enjoyed riding during the fashionable hour," she cooed with false charm.

In reality, the countess was livid. The fact that Traverston had ridden out with the pale beauty beside him when he had always flat out refused to accompany her to the park filled her with fury. From the moment she set eyes on Olivia with her former paramour, Beatrice took an instant dislike to the stately Miss Wentworth.

Traverston acknowledged his cousin with a barely perceptible nod before addressing his ex-lover. "I don't, usually."

"Oh?" Her intonation underscored her simultaneous disbelief and interest. "Then why are you here?"

Traverston turned to his companion, for once acknowledging the proprieties. "Miss Wentworth, may I present Lady Chisolm." His failure to introduce the gentleman accompanying the countess was noted by all present.

Strangely enough, the gentleman in question seemed to ignore the cut. "David Hamilton, your servant, Miss

Wentworth," he smoothly intoned, bowing from his saddle. Olivia's lips curled up slightly at the corners at his boldness. However, her smile faded immediately at his next words.

"I'm John's cousin."

Olivia eyed Traverston a few moments before turning gravely to Mr. Hamilton. "Not his favorite, I should think?"

His laugh was genuine. "I think not." An uncomfortable silence followed these words.

Olivia's horse reared up, restless at the continued inactivity caused by the conversation. She felt him becoming uncontrollable and moved quickly to pat his neck with her hand. "There, there, big boy," she muttered to him in soothing tones.

"That's quite a monster you're riding," remarked Lady Chisolm somewhat maliciously. "Hardly the mount for a lady."

Olivia's response was delayed by her attempts to stay seated on her horse. "Yes." She shot a meaningful look at the marquis. "Lord Traverston chose him for me."

"Really, Trav," scolded the lady in low, seductive tones. "How could you put Miss Wentworth on such a creature? Why, just look at him. I bet the veriest thing would put him in a fright." As if to demonstrate the veracity of these words, Beatrice waved her whip in front of the chestnut's face, making as if to hit him on his tender nose.

The horse's reaction was predictable. He bolted with Olivia clinging to his back for dear life.

The look Traverston directed at Beatrice was black. His voice dripping with venom, he addressed his cousin for the first time that day. "I'm surprised at you, David. You never used to take my scraps."

It didn't take Beatrice more than a second to realize she had made a grave error. In mute appeal, she looked at Hamilton, but he was white lipped with anger and unable to give her any support. In seconds, Traverston had wheeled his horse around and was heading off after Olivia at top speed.

For Olivia, the ride was harrowing. More so than the carriage ride with her husband the day before, for this time, she had no idea whether or not she would live to see the conclusion of the adventure.

She had no opportunity to try to control her mount. The reins had dropped to the ground when the horse had bolted and were dangling uselessly from his mouth. The best she could do was to hold on tightly and pray that the chestnut would tire soon.

As pedestrians out for a leisurely stroll scrambled out of her way, Olivia saw from the corner of her eye the marquis's stallion pounding the turf beside her. In moments, the white form of his horse drew closer, and Olivia knew that Traverston had come to her rescue. Leaning far out over his own steed, the marquis reached forward with one hand and grabbed the reins of the gelding. Bringing her horse slowly under control while keeping tight rein on his own mount was no small feat. By the time Traverston had brought both horses to a stop, Olivia's heart had been given a chance to resume a more normal tempo.

"This is worse than a scene in one of Mrs. Radcliffe's novels," Olivia said with more bravado than she felt. She stopped a second to take a deep breath and to steady her voice. "The hero rescuing the poor maiden before she succumbs to certain death." She had been trying for levity, but she wasn't quite able to keep a flash of admiration from her eyes, nor the quiver of fear out of her voice. Unnerved by her adventure but desperate not to show it, she dismounted and took the reins of her horse from Traverston's grasp.

Unable to sense her disquiet, the marquis aimed his

anger at the countess at her. "But you're not some poor maiden, are you?" His tone was bitter.

The question and its tone surprised her. She looked up and then away quickly, before he could really see her distress. "No, of course not." Her heart began beating rapidly again, and she thought he must be able to hear it.

"I'm surprised you have a knowledge of Mrs. Radcliffe's novels," he said in a seemingly swift change of mood. He also dismounted from his horse. He walked the animal to a nearby tree and tied its reins securely to a branch. "Do you have more than a passing familiarity with her works?"

Grateful for the chance to hide behind a topic other than herself, Olivia responded with alacrity. "Don't be absurd. Any woman who reads that drivel should be ousted from society. She deserves whatever treatment she gets from a man with that sort of trash as her guide." She followed his example and tied the gelding close by. As she made to turn from the horse, she was stopped by the low sound of the marquis's mocking voice.

"Are you a bluestocking then?" He was surprisingly close. She hadn't noticed his approach while she had been caring for the chestnut.

"No." She whirled around, her eyes hard as agates. But she couldn't make eye contact with him, because he was looking at her mouth.

"You always take the easy way out, don't you, Olivia?" he breathed. His gaze lingered on her trembling lips.

"I...I don't know what you mean."

He wouldn't look into her eyes. He wouldn't be rebuffed by their fearless nothingness. He concentrated on her lips. "You know what I mean."

She shook her head, but her eyes spoke other words. "I fear I have no idea."

Finally he looked up, seeing more in the deep, bottomless pools than she had intended. Her vulnerability was showing after all. His lips smiled at her show of weakness as he thrust home the dagger. ''I mean, my dear girl, you always take the path of least resistance, the one that will help you avoid conflict.'' Then his lips suddenly lost their twist and he stared intently at her. ''It's true, isn't it?''

A tinge of color crept into her cheeks. ''My lord, you have windmills in your head. You don't know the first thing about me,'' she said, desperately trying to keep calm.

He was persistent. ''Oh, but I do.'' He leaned in closer. ''I know that you can't sleep at night, Olivia.'' He watched her eyes go round with shock and he rushed on before she could recover. ''Oh, yes. You didn't know that anyone could understand you so well, did you? But it's true—I do. I know that you have disturbing dreams. I know that you see other young ladies your age and you watch them smile, laugh and cry, and I know that you wonder at their exuberance for life, their joie de vivre. You wonder what makes them tick. What makes them so different from you? How can they ignore the sensations burning in their breasts and screaming for freedom from the faceless, meaningless strictures of society? How can they act as if nothing preys on their minds?

''And then the doubts plague you, Olivia. I know that you wonder if those feathery whimsical girls with no substance feel what you feel. And then you wonder if you are real and all the things around you are real.

''I know that there is a deep, nameless yearning in your breast, one that becomes so intense at times that you don't think you can stand it. But you don't succumb to its seductive call because you think it will destroy you.'' He was so close he almost touched her. She felt smothered by his presence. His last words were whispered, but full of intensity. ''Don't try and pretend otherwise, my pretty little wife. I know it is true. Oh, yes, Olivia. I know you.''

Her hands held before her to ward off the despised insidiousness of his words, Olivia's response was a cry of desperation. ''You can't!''

He stared into her eyes, mesmerizing her with his smoldering gaze. She saw the winds of a thunderstorm in his irises and felt the tempestuousness of his inner soul pull at her and draw her in. She lost all sense of self. Her hands moved out in front of her and touched his chest, as if she could keep him physically away. But the pale, fluttering appendages had no strength.

And in trying to master her, to turn her mind to his own with its boiling, tempestuous sea of feeling, Traverston became unexpectedly stunned. Her eyes were wide, open and helpless, and he was absorbed by her look, her need. It was as if the void she was so afraid of succumbing to was actually trying to pull him in, too. He stood paralyzed. He couldn't move.

The seconds could have been hours for Olivia. With a strength she had no idea she had, she tore herself away from Traverston's mental hold. Her breath coming out in tight gasps, she leaned against her horse's flanks, willing the power of the animal to flow through her and give her its strength. She closed her eyes, not knowing how to recover from this encounter.

And then, a sound broke into the swirling chaos of her thoughts. Slowly, vaguely, she opened her eyes, her head still bowed against the horse's heaving side. Mutely, like a distant dream, the sight of Traverston's booted feet seeped into her consciousness. It was a moment before the words could percolate through to her brain.

''Let me give you a hand up.''

Olivia stopped breathing. The man offering her assistance was impersonal, polite. For a second, she almost wasn't sure she had heard right. No trace of their earlier conversation could be heard in his voice. Surely this couldn't be the same man who was determined to break her to his will? That man would never give her a reprieve.

But it was him. Thankfully, not daring to trust her luck or his generosity, Olivia gently and quietly began to breathe again. She gave herself to the marquis and allowed him to boost her into the saddle, keeping her eyes from him as he first assisted her and then mounted his own horse.

As the gelding began a strangely sedate pace back through the park, Olivia truly noticed her surroundings for the first time. When, she wondered in confusion, had the park turned so green?

The ride home was conducted in silence.

Chapter Seven

It had been several days since her adventurous ride with the marquis in Hyde Park, and until tonight, Olivia had not seen her husband since then. Lady Raleigh had sent word around earlier in the day to Traverston's town home that they would be attending the Merriweathers' ball this evening, but she had received no response from him on her request for him to be their escort. They had assumed the marquis had other plans.

Hours after their arrival, Olivia spotted him from the dance floor. A colonel in the light brigade was swinging her around the room with more enthusiasm than talent when Traverston appeared. As he moved through the throng of humanity, the crowd stepped aside to give him a wide berth. But he didn't seem to notice their movements. He only had eyes for the tall, statuesque goddess moving gracefully about the floor on the arm of another man.

As always, he was devastatingly handsome, and Olivia's breath caught in her throat when she sighted him bearing down on her and her dance partner. She tried to look away, but it was as if the marquis had some invisible hold over her. He captured her gaze, and kept it until he tapped her dance partner on the shoulder and claimed her for his own. She was vaguely aware of the officer's belligerent demand to finish his set, but the stranger's words had no more substance than that of a fly buzzing around them. Negligently, as if unaware that there was anyone else present, he took Olivia's hand and led her away.

When Traverston took her in his arms at the start of the next set, a waltz, Olivia felt as if he had taken possession of her. His hands moved on her back as if she were his to command and his to own. His steps were swift and sure, and he took Olivia around the room with him without a doubt that she would go where he led.

As Olivia felt the overpowering sense of the marquis and his masculinity seep through her, she immediately fought to release herself from his spell. Without conscious thought, she brought out the only weapon in her arsenal she knew how to use effectively—detachment.

The shift in her mood was palpable to Traverston, she knew. He looked down at her in puzzlement, but she resisted his every attempt to reestablish eye contact. She fought against his every bid for repossession of her soul.

But he knew her too well, and he knew how to fight her. Her aloofness wasn't enough for him. He wanted to make her react. He wanted to see the color come flaming into her cheeks and the fire into her eyes. He wanted her to be a real woman when he held her in his arms.

That was the source of his compliment.

"You look lovely tonight." Traverston felt Olivia stiffen perceptibly. Calmly, aware of exactly what he was doing, he pulled away from her a little in order to look at her face. Her eyes were removed from his and studying the floor beyond his left shoulder.

Seeking her gaze unsuccessfully, he gripped her a little tighter and returned her to his shoulder. "That bothers you, doesn't it?" he asked, already knowing the answer.

"I don't know what you are talking about." If she had had her teeth removed and cotton stuffed in her mouth, the quality of her speech might have been the same. Her words were dragged from between stiff and unmoving lips.

He pulled away from her again and scrutinized her immobile features. "That seems to be a rather typical answer for you, Olivia. And yes, you do know what I'm talking about." He gazed at her a moment longer before deliberately pulling her even tighter into his arms.

Olivia vowed not for the first time to get even with Lady Jersey for granting her permission to dance the waltz with Traverston. Their first whirl around the floor had taken them right by that monument of polite English society, but she had only smiled pleasantly at the rather handsome pair Olivia and Traverston made. Olivia knew then that despite all his outward appearances to the contrary, the marquis still had enough sense of respectability to clear the finer points of courtship through the proper channels. He had obviously gained Lady Jersey's advance permission to dance this waltz with her. Otherwise, she was sure nothing short of her undergarments catching on fire could have prevented Lady Jersey from cutting Olivia on the spot.

In truth, Olivia didn't mind the elegant dance in general; far from it. The waltz was a beautiful social pleasantry. She had imagined participating in the rite several times, always with mild anticipation. But that was before she knew her first partner was going to be Traverston. And the intimacy necessary between two people to dance the waltz gracefully made Olivia distinctly uncomfortable tonight.

Traverston's hand burned its way through the thin material of her sarcenet evening gown. She could feel each and every one of the thick, strong fingers where his hand rested in the small of her back. Vaguely Olivia had the impression that Traverston was a good dancer, but his nearness distracted her to the point that she couldn't be sure what her own feet were doing, much less his.

Traverston tilted his head closer to her and maneuvered his mouth next to her ear. "Why does it bother you, that you are so breathtakingly beautiful?" he whispered. He felt a quiver run through her body in reaction to his words. The responding thrill through his own quickened his pulse.

Without warning, Olivia broke from his clasp. She stood among the whirling couples, glaring at him, her body visibly shaking with emotion. Her face was a strange mixture of fear and dignity, and her eyes sparked as bright as the sun reflecting on water.

"Take me back to my grandmother." Although her voice was low, it carried a kind of power that was too hard for Traverston to try to ignore. Realizing that they were drawing the eyes of everyone around them, he firmly grasped her arm above the elbow and began leading her off the floor.

As he glanced around the crowd, careful to keep his gaze away from hers, he remarked in a soft voice that held a suspicious note of amusement, "You seem upset."

"You are odious, my lord." The words were hissed with more feeling than either party would have thought possible just scant days ago. He glanced at her quickly and then away, but not before he noticed the tension in her arms and neck. Traverston refrained from replying as they neared Lady Raleigh.

Olivia's grandmother was seated next to a plump matron crowned by a shimmering purple turban with a nodding white ostrich feather. Mrs. Silvia Fitzwater, a widow with three happily married and equally plump daughters, was in the middle of an animated conversation with Lady Raleigh when the young couple approached. She immediately broke off her train of high velocity gibberish to hold out a fat, dimpled hand to Olivia in a warm gesture of welcome.

"Olivia, darling! How are you this evening? Your grandmother and I were just having the most comfortable coze. I was telling her that you both simply must come to visit next week. Annabelle and Christine will be there, and I know you haven't seen them this age."

Olivia attempted something she hoped passed for a smile in response to this effusive speech before murmuring an appropriate response. Lady Raleigh, who had been only half attending her friend's prattle minutes ago, had not missed the slight altercation between Olivia and her husband on the ballroom floor. Noticing her charge's unusual pallor, she half turned to the empty seat next to her and patted it invitingly. "You look a little peaked, my dear. Why don't you sit here next to me for a while?" As Olivia sank down gratefully into the chair, Lady Raleigh turned to Mrs. Fitzwater in mock horror. "Gracious, what poor manners you must think I have, Silvia. Allow me to introduce to you John Markston, the fourth Marquis of Traverston." She indicated Traverston's politely attentive form with a slight motion of her hand.

Mrs. Fitzwater looked up at the darkly handsome marquis with what amounted to horror. Staring into his devilish gray eyes for a second or two, she turned back to Lady Raleigh as if to silently ask, "How on earth did you come to be associated with the notorious marquis?" Under the influence of Lady Raleigh's bland expression, however, Mrs. Fitzwater quickly regained her equilibrium. With an amazing change of attitude, she gave Traverston her hand, batting her eyelashes coquettishly at him. His amusement was evident as he made a sufficiently polite response to the introduction.

Keeping in mind Olivia's pale face, Lady Raleigh decided her granddaughter could use a respite from Traverston's imposing presence. She waved her fan a few times as if she were hot before cueing her companion. "Silvia, didn't I hear you say that you could do with a bit of champagne? I vow I myself am quite parched by this heat."

Mrs. Fitzwater was quick to take the hint. Relishing her new role as co-conspirator, she fluttered at the marquis. "Oh, indeed. I think some champagne would be grand." She batted her eyelashes a few more times for good measure.

Semigraciously the marquis bowed to the ladies. "Allow me." He eyed Olivia meaningfully before he strolled off to the refreshment table.

Lady Raleigh leaned toward her granddaughter and said sotto voce, "You look quite done in, my dear. Are you going to be all right?"

Horrified at the extent the feelings Traverston had aroused in her must be showing, Olivia colored. Quietly she replied, "I will be, now that you have sent him away."

Before her grandmother could offer a suitable reply, the ladies' tête-à-tête was interrupted by the arrival of David Hamilton. He bowed gallantly over first Lady Raleigh's hand and then Olivia's. His obsequiousness to Mrs. Fitzwater was sufficient to earn that good lady's immediate approval.

It was a moment before he finally came to the point of his visit to the ladies. "Miss Wentworth, I am sorry to interrupt, but I couldn't help but notice the ignominious way my cousin treated you out on the dance floor." He smiled apologetically. "I daresay you could do with a partner that won't tread on your toes. Won't you do me the honor?"

Taken aback by his willful misinterpretation of the earlier scene between Traverston and herself, Olivia was speechless. Lady Raleigh jumped quickly to fill the void left by her granddaughter.

"Olivia would be delighted, Mr. Hamilton."

Smiling the biggest smile she could muster, which was a very small one indeed, Olivia accepted Hamilton's hand as he led her out onto the floor.

The steps of the country dance don't normally allow a couple much opportunity for discussion, but such was Hamilton's determination that he managed to carry on one anyway.

"Allow me to apologize for the shameful way Beatrice treated you the other day in the park, Miss Wentworth," he began sincerely. "She's sometimes a little catty, I'm afraid, and it's regrettable that she chose you as her target. But you can hardly blame her. Beatrice and my cousin were an item not too long ago."

Although the news of Traverston's relationship with the lovely countess should have come as no surprise to her, Olivia couldn't help the tiny twinge of jealousy that caused her stomach to lurch at the news. "I'm sure you have no control over Lady Chisolm's actions, Mr. Hamilton," replied Olivia repressively.

He squeezed her hand and silently acquiesced to her attempt to turn the conversation. "I just wanted to let you know that, setting aside whatever is between you and my cousin, I am willing to offer you my assistance... should the occasion arise and you are in need of it."

Tongue-tied, Olivia replied simply, "Thank you."

He continued hurriedly. "It's no secret that the marquis and I are not great friends. But that doesn't mean that I can't be *your* friend," he added with a slight squeeze of her hand. As she remained silent at this overture, he plunged ahead with feigned nervousness. "I don't know what Traverston has told you about me, but whatever it was, it isn't true." He paused, obviously waiting for her to disclose exactly what nasty comments Traverston had made about him.

She answered him reluctantly. "He hasn't said much

of anything, actually." She refrained from adding that
their exchanges had been mostly of a hostile nature, not
an informative one.

This appeared to disappoint him. "Oh. Well. In that
case…we're half brothers, you know."

Olivia looked up in surprise. Her mouth formed a
small, startled O.

Judging by her reaction, evidently she did not know,
he thought. Maybe he had misinterpreted the look he had
seen his brother give this fair morsel? But, no. Any fool
with half a brain could see he was falling under her spell.

He kept his voice indifferent, as if the news were no
great secret. "Yes, it's true, although to all the world we
pretend we are merely cousins. Our mothers were related,
it is true, but the connection is actually much closer than
that. His father and my own were one and the same…
the third Marquis of Traverston."

"My lord," Olivia replied as she shook her head in
confusion, "I don't understand why you are telling me
this."

He shrugged his shoulders, the slight movement causing his blue superfine coat to wrinkle a little. "Intuition,
I suppose. I imagine John is going to marry you."

Again Olivia started in surprise. He laughed at her reaction. "Doesn't take a Bow Street Runner to figure that
one out, Miss Wentworth. John has never hung out for
schoolroom misses before." His forehead wrinkled immediately in consternation. "If you'll pardon the expression, my dear. I didn't mean any offense."

Her reply was barely audible. "Don't give it any
thought."

Before he could make any further apologies, Hamilton's arm was suddenly seized in a grip of steel. Making
the visual journey upward from the hand holding his arm,
Hamilton discovered the marquis's face at the end of his
trip. Although he had seen most of his half brother's dark

moods before, he was still somewhat taken aback by the marquis's expression.

Traverston's look was black.

The marquis's words were ground out between clenched teeth. "I'm sure you have other duties that need immediate attending to, David. Pray, don't let us keep you."

As Traverston released his arm, Hamilton's reply was almost drawled. A small, knowing smile played on his lips. "Of course, *coz*," he answered with sneering emphasis on the last word. With seeming indifference, he brushed the wrinkles from his coat where Traverston's hand had creased the material. Then, briefly, he locked gazes with his brother.

His eyes were murderous.

Painting a pleasant expression back onto his features, he then turned and bowed to Olivia. "Your servant, Miss Wentworth."

As the dance came to an end just then, Traverston took a hold of Olivia's arm and began propelling her to the open French windows on the far side of the ballroom. Away from Lady Raleigh, Olivia noticed.

While her mind whirled, she strove for coolness. Keeping the tone of her voice as if she were only mildly interested, she asked, "Where are you taking me, Lord Traverston?"

He kept his eyes trained on the open windows before them. "Outside for some fresh air, Lady Traverston."

Olivia winced involuntarily at the reprimand. Then she straightened her shoulders. He had no right to scold her, she thought. She hadn't done anything wrong.

At an almost military march, Traverston led her through the doors and out into the night. The air was sweet with the scent of the rose bushes beyond it, and a light breeze cooled Olivia's flushed face.

The marquis didn't release his grip on her, however,

when they reached the first flowers that marked the beginning of the garden. He led her past strolling couples and onto a gravel walkway. They walked for a full minute before he found what he was looking for. When he came across a stone bench in a secluded part of the grounds, he brought them to a sudden halt.

Unceremoniously he dumped Olivia onto the seat. Even through the dark, Olivia could see that his eyes were flashing. "Don't ever," he said in a low, commanding tone of voice, "and I mean ever, let me catch you with him again."

Confused, Olivia frowned up at her husband. "But I was just…"

He held up an index finger in front of her face. "No excuses, Olivia. There can be none where David is concerned."

Olivia grew angry, her own eyes beginning to sparkle with emotion. "You have no right to tell me who I can and cannot be with!" she declared with ill-concealed effrontery. "You have no claim on me."

"On the contrary, my dear," he replied, leaning into her face, his hands gripping either side of the bench on which she was sitting. "I have every right." His voice was deadly quiet, and Olivia leaned back away from him despite herself. "May I remind you that it is my name you bear, and if you don't do exactly as I say, that's a fact the entire world will know before this evening is out."

She glared at him. "That's blackmail."

His smile was wicked. "Yes, it is."

Pausing only to let him see her disgust, Olivia got up off the bench, pushing her way past him. He grabbed her hand as she flew by, pulling her back to him. The force he used was such that Olivia was yanked into his arms before she could stop herself. Her hands became trapped uselessly against his chest as he held her to him, his arms like steel bands around her. She struggled, but soon realized her efforts were of no use.

Capturing her eyes with his own, he leaned toward her and spoke with quiet intensity. His eyes burned with emotions she couldn't begin to identify. "Understand this, Olivia. This is a game you are going to lose."

"What…"

Olivia tried to get her brain to speed up enough to follow his thoughts, but her question died in her throat. Even as she comprehended what he was about to do, Traverston placed his lips on hers. The contact sent a shock wave through her body that left her feeling stunned. But more amazing still was the warm flood of sensation the shock wave left in its wake.

Traverston's lips were warm and insistent. The passion his mouth conveyed to her left her feeling weak and helpless but strangely exhilarated. His lips tasted musky and dark, with hints of brandy and mint. Unaware of what she was doing, she let out a low moan, her mouth parting slightly. Traverston moved quickly to take the opening.

When his tongue met with hers, Olivia felt an eruption take place somewhere in the depths of her loins. Without thinking about her actions, her hands moved up and around his neck and her fingers coiled themselves in his hair. Her knees gave in and her body melted against his. Every hard muscle in his body, each plane and contour, ached against her own. She vibrated with a sensation previously unknown to her—a dark, wondrous feeling that shook her entire body and left her curiously mindless.

But it wasn't enough. Suddenly she became obsessed by the desire to be held tightly by him. She wanted to feel his warmth throughout her and to be a part of it. Without really understanding the craving, she knew she wanted to be closer still.

Traverston's hands urgently caressed every part of her they could reach, leaving hot fiery trails across her skin.

His mouth left hers and his lips bathed her eyelids, her ears and her neck with hungry kisses. But he couldn't stay away, and his mouth once again found the sweet sensual pleasure of her lips. Delving deep to explore the honeyed catacomb, his tongue entwined with hers. At that point, Olivia completely lost the ability to think, wrapped up only in the need to feel, to be a part of this glorious sensation.

It was moments before Traverston's whispered words penetrated to her brain. "Olivia." His rasp was a passion-hazed sound in her ear. "Admit that you like it, Olivia."

Like a splash of cold water, Traverston's words finally broke through to her mind, their meaning clear. With sudden anger, she tore herself from his grasp and backed away from him.

He was manipulating her again. All of his caresses meant nothing more to him than a temporary ploy to amuse himself. He cared nothing for her. He never had. This tryst was just another one of his attempts at controlling her. It was just a means to an end.

"Get away from me." Her breath came out on ragged, rapid gasps. She had to repeat herself to be heard. "Get away from me." Her hands balled into tight fists of anger at her sides.

As the meaning of her words penetrated the passion-induced fog in his brain, Traverston's face registered his surprise. His own enthusiastic reaction to their embrace was still very much in evidence. Slow from the aftermath of the recent sensations she had aroused in him, he opened his mouth to question her, but she immediately cut him off.

"You're just like all the rest," she whispered. Her eyes signaled her anger and distrust, and her disbelief in her earlier reaction to his lovemaking was clear. "You use people for your own purposes, then you toss them aside once your amusement has waned." She grew more bitter as she spoke. "I mean nothing to you. You're only out to destroy me." She backed up another step. "But I won't let you. I won't!"

With those impassioned words ringing in his ears, Olivia turned on her heels and fled from him.

Olivia's disheveled state as she cautiously made her way back to the edge of the ballroom was noticed by surprisingly few people. However, three people in particular were quick to see and judge her appearance.

Two of them watched her progress across the crowded room with interest, their heads bent together in a conspiratorial fashion.

"Miss Wentworth appears to be slightly undone by her walk in the gardens with the dashing marquis," purred Lady Chisolm, her green eyes flashing. "What do you suppose happened out there?"

David Hamilton's lips curled upward in a smirk. "Something I'm sure you wished had happened to you— so you could take advantage of it, that is."

Beatrice's laugh was full throated. As she threw her head backward, her companion admired the pretty white column of her neck. He also didn't fail to miss the enormous emerald and diamond necklace gracing her throat and diving into her cleavage. He recognized her calculated gesture for what it was and smiled in appreciation at her unabashed skill.

"How well you know me, David, dear." She glanced at him mischievously from the corner of her eye, the double entendre unmistakable. "I imagine you would like to know what happened out there as well as I. Or am I wrong?" She threw the last question out like a challenge, confident that she was indeed correct.

He turned to her, giving her a tight smile, but he was clearly distracted by his own thoughts. His response was almost as much to himself as to her. "Only in as much as that knowledge would be useful to me, my pet. Although I already know that the beautiful Ice Queen means something to my dear brother, I do not know exactly what."

Lady Chisolm's eyes hardened. "She didn't appear to be a queen of ice just now."

His response was distracted, thoughtful. "No, she did not."

The conversational lapse gave Beatrice time to study her companion's profile. He was a handsome man, she decided, evaluating him frankly. The good looks that ran in the Markston family had definitely been passed on to the third marquis's by-blow son. His cheekbones had the same chiseled quality as his brother's, and his stormy gray eyes were every bit as expressive as the current marquis's.

But with those features, the similarity seemed to stop. While David Hamilton had a good figure, it did not compare favorably with the tall, strong physique of the fourth marquis. David wasn't weak or effeminate, to be sure, but he wasn't quite as long in the leg as John, nor were his shoulders quite as broad.

His dark auburn hair, thick with just the barest hint of waves, had to be his best feature in Beatrice's opinion. She loved to wrap her fingers in its fullness, and she never missed the opportunity to do so whenever the occasion called for it. Fortunately, that was becoming more and more often. She allowed herself a secret smile at the thought.

The countess pursed her lips and examined him closer. His lips were just a little too thin for true beauty, though. They were wide and slim, and they became almost hidden when he pressed them together in concentration, as he was doing now. In fact, more than any other feature, his mouth hinted at a secret and dark side to his personality. He held his lips too perfectly together in a habitual smug expression, and it was the best indication of the cold cruelty she knew he was capable of. And that he took pains to hide from the rest of society.

But she knew it was there. In fact, it was this very real hint of danger surrounding Hamilton that made him so interesting to her. That aura was probably his attraction for several other females, as well. They clamored to his side and away again, like dogs hunting a bear. They were at once attracted to him and afraid of him. They felt an overwhelming urge to take him on, but an unnamed fear of dire consequences if they did. The ongoing drama surrounding David was a never-ending source of amusement to Beatrice, but she doubted that the women who fluttered around him knew or understood the source of their interest.

Of a sudden, Hamilton turned his gray eyes to Beatrice's green ones, and his smile turned wicked, as if he had been reading her thoughts and knew she had been evaluating him. Involuntarily a shiver ran down her spine.

"Come, Beatrice." His voice was chillingly hypnotic. "Do me the honor of partnering me for this waltz." Without waiting for her reply, he swept her into his arms and off into the whirling couples on the dance floor.

The third person who observed Olivia's arrival from the gardens was Alex Buxley, the Earl of Monquefort. His well-trained eye didn't miss the slightly windblown look to her elaborate coiffure, nor did it miss the right shoulder of her dress where it hung just a tad lower on her arm than the left. But more telling still was the wide, unblinking stare she gave the crowd as she looked for her grandmother.

The earl had become sensitive to Olivia's subtle display of moods ever since he had assisted her several nights ago at the Eddingtons' ball. To be sure, he had seen her only infrequently since that night, but it was as if an invisible bond had formed between them. He felt tied to her in a way he couldn't explain and would have been at pains to put into words. Her thoughts were almost transparently clear to him now, and he wondered how he ever could have mistaken her for the Ice Queen that society so casually labeled its most delicate flower. And now, in his esteemed opinion, she looked upset.

With a brevity and clumsiness unusual for the highly regarded silver-tongued earl, Lord Monquefort broke off his conversation with the current toast of St. James and hurried over to Olivia's side. Trying to school his expression into that of a merely solicitous but distantly polite acquaintance, the earl interrupted the young woman's progress with his sudden appearance. Unfortunately, his attempts at discretion were a dismal failure.

"Olivia, my dear, what is wrong?" He took her hand and placed it on his arm, falling into step beside her.

Alex's palpable concern immediately set off warning bells in Olivia's head. Before his eyes, her face became the perfect picture of coolness and regality. Her magnificent eyes, so wide and distressed looking a minute ago, narrowed to their usual width. She stopped and turned to the earl with all the graciousness of the queen for which she had been given her nickname.

Removing her hand from his arm, she answered him as calmly as if she had just met him at an afternoon garden party. "Lord Monquefort, how nice to see you. Pray excuse me. I'm just on my way to see my grandmother, Lady Raleigh."

Monquefort stood a moment peering at her intently. Except for that last-minute darting of the eyes, she almost had him fooled. Almost.

Making up his mind in a flash, he took Olivia's hand and, before she could protest, led her into the waltz just forming. After giving her a few moments to adjust to her new circumstances, he said quietly, "I thought you were going to call me Alex from now on."

Her hesitation was brief. "Of course. Alex. I apologize. Please forgive me."

"No need for that, Olivia," he said, relieved. "We're friends, remember? Being friends means there is no need for us to stand on ceremony with one another, and that includes apologies." He pulled back a little so that he could look into her face. "Right?" His smile was returned with a ghastly echo of his own. He shook her a little for emphasis. "Right?"

"Ouch, Alex!" Her voice was indignant. "Be careful! You're trodding on my toes!" But the last of her scold was softened by a widening smile.

"But am I right?"

Her eyes glowed softly. "Yes, you're right, of course."

"Good." He pulled her back into the circle of his arms. "Then you can also tell me what had you in such a taking back there."

She remained quiet a moment. When she spoke again, all the earlier warmth in her voice had gone, leaving it a dull-sounding husk. "You're a dear to be concerned about me, Alex, but I really don't want to talk about it. Not now." She stumbled a little and he caught her and brought her upright. When her pale, serious eyes met his, they were full of pain. Her voice was tremulous as she softly added, "Please."

Alex drew her into his arms and resumed the rhythmic course of their steps. As his gaze left hers for the couples around them, Olivia concentrated on resuming her poise. Silently and with wonder, she repeated her last word to him. *Please.*

The word felt strange in her mouth. Over the past six years, she had gotten used to relying on herself. She had never asked for help from anyone, not even her grandmother. She firmly believed that relying on people only made you an easy target. Her father had gone out of his way to prove that.

Yet here she was, asking him to help her. And, she realized with a growing fear, she really did need it. Alex had offered her his friendship, and she had grasped at it with the desperation of a drowning woman. She couldn't take back her dependence on him now, no matter how much she wished she might be able to. She simply was not strong enough to keep fighting the world on her own. She only hoped he would be kind to her. She only hoped he would see the frailty of her trust in him and not abuse it.

He did. "All right." He felt her relax in his hold with his answer and he smiled in reaction. He squeezed her hand in silent understanding. "Now stop talking or I'll be forced to step on your toes again. I can only concentrate on one thing at a time, you know."

For a second or two, he held his breath. Then the slender muscles of Olivia's waist relaxed perceptibly beneath his hand and he was rewarded with what he could have sworn, had he only been able to see her face, was a silent chuckle.

Chapter Eight

The morning sunlight filtering into the yellow salon from the long mullion windows at one end of the room did nothing to ease Olivia's headache the next morning. Despite Alex's empathetic words to her the evening before, she had stayed up half the night tossing and turning in her bed. Her mind could not block out Traverston's words to her, and she was honest enough to admit that those words had hurt.

It was her own fault; she knew that. She had no one to blame for her current state of distress but herself. She knew now she had wanted Traverston to care for her, to like her, if only a little. Consciously she had fought the urge, but the desire had been there all the same. Now she knew definitively that all he cared about was getting through her defenses and wounding her. Just as her father had done.

Why did the men in her life have this power over her? Why after all these years was she still vulnerable to the pain they could inflict? She had tried so hard to shield herself from life's ups and downs, to be as motionless and calm as a placid lake, to let sensations slide over her like a river over a stone, without effect, but she had failed miserably lately, especially with her husband.

Traverston unnerved her. He could make her so angry, she could hardly believe the emotions emanating from her. And he could incite passion in her. She had found that out the hard way last night.

And he could make her sad. He could make her so unhappy, she thought the little part of her soul left intact from her childhood would break.

She seemed to have no more control over herself than a puppet on a string where Traverston was concerned. He played her body's sensations to affect her mind, and then he used her mind against her. She might as well give them both to him right now, without a struggle, before he ripped her apart by taking what he desired. He wouldn't leave her alone until he possessed her. She knew that. But she also knew she couldn't just give in to him.

Lady Raleigh's entrance just then was a welcome respite for Olivia from her own thoughts. "My, you're up early this morning, Olivia," she said as she made her stately way into the room. Lady Raleigh stopped just short of the girl and pointed her ebony walking stick at her. "But you still look pale. How are you feeling this morning?" Her voice was brusque, as if she thought she could startle a confession out of her.

Olivia's answer came reluctantly. "I'm afraid I have the headache, Grandmama." She shifted uneasily under her watchful gaze. "Perhaps I'll go lie down again in a bit."

"Yes," Lady Raleigh replied thoughtfully. "Perhaps you should."

The salon door opened, forestalling further conversation between the ladies. The butler entered the room bearing a large bouquet of lilies. He bowed deferentially in front of Olivia.

"These arrived for you, Miss Wentworth," he announced in a solemn and correct tone. He paused expectantly. When no response seemed forthcoming from either lady, he continued more uncertainly, "Shall I put them down somewhere for you, miss?"

Glancing at Olivia and seeing her lost look, Lady Raleigh decided to take the initiative. "Place them over on the corner table, if you will, Bates. Thank you."

Obediently the servant placed the flowers as directed and bowed himself out of the room.

As if the effort caused her head to hurt more, Olivia got up from the gilded winged armchair where she had been sitting and made her way over to the table. She placed her fingers on the white envelope encasing the card, touching it almost tentatively.

"Well," Lady Raleigh said from over Olivia's shoulder. "You are acting as if you have never received flowers before in your life. Heaven knows you receive enough of them. Why don't you open the card and see who sent them?"

Her fingers lingering over the heavy paper, Olivia weighed her options. Then, with sudden decision, she opened the envelope and scanned the few handwritten lines. Her heart had slowed down considerably by the time she turned around to face Lady Raleigh. With annoying nonchalance, in that venerable woman's opinion, Olivia finally said, "It's from Mr. Hamilton. He apologizes once again for Traverston's behavior last night, and regrets any discomfort it may have caused me."

Lady Raleigh gave a very unladylike snort. Olivia lifted her eyebrows in question.

She looked disapprovingly at her granddaughter. "Very pretty of him to apologize for your husband's behavior. It's hardly any of his concern."

"But Mr. Hamilton doesn't know that we are married," she replied reasonably. "Still it does seem a bit odd." Olivia tapped the card in a slow staccato against her open palm. "What do you know about him, Grand-mama?"

Lady Raleigh made another humphing noise before she turned around and eased herself into the chair Olivia had recently vacated. She looked disgruntled. "Not much more than hearsay," she replied reluctantly. Then she abruptly went on the attack. "I know I sent you off to dance with him, Olivia, but he was only an expedient means to end your discomfort. I'd steer clear of Mr. Hamilton in the future, if I were you."

Olivia raised her eyebrows again.

Lady Raleigh temporized. "Oh, it's nothing I can tell you specifically, but there is something about that young man that disturbs me a great deal." She paused to look off toward the window, her brow more furrowed than usual by the wrinkles there. "He has a very questionable past, Olivia. One that doesn't bear looking into."

Olivia walked over to the gold satin covered Sheraton sofa, her fingertips distractedly caressing the material over one arm. "I'm not surprised. He told me he's the bastard son of the third marquis of Traverston."

Lady Raleigh's look was sharp. "He told you that?"

Olivia was surprised. "Yes. Did you know?"

The older woman looked her granddaughter in the eyes, her expression unreadable. "I knew."

"Then do you also know why my husband hates him so much?"

Lady Raleigh dropped her eyes from their intense study of the girl's face. "No."

"But if it isn't over their relationship...?"

She glanced up at Olivia, her face suddenly tired. "I don't know why the marquis dislikes his brother so much, child. I doubt anyone but the two of them can answer that question. But I suspect the animosity is mutual."

That would explain his pronounced attention to her, she thought. Olivia's curiosity was piqued. As if she were totally uninterested in the conversation, however, she walked back over to the flowers, bending over them and inhaling deeply. She presently straightened up again but kept her back to Lady Raleigh. As casually as she could manage, she asked, "How did you come to learn about Mr. Hamilton's true father, Grandmama? Mr. Hamilton led me to believe it was a great secret."

Her grandmother's sigh was audible. "It's a very long story, and not one I'm at liberty to share."

Just as Olivia was about to respond that if she couldn't confide in her granddaughter, then who could she confide in, Lady Raleigh got up from her chair. "I'm going to get ready to make some morning calls. Are you coming, child? Or are you planning to lie down?"

Olivia was suddenly reminded of her headache and her desire not to be alone.

"I'll go with you. Just give me a minute to get ready."

If Olivia was unhappy that morning, the marquis's mood could only be described as a case of the blue devils. Midmorning found Traverston in his study, the scene strangely reminiscent of the one in his library some eight years ago.

The brandy decanter at Traverston's elbow was half-empty. His eyes were rimmed with red, and his hair was rumpled from repeatedly running his hand through the dark, gleaming strands.

To the servants who sat cowering behind their doors, it was apparent that the marquis's drinking bout had been going on for some time. Even before they had crept out of their cozy warm beds to tend to the early morning chores, Traverston had been locked away in the study with his brandy. When his normally pompous butler had tried to enter the room and serve him his breakfast, his ears had been blistered by his master's baleful remarks. Similar tirades had been granted to all of his employees who had tried to enter, regardless of their errands. Now, mindful of the marquis's black temperament, they crept around the town house on tiptoe, careful not to disturb his solitude with the slightest of sounds.

However, there was some improvement of this scene over the one eight years ago. Traverston's appearance in general was that of a gentleman. His cravat, freshly tied in the predawn hours of the morning, was free from spots, if slightly limp. His close-fitting breeches and jacket were perfectly cut and flattering to his figure, and his tasseled Hessians shone with a Champagne-based polish.

Traverston's surroundings had improved markedly, too. The massive writing desk with its fine wood finish and exquisitely crafted rolltop could have easily graced the most dignified houses in London. Red velvet couches, scattered attractively amongst satinwood furniture and towering bookcases, set off the oil paintings of hunting scenes in the English countryside to perfection. The Aubusson carpet under his feet, with its muted reds and yellow, together with the fire burning cheerfully in the grate, cast a warm and appealing aura over the entire room.

But these fine surroundings were lost on the young brooding nobleman at the moment. As he stared down with unseeing eyes into the reflective surface of one booted foot cast helpfully across the opposite knee for just this purpose, he noticed nothing around him.

Because the marquis was obviously distracted by his weighty thoughts, Lord Monquefort, standing uncertainly in the doorway to his friend's study, decided to clear his throat. He tried it once, softly. There was no response. He tried it a second time, much louder this time. Frowning when his attempts at courteous behavior prompted a result that was rather less than he had hoped for, the earl strode briskly into the room. He stopped a good ten yards from his companion and stood staring expectantly at the dormant figure before him.

Slowly Traverston looked up to where his friend stood, his eyes taking their time in focusing on the familiar visitor. "What," he asked laconically after a moment's delay, "are there no lightskirts to keep you occupied this morning, Alex? Must you come and bother me instead?"

Monquefort's grin was teasing. "Now I know something is wrong, Trav, when you deign to call me Alex." He came further into the room and seated himself on one of the sofas close to his host. His face grew serious as he said only half-jokingly, "You seem at loose ends this morning, friend. None of your servants would show me in here. They said I must risk my own neck if I wanted to be so foolish." He paused and looked pointedly at the cut crystal glass at the marquis's elbow. "I thought you gave up drinking before the nooning hour."

The marquis responded with a sigh. "I did."

The earl leaned back against the velvet upholstery, crossing his hands over his stomach and slouching resignedly. With remarkable perception he commented, "You look about as brooding as Olivia did last night."

Traverston raised one eyebrow. "So it's Olivia now, is it, Alex?"

"Don't raise your hackles at me, Trav," Monquefort said, and laughed, sitting upright again. "I know you consider her your affair, although God knows why. You two don't seem to get along very well." He lowered his brows. "We're just friends, Olivia and I. That's all."

Traverston took another drink, his eyes dropping away from the earl's. "I'm not worried about you, Alex."

The earl, who took great pride in his prowess with the ladies, immediately became offended. "Well! I say! There's no need to go and get insulting!"

Traverston laughed bitterly. "You misunderstand me, Alex." He smiled mockingly. "I merely meant that your honor would preclude you from taking advantage of Olivia when you knew I was an interested party.''

Monquefort's shoulders relaxed a little at this salve to his pride. "Well, of course not." Then he peered intently at him. "That is, if I knew you had honorable intentions toward her."

It was stated as a question, but the marquis didn't miss the implied warning. Mumbling into his glass, he replied sourly, "The highest."

That was the heart of the problem, thought Traverston. He had married the girl. There was no way out of that now. But God knows, if he could run, he would. And fast.

Traverston had realized last night that he was coming to care for Olivia. He was beginning to care a great deal, as a matter of fact. The knowledge had struck him yesterday with the same blinding power as her impassioned kiss. And that knowledge bothered him.

Eight years had done a lot to temper his outlook on life, but they had not completely changed it. He didn't want to be tied to anything in this world. He didn't want to care for anyone or anything, least of all a woman.

Why couldn't he have become fond of a bloodhound, instead? Why couldn't he have cared for a faithful steed to ride on during the winter hunts? Why not a bird, a cat, or a rat for that matter? But, God forgive him, it should never have been a woman.

The last decade of Traverston's life had been spent with people he could read, people whose motives he understood. They had been courtesans with nothing on their minds but greed, gaming partners with similar motives, and bits of fluff he could toss to the wind without a second thought. Or they had been women like Beatrice, whose greed for money and power was so transparent as to have been laughable. But at least it was understandable, and therefore controllable.

The exception had been Monquefort, who from some misguided motivation only the earl knew, had seen something worthwhile in the marquis and pursued the friendship. Perhaps out of loneliness, or perhaps out of some other long repressed emotion, Traverston had welcomed the friendship, and that relationship had grown into the easy companionship it was today.

But Alex was a man well able to take care of himself. Olivia was an altogether different matter. She was a woman, and a fragile and wounded one at that. She didn't need more pain from him—and Traverston didn't want to hurt her. He didn't want to taint her with his past. He didn't want to contaminate her with who he was intrinsically. And he would wind up hurting her if he didn't leave her alone. He knew that. It was unavoidable. It was inevitable.

And yet he was consumed by her. She ate at his senses. When he wasn't with her, all he could do was think about her. When he consoled himself by being with her, her damned indifference inflamed him. He couldn't refrain from trying to make her react. It was as if her shell of coolness begged his touch, pleaded with him to make her into the woman she was meant to be. He was at once tempted and damned. He desired her and despised himself for the emotion. To be near her and not touch her, not make her look at him with those bottomless eyes was maddening for him.

But Olivia couldn't stand him. He had made sure of that by his treatment of her. He had gone out of his way to be insulting to her. From their first encounter, he had sought to make her despise him. The results were at once satisfying and infuriating.

If she couldn't stand him, then at least she would stay away from him. He reiterated to himself that his original objective remained clear. She had to avoid him at all cost, thereby not risking her person or her feelings by associating with him. Traverston was satisfied he was making good progress toward that goal.

At the same time, what he desired above all else was to be a part of her; to know her body and mind completely. He desired to have her trust, to hold her in his arms like he did last night and know that *that* was where she longed to be more than anywhere else in the world.

His body grew heavy at the thought of the previous night. Olivia's impassioned response to his kiss had been electrifying for him. Partially because it was so unexpected, so unsought for at the time, and partially because her chemical reaction to him snapped the iron control he always felt was necessary when he was around her. She made him want to take her immediately and make love to her without giving a thought to the consequences. He didn't know what he would have done if she hadn't broken the spell last night.

He wanted her badly, but he also wanted her to stay as far away from him as she could.

The dichotomy was killing him.

Traverston's dilemma was borne in every deeply etched line in his face. Troubled, the earl looked on in silence as he watched his friend struggle over the internal battle, unaware of its cause.

Looking down at his hands, Alex confronted his own silent battle. He could say nothing. It was clear that his friend wouldn't talk. The marquis had never been one for confidences of an intimate nature, and Alex doubted he would start with one this morning. Still he wanted to help.

More than anyone else, the earl knew that the marquis was a troubled man. When he had made his acquaintance some five years earlier, he had fallen in with the marquis out of a mischievous sense for trouble. Traverston seemed to have an uncanny knack for finding danger and thwarting it, and Alex had wanted to be a part of his exciting adventures. But where the earl pursued his adventures with an innocent passion for new and fresh excitement, the marquis pursued his with a recklessness born of abandonment and desperation. It hadn't taken Monquefort long to see his friend was a tormented soul.

Over the succeeding years, the earl had done what he could to mitigate the marquis's darker passions, and he felt he had met with some limited success, but not to the extent that was necessary. Now, finally, just when he thought that Olivia might hold the key to bringing his friend back to life, it looked as though the very opposite were true. And so simply, in the only way he could, Alex sought to help his friend once again.

Perhaps a breath of fresh air would put the world to rights for Traverston, he thought brightly. It usually did wonders for him when he was having problems.

Getting up from the chair, Alex strode over to his friend and slapped him lightly on the thigh with one of his leather gloves. "Let's go for a ride, Trav," he offered, strolling over to the desk and toying with a gold ink pot. "I have a sweet goer I picked up at Tattersall's last week and I'm dying to put her through her paces." He looked over at the marquis, his tone artificially cheerful. "What do you say, old man?"

It was a few seconds before Traverston moved, but when he did, it was to slowly set his brandy glass down next to the decanter. Using his hands to lever himself out of the chair, he rose by inches, moving as though the earth's gravity had suddenly increased its pull on his body by tenfold.

"All right, Alex," he said tiredly, his eyes wandering to a place on the rug near the earl's boots. "Meet you back here in one hour."

Olivia's beige cotton habit piped in maroon was an outstanding ensemble. The delicate bolero jacket with its giant puff sleeves swept in toward her waist and exaggerated its tininess. The blouse, a brick red that exactly matched the trim of the jacket and skirt, was a filmy soft silk that revealed the perfect round swell of her breasts.

David Hamilton whistled under his breath at her audacity in wearing such an ensemble. Not many younger members of the *ton*, especially ladies in their first season, could wear a getup like that and get away with it. The gesture showed she had more spirit than anyone had previously thought. Smiling appreciatively, he slapped his horse's flank with his whip and trotted over to Olivia's side.

"Allow me to compliment you on your outfit, Miss Wentworth." His feral smile grew wider as he examined the delicate pointed hat with its expensive lace veil perched precariously on her perfect curls. "I don't remember the last time I saw such a charming sight."

Olivia nodded her head at him. "Good afternoon, Mr. Hamilton. How do you do?" She looked over her shoulder without waiting for a response from him. Her groom was still keeping a respectful distance from his mistress. Her eyes returned to the man next to her. They were decidedly cool.

"Have I done something to offend you, Miss Wentworth?" he questioned, immediately concerned. "Don't tell me you are allergic to flowers."

She gave him what could pass for a tight smile. "No. Thank you."

"Then what could it be? I had thought you would appreciate my comparison of you to the slim and elegant lily. Perhaps I was wrong. Perhaps I should have sent you roses after all."

He wasn't fooling her for a minute. He wanted something from her...they always did. She just wished he would come out with it. Didn't he realize she didn't play this game? All of society knew it, else she wouldn't have been dubbed with her ignominious title. She grimaced internally at the thought of it.

She decided to be blunt with him. "Why do I get the feeling that you were lying in wait for me, Mr. Hamilton?"

He laughed, the sound not coming quite as easily as he would have liked. "But how can you wonder? Such a beautiful young woman as yourself must have thousands of admirers."

Olivia turned back to face the front, guiding her mare with an easy hand. She delivered her response in an even tone. "As you can see, I am alone."

"Then allow me to remedy that situation. Not only today but also in the future. Let me accompany you on a ride through the park on the morrow." He threw up a hand, intending the gesture to be casual. "But not during the fashionable hour. There are too many people around then."

He shot her a sideways glance. "May I be so bold as to suggest that judging from your ability to control my brother's chestnut the other day, you'd enjoy an early-morning gallop in the park when there would be few people around to censure such an activity? Say, seven o'clock?"

Olivia turned to look at her companion again, her expression openly contemplative. A few moments later her eyes shifted away as she responded, "Mr. Hamilton, may I ask you a question?"

"But of course." It was a firm reply, full of self-confidence.

"Why are you showing an interest in me?" she asked, sliding her gaze back to her companion so as not to miss his reaction.

Again his laugh was slightly forced. "But what do you mean? I never thought you were the kind to fish for compliments, Miss Wentworth."

A look of irritation crossed her face. "And I didn't take you for a ninnyhammer, Mr. Hamilton."

The lines of his face tightened, and she was inadvertently reminded of her husband. "Then I am at a loss to respond. Could it be that you are truly unaware of your charms?"

Her look was chilling. "Mr. Hamilton, don't play me for a fool. I have a feeling your real interest in me has nothing to do with any attraction you may feel. I believe you are merely showing an interest because the marquis has demonstrated a marked attention to me. You said yourself you thought he would offer for me, did you not?"

"Miss Wentworth, I must protest. I don't make a habit of casting out lures in order to steal my brother's women, if that's what you're implying. I merely thought to further our acquaintance. I had assumed, perhaps wrongly, or so it now appears, that you would be amenable to the idea of getting to know your future husband's brother."

Olivia studied him, taking in his whole appearance and attitude. She could swear his offended air was genuine. She relented after a small hesitation. "I apologize, Mr. Hamilton," she said with more warmth in her voice than she had shown before. "Although I think your assumptions about the marquis and myself are a little premature, I would like to get to know you better."

Olivia concentrated on guiding her mare forward through the afternoon crush. Then, she let her gaze flick sideways to her companion. He was still correct and firm in his saddle. Before she could stifle the apology, it was out. "I'm sorry I took you to task for being kind to me." Grimacing at her inability to sound sincere, she added, "If the offer still stands, I'd be very pleased to go riding with you tomorrow."

He bowed stiffly from the saddle, his wounded pride still evident. "Tomorrow at seven, then." Without another word, he wheeled his horse and trotted it off in the opposite direction.

With a nameless regret for her acceptance, Olivia watched him ride away before she guided her own mount on through the crowd.

Chapter Nine

The Marquis of Traverston was in a foul mood. Twice already he had attempted to claim his driving gloves from the gentleman's shop in Picadilly, and twice he had been turned away. Both times the shopkeeper had made extravagant excuses to the marquis, accompanied by fulsome compliments meant to soothe that gentleman's pride. Both times the shopkeeper had barely succeeded in retaining his head.

But not today, thought the marquis darkly.

If his gloves were not ready today, Traverston was determined to do his very best to undermine further patronage of the store by any of his acquaintances. He would run the fat little owner out of business, and he would take great pleasure in doing so.

Ordinarily the marquis was not quite as vindictive when it came to his apparel. After all, if he really examined his complaints against the shopkeeper, he would have seen that they were the merest trifles in the ongoing saga of his life. In truth, he didn't need to come to the store himself. He could have sent his man of affairs to see to such a minor errand.

In addition, it wasn't as though he really needed the gloves. He had ten pair already. He had only commissioned them out of a desire to seem as though he had a purpose in going out to the shops with his friend, the Earl of Monquefort.

That trip was ten days ago. The marquis still didn't have a purpose in going out. He just knew he wanted to be out.

The past few weeks had been hell for him. More than at any other time in his life, the marquis felt like a caged beast. It seemed to him as though circumstances had conspired against him for the past eight years. Ever since his grandfather had died, his actions had not been his own. But now, more than ever, this was true. It was true because of Olivia.

Olivia. Dear God, what was he to do about Olivia? She was like the proverbial candle to him, and he the moth. He couldn't stay away, and yet he had to. Only this time, if he were to go to her side, he would wind up burning not only himself, but her, as well. His interference in her life would mean destruction for both of them.

But, if he only could stay away! If it were only that easy. Look at him. It had only been a few weeks and already he felt as if pieces of himself were falling off and being lost forever. To stay away from her would drive him crazy, he was sure.

No matter what he did, he was doomed.

This mental torment, and not the petty problem of the unfinished gloves, was the true source of Traverston's black mood. But he did not want to recognize it as such. Grumbling to himself, he pulled the door to the gentleman's shop open with a hard yank. The little bell attached to the top of the door jangled violently, startling both the shopkeeper and the only other patron currently present within the narrow confines of the tiny store.

"Traverston!" exclaimed the stunning blonde standing before the store's counter, using the same pleased tone she would have if she had been met with a particularly tasty treat from her paramours. "What a nice surprise!"

The marquis hesitated only a second in the doorway before moving inside with brisk steps. "Lady Chisolm," he intoned coldly, giving her a tiny nod of his head. Immediately he shifted his attention to the store's owner, a fat, timid man who seemed to shrink where he was standing at the marquis's abrupt entrance. "You have something for me, I'm sure," he growled at the shopkeeper, not bothering to attempt any pleasantries.

"Ye-yes, my lord," stuttered the balding, portly man. His wide eyes shifted with the frightened urgency of a rabbit from the countess to the marquis and back again. "This will just take a minute, my lady," he whispered at her with extreme supplication, as if he somehow worried that the noblewoman might be a greater threat than the marquis.

"Of course," she replied airily, and shooed him off toward the back of the store with the negligent wave of one hand. As soon as the shopkeeper was out of hearing range, Beatrice turned to the marquis once more. Leaning an elbow on the countertop, she threw one shoulder back and looked at him archly. "I declare, Trav. You have that man in a terrible fit. Shame on you to frighten a poor defenseless man of his ungainly proportions like that! One would think you are a bully."

Coolly Traverston turned his baleful gray eyes on her. "You would know, Beatrice."

She smiled with all the seductive powers she possessed. Lowering her voice, she replied, "Yes, I do know. You are a horrible bully, but I forgive you."

He cocked one eyebrow in amusement. "Do you now?"

Taking her elbow off the counter, Beatrice stood up straight before swaying slowly to his side. Gently, as if calculating the size of the muscles underneath his coat, she laid one gloved hand on his arm and looked up at him from beneath her bonnet. Her eyes were very green and very inviting. "Yes, I do. You were very bad, Traverston, but you know me." She licked her lips slowly and savored some flavor only she could taste. "I like men who are a challenge. And you are definitely that." She tossed her head back so that the arch of her neck could be exposed. "So I'm willing to overlook the other night if you are. We could go on as before. Like nothing ever happened." Her last words came out on a whisper.

One corner of his mouth twitched up a tiny amount, but other than that, his expression was unchanged. "And the fact that I'm married doesn't bother you?"

Abruptly she pulled away, but just enough to distance herself a little bit from him. "Why should it?" she asked in a casual tone of voice. "Not that I think you really are, but I've been with married men before. Your wife must be pretty awful, or society would have known about her by now. But you aren't really married, are you, Trav?" She looked at her gloves for a few moments, as if his answer couldn't possibly make a difference to her. But then, through her eyelashes, she brought her cat's eyes to bear on him.

It was a tempting offer. The countess was a delectable woman, and it was possible that she could slake some of the frustrated burning desire he felt for Olivia. He narrowed his eyes and dropped his gaze to her chest, where her ample bosom was heaving with excitement or fear. Bringing his gaze upward to her face again, he saw her small, knowing smile, and he was sure she had planned every breath for his own pleasure.

Yes, the countess was a woman who could take care of herself. He didn't have to worry about her feelings, and he didn't have to wonder what her motives were. He could use her, because she expected to be used, if only so that she could get something material back in return.

And yet, he couldn't. The knowledge brought more chagrin than regret, because he had known from the first sound of his name on her lips that he would have to turn her down. For better or for worse, Olivia was the one he wanted, and no other. And if he could not have her, he didn't want anyone at all.

But for Lady Chisolm's sake, and because Olivia had already begun to change him in ways he couldn't yet fathom, he was much gentler with her than he would have been before. As the shopkeeper handed him his gloves and he counted out the money, he reached for the words that would let her down gently. Finally, just before he walked through the door, he turned around once more to face her.

"I'll think about it," he said, but his eyes gave a different answer completely. And as he moved to vanish through the open door, he missed the answering flash of venom in the countess's emerald green eyes.

"So tell me, Mr. Hamilton. How is it that you come to know so much about the gardens?" Olivia asked, after listening to the gentleman comment on Vauxhall and its history for nearly a quarter of an hour. She stopped her measured tread and turned to face her companion.

"My dear Miss Wentworth," he replied with a twinkle in his eye as he took her by the elbow and led her from the center of the paved walk to its edge, "I hardly think that question is within the bounds of propriety." He watched her for a moment, waiting for the telltale blush that usually accompanied his burlesque banter with other women, but it was not forthcoming.

As she continued to gaze at him with an unblinking, solemn stare, he smiled at his own folly in expecting the Ice Queen to show any emotion, much less embarrassment. He turned his head and gazed out over the well-patterned walkways that formed the latticework of the maze of gardens they had just walked through. Vauxhall was indeed a lovely place to visit on a sunny afternoon. And he did know a lot about the place, although he usually reserved his visits for those times more suited to his nocturnal habits.

"I come here often," he replied after a while, choosing to let go the choice remark uppermost in his mind. He turned his sparkling eyes back to hers and once again marveled at the bland front they offered to the world, with no clue as to what lay behind them. "I find the air here is fresher than in most places, and I get a certain pleasure out of watching the other people who come here to spend a quiet afternoon."

She lifted her eyebrows in what, had her face been capable of more expression, would have passed for astonishment. "Do you like to observe people? I wouldn't have guessed."

"Really? I am astounded. I thought you would have noticed by now how often it is that I watch you."

She looked away, letting her gaze drift to a huddle of children playing with a ball. Her expression remained frozen, but inside her heart was racing. She didn't know what game her husband's brother was playing, but she was sure that it wasn't one she wished to participate in.

When she looked at him again, her eyes were cool and distant. "I fear I have been negligent about the time, Mr. Hamilton. I'm sure I never intended to stay out so long with you. Would you be so kind as to escort me home now? My grandmother will be worried."

"Miss Wentworth, I pray you, don't take that tone with me," he responded contritely. "I beg your forgiveness for being so blunt about my admiration for you. I fear that it has been a long time since I have been out with anyone as sweet and innocent as you, and my manners have rather rusted as a consequence. I shan't speak of my affection again. I assure you." He patted her arm and placed her hand once again in the crook of his elbow, then began the walk back the way they had come.

Olivia glanced once over her shoulder to be sure that her maid was still following at a discreet distance. When she had assured herself she was, she spoke. "Mr. Hamilton, since you have been so kind to me these past few weeks, I think it only fair to inform you that your first guess about your brother and myself was right. We are to be married. So you see, your attention to me is unwarranted. I will completely understand if in light of this information, you decided your time was better spent elsewhere." She glanced at him, her normally smooth brow marred with tiny wrinkles. "I'm sorry I didn't tell you sooner. I wasn't at liberty. But your comments lead me to believe you deserve to know."

It was a few moments before he broke the silence. "Thank you for your honesty. Still, Miss Wentworth, I think of you as a friend. Would you mind it if I continued to call? I promise to treat you with nothing less appropriate than the affection of a brother."

Olivia watched the path before her feet as they slowly progressed across the grounds. "No, of course not," she replied softly.

He laid his hand over hers where it rested on his arm and gave it a squeeze. "Good. Borrow!" he cried then, and raised his hand to capture the attention of his pacing coachman. "Bring up the carriage, my man. We're going home."

Two days later, David Hamilton waited impatiently behind a potted palm, listening to a "diamond of the first water" warble out her aria on a makeshift stage. The lady was lush enough, he decided as his eyes drifted once again to her ample bosom, but any man foolish enough to marry her would wind up deaf before too long. He shuddered with ill-concealed distaste as she hit another high C.

Fortunately for Hamilton, he was hidden from general view and his feelings about the soprano and her performance could go unobserved. That was why the light tap on his shoulder caught him by surprise. Jumping up, he tangled his head in the leafy fronds that were shielding him from the room at large. By the time he disengaged himself from the offending plant, his mood had gone noticeably sour. Frowning heavily, he jerked around to find the source of his distraction.

"Well, David," smirked a familiar silky voice. "I didn't think that this was your type of entertainment." Beatrice Chisolm's eyes glowed with amusement. Nonchalantly she picked a strand of green from his hair with her long, slender fingers. "I'll have to hold a hopelessly amateur musicale myself, if it'll ensure your attendance, even if you do find the plant life more interesting than the guests. Or should I just hold a garden party?"

Hamilton snorted derisively, his eyes moving back to the crowd on the other side of the plant. He shrugged off her gibe about his surveillance abilities as if it were of no import. "That's a leveler—your holding a musicale. I can't imagine you entertaining such an insipid crowd as this. Please, don't change on my account, Lady Chisolm." He glanced briefly at the seductress beside him. When he noticed she wasn't making any attempt to hide, he said, "Do go away, Beatrice." He turned to face the crowd again before declaring dismissively over his shoulder, "You stick out like a sore thumb. In case you haven't noticed, I'm trying to be discreet."

She half crouched down beside him, making her full bosom in its plunging neckline easier for him to view. "Not until you tell me why you're trying to merge with the greenery, my love. Besides, you have to admit, hiding in the bushes at a party is hardly discreet."

"It is unless you have a shrew looking for you," he muttered to himself. He half turned in her direction, giving up watching the audience seated in front of him for the moment. "I'm attempting to discover if my charming brother is here, if you must know." His voice was soft but with a dangerous edge. He was irritated by the interruption to his activities. He paused while he let his glance dip and linger on her exposed cleavage. "Although why that fact should interest you I can't imagine."

Astonishingly she felt her face grow warm from Hamilton's gaze. She had thought she was long past the point where she was capable of blushing. Apparently she was not. "Oh, but it does." She straightened her shoulders a tad in an effort to bluff her way through the ruse that had now gone sour. Her face grew warmer when she caught his crooked smile. He obviously found her discomfort amusing. She glared at him before continuing. "I'm very interested in anything having to do with the unassailable marquis."

"Oh?"

Beatrice couldn't misinterpret the invitation to confide. She studied Traverston's half brother through her slanted green eyes. She decided to gamble; perhaps she and Hamilton could work something out. With a tiny shrug of her rounded shoulders, she said, "Yes." Her eyes grew hard. "I owe him for something."

"Ah." The single syllable conveyed a wealth of understanding. But Beatrice was taken aback when he turned around and faced the audience again. It was a singularly dismissive gesture.

Although she was a little daunted by his response, England's reigning queen of beauty had never been one to give up. She leaned close to him, brazenly thrusting her cleavage under his nose and daring him to look where he had just a moment before. Then she laid one hand on his back and whispered determinedly, "I think we can help each other, David."

When no answer seemed to be forthcoming from him, she continued, louder this time. "I want to help."

At that provocation, Hamilton spun around so quickly that Beatrice had to retreat a few steps. His body was rigid with tightly controlled anger. His eyes were hard agates of distaste. At the violence of his response, her mouth dropped open in surprise.

"Listen, you *minx*," he began, practically spitting out the descriptive noun, "I didn't spend the last few weeks trailing after Olivia to have you spoil the game now." He glanced around them and then lowered his voice. His tone was quieter, but his words still forceful. "What I may want with my brother is no concern of yours. Neither are any thinly veiled plots of revenge you may have any concern of mine. I suggest you look elsewhere for help in your petty schemes against your ex-paramour."

Anger flashed across Beatrice's fine features like white-hot lightning, but as Hamilton again turned his back on her in contempt, he missed the devastating effect of his words on the enchantress. Seething, the countess shifted onto one foot and regarded her companion's back with fury. He wasn't going to dismiss her so easily, she thought. But there would be more bees caught this evening with honey than with vinegar. One raw and unrestrained temper between them was enough. But she would have to show him she meant business. She wouldn't be brushed off in this.

Regaining her equanimity rapidly, Beatrice laid her hand on Hamilton's back more forcefully this time, using enough pressure that he had to turn and look at her. When his eyes shifted with impatience to hers, she was the picture of arrogance and sophistication, and her eyes flashed with relentless determination. "I have no wish to be at daggers drawn with you, David, but I think you should listen to me. I may be of more use to you than you think.''

When he rolled his eyes and began to look away, she rushed on. ''Who is it who's going to draw Traverston off when you make your move on the little iceberg out there.'' She nodded in the audience's direction. ''Huh? Traverston's been conveniently absent from the social whirl these past few weeks, but don't think for a minute he will stay out of your way.''

She nodded at him, seeing his look and noting the stiffness that had overtaken his body. ''Oh, yes. You're not the only one who has watched his movements, or Miss Wentworth's for that matter. That surprises you, doesn't it?'' she asked rhetorically. ''It shouldn't. You haven't been nearly as discreet as you think you have. I've seen you tattling about after her—taking her riding in the park, sitting with her at parties, escorting her to the opera. You've managed to be everywhere she is, David, even if you don't seek her out to speak with her.

''And I'll tell you something else. I'm not the only one who has noticed your pointed interest in the lovely chit, my friend. If you think your activities have gone unnoticed by the marquis, think again. I wouldn't be surprised at all if he happened to choose this evening to show up and declare for the girl, if not out of true affection for her then just to spite you. And if he does, David, your game is finished.''

Hamilton's face grew stony as he listened to Beatrice's tirade, but in the end, he had to admit she was right. ''And what,'' he asked softly and with warning in his tone, ''do you think you can do to improve things?''

''Well now,'' she purred, coming up close to him and leaning on his shoulder. Her gloved hand caressed the muscles of his upper arm, lingering on the firm biceps encased in tightly fitting superfine. Her emerald eyes peeked up at him from underneath heavily lidded eyes.

"Quite a lot, actually. A man like the marquis must be frustrated by now, having been so long away from his ladylove. It must be taking a lot of restraint and patience to stay away from someone as attractive as the little ice princess, and we both know that those are two qualities the marquis is rather short on. All it will take is a little feminine charm from yours truly to bemuse him for a few moments, and then you can play whatever hand it is you intend to play with the lovely Miss Wentworth."

"You're not half as silly as I thought, Bea." Hamilton took her hand from his chest and lifted it to his mouth in a courtly gesture. "You may just be right, my dear. I think I could use your help in getting Olivia away from my dear brother. She's not right for him, anyway."

Suddenly the countess pulled away from him, her kittenish expression disappearing in a flash. "Are you planning to marry her yourself, then?"

He laughed harshly. "And just when I thought you had a brain in that lovely head of yours. Don't be ridiculous." His eyes turned frosty. "She's not my type."

"What, then?" she asked, still suspicious.

He looked at her smugly, self-confidence oozing from him. "You leave that to me, my dear," he said as he condescendingly patted her arm. Then he turned his attention back to the seated audience on the other side of the plants.

Olivia yawned discreetly behind the delicately carved panels of her ivory fan. She was the first to admit she wasn't terribly musical, but this gathering had been hard even on her ears. Beside the horribly amateur soprano that was currently testing the audience's ability to tolerate pain, there had been a hopelessly incompetent violinist, a maudlin piano and cello duet and several renditions by a small-time opera singer who had never made it past the chorus in any particular show. Olivia yawned quietly once again before waving the fan a few times in an attempt to give truth to the lie she was warm before setting it in her lap.

Moving her head slightly first to one side and then the other, she looked for perhaps the hundredth time for a glimpse of her husband in the crowd. He was nowhere within her range of vision. With a small sigh of resignation, she gave up searching for the moment. Half an hour ago she had given up pretending that she was not looking for him at all and that she was just perusing the gathering in her ennui. She could deny the truth no longer, however.

It had been weeks since she had seen Traverston. Three weeks, five days, to be exact. Again she winced mentally at the admission she had been keeping track. Olivia had tried to drive him from her mind, but he was always there. He and his burning embrace.

Actually, she had no idea if he planned on being at the musicale. It was the kind of party that he would have hated, so she rather doubted it. But still, even though the chances were slim, she couldn't refrain from letting her eyes dart around the room on the off chance he might be there. After all, he might have come if he had known she was going to be there. Mightn't he? Olivia drooped a little in her chair. Or perhaps not.

The past three weeks had been hell. The only thing that had made this period in her life bearable was Alex's occasional visits to her. But he had so many other friends and acquaintances, he wasn't able to call on her more than a few times a week. Not to mention the fact that he had some kind of special assignment work he was doing for the government right now. That made his visits even more few and far between.

David Hamilton's visits had helped, as well, she thought belatedly with a twinge of guilt. That gentleman could be rather charming when he tried, and it was ob-

vious enough that for whatever reason, he was trying very
hard. But his presence always seemed to make her grandmother uneasy. She was barely civil when he was around,
and occasionally his calls to the ladies at Wimpole Street
had been difficult to get through.

And when Hamilton came, Olivia was always reminded by his presence of the marquis. His cousin not
only looked like her husband to some degree, but he was
a blatant reminder of why they had fought in the first
place. She worried her bottom lip with her teeth and con-
templated telling Mr. Hamilton that she was unwilling to
continue seeing him. Still, they had had a few decent
rides in Hyde Park together.

With a start, Olivia realized the soprano had finished
her piece. Reluctantly she joined in the applause, fervently hoping that this signaled the end of the recitation.
Relief poured through her body as it soon became apparent the soprano was indeed the last performer.

Getting to her feet, Olivia turned around to help her
grandmother from her chair. She was surprised to see that
woman fully alert and sitting with her back straight, almost as if she had been attending a military parade instead of a musicale. Even in this immense test of will,
the old woman had come through with flying colors. Her
grandmother's strength of character never failed to surprise her.

Lady Raleigh's eyes met her granddaughter's, an
amused twinkle sparkling in their depths. "I vow, that is
a relief," she said none too quietly. "I thought that
trumped-up little songbird was going to keep on trilling
forever."

Olivia looked about them with embarrassment. But if
any of the nearby couples had heard her grandmother's
commentary on the performance, they were too well-bred
to show it. Or else they were in agreement. Ignoring her
elder's remarks, Olivia rose from her seat and held out

her hand. "Come, Grandmama. Let me get you some refreshment."

"That would be a relief, as well." She leaned heavily on her cane, preferring to struggle out of the chair on her own rather than rely on Olivia's help. Olivia withdrew her proffered hand respectfully, remembering just a tad too late her grandmother's edict not to make her look weak in public.

Setting her pace to the more measured walk of her elder, Olivia accompanied Lady Raleigh out of the small impromptu auditorium and into the ballroom. Tonight the wood-paneled room with its intricate parquet floor was sparsely adorned with delicate orchids. The hothouse flowers scented the room with their sweet perfume. Olivia breathed in deeply, enjoying the fragrance. She casually looked up at the giant Austrian chandelier with its profusion of candles suspended from the ceiling by a slender silver pole.

Bringing her gaze back down she met the bright and wizened look of her grandmother. They shared a secret smile and a knowing look because they were in agreement. Overall, the room was decorated tastefully and with restraint. Not, therefore, the work of their esteemed hostess.

As Olivia and Lady Raleigh made their way over to the refreshment tables, they were waylaid by the same woman who had preoccupied their thoughts just a second before. "I beg your forgiveness, Lady Raleigh, Miss Wentworth," the societal dragon began, her gold turban bobbing up and down like the head of a turkey, "for not having this little gathering adjourn to a more appropriate room." With a flutter of her hands, Lady Sommerby indicated their surroundings. "But my salons are being redecorated, and rather than postpone my party until later, I decided to make different accommodations for my guests."

"It's quite all right, Millicent," interrupted Lady Raleigh before the matron could be any more obsequious. "I doubt anyone noticed where they'd been led to after that performance back there."

The woman's face lit up. "Oh, yes. Miss Elizabeth has a lovely voice, does she not? I simply adore having her at my musicales."

"An interesting technique to be sure, my dear," commented the old woman dryly. She slid her glance toward Olivia before adding, "My granddaughter and I were just admiring your lovely ballroom. However did you think of such understated elegance?"

Olivia did not wait to hear how her hostess was going to respond to this comment. Instead, she let her eyes drift over the crowd as she had done earlier. This time, however, she met with limited success. True, she did not find the one she was looking for, but her eyes met with a familiar face.

Seeing Olivia notice him, David Hamilton immediately broke off his conversation with a rather insipid young miss and her overbearing mother. Olivia's mute plea for his company was just the opening he had been looking for. Coming over to her side, he led her a little away from her grandmother and Lady Sommerby.

"I feel sorry for Lady Raleigh," Hamilton whispered with amusement, nodding casually at the two older women still locked in conversation. "Having to listen to our hostess search for praise on the success of her party can't be the most pleasurable of pastimes. I would not wish to be in her slippers."

"I collect Lady Sommerby does not have much of an ear for music," replied Olivia. The hint of a smile played at her lips.

He looked at her conspiratorially. "What do you say to us exiting this quaint little gathering for a moment, Olivia? You look as if you wouldn't mind a few moments' peace from mouthing pleasantries and listening to empty observations. Think of your absence as a well-earned respite.''

Her face grew uncertain. "I don't know, Mr. Hamilton. That would be unseemly.''

"Oh, come on, Miss Wentworth," he replied cajolingly. "You are the very pattern card of respectability. You can relent your adherence to societal dictates for a few minutes, can't you? And your grandmother won't miss you for a short time. Besides—" his look grew sly "—I happen to know that Lady Sommerby has a rather interesting portrait gallery here.''

Olivia could think of better things to do than to stare at the long-dead faces of Lady Sommerby's ancestors, but in truth, remaining at the party and listening politely to "empty observations," as Hamilton had put it, was not one of them. She hesitated only for a moment. "All right. But just for a minute or two.''

She took his arm as he led the way toward the hallway leading off the ballroom. Glancing around surreptitiously to ensure no one was watching them, he put his hand over hers and pulled her with him quickly down an opening to their left. Scant minutes later, they arrived at the long hallway of the portrait gallery.

The hall was empty save for the slightly dusty oil paintings gracing the length of its walls and a few strategically placed settees. This part of the house was not well lit. Only a few candles sputtered in their sconces by the paintings. It was obvious the hostess was not expecting her guests to venture this far from the party.

Olivia cleared her throat nervously. "The house doesn't look this large from the outside," she commented. Her tone betrayed her second thoughts at sneaking away from the party with her companion. "I think my grandmother must be starting to worry about me.''

Hamilton turned to her, his face not quite hiding his

contempt. "Don't tell me you've changed your mind, Miss Wentworth?" The daring note in his question was unmistakable.

Her bristles immediately rising, Olivia denied the implied accusation too quickly. "No, of course not! I...just think perhaps we shouldn't linger."

"What?" His eyes gleamed dangerously. "Afraid to be alone with me?"

Something in his tone sent chills down her spine. "Of course not," she repeated. She mentally took hold of herself and smiled a little tentatively. "As you are the expert here, what do you recommend we look at first, Mr. Hamilton?"

He pulled her forward, keeping a firm grasp of her hand on his arm. "Don't you think it's about time you started calling me David, Olivia?" They stopped before a portrait of a bearded middle-aged man. His neck ruff, close-fitting doublet and padded trunk hose informed Olivia that they were looking at one of their hostess's Elizabethan ancestors.

Gulping nervously, she moved a little closer to the painting, pretending to study the method the artist had used to get the jewels in the doublet to reflect the available light. Choosing her next words with care, she was just about to open her mouth to reply when his next sally caught her off guard.

"Do you know who this is, Olivia?" His voice was astonishingly close. She could feel his warm breath on her neck, causing the little hairs there to stand on end.

Using every muscle in her body to control the motion, she backed away very slowly from the painting. When she turned around, it was to discover Hamilton's face uncomfortably close to her own.

His gaze was intense, predatory. Her lips were dry, and instinctively she wetted them with her tongue. His eyes followed the movement before coming back to meet with hers. Her breath started coming in shallow pants. "Who?" The question was barely audible.

He came even closer. "He was the first Duke of Emery, granted his title by Queen Elizabeth for saving her cousin's life. Some say they were lovers." His last words were whispered against her lips.

Olivia couldn't move. It was as if Hamilton had weaved some magic spell around her, wrapping her in his web of danger just as he was wrapping her in his arms.

His lips were hot, dry, not at all like the marquis's. Even as he deepened the kiss into something less chaste, the thought sank its way into her brain. The pressure on her mouth was strong but not brutal. She had the fleeting impression that he was seeking to seduce her, but his kiss left her cold and distant, almost as if she were watching the embrace from a small remote part of herself.

"What the devil!"

The exclamation caught Hamilton off guard, and he spun toward the outburst. His lips curled back in a sneer as he saw the marquis's tall frame silhouetted in the entrance to the hall. His body became taut, braced for the onslaught he knew would come. He did not have to wait for long.

In three bounds the marquis was there, looming over the couple. Without any hesitation he reared back with one fist and smashed Hamilton in the face. Hamilton spun back with the force of the blow before whipsawing forward into a hunch. He straightened a few moments later, gently touching his mouth. His hand came away with blood.

Olivia had flinched reflexively with the marquis's attack on his brother, but otherwise she had remained still. Her eyes were frozen on Traverston, and she wasn't quite able to believe his presence there. Had her thoughts of him summoned up this specter of anger? But no, that was ridiculous. She blinked twice rapidly and tried to school her mind into coherent thought.

Hamilton warily faced his opponent, repeatedly touching his mouth and checking his fingers for blood. Slowly he lowered his hand to his side. Using his other, he pushed back a lock of hair that had fallen over his forehead in the fray. The action was meant to be nonchalant, but it actually betrayed his pain. He worked his jaws a few times tentatively, as if testing their strength. "Hello, brother," he finally said, his voice dripping with venom. "You seem a tad overset. Something wrong?"

Traverston's eyes narrowed and he began reaching for his enemy's lapels with renewed determination. Within a second, Hamilton lay on his back on the polished wood floor, clutching his middle in anguish. The marquis merely watched him from his awesome height.

When Hamilton could speak again, his voice still held the calm note of earlier. But beneath the pleasant tone was a hint of steel. "I owe you one for that, brother. Just be glad there is a lady present."

Traverston's look was filled with disgust. "Get out," he growled between clenched teeth.

Hamilton spared a single glance for Olivia before getting to his feet. She was still locked in her trance. He moved forward, stopped mere inches from Traverston and glared meaningfully into the other's eyes, letting all of his hatred show through as he repeated softly, "I owe you one." He turned and strode out of the hall before Traverston could rouse himself to a suitable reply.

After the marquis had made sure of Hamilton's departure from the hall, he turned back to face Olivia. He noted she was once again in control of her faculties. She stood staring at him, her eyes defiant. He could see the challenge there in the set of her jaw, and it ate at him, snapping his control.

With a swift, sudden movement, he grabbed her arm,

his face a mask of fury. His voice was like little pieces of sharp metal, grinding into her soft skin. "Did you enjoy your little tête-à-tête with David? Did it give you pleasure knowing you were defying me, tossing my request in my teeth?" He shook her for emphasis, his fingers biting into her skin. "How was he, Olivia? Did he ignite the long-dead fire in you and make you feel like a woman? Is that what you wanted from him? Did he get what you won't give to me? Answer me!"

She stood mutely, her lips held together in a white line, but her eyes glared her answer.

Like a snake, he hissed his response. "Is it kisses that you want? I understood from our last encounter that lovemaking was the last thing you wanted. Apparently I was wrong."

His mouth came crashing down on hers, engulfing her. His kiss was passionate, desperate, consuming—everything Hamilton's was not. Olivia felt overwhelmed, as if she were losing her sense of self. This was no kiss she could hide from or shield herself from as she could with his brother's. This kiss threatened to destroy her.

With a strength born of desperation, Olivia tried to push herself out of Traverston's arms. They were like timber oaks, keeping her from escaping. She twisted her head first one way and then another. Always his lips were there, his mouth devouring her. Heartrending gasps, ardent pleas for mercy, all were swallowed against his lips. There was no escape.

Then, with a suddenness that caused her to gasp, Traverston broke away. His eyes raked over her face, taking in the tears that had at some time during his onslaught left wet trails down her cheeks. Her eyes were huge pools of misery as they met his own, seeking some understanding for his desire to wound her. An emotion he couldn't name stabbed his heart, but it was quickly squelched by a renewed surge of anger.

He flung her away from him, sending her crashing to the delicate French settee by the painting she had been studying earlier. A sob escaped her lungs before she could stifle it, and she covered her heaving chest with one hand.

His words were angry and clipped as he stared down at her. "Go home and get your things together. We leave for Surrey in the morning." He turned on his heel and strode from the hall.

Chapter Ten

Olivia heard the muted sobs as if they originated from a long way off. The sound moved thickly and slowly, creeping down the hollowed and padded corridor, soft and strangely quiet at the beginning, then crashing into a wail on a long-drawn-out note. Like waves, the sound hit her, distorted and yet distinguishable nonetheless.

Concentrating, she listened harder. The cries were pathetically moving, bringing to mind the image of someone completely alone in the world with no one to turn to. They were a plea for help and for mercy, and she almost recognized them, but then lost the familiarity of their ring as she dropped back down into the depths of her own wounded soul.

Hours or minutes later, Olivia regained clarity of thought again. The crying had died to a soft snuffling sound. Bringing her hand up to cool her heated cheeks, she gasped in shock as her hand touched the wet surface of her skin. In horror, she brought her hand back into her line of sight, staring at it as if it were a detached, live thing. Salty water glistened on the fingertips as it suddenly became all too clear that she was the source of the sounds she had heard.

With trembling hands, she reached down and clutched

the material of her sky blue muslin gown with both fists. She meant to grab hold of something solid and use it as an anchor for her senses, but the moment she brought her eyes back into focus on her hands she was sorry. They looked pale and bloodless against the material in the guttering candlelight. Her eyes moved elsewhere, seeking another, less disturbing source of concentration.

They landed on her beaded reticule lying some five feet away. The tiny sparkles scattered around the bag suggested that she had dropped it sometime during the past drama, although she couldn't remember having done so. Her gaze wandered back to her hands, still in their death grip on her gown.

A renewed surge of unhappiness welled up in her, spilling fresh tears down her cheeks. Damn him, damn him, damn him, she thought. Would he never leave her alone?

She brought one hand up to her face, the fingertips brushing the soft skin of her cheek and tentatively exploring the damage her watering eyes had done. The flow of tears came faster as she thought of the last time she had been moved to cry. She had sworn then that it would be the last time she would let someone affect her so deeply. She had been wrong....

Her twelfth birthday had been a nightmare. The morning had dawned bright and clear, promising all sorts of treasures to the young girl who awaited it eagerly. Just the day before, her father had promised her a special treat for her birthday. He had acted like his old self, smiling down lovingly at her, his brown eyes warm with feeling as he looked at his beautiful, delicate child. At supper, before he had sent her off to bed, he had held her hand tenderly, enveloping her in his adoration and pride.

Hurriedly Olivia had gotten dressed the next morning, the blue dress she had been given on her tenth birthday too small and childish on her fast-maturing figure. But she wanted to show her father how much she loved him, how much she cared for him, and this was the last real gift he had given her.

Her long hair held back with a pale blue ribbon, Olivia had rushed down the stairs, longing to get to the breakfast room first so as to be there when her father appeared.

She had arrived first! A sense of excitement welled up in her as she waited for his appearance. Too thrilled to eat, she had waved away the steaming kippers Maddie had placed under her nose. She would wait and eat with her father, she told the disapproving nanny. And so she waited. And waited.

Hours later, her face a picture of disappointment, Olivia slowly made her way from the room and her untouched meal. Her dragging footsteps had taken her down the main hall and past her father's study. It was then that the paneled door, closed as was customary against the cool autumn air, suddenly swung open to reveal her father.

His formerly portly frame, made gaunt by a full year of hard drinking and poor nutrition, swayed unsteadily toward her. A large hand came down on her shoulder, startling her with the weight behind it. She staggered as he leaned on her, using her smaller body for support.

Wentworth blinked several times trying to clear his vision sufficiently to see the small person in front of him. With a beatific smile, he identified his daughter.

"Olivia," he slurred happily, "what a pleasant surprise." He swung her around with his heavy hand, dragging her into the study with him. "Come to see your old papa, have you? Such a good child."

Olivia warily noted her father's features, twisted askew by drink. She made some resistance to follow him, but he didn't seem to notice. She was worried because she never knew how he was going to act when he was this far in his cups.

The room was dim. All the curtains had been drawn against the windows and only a single brace of candles lit an area near his favorite sofa. Olivia wrinkled her nose against the dank, sour smell of the room, resisting the urge to pull out of his grasp and run from the room. Her father never let Olivia or Maddie into his study unless specifically invited, and recently those times had become fewer and fewer. Consequently the room showed hard use. But the clutter and mess of the room were only slightly worse than the owner.

Let loose from his grasp while he took another swig from the glass in his hand, Olivia noted the spotted coat he was wearing, smudged by both grime and spilled brandy. The points of his shirt were unidentifiable, his cravat tied around his neck like a scarf. He didn't wear a waistcoat, she observed, most likely because he had forgotten to put one on. One buckle of his pointed shoes was missing and the other so dirty the metal no longer resembled brass. His appearance in total gave the impression that he had rolled in the ashes of the long-unlit fireplace at the end of the room.

"Olivia." The sound of her father's voice pulled her attention back to his face. His fogged brown eyes were beaming happily. "What did you come to see your papa for today, my child? Do you want me to tell you a story?" he asked, gazing at her with the unfocused stare of a man whose mind was elsewhere.

Her face was serious, reproachful. "It's my birthday today, Papa. You promised me a surprise."

He stared blankly at her for a second or two, taking his time to understand her words.

When he spoke, he sounded vague. "I did, eh?" He scratched his head and shrugged his shoulders. "Then a surprise you shall have." He laughed at his own generosity, reeling sideways as he attempted to turn and walk to the table by his chair. He grasped the table just before he threatened to go over it, righting himself with the painful slowness of a drunk man. After spending a moment to regain his balance, he scratched his chin thoughtfully, sending dust flying from the whiskers growing there. Then his eyes lit up as he hit on a thought. "Just the thing," he murmured excitedly, "just the thing."

Picking up a dirty glass, he poured a bit of brandy into it from the decanter next to it. Peering intently into the glass, as if determining whether he had poured the right amount, he turned around to face his daughter. With a flourish that included a lopsided bow, he presented the glass to her. "Your first taste of brandy, my dear."

Olivia looked sadly at the gift before her, her eyes unable to hold back the tears gathering there. When Wentworth managed to look past his proffered glass into the miserable eyes of his daughter, an unspeakable rage seemed to explode from him.

He threw the glass and its contents past Olivia, missing her head by bare inches. His body shook with anger, and his face grew red as he raised one clenched fist in front of him. "So my gifts aren't good enough for you, are they?" His choler caused him to make little choking noises as he drew in breath for his next impassioned speech.

"Don't like what your father picked for you, do you?" He seemed to turn purple before her eyes. "What do you mean looking at me with those reproachful eyes? I'm your father! I know what's best for you. I've always taken care of you, haven't I? Don't look at me like that!" His last words ended on a shriek.

Olivia turned and ran from the room, her father's tirade dogging her steps as she went. "What the hell are you wearing that dress for? Burn it! Burn it this instant! If I ever catch you in that dress again, you little hoyden, I'll tan your hide to within an inch of your life!"

As she raced up the main staircase, almost tripping

over the holes in the carpet, Olivia finally managed to escape him. She ran into her room and locked the door. Still breathing heavily from her flight, she immediately turned and flung herself onto her bed with all her might. But his words, faint though they were through the door, still followed her.

The sobs came out in gasps, her sides heaving. She was upset at her father's words, but she was more upset at herself. She had let him hurt her. She had taken his words yesterday to heart, but now she knew he was just setting her up to wound her. What he really wanted was to destroy her.

Just as Traverston was trying to destroy her now. The agony she felt was crippling. He must have known how she had hung on to his image in her childhood. He must have known how she had built up their first meeting into something magical and wondrous, and that she had harbored the hope that one day Traverston would come back and rescue her from her miserable existence. It was the only explanation she could find for his singular persistence in making her wretched, and for his being so successful at it.

Eventually the last teardrop wound its way down her face. With unseeing eyes, Olivia stared across the hall to the painting opposite, thinking about how she might handle this disaster now. Somehow she knew that but for the damage her fists had wreaked on the soft material of her gown, it had miraculously gone untouched during the fray. But the same could not be said for her face. If she appeared in the ballroom now, even in the dim candlelight, there could be no doubt that she had been crying. Her eyes had that distinctly swollen and gritty feeling that came only after serious crying, and her tears had undoubtedly left tracks in the light film of powder over her cheeks.

She bit at her swollen lower lip knowing it, too, showed the aftereffects of Traverston's rage. It felt tender and puffy as she worried at it with her teeth. A hand strayed up to the complicated coiffure, confirming the damage there. No, there was no way she could rejoin the party without causing a scene.

Tentatively, as if testing the strength of her legs, Olivia got up from the seat and made her way over to her fallen reticule. She picked it up gingerly, making sure the contents were still intact even if the stylish exterior was not.

Using her hand for support against the polished mahogany paneling of the hall, Olivia made her way toward the nearest exit, praying her sense of direction would not play her false. She felt sure that there had to be multiple exits to a house this large. All she had to do was avoid Lady Sommerby's gathering until she could find one.

After a longer period of time and more turnings than Olivia would have guessed possible, she found an exit used by the servants near the kitchens. Through a stroke of exceptional good luck, she managed to make her way out the door without being seen. She worried momentarily about the cloak she had left with the footman, but a gold sovereign to her maid should ensure its safe return.

Making her way down the side entrance to the street beyond, Olivia walked cautiously, her eyes moving about warily for observers. Except for a few passersby who paid her no heed, she believed she went unnoticed. A hackney, persuaded to pick her up by the flash of gold in her palm, took her the short distance to her grandmother's house on Wimpole Street.

Ignoring the butler's worried inquiries about her appearance, Olivia rushed past him to her bedroom. She penned a hasty note to her grandmother, then rang for a maid to deliver it to Lady Sommerby's house and to collect her cloak. She then changed her clothes without the help of her abigail, slipping into a dark russet traveling gown trimmed in black. After unpinning her hair, she was in the process of pulling it back into a chignon when her grandmother came bursting in through her door.

The old woman's glance took in Olivia's changed appearance in a flash. She hurried to her side, taking Olivia into her arms as she cried, "Oh my dear, what has happened?"

Olivia pulled gently out of the embrace, her face calm now that she had had a chance to remove the worst evidence of the ravages to it. Still, she couldn't quite hide the sorrow in the depths of her pale eyes, nor the force that pulled down the corners of her mouth a tiny bit. "He's taking me away tomorrow, Grandmama." She paused as she let her aged relative take in the significance of those words. There was no need for her to say who the "he" was.

"Oh, my dear!" Lady Raleigh repeated again, but the words were muffled by Olivia's shoulder as she pulled the girl into her embrace once again, her grip surprisingly strong for one of her advanced years. Olivia patted her on the back reassuringly, thinking how odd it was that she should be the one to give comfort. But her grandmother really had come to depend on her a great deal over the years.

Lady Raleigh moved out of Olivia's embrace but held firmly onto her arms. Her forehead was even more wrinkled than usual, and Olivia noticed a hint of moisture in her eyes. "However did this happen?" she asked unsteadily.

Olivia disengaged the clawlike hands on her arms, but not ungently. She turned and walked to her dressing table, gathering a protective wall around her as she went in order to fend off the threatening wave of memories and painful feelings. She picked up a silvered comb and put it down again almost immediately before answering.

Her voice was low as she replied, "He was there... tonight...at the musicale."

"But I didn't see him!"

"Neither did I at first." She grimaced internally as she remembered how hard she had looked for him the first part of the evening, and how he had come just as she wished he were anywhere but at the party. With difficulty, she hid her feelings. "We had an altercation. He demanded that I leave with him tomorrow morning." She glanced at the ornamental gold and crystal clock surrounded by cupids on the mantel and noted the late hour. "This morning, rather."

Lady Raleigh made a soft choking noise. Olivia gazed at her in alarm, but soon found she was all right, given the circumstances. She was just upset, an unsurprising reaction to the news. Olivia rushed over to her side nonetheless, her dress and petticoats making a soft rustling sound as she moved. She took her grandmother's hands in her own in a loving gesture.

"You mustn't fret, *grandmère*," she said softly, using the term of endearment she saved only for the most special of occasions. "I will be all right."

Lady Raleigh grasped her granddaughter's hands tightly, the tears that had been swimming in her eyes finally brimming over to course down her withered cheeks. She gripped Olivia's hands tighter as she found her voice.

"I wish I could believe it."

The steady, rhythmic clip-clop of the horses' hooves pulling the elegant traveling coach did nothing to relieve the tension in Olivia's neck and back. Vainly she leaned her head back against the burgundy-colored velvet squabs, trying to find some release for her aching muscles. But she couldn't keep her eyes closed, and she couldn't relax.

Pulling her head upright again, she rubbed at the offending parts of her anatomy, rolling her head back and forth and seeking relief from the bone-deep ache. But she knew her body was simply telling her what her mind had been trying to forget about for the past hour. It had been a terrible morning.

Traverston had arrived promptly at seven o'clock, throwing the Raleigh household into a turmoil. Olivia looked tired and wan as she came down the steps to meet her husband, her eyes unnaturally dark and unreadable. Semicircular bluish green rings shadowed the space between her eyes and cheekbones, giving mute testimony to a sleepless night spent packing.

She didn't try to meet Traverston's gaze as she completed the bottom stair, instead choosing to look past his shoulder and out the open door to the entourage he had brought with him. At least he was letting her travel in style, she thought without satisfaction. He had brought his smart traveling carriage and two other vehicles, one to pull the luggage and the other to carry the servants.

She counted six outriders dressed in forest green and black livery. Surprisingly they wore their uniforms smartly and carried their heads high, as if proud to serve the marquis. As she stared at the milling group of people and horses on the street below, she wondered mildly why she had assumed Traverston would come for her on a single horse, allowing her no baggage for the journey. She imagined it was her less than favorable impression of him so far.

Olivia's parting with her grandmother had been short and restrained, neither lady wishing to appear overly emotional in front of the coolly distant marquis. His responses to Lady Raleigh's inquiries had been clipped and to the point. He wasn't exactly rude, but he wasn't a fountain of polite behavior, either. He was obviously relieved when Olivia was ready to go.

Olivia's first true test, however, came when Traverston flatly denied her request to bring along Isis. He had looked with intolerance upon the dignified white cat wrapped securely in her arms when she had made to bring it with her in the coach. Olivia ignored his icy glare and started to climb in the carriage anyway, but his next words stopped her cold.

"Bring *that* in my coach and I'll have you both bodily removed from it." His flat tone told her he wasn't jesting.

Olivia brought the booted foot she had placed on the first step of the carriage back down and turned around to face him. She stared at him with eyes meant to bring an apology rushing from his lips, but the apology never came. His glare was just as frosty as her own. Biting back the unladylike words bursting into her mind, Olivia walked the few steps to her husband and confronted him, the angry feline hissing its displeasure.

"Is that a threat or a promise, my lord?" she asked with contempt.

He eyed her dispassionately. "Neither," he said, and he plucked the cat from her arms before she could protest, depositing the furry ball into the trembling arms of her abigail.

Olivia watched the marquis return to his directing of the servants, hotly aware that to him, the matter was concluded. Marshaling her strength in order to appear calm, she walked over to her maid and stroked the cat she held uncomfortably. "You have Isis for the trip, Bess," she told the abigail without inflection. "Take good care of her, please." After the nervous woman darted a glance at her new lord before dropping her mistress a curtsy, Olivia climbed back into the vehicle with as much dignity as she could muster, not daring to look her husband in the eye as she went.

Fortunately Traverston did not get into the coach with Olivia as she had been half-afraid he might. Instead, he had taken off on his white stallion almost the moment he had seen she was safely ensconced in the well-appointed carriage. His desire to keep her company for the absolute minimum amount of time required appeared to be as strong as her wish to stay as far away from him as possible.

Olivia leaned back against the squabs again, her eyes moving restlessly to the window, its plush curtains gathered away from the smudged pane. They had left London a short while ago, but the roads were still choked with traffic. Tradesmen and farmers entering into the city competed with mail coaches, hired chaises, and private carriages exiting it, generally turning the dirt road into a churning, riotous mass of dust.

Leaning up close to the pane, Olivia looked as far forward as the window's design would allow. She knew Traverston would never ride close to the entourage with all the dust the carriages and outriders threw up, but she looked for his charger anyway. Just to reassure herself that he wasn't close by...or so she told herself.

Leaning back again after shifting restlessly in her seat, Olivia put out her hand and pulled the curtains over the window. With quiet determination, she closed her eyes, willing herself to sleep. Although she thought it was a futile exercise, she knew she had to try. She was weak with fatigue, and if her future encounters with her husband were going to be anything like her past ones, she would need all the sleep she could get in order to marshal her strength.

Hours later, Olivia sat up in her seat with a start. The foggy sensation in her mind informed her she had miraculously fallen asleep sometime between fretting about her journey and trying to imagine her future life with Traverston. Still groggy, she pulled back the curtains from one window, confirming what her senses had told her when she had jolted awake. The carriage was not moving.

Reflexively Olivia recoiled a little as the coach door swung open. Her husband's tall frame partially blocked the fading light coming through the portal. But she could still make out the way his sardonic smile twisted his features into an expression that was less than inviting.

As if reading her thoughts, he said, "What are you waiting for, my dear? An invitation?"

Traverston's smooth tone held a note of impatience that grated on Olivia's nerves. With equal unpleasantness she replied, "If you'd move out of my way, I might be able to get out."

His smirk grew a little in acknowledgment of the repartee, and he surrendered his position in the door with a mocking bow.

As gracefully as she could manage with the cumbersome skirts of her heavy traveling gown dragging at her heels, Olivia grasped both sides of the doorway and pulled herself through. She was so intent on glaring at her husband as she went through the small opening, she didn't notice that the coach steps hadn't been let down. Before she knew it, she felt herself free-falling through the air and the ground approaching much too rapidly for her taste.

Quicker than the human eye could distinguish the movement, Traverston was there in front of her, catching her as she fell. Instead of meeting the ground in the rather nasty impact she had anticipated but a half second before, Olivia was caught in the marquis's firm grasp.

Breathing hard from the shock, a second or two passed before Olivia could take in her surroundings. The first thing she noticed was the steel grip Traverston had on her and the way she was pressed against his body. The second thing she noticed was how rapidly his heart was beating…even more rapidly than her own.

Another few seconds ticked by before she felt Traverston relax his hold on her. As she secured her own footing and casually distanced herself physically from him, she peeked at him from under her eyelashes. His expression caused her heart to skip a beat again, only this time not from fear.

Traverston's face was ashen. A haunted look ricocheted in his darkened eyes, and the lines around his mouth were hard, as they would be if he were extremely angry, only now the expression he wore was one of profound relief. Olivia dropped her own eyes to her half boots, pretending to be nonplussed by her clumsiness as Traverston took her elbow and began walking her across the coach yard.

His grip was firm and hard on her arm, and he rushed her steps with a seeming lack of concern for her near accident. Surreptitiously she glanced at him again out of the corner of her eye. She wasn't surprised to find that his features had fallen once again into their regular cynical lines. But she hadn't been mistaken, she was certain of it. He had been concerned for her when she fell. And although his face denied it, she would bet a monkey that his heart was still pounding frantically, too.

As they neared the door of the building, Olivia looked up to see the whitewashed outline of a squat, neat-looking building that had to be an inn. Traverston held the stout oaken door open for her as she carefully negotiated the two steps from the yard to the entrance, lifting her skirt a tad higher than might have been absolutely necessary. As her back was to her husband when she crossed the threshold, she missed Traverston's secret smile at her slow and deliberate progress.

The innkeeper showed the couple to a private parlor, uttering obsequious phrases as they went, which were largely ignored by both Olivia and Traverston. The room was reasonably comfortable, and as Traverston made the arrangements for their late dinner, Olivia went immediately to the roaring fire at the opposite end of the room to warm her numbed bones.

Olivia's thoughts were in a turmoil. What had Traverston's expression after her nearly tragic fall meant? He couldn't have known she was watching him or that she had seen his reaction. Therefore his face must have been unusually open to her, not shuttered as it always was when they were together.

But that didn't make any sense. If he was genuinely concerned for her welfare, why did he treat her so poorly? Why did he act as if his sole objective in life was to drive her insane?

Traverston's sudden appearance at her elbow drew Olivia from her reverie. She had no idea how long she had been staring into the flames. With the confusion of her thoughts readable in her expression, she sought his gaze, her pale blue eyes demanding an explanation. Traverston's gray ones stared back, offering nothing to her.

Unable to train her mind into a nonsensical pleasantry, she said the first thing that occurred to her. "Why?" she asked softly.

He swirled a Bordeaux in his glass, watching the dark red liquid swish to the rim of the cup and back to the center again. "Why what?" he countered.

She moved nearer to him, silently demanding that he meet her gaze. "Why are you tormenting me?"

The glass stilled in his hand. He looked up at her, the dividing wall between them firmly in place. "I don't know what you are talking about."

"It sounds as though we have changed roles. That's what you accuse me of saying." Her pause was pregnant with meaning. "I think you do know." Her voice was soft, persistent, but without a trace of anger or accusation. Silently she wondered at her own temerity in confronting him.

Traverston's heart beat unnaturally fast as he stared

into her unusual eyes. They were eyes that followed him everywhere, even into his sleep. To him, they seemed to absorb everything around them, taking in light and knowledge while being strangely reflective at the same time. The thoughts and feelings behind them, so well sheltered to the rest of the world, spoke volumes to him. They tugged at his soul, begging him to be honest, to play straight with her. They were eyes that asked for the truth and accepted nothing less.

For the hundredth time, Traverston felt caught in a force he was powerless to resist. He had a sudden desire to take Olivia in his arms and tell her how much he cared for her...tell her how much he loved her. But he wouldn't, he couldn't dare tell her that.

His tortured eyes locked with her childlike ones for a seeming eternity. Traverston opened his mouth to say the words burning lines into his brain, and was interrupted by the parlor door opening.

Relief poured through every fiber of Traverston's being as he ripped his gaze away from Olivia, narrowly avoiding the disastrous confession. He gathered his pride around him and relished the chance to recover from Olivia's strange effect on him by playing host. He helped to seat her at the oak table. Pulling back the covers to the sturdy china dishes, the innkeeper acted as their server, offering them pheasant, salmon in dill sauce, smoked ham, beef tongue, oysters, turnips and leeks. The man's presence offered the couple the excuse to remain silent, both wondering to themselves exactly what had happened between them just minutes ago.

After the final course was served, Traverston dismissed the innkeeper for the evening. He sat back in his chair, swirling his glass of wine thoughtfully once again. Olivia picked dissatisfyingly at the remains of her plum cake, finally laying the fork to rest beside her plate. She looked up at him, wondering what would happen now.

As if in answer to her unasked question, he spoke into the void created by their prolonged silence. "I have procured a room for you for the night. It's at the top of the stairs and down the hall a few doors. The innkeeper's wife can show you where it is when you're ready."

His words implied that he would not be coming with her. A moment of relief and acute disappointment flashed through her breast. To hide it, she asked, "Where will you be staying?" She held her breath, waiting for the answer.

He set down the glass and pushed his chair away from the table. Moving restlessly to the writing desk by the window, he ran his fingers over the polished wood surface before saying over his shoulder, "I'm going on tonight."

Olivia frowned slightly in reply, not quite understanding. "You're going on? To where?"

"Norwood Park." Slowly he moved to face her, his countenance unreadable. "It's only about four hours from here. I'll be leaving shortly with my valet. We should get there sometime in the early morning hours."

She shook her head, not quite understanding. "You're leaving tonight?"

"Yes." *Because I can't be here under the same roof with you and not make love to you.* But the words stayed firmly inside his head.

The transparent eyes fixed him, a flame shooting in their depths. They answered the unspoken desire in his own. "Then I'm coming with you."

"No." His response was sharper than he had intended. More softly, he repeated, "No. There's no reason for you to travel in discomfort in the middle of the night. Besides, it would take much longer to reach the estate with the entire entourage tagging along. You will stay here and make the journey more comfortably in the morning."

Olivia got up from her place at the table, and moved

hesitantly toward him. As she closed the distance, the air between them seemed to crackle with some emotion neither one could, or would, have been willing to name.

And then she saw it. There in the flickering candlelight, she identified the same haunted look in his eyes that had spoken to her so many years ago. His eyes spoke to her soul and begged her for mercy. "Please," she could almost hear them say, "save me."

Meeting his need with one as deep as her own, she said his name like a benediction. "John," she whispered, and her voice was strangely compelling, "I want to come with you."

He stared at her, the odd sensation of being powerless seeping over him once again. Her body seemed to vibrate to him, begging for his hands to touch her. Her lips quivered, and he couldn't pull away from his mind's image of kissing her passionately, insatiably. Of their own accord his hands moved from his sides, and he took a step in her direction.

Insanity. The pronouncement of his fate rang through his head with the clang of a gong. It was inescapable. With a swiftness too quick for Olivia to follow, his dark, sensuous mood changed. She read anger, barely controlled and laced with resentment, on his face.

"I don't remember giving you permission to call me that."

The chastisement cut across her heart like a knife. Striking out blindly, her own temper flared in response to his heartless words. "Oh yes, how kind of you to remind me, Lord Traverston, that this travesty of a marriage is nothing more than a terrible sham."

He glared at her for a fraction of a second, his eyes glacial. Then he brushed past her, and with rigid movements he opened the parlor door. Holding the knob firmly, he looked at her, all warmer emotions wiped clean from his face.

"Good night, Olivia."

She stared at him a brief moment, her thoughts inscrutable, before walking past him and through the door.

Chapter Eleven

April 18, 1816

Dearest Felicity,

I have never questioned your happiness, never re-
proached you for the choices you made in your
youth, never demanded that you return to the country where you were born.

Until now.

If this letter is abrupt, without all of the usual
pleasantries you are accustomed to from me, I beg
you excuse me and realize it is my distress that
causes me to write so.

My dearest friend, I am in dire need of your help.

This morning, your son has taken away from me
the only thing of real value to me in this world—
my granddaughter. And while I wouldn't deny you
anything that is mine, I know you would never ask
this sacrifice of me.

Do you know your son, Felicity? Do you know
who he is and what he has become in the more than
thirty years since you've seen him last? He is a
haunted man, Felicity. Haunted, dispirited and des-

perate. I fear him, and I fear what he will do to
Olivia.

I told him that you were still alive when he came
to collect my girl originally some four weeks ago. I
wouldn't have willingly betrayed your trust in me
but I saw I had no choice. He told me that they had
married some years ago, and that Olivia was igno-
rant of the ceremony. As difficult as this may be to
believe, I believe it to be the truth.

I managed to postpone his taking possession of
her for a little while, but I fear not long enough.
This morning they set out for Norwood Park, and I
dread their arrival there. I don't know why, Felicity,
but I believe he is out to hurt her, to wound her
mortally. He reminds me so much of your husband,
my dear friend, that I am frightened, both for her
safety, and for his sanity.

Only you have the power to save her, Felicity,
and I beg that you use it. I know only some of the
reasons you left England so long ago. I suspect there
were others you never told me about. In any case,
it is imperative that you intervene on Olivia's behalf,
for I have tried to do so and failed.

Please, Felicity, I beg of you. Come home to England before it is too late.

Beseechingly,
Leticia

As the coach lurched along the pitted dirt road, Olivia
pushed back the dread rising in her throat at the thought
of her final destination. Deliberately she pulled back the
curtains and squinted into the early-afternoon sun. But it
was no use. Her thoughts would not be banished.

In her mind's eye, Norwood Park was a fairy-tale
place, full of handsome princes and beautiful maidens.
Even at eighteen, Olivia still hadn't managed to com-

pletely forget her first impression of the noble estate, an impression that had been made when she was barely ten years old. The cool gray stone building, with its blocky Elizabethan architecture and sweeping cobbled driveway, had housed a thousand-page book filled with happy, romantic stories for her.

But she knew the house couldn't possibly live up to eight years of fantasies, and she despaired of having this last illusion from her childhood shattered. She didn't want it destroyed completely, as her hopes about Traverston had been destroyed.

As the carriage made the sweeping arch of the driveway, Olivia closed her eyes tightly. The action was childish, she knew—like trying to wish away a monster under the bed—but she did it anyway. The longer she could postpone the inevitable, the happier she would be. Or at least, the less distressed.

Iron-shod hooves ringing against the cobblestones signaled an end to her vigilance against reality, and she opened her eyes as the coach door swung open to reveal a smartly dressed footman in the Traverston green and black livery. He stood respectfully by the door, waiting to assist her descent down the steps whenever she was ready. She hesitated only a moment, bending over a little to look at the tunnel-like vision of the gray house made by the limited view through the door. Giving one hand to the footman, she gathered up her skirts in the other and descended the stairs, mindful all the while of the eyes staring at her.

When she looked up from watching her feet make the descent, the front of the house overwhelmed her senses. The massive structure was much larger than she remembered, its stone front threatening to swallow up her tiny inconsequential form. She tilted her head back to look up the four-story height, noting the plain yet majestic architecture with its simple lines and regal appearance.

After one last long look that swept all the way across its exterior, Olivia started the short walk across the driveway to the bottom of the stairs. The huge front doors, recessed several yards inside of a square arch, yawned open before her. Conscious of the rapid beat of her heart and the sudden stillness of the grounds around her, Olivia crossed the final steps into the house.

Like a scene out of some play, the house and ground servants were lined up on either side of the entryway ready to greet her. With only half her mind on the unexpected welcome, Olivia made the acquaintance of every Norwood Park employee, from the butler and housekeeper all the way down to the lowest groomsman and chambermaid. Ten minutes later after all the introductions had been made, it was with heartfelt relief that Olivia allowed the housekeeper, whose name she managed to catch as Briggs, to show her to her room.

Climbing the beautiful main stairway to the second floor, Olivia had time to let her eyes roam over the great hall. She noted the exquisite Persian carpet lining the stairs all the way up, the patterned marble floor of the hall where she met the servants, the intricately carved banister that could only have been designed by Adam, the gorgeous tapestry gracing the back wall where the staircase parted to the left and right halfway to the second floor, and the fabulous Waterford crystal chandelier illuminating the entire ensemble. Bringing her attention back on the housekeeper for a moment, she realized she was being addressed.

"...been expecting you, my lady. Fortunately, the marquis has the master suite constantly attended to, as well as several guest bedrooms, in the event he has an impromptu house party. I trust you'll find the suite adequate."

"I'm sure I will," she murmured, beginning to look around again.

Briggs led Olivia down an elegantly appointed hallway lit by tapers in brass holders at regular intervals along the walls. She glanced briefly at the oil paintings and mahogany furniture gracing their path, conscious that all of the decorations had been done with incredible good taste. Turning down what must have been the middle wing of the huge building, Briggs finally led her to a pair of white double doors ornamented in gold.

The doors opened to reveal a light, airy room decorated in sea green, white and gold. Olivia moved into the room, a soft smile of delight creeping across her features. The twenty-four karat gilt furniture was set off beautifully by the white velvet upholstery and low pile sea green rug. Olivia crossed the room to the full tester bed, her fingers itching to feel the airy softness of the white gauze hanging curtains. Her eyes traveled up the bedposts to the gilded cupids holding the material in their carved hands. Out of the corner of her eye, she detected the rotunda set in the center of the ceiling. Moving to get a better look, she admired the cherubs and angels painted there, their rosy bodies ringed by gold carved flowers.

Turning around to face the servant, Olivia smiled at her, her eyes shining for the first time since she had departed London. "It's a lovely room."

An answering smile lifted the corners of Briggs's normally dour mouth and she nodded in acquiescence to the comment, as if she had been solely responsible for the room's current state. "I'll have the chambermaid bring you some hot water. I imagine you'll be wanting a bath." She indicated the fire burning in the marble fireplace, protected by a black iron grill. "The hip bath will go just over there, my lady. If there is nothing else…?" She let the words trail off expectantly.

"No, everything is perfect."

"Very good, my lady." Briggs nodded again and

moved to the door. She began closing it behind her before she was stopped by Olivia.

"Um, Briggs..." She hesitated, aware of how strange her question would seem to the servant. She turned around and attempted nonchalance as she moved back toward the massive but elegant bed. "Do you know where my husband is this morning?"

As her back was turned, Olivia missed the pitying look the housekeeper bestowed on her. "I believe he's out on the estate today, my lady."

"Thank you." Olivia's quiet voice was lost in the large room, and to her ears the muted thump of the closing door sounded horribly lonely.

After her bath, Olivia wandered alone through the gigantic house. Not once during the entire afternoon did she tire of the delights the house imparted to her. From the largest oil painting to the smallest piece of Sevres china she gazed with enchantment at its treasures. In all her dreams, she had never imagined the house could be as beautiful as it was now. Wandering the house was like touring Versailles, she marveled. There was so much to see she couldn't imagine how she would see it all in one lifetime, even if she was going to be living here.

So far on her journey, only one room had been locked to her. From a passing footman, she learned the walnut doors hid the contents of the library. With a dissatisfied sigh, she had turned away from what she was sure would have been one of the most delightful rooms in the house. As she made her way on to the next suite, she decided to get the key from the butler before the week was out. In the meantime, however, there were plenty more rooms for her to see with much less trouble.

Around six o'clock, Olivia returned to her own suite of rooms, once again reveling in the glowing delicacy of them. Her abigail came to help her change for the evening, and as Bess dressed her hair, Olivia was conscious of a strong desire for Traverston to be present at dinner.

She had had no word from him all day, nor had she looked for any. With a vigilance, Olivia had started exploring the house in order to school her mind away from thoughts of her husband. Soon the charming house had made the task an easy chore, giving her pleasure room after room. But now that she was preparing for dinner, thoughts of him again encroached on her consciousness.

Opening her jewel case, Bess advised her quietly on the choices that would look best with her alluringly cut gown of soft pink silk set over a slip of satin. After a moment's hesitation, Olivia chose long pearl drops, disdaining any jewels around her neck that would take away from the daring cut of her gown. With a thankful nod, Olivia dismissed her maid to finish the last moments of her toilette alone.

As Olivia bent down to stroke Isis, who was rubbing up against her legs, she caught a glimpse of a blue velvet box in the jewel case out of the corner of her eye. Purposely ignoring the seductive call of the box, she gave Isis a few more strokes and then finished placing the pearl earrings on her lobes. Then, when she was sure she could have resisted a while longer if she had wanted to, she reached down into the case to touch the soft exterior of the box.

In her mind's eye, she could already see its contents. She had stared at it so often in the past, wondering at its origins, it hardly took any imagination at all to see it now. But soon, knowing her memory could not perfectly recreate the sparkle within its interior, she reached in and pulled the case out. After staring at it a moment longer, as if gearing herself up for the wonder of the treasure inside, she opened the box to reveal the glittering diamond and sapphire ring set securely within.

Olivia pulled the ring out, handling the gold carefully

so as not to smudge the stones. She had never worn the ring before. Her grandmother had never been able to identify it as one of the Raleigh heirlooms, and she knew her father had been too poor to buy such a magnificent piece of jewelry for her mother. To date, the ring's origins had remained a mystery to Olivia. It had therefore seemed like a blasphemy to wear it.

With sudden decisiveness, Olivia slipped the ring onto her finger. It fit perfectly, and she held up the back of her hand to the mirror, studying its brilliance. It felt right on her hand. Its weight was not an encumbrance, as she had thought so large a piece of jewelry might be, but pleasantly heavy and secure against her third finger.

Tearing her gaze from the mesmerizing call of the stones, Olivia rushed to finish the rest of her toilette. Finally, once she was ready, she closed the jewel case with a snap and got up from the dressing table in time to hear the ring of the dinner gong coming from below.

The anteroom outside the dining room was as plain as the rooms in this house seemed to come, thought Olivia, as the butler showed her in. The patterned carpet beneath her feet was of the finest, its Far East origins proclaimed in the elaborate design. Candles in silver candelabras lit the room with a soft glow, showing to advantage the few scattered pieces of Chippendale furniture against the walls.

A strong step muted by the carpet over the wooden floor alerted Olivia to a second presence. As she turned toward the sound, she smiled reflexively at the newcomer before she could stop herself.

Traverston was outstandingly handsome in his formal black-and-white evening attire. In a way she wasn't really aware of, Olivia was flattered that he had dressed so well for a dinner just with her. The action made up for his lack of communication with her earlier in the day, and for his distant behavior last night.

At Olivia's smile, as timid as it was, Traverston's heart turned over in his breast. His nobler instincts had told him to avoid Olivia at all costs tonight, but his baser instincts, the ones that drove him to see her regardless of the consequences, had won out. He stood for a moment just inside the room, stunned by her beauty as he always was whenever she was near.

Collecting himself, he gave her a tight, forced smile. Prodding himself to stick to the banalities in order to guard himself from her unwitting influence, he held out his hand in invitation. "Shall we go in?"

Nodding her head, Olivia allowed him to lead her to the doors at the far end of the room. He opened one of them, taking her into the magnificent dining room she had noted earlier in her exploration of the house.

Only one end of the long, gigantic table was set for dinner. Olivia couldn't help the thrill of excitement that ran through her body at the thought of sitting next to her husband during the meal rather than at the opposite end of the monstrous table as she had feared he would insist. He led her to an intricately carved chair whose rosewood gloss matched that of the table. Another thrill ran through her as he pulled the chair out for her. It was an intimate gesture, and she was highly conscious of it. His was a courtesy usually taken care of by the butler.

As Traverston seated himself, the butler came in bearing a tray of covered dishes. As the dignified servant began setting dishes directly on the table, the marquis spoke. "I hope you don't mind, Olivia, but I thought on your first night in your new home you'd rather we served ourselves."

She caught his eye, a small questioning expression creasing her normally smooth features. She hesitated only a fraction of a second. "No, I think it's a splendid idea."

"Good." Traverston snapped out his napkin in a businesslike manner as the servant finished bringing in the dishes.

The clink of the heavy silverware against the patterned china echoed strangely in the quiet room. As the silence stretched on, Olivia rapidly lost the appetite she had built up from her lengthy journey through the house earlier in the day. Her taste buds registered the creamy richness of the béarnaise sauce over the roast only remotely, and instead, her thoughts focused on what means she could use to break the quiet. Traverston must have been suffering from the same discomfort, however, because it turned out he spoke first.

"What do you think of our house?" His question was conversational with no detectable ulterior motives behind it, but he gripped his fork a little tighter as he spoke the words, and kept his eyes on his plate.

Olivia let her own fork rest on the side of her plate, ignoring the way her heart jumped at the word "our." "It's better than I imagined," she replied honestly.

"Oh?" he asked casually, his heart leaping at her praise. "How so?"

She was silent until he looked up. He noted her concentration with something akin to wonder that she was devoting so much thought to the question. "When I first came here, I don't think I really noted the surroundings. I just sort of made them up. I let my mind fill in the details I had missed," she replied.

"When you first came here?"

Her look was amused.

A little abashed, he dropped his eyes and muttered, "Oh," before spearing another bite of the capon on his plate.

"When I first came here," she continued, "I couldn't tell you what was really here and what was just a figment of my imagination." She picked up her fork again and pushed her food around. "I have thought about it a lot, and this house surpasses all my expectations. And believe me, I had quite a few.''

He was silent, unable or unwilling to comment. She suddenly pierced him with her frank gaze. ''Why weren't you there this morning when the servants came to greet me?''

He studied her, again noting with surprise the absence of accusation in her face. She was not judging him. She just wanted an answer. He temporized. ''I had estate business to attend to. I've been gone from the Park for some time.''

''It looks as if you've never been away at all.''

He chewed the food he had taken from his fork during her response. ''I always have the house ready for my return. I never know when I'll make it back.''

''Oh.'' She looked crestfallen. ''Still, I had expected you might be there.''

''I made sure Briggs would see to your needs.''

More silence. With her next question however, she caused him momentarily to stop eating. ''Why is the library kept locked?''

He took his napkin and wiped the corners of his mouth. Taking his hand and placing it on the table next to his crystal wineglass, he looked at her, his face as expressionless as hers. ''Why do you want to go into the library?''

''I want to see all of this house, if I'm going to live here from now on.''

He picked up his fork again as he said, ''I'm not sure that will be the case. We'll most likely stay in London for the season. And I have a few houses abroad.'' When she resisted his attempts to put off the question, he finally groused, ''The library is off-limits. Only I go in there. It's my personal sanctuary, if you will.'' His face denied his anger, but his tone made the statement a warning.

Olivia's continued silence eventually forced him to

look at her. Her face was pale, and he could discern a hunted or haunted expression in the depths of her eyes. She looked up and met his stare with an unnatural one of her own. "My father was like that. He had a room he wouldn't let anyone in, too. It was a mess." The last words were barely audible, as if Olivia were caught in the throes of unpleasant memories.

Traverston could feel the beat of his heart pulsing in his neck. He didn't understand the sudden tension infusing the room, but he was aware of Olivia's horror—a feeling she was trying desperately to hide.

A flash of brilliance caught his eye and he looked down at Olivia's hand to seek the source. Glittering in the candlelight on her third finger was a diamond and sapphire ring. He swallowed with difficulty.

It was his mother's ring.

Time stopped for Traverston. How long had it been since he had seen that ring? Did she have any idea what it meant for her to wear it? Trembling, he felt the sweat begin to break out on his brow. Ye, gods! He had forgotten he had even given it to her. At the time, the gesture had been made in contempt. He had been out to goad the smug and self-satisfied Wentworth, and he had succeeded. For decades, Traverston had hated that ring and all it had stood for. And now she was wearing it.

The stones twinkled again, and the sparkling light broke into his memories. Looking back up at Olivia's face, he saw that she was still pale and upset, still fearful. Whatever past associations that ring held for him, they did not exist for her. With an inscrutable expression, Traverston reached into his pocket and took out a brass key. He waited until Olivia looked in his eyes again, the mysterious emotion still there.

"Here. This is the key. You're welcome to go there anytime you like." His voice was gruff but not unkind.

He placed the key next to her plate and waited for her to take it, noticing the slight tremor in her hand.

Keeping his eyes averted from her face and the conflicting emotions warring there, he picked up his fork and began eating his dinner once again.

Olivia turned the key in the lock and heard the faintly audible click as the latch on the other side was released. Aware of the pounding of her heart, she closed her eyes briefly and tried to steady her breathing. She had no idea why coming to see the library was so important to her, but it was. She couldn't think about Traverston's generosity in letting her have a key right now. Her mind didn't have time to ponder the implications of his decision. She simply *had* to see what lay on the other side of this door.

Inhaling deeply and willing herself to be ready for any-thing, Olivia pushed the door open using her shoulder, her hand firmly grasping the knob. She slowly let out her breath as her eyes adjusted to the dim lighting of the room, taking in the interior. She stood still, not quite believing what her senses were telling her, before she moved forward into the room to light the tapers.

Once she had lit three braces of candles, she turned around again to survey the room. It was exactly as she had thought. There were no dirty glasses lying around, no smudged and worn furniture, no ripped curtains or carpeting as she had half feared she would find. The room was comfortable and masculine, lacking the polished presentation of the house's other rooms but refined all the same. Olivia walked to the fireplace and knelt down to light the logs piled expectantly there, basking in the faint pine smell of the room that seemed to pervade everything. Within minutes the fire was burning cheerily, and she moved to the bookshelves, which seemed to line every wall.

Running a light hand over the finely tooled leather

covers of the books stacked neatly in their shelves, she came across a book of poems and immediately took it down and over to the red leather armchair by the fire. Smiling in anticipation, she curled her feet under her as she opened the book and began to devour the verse written there. She never noticed the measured tread of her husband's walk until he spoke from the doorway, his shoulder negligently lounged against the frame.

"No monsters in this closet, I presume?" His voice was lazy, oddly content as he watched his wife snuggled down in the chair, reading her book.

She smiled up at him, causing a responding reaction in him at its warmth. "I feel quite inexplicably at home here."

He pushed his lean frame off the doorway and moved toward her at a sauntering gait, one hand in his pocket, the other on the bowl of his wineglass. To Olivia, he looked supremely elegant and masculine in his formal attire, and she felt a momentary start of guilt for the way she had abandoned him during dinner to explore this room.

"Mind if I join you?" The question was soft, confident of the reply.

"Of course not."

He sat in the armchair opposite her and leaned his head against the leather backrest. With his eyes closed, Olivia thought he looked peaceful, even approachable. When she realized she had been staring, she dropped her eyes again to the lyrics of the poem she had been reading before he had come in. But the words wouldn't come into focus for her. Giving up, she looked from the book to see his dark gaze examining her. But his look was contented even while it was penetrating. He seemed to be watching her, but not waiting for her reaction as he always did in the past.

Olivia shifted uncomfortably, bringing her shoulders

up a little straighter as she closed the book, leaving her forefinger to mark her place. "I…" She looked hesitantly at him, as if unsure of how to proceed, or even if she should. With visible effort she did. "I want to thank you for giving me the key. It was…very generous of you."

He shrugged, the movement belying the inner turmoil he felt as he watched her, his wife's uncertainty with him strangely moving. "You seem to belong here."

The appropriateness of the phrase amazed her. "Yes, I do, don't I?" She looked down at the book in her hand and ran a finger over the gold-stamped letters of the title. "That's strange, isn't it? I was actually afraid to come in here."

His breath caught in his throat. But he managed to make his voice sound normal. "Why?"

She kept her head down. "I don't know. I guess…I guess perhaps I was afraid you'd be like my father." She looked up at him then, her pale eyes quietly beseeching.

His glittered back. She thought he might be angry at the comparison, but his voice was calm when he spoke. "Tomorrow I am going to ride out and see some of the tenants. Would you care to join me?"

Traverston was amazed at his own words. A moment before he had had no idea what he was going to say to her. But the offer had been made, and he couldn't take it back now.

She stared at him, trying to figure him out. But it was a useless task. He was an enigma to her, a mystery. Instead, she decided to follow her instincts.

"I'd love to," she replied sincerely.

"Good." He stood up, quelling the desire to take her in his arms as she evaluated him, her desire to believe in him etched openly on her face. He set down his wineglass on the tiny cherry wood table next to the chair. "Come to the stables at eight. A footman can show you the way."

He turned to leave but stopped at the entrance to the library. He hesitated, as if searching for the proper words. Finally he just smiled tightly. "Good night, Olivia."

"Good night...my lord," she whispered, but she didn't think he heard her as he walked away.

Chapter Twelve

The glowing coals framed by the elegantly carved wood mantel of the fireplace gave off a remarkable amount of heat. Traverston closed his eyes and basked in the vaguely numbing sensation of his superheated skin. The heat made his eyelids feel heavy and weighted, as if an extra effort on his part would be required to open them again. The warm feeling crept down his neck and into his chest, and the silk fabric of his embroidered robe felt hot and crispy against his skin.

Regretfully the marquis opened his eyes again, staring unseeingly into the wavering, shifting patterns created by the air coming off the coals. His hands rested lightly on the carved arms of the seventeenth century chair, the wood gently warmed beneath his fingers, but his hands ice-cold despite the fire.

His feet were planted firmly on the floor, placed evenly from one another shoulder width apart. Distractedly one hand moved with painful slowness to comb back the lock of starkly black hair that had fallen forward onto his brow. With equal slowness, it returned to its place of origin on the armrest.

Traverston sat lost in thought, oblivious to all of his surroundings save the vague sensation of heaviness caused by the heat of the fire. In his mind's eye, none of the current world was real. He was young again—very young. He watched the scene unfolding in his memory as if he were an uninvolved observer, not seeing the boy of five or six as himself, though he knew in some remote, detached part of his brain that the child was indeed he.

The boy in his mind was playing with a set of tin soldiers, deploying them with careful concentration and attention around a great battlefield in the American colonies. His tutor had just taught him about the war for the colonies' independence, and the boy was imagining what his soldiers could have done to General Washington's army, given half the chance.

Voices raised in anger penetrated his consciousness and caused his hand to still over one of the tin figures. With trepidation, the youngster got up and crept to the nursery door, which had been left slightly open after his tutor's departure. The crack between the door and its frame illuminated a small portion of the hallway outside, empty at the moment but for the worn carpeting and a few flickering candles.

He inhaled sharply as his mother came into view, her dress with its mauve flowing skirt billowing around her as she fell. His father came into the range of his vision a few seconds later, striking the fallen woman as she cried out in anguish. The boy's lower lip quivered, and tears began to form as the familiar feeling of helplessness rose in his breast. This wasn't the first time he had witnessed such a scene, and he had learned long ago that to interfere was to ensure a similar treatment for himself from his father.

Softly, with as much control as he could muster, the child closed the nursery door all the way and leaned back against the stout wood. Tears streamed down his face as he attempted not to think about the beating his mother was receiving. His pretty, soft, lovely mother, who looked so tiny next to the bullish marquis.

Slowly Traverston's eyes came back into focus on the small but intense flames produced amongst the coals. Wearily he turned his head to look around at the master bedroom that had once belonged to his father, the grim memories of him fresh in his mind. The low illumination provided by the almost extinguished fire didn't let him see the room distinctly, but he knew its surroundings well. The huge tester bed in the corner, decorated in a deep, masculine forest green, complemented the beautifully carved black oak ceiling and molded wainscoting. With a grim smile of satisfaction, the marquis thought that none of the furnishings he half saw, half envisioned had belonged to his father, the third marquis.

When Traverston inherited his fortune from his grandfather, the first action he had taken with his newfound wealth was to completely redecorate the huge estate house. He spent a year on the Continent looking for pieces to fill his home, choosing the furnishings, paintings, china, silver, panelings, ceilings and tapestries with exquisite care. He wanted Norwood Park to be his home, not the home of the third, second, or even the first marquis. When he was finished, he didn't want there to be a single reminder left of his family or his heritage in the mansion.

Five years after his task had started, Traverston knew he had been successful. Norwood Park was a creation of his own imagination and taste and none other. Now the house only rarely caused him to relapse into reflective bouts on his childhood, even as he was doing now.

But the house hadn't triggered these memories. Traverston wasn't foolish enough to try to convince himself of that. Thoughts of Olivia had started this disturbing journey into his past; thoughts of her he shouldn't have been entertaining.

He reached over for the ever-present glass of brandy at his elbow. He picked up the glass and swirled its contents, gazing into the whirling liquid as if it could help pull him out of his dilemma. He moved the glass away, ambivalent about taking another sip, and finally set the finely cut crystal down on the table again.

He pushed himself out of his chair, marveling at how tired he felt and how restless at the same time. He desired sleep, longed for it, but he knew it wouldn't come. Sleep was too easy an escape, and his brain would never allow him to take the easy way out.

He tugged on the sash of his robe, pulling the separate ends of the dressing gown closer together. Of a sudden, his eyes fell on the connecting door to the second bedroom. He stood transfixed, caught by the thought of what lay on the other side. She was so close, and yet a million miles out of his reach. He took the first steps toward the door before he was even aware of what he was doing.

Traverston stared at the brass handle in his hand, not remembering how it had gotten there. His body must have been propelled to the door by some force out of his control, but now he was there and he could not, would not turn back. Quietly he turned the handle, for the first time ever grateful that there was no lock on the other side of the connecting door.

He pushed the door inward, holding his breath for fear of making the slightest noise. With light steps so soft he couldn't distinguish their sound himself, Traverston crept into the room.

She lay on the bed several feet from where he stood. He could just make out her dim form in the moonlight streaming through the window. After perhaps a minute, he moved forward again, drawn to her side as he had been drawn into her room, by an unexplained, undeniable force.

She was so beautiful. She lay on her back, her head

turned away from him so that the line of her jaw was outlined by the moon while the rest of her face was in shadow. Her right arm, the one furthest from him, was cast out to her side, palm up, fingers curled gently. The covers were pushed down around her waist, leaving her upper body covered only by a thin night rail. He could make out the tip of one rosy breast, moving up and down slowly in sync with her deep, even breathing.

He moved closer still. The desire to touch her, to lie down next to her and hold her in his arms was almost unbearable. But the thought was impossible. He stayed there, watching her countless minutes before finally tearing his eyes away and closing them in agony. With heavier steps than those that had brought him to her, he made his way back across the room and to the connecting door.

After she heard the door give an almost inaudible click as it closed for the second time, Olivia let out a sigh. She opened her eyes, turning her head in order to verify her husband's departure.

Why had he come? What did he want? Was he angry with her, or were his feelings of a different nature?

She couldn't understand what was going on in Traverston's head or why he acted the way he did with her. Her thoughts tumbled about like a sea in a storm, confusing her more than ever. Then a single question popped into her mind, so clear and overpowering as to frighten her.

How did she feel about him?

Her mind began to whirl again, more frantically than before. How could she tell? First she remembered her fantasies about him as she was growing up, then the scenes between Traverston and herself as an adult. Her heart ached when she thought of the awful things he had done to her, then leapt with joy when she thought of the equally kind way he had been moved to treat her recently.

The way he had been moved to treat her. Her mind scurried away from the obvious question. She moved to the more pleasant thoughts of a moment ago, and then lingered on them for a moment, giving special attention to the way he had paled when she fell from the carriage yesterday, and the way he had given her the key to his private sanctuary tonight.

With a catch of breath, she pushed all thoughts of him out of her mind, trying diligently not to think at all. She would think of her grandmother. She would think of her cat. Anything, she told herself, anything but Traverston.

She could not answer the question her brain had posed. To do so was too dangerous.

The morning air was sharply sweet. It was air with the unmistakable taste of spring. Olivia breathed deeply, silently rejoicing at a day that had dawned so perfect for riding. She moved across the lawn toward the stables with long, brisk strides, her dark blue riding habit occasionally catching at her legs. After a minute or two, she gathered the voluminous skirts in one hand, freeing them from her long, tapered legs. She was anxious to feel a powerful horse beneath her. She wanted to feel him galloping with breathtaking speed, taking her away from all her worries and cares. Unconsciously she quickened her step.

The tangy scents of horseflesh and hay greeted Olivia's nostrils as she closed with the elaborate building that housed the marquis's cattle. She heard the easy slang of the groomsmen and smiled to herself as they suddenly broke off their conversation when she appeared.

Moving down the multipartitioned corridor of the right half of the building, Olivia noted the horses in their stalls with quiet pride. Her husband had obviously chosen his animals with great care, for they were all magnificent examples of the species. Now they were hers to use, as well.

She found Traverston at the end of the row, consulting with the head groomsman about a mount for her. She nodded in approval at the bay mare whose stall they were standing in front of, and within minutes she was saddled up and riding across the fields with her husband beside her.

Olivia had noticed the superb style with which Traverston rode a horse on their first adventurous horseback ride together in Hyde Park, but she was impressed by his skill all over again today. He seemed at home in the saddle, a part of the horse beneath him, and he took the small jumps they rode over with amazing graze. Unknown to her, Traverston was having similar thoughts about his wife.

It was several minutes before Traverston slowed his own horse to a walk in order to converse with Olivia. As she had gotten on her mare, he had kept his remarks to the barest minimum, only speaking in order to inquire about the length of her stirrup and the tightness of her saddle's cinch strap. Now, however, he seemed inclined to converse on more intimate grounds.

"I want to thank you for riding out with me today. It's kind of you to show an interest in the people in my care."

She looked at him, her eyes wide with genuine surprise. "You must think me coldhearted indeed, my lord, to assume I would come along this morning only condescendingly. Is it not natural and proper that I should be interested in the affairs of my husband and the people whose lives are now also in my care?"

He grimaced ruefully, realizing he had unwittingly brought her hackles up when he had for once truly not intended to. He shook out his reins, causing his stallion to shake his head likewise. He had told her his real feelings on the issue unintentionally, even as he groped for a less personal response. Unable to find one, he replied, "My parents would never have thought so."

Olivia was at a loss as to how to reply. "Indeed?" she said, wincing internally at the inadequacy of her answer. Firmly she clamped her lips together. She decided to keep quiet, rather than add something foolish she would only regret later. If Traverston desired to tell her about his parents, then he would. She could not force a confidence from him.

But he, too, remained silent. Seeking to disburse the cobwebs cluttering his mind and confusing him, he asked in a more impersonal tone of voice, "Shall we run them?" His eyes were trained between his horse's ears on the ground ahead of them.

A small, devilish smile cut across Olivia's face. Before Traverston had any idea what had happened, he saw Olivia's form bent low over the back of her mare, racing away ahead of him. With a low exclamation, he whipped up his own stallion and set off in pursuit.

A feeling of exhilaration coursed through Olivia. She was here, riding across the vast fields adjacent to Norwood Park, far away from the prying eyes of society. She reveled in the hitherto-unknown feeling of freedom. The wind ripped at her hair and clothing, sending the mare's mane flying in her face. She smiled as she felt the delicate tricorn hat of her riding outfit torn from her head by its force.

A dark form appeared next to her, and Olivia looked over her shoulder to see Traverston urging his mount faster. With renewed vigor, she gave her attention to her own horse, urging the bay on to even greater speed. Slowly the stallion took over the lead, and Olivia smiled broadly as she conceded defeat and eventually brought her horse to a slower pace.

Minutes later, she came upon Traverston trotting his

horse back toward her own. His smile was as wide as hers.

"That was famous!" she exclaimed, unaware of the dazzling effect her windblown hair, sparkling eyes and brilliant smile were having on the marquis.

"Yes, it was rather a lark," he replied, unable to stop grinning like a foolish schoolboy.

Olivia distractedly moved a strand of hair that had escaped from her coiffure back from her face. "I can't remember when I enjoyed anything half as much. It's rather too bad one is not allowed to gallop through Hyde Park."

"But there are no such restrictions here."

His voice was low and its timbre sent a pleasant shiver through her body. Suddenly she was aware of his intense gaze and the hidden implications in his words. Disconcerted, she looked down at the horse's mane and then at her hands. She had to focus her eyes anywhere but on him.

Finally he spoke again, his tone more neutral. "Shall we retrieve your hat?"

"Yes." Olivia tried and failed to keep the relief out of her voice. In her attempts to avoid being scrutinized, she missed his quizzical expression as he turned his horse to lead the way back over the field at a trot.

Not long after the start of their renewed journey, Traverston veered left onto a dirt track. The trail led to a small but neat cottage with a thin trail of blue smoke coming from the chimney. He dismounted and tied his horse's reins to the branch of a tree close to the house, then assisted Olivia in doing likewise.

Softly in an undertone, Traverston informed her as to the cottage's owners. "A tenant farmer lives here, one of the more prosperous ones on the estate. I want to consult with him about a crop rotation technique he has tried with some success. I believe the idea can be reasonably applied elsewhere. There is no reason others can't benefit from his experiences.''

Olivia looked at her husband curiously. ''And would you communicate these ideas to the other tenants?''

He returned her look with interest. ''Who better?''

The cottage door was opened as they approached it, and the farmer and his wife greeted the marquis with embarrassing gratitude. Olivia felt like a queen rather than a simple member of the nobility. But then she remembered that to these people, a marquis and his marchioness were royalty.

As Traverston moved off with the farmer into the nearby field crowded with wheat, Olivia was invited inside the house by the wife. She listened a moment to the woman's effusive apologies about the state of her poor house before interrupting quietly.

''Please, my good woman, no more apologies. You have no idea how poor I was growing up. I'm quite happy indeed to be invited into your home.''

The woman smiled gratefully. ''Your ladyship is too kind.'' Olivia shrugged off the compliment and instead began with embarrassment, ''I'm afraid that my husband is terribly lax in his attitude about keeping me properly informed. It's my fault as well, really. I probably should have asked him before we came, but I'm afraid I don't know your name...?'' She let the end trail off as a question.

The farmer's wife blushed at the lavish explanation from the master's wife. She had no idea that such a well-bred gentlewoman like Lady Traverston would want to know anything about her. ''It's Mrs. Parks, my lady,'' she replied, her eyes on the ground.

Much to that woman's surprise, Olivia offered her hand. ''It's nice to meet you, Mrs. Parks.''

Mrs. Parks blushed bright red all the way to the roots of her hair as she gave Olivia her hand. She was embarrassed to take the delicate white hand with its buffed and polished nails into her own red and rough one. But secretly she was pleased.

Mrs. Parks indicated the rough table in the main room where they were standing. She ducked her head as she admitted, "We've never had a member of the gentry here, my lady. I can only offer you a seat at our table."

Olivia glided gracefully to the table, her booted feet making a minimum amount of noise on the wooden floor. She sat down as she replied, "I'm quite grateful for the chance to sit. I'm not as used to riding a horse as I once was."

Although it was a white lie, the words helped to put Mrs. Parks at ease. She turned to the fire a few feet from the table and removed a kettle from its hook. "Would my lady care for some tea?" she asked nervously.

Olivia nodded and began to remove her riding gloves. Mrs. Parks poured out the tea into a plain but sturdy earthenware cup and saucer. When Olivia saw that Mrs. Parks planned on remaining on her feet, she indicated one of the other chairs and asked her to sit down and have a cup of tea with her.

Mrs. Parks looked shocked and grabbed her hands to her chest. "Oh, no, my lady! I couldn't very well do that!"

"I don't see why not, Mrs. Parks. This is your house, after all. I am but a guest."

"But your ladyship! I could never pretend to be half as good as you!"

Olivia smiled patiently and then spoke slowly, as though to a small child. "Please don't stand on ceremony with me, Mrs. Parks. You're the first local person I've talked to since arriving at Norwood Park, and there are some questions I'd like to ask you. I can't very well ask them if you go on treating me like royalty. It would make me uncomfortable. You don't want me to be uncomfortable, do you, Mrs. Parks?''

The woman's face contracted with firm denial. "Oh, no, my lady. I wouldn't want that."

"Then please say you'll sit with me." Her face wore an unusually open and sincere expression as she asked the woman to humor her.

Her doubts about the propriety of the situation showing on her face, Mrs. Parks sat down gingerly on the edge of one of the other chairs, her hands clasped tightly in her lap. She waited patiently for Olivia to speak again, acting like a servant allowed to sit in King George's throne, stiff and afraid to move.

Olivia leaned forward onto the table, determined to show the woman how at ease she herself was. "Do you have any children, Mrs. Parks?"

"I have three, my lady," she replied, wondering how it was that the marchioness had come to ask after her family. "Are any of them in trouble, my lady?"

Olivia smiled and shook her head. Being the mistress of a huge estate was not going to be an easy task, she could tell. "No, no, Mrs. Parks, nothing like that. I'm merely interested in knowing something about you."

Mrs. Parks was confused. "Why should your ladyship want to know anything about me?"

Olivia looked her in the eyes, trying to convey her sincerity to this woman. "I want to know about everyone who works for my husband. Are your children boys or girls?"

"All three sons, my lady." She couldn't help letting a note of pride creep into her voice. "And bonny lads they are, too." Then she looked immediately worried, as if she might have said something that offended her mistress.

Nodding her head encouragingly, Olivia smiled. "Tell me about them."

Mrs. Parks took a deep breath as if to plunge into a story, then abruptly held it, looking at Olivia questioningly. When she saw that the marchioness was actually waiting for her to go on, she let it out in a rush. "There's Davy, he's the oldest. A fine strong man, just like his father. Matthew is second. He's awfully quiet. And Peter—" she smiled fondly in memory "—he's the youngest. He likes to dream, but he's a good boy at heart."

"Do they help Mr. Parks in the fields?"

"Oh, yes, my lady! There are no slackers in my family."

Olivia sighed. She had not meant her words to be construed that way, but to protest the fact to Mrs. Parks would probably not have been productive. She took a sip of the tea the older woman had poured for her and savored its hearty flavor. She let her eyes slip around the room to take in the simple and plain furnishings. They were a wealthy family by some standards, Olivia knew, but she couldn't keep the contrast between this cottage and Norwood Park out of her mind. No wonder poor Mrs. Parks was in awe of her.

Mrs. Parks cleared her throat as if gathering her courage. Olivia looked at her kindly, encouraging her to speak without actually pushing her to do so. Finally the woman said, "It's awfully kind of your ladyship to show an interest in my family. The last marchioness never would have done so."

She raised her eyebrows in interest. This was similar to what Traverston had hinted at earlier. "Oh?"

Mrs. Parks nodded vigorously. "Yes. The previous Lady Traverston, God rest her soul, never accompanied her husband out on his rounds." She dropped her eyes to her lap. "That is, the few times his lordship came around."

Olivia kept her voice politely interested although she was dying of curiosity. No one had told her anything about the previous marquis and his wife. "The third marquis didn't visit his tenants very often?"

The farmer's wife looked at her conspiratorially. Obviously gossip was a class leveler in Mrs. Parks's eyes. "Not unless it was to raise the rents. He was a mean one, that one." Suddenly she seemed to remember who she was speaking to and dropped her gaze again. "Although I'm sure he had his good points."

Olivia decided to be blunt with her. "I didn't know the previous marquis." She watched a look of relief pass quickly across Mrs. Parks's face. "Tell me, what was your impression of my husband's father?"

Mrs. Parks had very strong opinions about the last marquis, that much Olivia could see without stretching her imagination. The farmer's wife immediately lost her stiff posture and leaned over the table toward Olivia as if imparting a great secret.

"His lordship, the third marquis, that is, was a brute. He'd come here after tipping the bottle and demand to see Dick...Mr. Parks, I mean. He didn't care a tuppence for his tenants but for what they could pay him. That was before the war with Boney, and farmers on Lord Traverston's land were starving, while on other estates they were flourishing. Things would still be bad but for his current lordship. Things were hard for a while even under him. Eight years ago we despaired of ever having a decent landlord, but then his lordship seemed to have a change of heart. Overnight he went from being a chip off the old block to being the man he is today. We couldn't ask for a better overlord. Well, you see...right now he's figuring out ways to make the harvest more productive. And not to line his own pockets, neither. He's already rich enough. His father never would have done that."

Olivia sat for a moment in thoughtful silence. Then she asked, "What changed him?"

"You mean you don't know?" Mrs. Parks looked

shocked. "I beg your pardon, my lady, but I just assumed you knew, what being married to him and all." She paused for dramatic effect. "Well, his father finally died of a weak heart, or so I'm told, and the Lord forgive me but that was a blessed day. We all thought that the new marquis would be a big improvement. He was such a sweet child, you see. Then he up and went through what was left of his father's money. He gambled day and night, drank heavily and sold off everything that was left on the estate to pay for his excesses. In the end he was so poor he couldn't afford a single servant.

"We were all terribly disappointed, the other farmers and their wives, I mean. The servants that had worked at the big house for years were left without pensions. But the new marquis didn't seem to care. He kept to himself and was hardly ever spotted anywhere on the estate. When he was seen by an occasional villager every once in a while, rumor had it he looked terrible. Headed for an early grave, they said. And then it happened." She stopped and looked expectantly at Olivia.

"What happened?"

"Why, his inheritance, of course. His grandfather on his mother's side left him a bleeding fortune. They say it gave him a new lease on life. And here he is, speaking with Mr. Parks about crop rotation. It's a miracle!"

Olivia looked thoughtful. "Yes, it is." She gazed into her teacup. "And when did you say this change in the marquis occurred?"

"Eight years ago, my lady. I remember it well because young Peter was born the year before, and I couldn't help but think how lucky we were to be able to bring him up proper like when I had despaired of having another child the nine months before."

Olivia shook off her own depression. "You poor woman," she empathized.

Mrs. Parks smiled and shook her head. "That's just the way things are, my lady."

There was an unusual companionable silence between the two women, which lasted for a moment. It was soon shattered, however, by the entrance of Mr. Parks. His big frame filled the doorway to the small cottage, and he looked pitifully embarrassed. He shuffled his feet awkwardly and screwed up the cap in his hands as he stuttered, "The marquis requests that you join him, my lady."

Mrs. Parks got up from her chair quickly, her husband's entrance reminding her forcefully of her subservient position. Olivia got up more slowly and moved to the side of the now-nervous woman. "Thank you for your hospitality, Mrs. Parks. I appreciate your candid answers to my questions."

Mrs. Parks ducked her head and mumbled something about her inadequacy to serve her ladyship properly.

Olivia left the couple and rounded the corner of the small building to see Traverston waiting by the tree where they had left the horses, both sets of reins in his hands. He helped her into her saddle quickly and efficiently. Then they began to move back down the dirt track.

Olivia was the first to speak. "Did you learn anything useful?"

His reply was distracted as he stared off to his left at a field lying fallow. "Yes, I believe so."

She watched her husband with interest. What had changed him? Mrs. Parks was right. He was genuinely interested in his tenants. After a moment she asked, "Do we go on to see anyone else?"

He looked over at her, as if seeing her for the first time since they had remounted. "I'd like to visit a few more tenants, if you don't mind," he replied carefully.

She looked ahead with satisfaction. "No, I don't mind at all."

Chapter Thirteen

Olivia stared thoughtfully out into the moonlit night, her hands resting lightly on the stone balustrade in front of her. The spacious balcony outside of her bedroom overlooked the formal gardens, and beside them was the luscious expanse of the park. She took a deep breath, exhaling slowly and savoring the sweet, wonderful smell of an English spring in the south.

Dinner had been a quiet affair much like the night before, but more companionable. They had talked at length about their visit to the tenants, and Traverston had shared some of the details of the new farming techniques with her when he saw she was truly interested. Olivia had found that the other tenants were to some degree more or less like Mrs. Parks. They had all treated her warily at first, but with more enthusiasm as she spent additional time talking with them.

After dinner, Olivia had excused herself to go to her own room, intending to retire early. Now that she was here, however, she found that she wasn't in the least tired. The night seemed strangely inviting to her, especially the well-laid gardens beneath her, and so with sudden decision, she turned from the balcony to pull on a light cloak.

She didn't feel especially deceptive, nonetheless she

trod lightly down the main staircase. Not wishing to disturb the servants or cause a disturbance by her departure, she chose to leave the house via the tall French windows of the music room on the ground floor. Normally they were locked for the night, but it was an easy chore for Olivia to unlock one and slip out swiftly before she was accidentally seen.

As her thin slippers made contact with the dew-damp grass outside, Olivia took another deep breath. This night was magical, she could feel it. The moon was full and large and totally incongruent with late spring, but there it sat, burning in the sky with bright luminosity anyway. Down here at ground level, the scent of roses and honeysuckle was more potent than from above, and the smell caused Olivia to smile contentedly. Then the realization struck her—she *was* content...but she didn't know why.

Olivia had been staring at the moon for so many minutes, thinking about all the events of the past few days, that Traverston's appearance by her side seemed completely natural. She turned to give him a warm smile, one that seemed to come much easier for her now than it ever did.

"I was just thinking about you," she said.

"I thought you were going to retire early."

The fact that his statement did not come out as an accusation surprised her. She looked back at the moon, the movement exposing the gentle curve of her neck. "I was, but somehow I felt called out here. I can't explain it. I went out onto my balcony, looked down, and now, here I am." Her eyes again sought his in the semidarkness. "Isn't it lovely?"

"Yes." But he wasn't looking at the moon.

Olivia didn't seem to notice. "Will you walk with me? It seems silly, but I haven't yet seen the roses."

"I'm not sure evening is the best time for viewing flowers."

"Isn't it? I would think it an especially good time." She began moving toward the bushes.

Bemused by her mood, Traverston followed. They walked for some time among the flowers, following the carefully laid stone path cared for by the army of gardeners at the Park. Their pace was leisurely and in keeping with the tone of the evening. At length, Olivia stopped at one of the many stone benches and sat down, carefully fanning her skirts and cloak out as she did so. Her eyes gravitated up toward the bright celestial body once again.

"You've been terribly quiet, my lord."

He stood beside her, looking at her as she looked toward the heavens. "Perhaps, like you, I don't feel the need to expend breath on useless words tonight."

That caught her attention. "Words are never useless, my lord. Generally speaking."

"And if I asked you what you were thinking just now, what would you say?"

She tried to see his expression, but his back was to the moon and his face in shadow. She decided to be brave and use the cover of darkness to answer truthfully. "I'd say I feel content, and that I was thinking I haven't been this happy in a long, long time."

"And are you happy?"

There was a strange note in his voice, but again she couldn't make out his expression. "Yes, I am. Realistically, I suppose I have no reason to be. I've been all but kidnapped and brought against my will to live in a strange house with an even stranger man, and yet I feel...safe."

He was silent. After a moment he asked neutrally, "Weren't you always safe, Olivia?"

She looked down at her lap, suddenly shy. "No." The word came out softly, almost inaudibly.

Traverston kept standing where he was, but Olivia felt as if he had moved closer. "Tell me about it."

The call of his request to her soul was irresistible. She opened her mouth to respond to the question before she was able to ponder the wisdom of doing so. Perhaps it was his tone, or perhaps the strange beauty of the night, or perhaps it was simply that she had kept her burden to herself for so long she was ready to share some little part of it with someone else. She did not know. All that Olivia knew was that she felt compelled to explain to him her feelings tonight.

"My father never loved me." She stopped and almost immediately began again. "No, that's not true. I remember a time when Margaret, my sister, was still alive, and he did love me then. But I lost that love somehow. I don't know how. Worse than that, though, my father sought to torment me. He actively sought my affection and then turned on me whenever I was weak enough to give it to him in the hopes of receiving something in return. Pretty soon I stopped trying to care for him. I let him do whatever he wanted and stayed out of his way." She looked up at her husband earnestly. "It's best that way with all people, though, don't you think? If you never let them get to you, they can never hurt you. I've learned that the hard way."

Traverston looked down at her, her face turned up to him in mute appeal and her eyes glowing in the moonlight. Her unconscious request to him wounded him terribly. He knew she was begging him to leave her alone. *Look at me,* her eyes declared. *I'm not strong enough to stand another betrayal. Please don't hurt me.*

A tenderness he thought would surely break his heart welled up inside him. A single step and he was next to her, his own features clearly delineated in the moonlight. Concern lined the place between his brows. His eyes were troubled and they mirrored the pain of her own. He lifted a hand as if to caress her cheek, and caught the glistening of unshed tears in her eyes. "Dear God, my girl," he uttered with feeling. "It's not like that. What happened between you and your father shouldn't color your outlook on the entire world." Against his will, he completed the gesture and let his hand rub against the silky softness of her cheek.

Immediately the tears spilled over her lids to wet his fingers. His heart contracted as she held his gaze, too brave or too scared to break the contact.

"But he sold me." She whispered the words so softly, had he not been watching her face, he would have thought they were a murmur on the wind and nothing more.

As her desperation reached out to him, Traverston was consumed by the desire to hold her tight and assure her that the world was not the harsh place she had grown up assuming it to be. There is love here, he longed to say. There is hope here.

And then, abruptly, he was reminded of his own past. Who was he to offer this child a new and better life? Who was he to open his arms and ask her to come into them? Look at her, the dark side of his mind commanded. She had said she was happy, and now look what he had done. This was only the beginning. This was only an indication of the harm he was capable of inflicting on her. As if branded by fire, he quickly brought his hand back to his side and moved away from her, turning as he did.

Olivia bowed her head, her shoulders slumping forward. Traverston stood still for a moment, struggling for something to say. But what could he say? His fate was predetermined. He had no right to interfere in her life, no matter how much he might wish he could. Then, without looking back, he strode forward off into the garden and back to the house.

The morning room was empty at eight o'clock when Olivia came in to eat her breakfast. She hadn't really thought Traverston would be there, especially after last night, still she had hoped he would be.

With movements that underscored her deflated mood, Olivia picked at the food left in the warming tins on the buffet. Nothing looked appealing to her, especially not the kippers or poached eggs. After picking up a single piece of toast three times and setting it down again, Olivia finally deposited the piece of bread on her plate and slowly made her way to the table.

The butler came in and poured her a cup of hot tea, but its aroma did little to hearten her spirit. She took a tiny sip of the hot liquid, then a bigger one. She had just set the china cup back on its saucer when Traverston came down the hall and stood hesitantly in the doorway, a newspaper in his hand. Olivia perked up noticeably at his entrance.

"Olivia..." he began, but almost immediately he was cut off by a loud, familiar voice ringing somewhere in the distance.

"Shipley, be a good fellow, would you," the disembodied voice demanded of the butler, "and get out of my way? You know Traverston would never stand on ceremony with me, so I don't see why you're so determined to announce me." The voice got steadily closer during this speech, and soon the strident footsteps Olivia and the marquis had heard coming down the hall were accompanied by the sight of the Earl of Monquefort struggling to get in front of their determined butler.

"Monquefort, you scoundrel!" exclaimed the marquis, genuinely glad to see his old friend. "What in heaven's name brings you out to Surrey?"

The earl turned to the startled butler, who had stopped in his tracks at his master's warm greeting to the young upstart. "There, you see, Shipley? What did I tell you?"

He patted the butler on the back with good-natured swats. "Get me some coffee, will you, old man? There's a fine chap." He turned and came into the breakfast room, dismissing the servant from his thoughts.

"Olivia, my dear," he said warmly, coming around the table to take her hand and then bending over to kiss her cheek. She blushed charmingly. "Let me be the first to congratulate you." He straightened and looked at her fondly, still holding her hand tightly. After a moment, he went hurriedly over to Traverston, as if just remembering his friend's presence. "And to you, too, you old dog."

"Your congratulations are appreciated, Alex," said Traverston sarcastically. The earl's effusive behavior with Olivia had not escaped his notice.

Monquefort shrugged deprecatingly, the hint of a roguish smile teasing the corners of his lips. He turned from the marquis to speak with Olivia.

"Alex," she said warmly. "It's so nice to see you. But whatever are you doing here?"

"Why, I've come to see my favorite couple and share the latest gossip from London, of course."

Traverston moved to join the intimately chatting couple. "Can we offer you some breakfast, Alex?" he asked with a slight edge to his voice.

The blond Lothario unhesitatingly replied in the affirmative and began immediately to secure his breakfast from the repast already laid out. As the earl dug in with enthusiasm, Olivia and Traverston shared an amused look behind his back. After a moment, Traverston sat down with Monquefort across from Olivia.

"And what news do you have from London, friend?"

Monquefort waved his free hand dismissively as he finished off the bit of bacon on his fork. He spoke around his mouthful. "Well, you know most of it already, actually." He took another bite as he continued. "After all,

the biggest news is your elopement. Couldn't believe my
own eyes when I read it in the papers.''

Olivia met her husband's gaze briefly and then shifted
in her seat. But it was Traverston who managed to respond first. ''We didn't elope. Not really, anyway. Olivia
and I were properly married with her grandmother in attendance. We just didn't want to have a large wedding.
Didn't Lady Raleigh explain that to you?''

Monquefort hadn't missed the silent exchange between
the newlyweds. There was obviously something more to
the story than either was willing to let on. Still he pretended ignorance as he replied, ''Well, yes, but no one
believes that story.''

Traverston's visage seemed to grow darker before the
earl's eyes and he rushed to get in an explanation before
the storm could break. ''I mean, you hardly saw one another for weeks before you ran off. Before that you were
kind of thick, but not for any extended period of time.
Rumor has it that you were just trying to throw the old
dragon off the scent. Lady Raleigh, I mean. As Olivia is
her only grandchild, she had no choice but to lend countenance to the marriage once the deed was done.''

Olivia's shocked ''Alex!'' was simultaneous with
Traverston's ''Now see here!''

Monquefort dropped his fork and raised his hands de-
fensively. ''I didn't say it! I'm just repeating what I've
heard. That's why I'm here. I thought you'd be glad to
know.'' He watched the pair digest his words and the
outrage slowly leave their faces. When he judged himself
safe, he picked up his fork and began shoveling food into
his mouth again.

''And what do you think, Alex?'' asked Traverston in
a low voice.

The earl lifted his gaze to meet the keen look in his
friend's eyes. ''I think you were married properly. Olivia
would never deceive her grandmother.'' But something

in his tone told the marquis that wasn't all he thought. The earl held his gaze as if asking silently what the true story was, but Traverston chose to ignore the invitation to disclose it.

"Quite right," he responded noncommittally instead.

Monquefort studied him a moment longer before bringing up a new topic. "Two of our friends aren't responding very well to the news of your marriage, Trav." He put special emphasis on the word *friends*.

"Really?" inquired Traverston disinterestedly. "And who might that be, Alex?"

"Oh, these are particular friends of ours. You remember Lady Chisolm and Mr. Hamilton, don't you?"

Traverston put his hand down firmly on the table. "I, for one, am not interested in anything having to do with either of them."

Olivia looked at her husband uncertainly for a moment before turning to Monquefort. "Anything terribly unusual?"

"Only that Hamilton is in a rage for having Trav here steal away the woman he was planning to marry."

"What? That's ridiculous!" interjected Olivia angrily.

Monquefort shrugged his shoulders. "That's what he is saying."

"Why, that mongrel!" muttered the marquis, with a few choice oaths following the pronouncement.

"Don't you have any good news, Alex?" asked Olivia with exasperation.

He smiled. "Lady Chisolm is put out about the whole affair," he replied. "That ought to make you happy, Trav. She's going about London like the proverbial jilted woman."

Traverston smiled bitterly. "Not terribly satisfying news now, Alex. Sorry to disappoint you."

"How long were you planning on staying, Alex?" asked Olivia in a bid to change the subject.

He looked at her and gave her one of his famous smiles. "As long as you and your husband can stand me, my dear," he replied with a twinkle in his eye.

Traverston snorted. "Well, that settles it then. Tell the servants to expect a very short stay by our guest here, Olivia."

Alex gave a bark of laughter, causing Olivia to smile again. The earl caught her expression and grinned even broader when he realized he had never seen Olivia looking so relaxed. Holding her eye a moment longer, he broke the contact to finish the last muffin on his plate.

The gleaming polished wood of the grand piano caught the mellow rays of the setting sun from the mullion windows of the music room and filtered them, sending soft, sweet light in all directions. Olivia looked up from her petit point, her hands unmoving in her lap. She gazed with quiet fondness at her friend, his upper body bent over the ivory keys.

When Monquefort had come into the room some two hours ago dragging a reluctant Olivia with him, she had had no idea what a maestro on the giant instrument the earl was. She had agreed to play for him, albeit reluctantly, and he had listened with great attention as she had attempted a two-part invention by Bach. *Attempted* was the operative word, for Olivia was not much of a musician. Her grandmother had insisted that she take lessons on the piano, but even Lady Raleigh, who was normally Olivia's greatest fan, winced when her granddaughter was cajoled into playing before some of their friends.

But when Olivia had ceased playing and Monquefort had "tried his hand," as he had put it, the new mistress of Norwood Park was astounded. The earl played beautifully. From his cheeky grin, Olivia had guessed the real reason he had dragged her into the music room was not to hear her feeble attempts at the pianoforte, but to admire his own very vast skill as a musician. And indeed, she did not mind.

The tune the earl played now was a favorite of Olivia's, *The Moonlight Sonata* by Beethoven. The music, when viewed in written form, was deceptively simple. Yet in Olivia's mind, only the most sensitive of pianists could play the melody properly. Monquefort was definitely one of those musicians.

She studied him now, watching his face with open interest as he played. His eyes were closed and his features set in an unreadable expression, almost as if he were listening to some music inside himself as he played. Olivia leaned forward, giving the rigid posture demanded by polite society no second thoughts as she abandoned it. Her elbows came down on her knees, her embroidery forgotten. Minutes later, she was still in the same attitude staring dreamily at the earl as he finished playing and slowly opened his eyes.

"If you sit like that any longer, Olivia, I shall have to throw my friendship with Trav to the wind and run off with you myself. You look quite adorable—just like a little girl watching a ball from behind the banister at the top of the stairs." Monquefort's tone was amused, but there was something a little unnerving in the depths of his warm blue eyes.

She sat up slowly, stretching like a cat in the process. "That was positively wonderful, Alex. I feel quite as though I could go to bed now and be assured of beautiful dreams all night."

His smile stayed on his lips, but it seemed to harden just a little. "Surely all your nights are filled with lovely dreams?"

She avoided his eyes. "Oh...no more than anyone else's."

She tried to make her words in keeping with the playful tone of conversation the earl had set, but he would not let her off so easily. He got up from the bench and came around to her side. Looking down at her with a sincerity that caught at the breath in her throat, he asked, "Are you happy, *chérie?*"

"Of course!" she answered brightly. A little too brightly. She got up from her chair and moved nervously over to the piano. Her hands flipped through the mound of musical sheets stacked untidily on top on the instrument. She looked over first one piece and then another, without really seeing any of them. "Do play some more, Alex," she begged, careful not to look at him. "I do so adore the way you play."

"Olivia." The single word vibrated in his throat and caused her hands to stop their frantic movements. She felt his hand on her chin, its light touch gentle and yet unrelenting in its effort to turn her face toward his. She met his eyes with reticence. Alex was too good at ferreting out her secrets.

For the second time in as many days, Olivia felt the tears gather in her eyes. It was only a moment before the first drop brimmed her lower lid and slid down her cheek. Angrily she brushed the tear away, moving out of the earl's grasp as she did. "I didn't cry for eight long years, but all of a sudden it seems I've turned into a veritable watering pot. I do wish all of you men would leave me alone."

She had delivered this speech with her back to Monquefort, and he watched her shoulders shake with the strength of her unhappiness. Without a word, he walked up to her and put his hands on her shoulders. She turned around and fell into his arms in one smooth, swift motion. He held her tight as the worst of the storm swept over her. A minute or two later, as she kept her head bowed, he released her and retrieved a handkerchief from his coat pocket. She took it silently and proceeded to use it to mop at her face. But it was some time before she could meet his eyes again.

His look was tender, but the crook of a half-buried smile teased his lips. "Better?"

Her own sense of the absurd imbued her with strength, and she gave him a weak smile in return. Her short nod confirmed her improved mood.

"Now," began Monquefort as he led her back over to the pair of chairs where she had listened to him play, "tell Uncle Alex all about it."

"Oh, Alex." She sat down feebly, her friend's gentle and caring attitude threatening to bring on another bout of weeping. But she was able to bring this burst of emotion under control much better than before. She looked at him, her pale eyes rimmed with red from crying. "I'm so miserable. But then I'm not. That's the problem, you see. My feelings have been on the sleigh ride of their lives ever since I met the marquis, and I just don't know what to do."

He gave her the full benefit of his empathy, but he was careful not to touch her again. "What do you mean?"

She got up from the chair, her earlier restlessness returning. "I don't know what I mean. Traverston is so mean to me sometimes. Well...you saw him. For instance, when you introduced us at the Eddingtons' ball, and he responded, 'Your husband, I believe.' What was all that? What kind of human being throws another into shock like that? I thought I was seeing a ghost, Alex. Another one from my past."

"What do you mean, a ghost, Olivia? Are you saying that you and Trav *were* married some time ago?"

She dropped the hand that had been busy dabbing at her face and turned to look at him with incredulity. "You mean he didn't tell you?"

"Tell me what?" He interrupted before she could interject anything. "Olivia, you must understand that Traverston and I do not pry into one another's affairs. I heard him tell you that at the party, it's true, but I just thought it was a novel entrance line gone sour. He never explained himself, and I never demanded an explanation.''

"Oh!" cried Olivia in vexation. She couldn't believe that he hadn't been the least bit curious as to why she had responded so dramatically in front of hundreds of people to a few simple words from the marquis.

"I'm sorry, Olivia, but I just thought that Lady Raleigh wanted to see him in private so that she could take him to task for his shoddy treatment of you. I had no idea there was anything more menacing in their conversation.''

Suddenly she lost all of her anger. "Well, now you do.''

He gripped the arm of his chair hard, searching for the right words. Failing their discovery, he gave in to his own natural curiosity. "How did it happen?"

Olivia looked at him strangely as if trying to determine the meaning of his question. Then her face cleared and she began to walk back to her chair. "I don't know, really. This may sound ridiculous, but I never asked.'' She sat down in her chair with a defeated, lost air. "I mean, I remember the ceremony. How could I forget? Traverston was incredibly handsome. And he was so nice to me. He took my hand and told me everything would be all right. But I had no idea what was happening. My father never explained, and I think I was distracted…I can't remember now. I don't remember anything before the ceremony, or anything after it was all over. Whenever I mentioned the affair to my father, he pretended I was going insane. He denied there ever having been any kind of a service that we attended that night. After a while, I think it did become a dream of sorts for me. The memories lost all their sharp edges. I don't know, Alex. I simply don't know.''

"But surely Traverston must know."

"I suppose he must. But…well…it hasn't come up."

His look was incredulous. "What? It hasn't come up? Olivia, do you have maggots in your brain? The man shows up, says you married him, and you never asked him about it?"

"Well, I don't know." She shrugged her shoulders helplessly. "It never seemed important, Alex. In my heart, I knew he was right. There didn't seem much point in discussing it."

"Olivia!"

"Oh, come on, Alex. Don't tease me about this now. It isn't fair. I suppose I haven't been thinking all that clearly about the whole mess from the beginning. My mind seems to be in a permanent muddle. Traverston has done this to me. He's so cruel sometimes, as if he can't stand the sight of me. Then he goes and does something really batty like saving me from a fall. I saw his face, Alex. He was scared to death that I might have hurt myself. I'll never forget it. My heart almost stopped beating, I was so surprised.

"And then there was the library."

"The what?"

"The library. You know, you have seen one before, haven't you? It's got books all around the walls and is really quite cozy generally."

"Oh, stop it. Get on with your tale!"

"Well, I was walking around the house a few days ago, just to familiarize myself with my new surroundings, you understand, when I came upon the library. The door was locked."

Alex nodded his head. "He doesn't like anyone to go in there. Only caught a glimpse of it one time myself."

"That's just what I mean. At dinner that night, I happened to mention that I wanted to see the library. He gave me the key."

"Blimey!"

She looked away at the piano. "Yes."

After a moment, Alex said, "Well, I don't know, Olivia. Trav is a strange cove, always has been. I definitely don't know everything there is to know about him, but I do know that he had a rotten childhood." He continued when Olivia shifted in her seat in order that she could look more directly at him. "His father was a brute. He used to pound everything in sight. Always in his cups, too. He never mentions his poor mother, but I think she was killed by the third marquis or something when she tried to run away from him with her lover. Trav was just a tot in leading strings then."

"Poor John," she murmured, looking shocked.

"Yes. I imagine he stays in the library all the time because his father would never go near it. The old bastard hated books. He only kept them because they were entailed with the estate and he couldn't sell them."

He hesitated, debating the wisdom of telling her any more. Finally he made up his mind. "And then there's Hamilton. He's Trav's half brother."

Olivia moved slowly to pick up her needlepoint again. Her voice was quiet but unsurprised. "Yes, I know."

Monquefort decided not to probe, though he couldn't imagine that Traverston had told her. He finished, much less certain than he had started, "So you see, you can't blame him if he's a little spotty at times."

Olivia picked at a couple of loose strands in her hoop. Finally she looked up. "I suppose we had better get dressed for dinner. Cook says she has something special for you tonight."

Monquefort immediately brightened. "Jolly ol' Mrs. Wilshire. She's got a heart of gold, that one. Why on earth didn't you mention food earlier?"

She smiled a little, his personality too forceful to fight

against. "I don't know how you stay so thin, Alex. You have an incredible affection for food."

"And for the ladies," he said wickedly as he pushed off from the chair. Without warning, he grabbed Olivia up out of hers and began spinning her around the room in a wild mockery of a waltz, mouthing wordless nonsense to the tune of one of the day's popular songs.

Olivia shrieked and laughed alternately, unable to loosen his grasp. A few minutes later, he finally broke his hold from around her waist, too tired to keep dancing. He panted breathlessly as he watched her escape to the far side of the room, her face flushed and her eyes bright. She grinned at him, her own breathing coming in pants. "Alex, you devil!"

"Aye, that I am, my lady," he responded with a deep bow in her direction.

She laughed as he started to whirl around again, this time with an invisible partner.

Traverston heard the melodious sound of a woman's laughter and his heart filled with agony. Up until now he had never let himself long for Olivia's laughter, or wonder what she sounded like when she did laugh. And he had never realized how much he had wanted to be the one to cause that joyous sound.

He stopped short in the hall outside the music room, growing more depressed by the second. Monquefort was such a droll fellow. Indeed, his sense of humor was one of the reasons the marquis had formed a friendship with the younger man in the first place. Therefore, it should have come as no surprise to Traverston that Olivia had taken to the earl as well as she did.

But he was conscious of the fact that their friendship was a surprise. Traverston had always thought of Olivia as *his* wife. He was slightly disturbed by the idea of sharing her with anyone.

Apparently, however, the couple inside the room had no need of the marquis. If he went in now, he knew he would be *de trop*. The scene flashed before the marquis's eyes. They would probably spring guiltily apart like naughty children. Then they would shuffle their feet and look for some topic of discussion that wouldn't indicate the pleasure they had had without him. And the entire time they would be wishing him away.

No, he decided, he would not go in. Although he longed to do so, if only to be able to share in their warm, carefree attitude just for a second. He had no one to act as his confidant and no one to lighten his burden. With a heavy heart, Traverston turned away and quietly retraced his steps the way he had come.

Chapter Fourteen

Three weeks had passed since Monquefort's arrival at Norwood Park. The earl had yet to show any inclination to leave the Surrey countryside, which Traverston believed was just as well. His visit had done no end of good for Olivia. He had noticed that a hint of color had started to appear in his wife's cheeks lately, and her mood seemed lighter. In addition, his impression was that she smiled more often and with greater ease, especially at dinner when all three of them were present. Traverston smiled to himself as he reflected on last night's meal.

From the beginning, Monquefort had insisted that they keep with the tradition of dining informally, started by Olivia and Traverston. They camped out at one end of the giant table in the great hall, helping themselves from the heaping silver platters brought in at the beginning of the meal by the butler. Once everyone's plate was filled with the delicious delicacies prepared by the cook, Mrs. Wilshire, the earl would proceed to regale them with outrageous tales from London. Last night had been no different.

During the meal, Traverston had surreptitiously studied his wife. He had felt both pleasure and pain when he saw her flushed cheeks and sparkling eyes brought on by

Monquefort's attention. Pleasure, because she was incredibly beautiful when she was happy. Pain, because her happiness was caused by the earl's presence, and not his own.

Traverston brought his attention back to the ledger open on the flat-topped desk in front of him. But the figures in the long spindly columns on the pages refused to cooperate with his will. In a moment's time, the numbers dissolved in front of his eyes, and he was again seeing Olivia as she was last night.

He didn't begrudge Alex's time with his wife, but he was envious. He could never have the easy and casual relationship with her that the earl seemed to enjoy. He would never allow himself to get that close to her.

For the hundredth time, Traverston silently damned his family history. His father's personality was no quirk of fate, of that the latest marquis was sure. All through the generations, the Markstons had been plagued by a series of rogues and madmen in their lineage, most of whom had a penchant for cruelty. Traverston had not the smallest doubt that his own bout of sanity was merely temporary. He expected to lose control of his rational capacity in a few years, maybe less. The worst part of it was he wouldn't even realize what was happening to him. Not a single member of his family had ever had any notion that he was unstable. On the contrary, each of his more eccentric ancestors had been sure that he or she was an elite part of humanity. They had never had any tolerance for the "weaker" forms of the human race, as they had put it.

And with this as his legacy, Traverston knew he could never become romantically involved with Olivia. He would doom their relationship from the moment it started. She would be better off hating or despising him. He had to keep her at a distance. In fact, if Olivia de-

veloped a sincere attachment to the young earl, she would
be far better served still.

The thought made logical sense to the marquis, but it
stabbed like a knife into his heart. He didn't want anyone
to possess Olivia but himself. She was his! She always
had been. He was a hypocrite, of that he could be sure,
but the feeling remained all the same.

A sharp rap on the study door brought an expression
of relief to Traverston's face. If he had thought about his
feelings for his wife any longer, he was positive that he
would immediately set out in pursuit of the earl and Olivia on their afternoon ride together and succeed in doing
something rash. Something he would surely come to regret later.

At his command, the door opened to admit his butler,
Shipley. Shipley was normally the ideal servant, all starch
and self-importance, but this morning he was not. Traverston took a hard look at his butler as the man stuttered
out an unclear pronouncement regarding some visitor. A
lady, if the marquis was to interpret the butler's blathering correctly. With a rising sense of irritation, Traverston got up from behind his desk in order to follow the
servant out.

The butler hurried to get in front of the marquis as his
master took the lead down the hall. Vainly attempting to
regain the shreds of his dignity, Shipley led the way to
the blue salon. Unfortunately, he was unable to keep from
looking over his shoulder at the marquis in a rabbity fashion. This caused Traverston to grow angry, especially
when he saw his butler actually shaking. What on earth
could put such a normally reliable servant into such a
state? His vexation grew by the second.

The answer was not immediately apparent when Shipley finally opened the salon door to admit the marquis.
Traverston moved forward into the room, confused by
the unobtrusive appearance of his visitor. A second after

he crossed the threshold and into the room, the door shut behind him. Bewildered, the marquis looked at the door he had just come through. Obviously his butler did not want to be a witness to whatever was about to take place.

His guest looked harmless enough, he thought as he studied the woman who had risen upon his entrance. She was probably in her sixties. Her hair was completely white and styled neatly in a French twist. Her clothes were tidy without being too stylish or too dowdy. She had a fair number of wrinkles around her face, but no more or less than any other woman of her apparent age. He noted that she did hold her head proudly, though, as if she were a person of some consequence.

Traverston came to a standstill halfway across the room. As good manners had never been his strong point, he wasn't overly concerned with them now. He tried not to be unkind, but he couldn't help remembering that whoever she was, she had agitated his butler. As it turned out, when he did speak, he came across as forceful and to the point.

"Who are you and what do you want?"

The elderly woman in front of him merely looked at him, not responding immediately to his questions. Her expression was a trifle sad, as if she were feeling regret or remorse. The marquis stood his ground and waited impatiently.

Finally she spoke. "Don't you recognize me, John?"

Her voice was gentle and wistful, amazingly absent of any trace of old age. But her eyes were her most poignant characteristic. They were a light gray in color; the color of misty days in London, thought Traverston. They spoke to the marquis about tragedies and wasted youth, and in spite of himself, he began to soften toward the old woman standing before him.

His brows lowering in mystification, he asked again, but softer this time, "Who are you?"

She looked at him a moment longer, trying to see in him something that was no longer there. "Your mother," she answered uncertainly, not quite sure what else to say.

Traverston stood as if fixed to the carpet beneath his feet. His body went stiff with shock, but his mind was whirling. His brain didn't seem to be capable of absorbing the announcement. Finally his lips moved and a single word escaped. "No." He didn't look at her as he said it, but he caught her eye a second or two later. "No," he repeated, with more strength. Abruptly he changed, his eyes becoming glacial. "I don't believe it." The words were a judgment, a final summation that brooked no argument.

His mother stood there and slowly shook her head from side to side. "It's true."

The pain behind the simple statement tore at him, begging him to be heard. Traverston spun away from her, angrily striding toward the door. "I won't listen to this, whoever you are. Get out of my house!"

He had reached the door before she could react. "You know it is true!" she cried, her voice ringing across the distance.

Traverston stopped, his hand on the doorknob. Defeated, he turned around again, slowly, painfully. He did indeed know it was the truth.

He recognized her voice.

And in that moment a dozen almost forgotten, definitely unwanted, memories flooded through his head. His mother singing to him softly in the night, her playing with him in the nursery, her delighted laughter as he sought to amuse her with his antics...his mother calling out in pain as his father beat her. The fleeting impressions tumbled together in one riotous mass, coiling and churning in his mind. For a moment, Traverston had to close his eyes in order to block them out. He would not allow himself these thoughts—he could not. He had to think clearly right now.

When he opened his eyes again he had regained a semblance of self-control. "What do you want?" he asked.

The woman before him sighed sadly, shrugging her shoulders as if to say, *What can I do?* But instead she replied, "What does any mother want? To know her son, of course."

His eyes narrowed. "I don't believe you." She stood her ground and didn't flinch as he continued, "After all these years, it is incomprehensible that you now have a sudden desire to see me." His voice got even harder. "What are you after?" His eyes narrowed even further until they were mere slits. "You're here for your father's money, aren't you? You've just now found out that he left it all to me, didn't you?"

She laughed. The sound of it immediately made Traverston feel ridiculous.

"Oh, no, John. I don't want the money. I never did. You're welcome to it and with my blessing."

But to all outward appearances, he was unmoved by her levity. "What, then?"

Moving physically away from the confrontation with her son, the dowager marchioness strayed a few steps to the side, her movements still graceful after all these years. "I only wanted to see you. I don't know how to convince you that it is the truth," she answered with a sigh.

She's giving in too easily, he thought. She was probably trying to fool him into believing she was throwing in the towel. His inner feelings wouldn't allow for any other explanation for her behavior. "Don't even try." The slow, evenly spaced words made his suspicions evident.

She turned to look at him, her own temper beginning to show. "What do you want me to say, John? I'm sorry. I'm sorry I ran out on you when you were only a boy.

I'm sorry I left you with a beast of a man who hadn't the ability to care for you, to love you, or even to like you. I'm sorry I've been a failure as a mother. I've said it. I am sorry.'' She said the last three words with slow emphasis.

"It isn't good enough," he said with a sneer.

She looked at him hard. "You would have me tried like a witch, wouldn't you? Well this isn't the Spanish Inquisition. You have no right!"

"I didn't invite you here."

His words hit her like a splash of cold water. "No. No, you didn't. But that doesn't give you the right to act like a spoiled child."

"Why not? I am my father's son," he proclaimed.

"And mine."

"Yes." The drawled word made it an insult.

In frustration, the dowager marchioness rubbed at her temples with both hands. After a moment, she dropped her hands to her sides and moved to the chair where she had been sitting when Traverston had come in. Traverston watched as an aged hand, lined with delicate blue veins, moved agitatedly to her hair. But the strands were in place and, with nothing left to check on, the hand moved back down again. She turned watery eyes to him. "Is there nothing I can say to you?"

"Nothing comes to mind."

She turned her head away. "I was hoping to stay here, but…''

"I advise you to pack your bags and go back to wherever you came from. I have nothing more to discuss with you."

A noise from outside the room caused Traverston to stiffen, and a second later the door was opened by a mystified Olivia. She paused in the process of entering, her hand still on the handle as she inquired, "Shipley said something about your mother being here?" Then she spied the older woman sitting on the far side of the room. Immediately she left her position in the doorway to cross to her. Ignoring Traverston's black look, Olivia was by the dowager marchioness's side in a flash, her hand extended and a welcoming expression lighting her face. "How do you do? I'm Olivia, your son's wife."

The woman's features immediately cleared and she returned Olivia's smile. "You're just as your grandmother described you, my child."

Olivia was mildly surprised. "My grandmother? Are you acquainted with her, my lady?"

"Oh yes!" enthused the older woman. "She and I were the best of friends in school."

"What an odd coincidence!" She turned to look at her husband, momentarily taken aback by the anger he was exuding. "Trav...did you know about this, my lord?"

Stubbornly he refused to answer. Olivia frowned in puzzlement, but her attention was drawn back to the marchioness as the woman interjected, "Leticia told me that he knew."

"That is beside the point," Traverston declared. He walked with long, hard strides toward the two women. Speaking harshly as he put his hand under his mother's elbow to lift her bodily from the chair, he continued, "Mrs. Markston, or whatever she calls herself now, was just leaving."

"John!" exclaimed Olivia, horrified.

"This is none of your affair, Olivia, so just stay out of it!"

"On the contrary," she denied vehemently, "this is my house now, too, and anything going on within it is my affair. I'll not have you treating one of our guests this way."

He froze. "What are you saying, Olivia?" His voice was deadly quiet.

Olivia had to swallow a sudden lump in her throat, but

she would not back down. "The dowager is my guest."
She hushed Traverston's mother's feeble protests with a
look. "She is staying here in this house and you will
unhand her."

"You don't know what you are doing," he warned
glacially.

She glared daggers back at him. "I will be the judge
of that."

Traverston dropped the woman's arm and straightened
up, pinning his wife with his gaze. He said in a low,
intense fashion, "If you insist on having her here, I will
have nothing to do with her."

"Well," she replied as easily as she could, "you will
have to act as you see fit."

Traverston stared at her for another moment, then
abruptly spun on his heel and marched across the room.
He pointedly ignored the white-haired woman sitting in
quiet astonishment in the armchair. The door to the salon
banged shut almost upon his heels as he left the room.

The elegantly appointed room seemed terribly quiet
after the marquis had left. Olivia stood in bewildered silence, not quite sure what she had just done or what she
had committed herself to. A glance at her mother-in-law
told her that the poor woman was in almost as much
shock as she was herself. But it was the dowager marchioness who first seemed to find her tongue.

"I'm terribly sorry about all of this. Perhaps you
should have just let him throw me out."

Olivia was immediately reminded of her duties as hostess. "Don't be ridiculous. I wouldn't have heard of it."
She sat across from her guest, now taking the time to
evaluate the woman openly. "Can I get you some tea?"
A nod from the dowager sent Olivia to the bellpull. She
gave brief, expressionless commands to the pale butler
who answered her summons. When he had gone to carry
out his mistress's instructions, Olivia walked back across

the carpet and reseated herself with a graceful ease that belied her tumultuous inner feelings.

"He has cause to be angry, you know."

As Olivia was still somewhat distracted by the argument she had just had with her husband, she didn't hear what her visitor had said. She shook her head, bringing her gaze back into focus. "I'm sorry," she replied vaguely, "what did you say?"

"I said he has reason to be so angry with me," replied the woman. "I abandoned him as a small child, leaving him in the hands of a brutal man. If I were he, I doubt that I could forgive me, either."

Just then, Shipley came in bearing a silver tray laden with the tea things. He set the tray beside Olivia, but for once she forgot her good manners and ignored the tray's presence. She waited impatiently for the butler to leave.

When he did, she jumped right back into the conversation, her previous offer of refreshment completely forgotten. "My lady, forgive me for prying, but..."

"Actually, it's Mrs. Nottingham now. I remarried many years ago. But I would prefer it if you would call me Felicity."

Olivia's mouth opened once or twice, but her mind seemed unequal to the challenge of forming a reply. Finally she said weakly, "Felicity," and this seemed to be sufficient.

Traverston's mother smiled encouragingly and continued. "Yes, I know. It is all rather confusing. You see, it all started when I was a girl, probably a little younger than you are now. I was sixteen and horribly in love with an impoverished young man in the neighborhood. My father was a wealthy merchant, and title hungry for his daughter. When the third marquis, John's father, that is, made an offer for me, my father practically ran over a whole village in his rush to say yes. I had no say in his decision at all.

"When my father told me what my fate was to be, I was terribly heartbroken. The third marquis seemed like a brutal man to me, and I was already in love with somebody else. I tried to run away, but my father found out and dragged me home in disgrace. To my surprise, the marquis was actually kind to me when he found out about it. He took my hand and assured me that he would try to be a generous husband. My problem was that I believed him.

"Three months later, we were married and my nightmare began. I wish I could explain to you the kind of torment John's father inflicted on me. It wasn't just physical abuse, although there was plenty of that, but it was mental abuse as well. He threatened to kill Thomas—that was the name of my first love—if I ever saw him again. But that wasn't the worst of it.

"The worst part came when he had a bastard child outside of our marriage. Would you believe it? He told everyone that it was my baby by Thomas, and that we had paid my cousin to take care of him. Frankly, I can't imagine how she came to have his child. I was shocked when I learned of it, to say the least. Anyway, in order to show the world what a wonderful person he was, he lavished money on 'my child,' all the while screaming about what a faithless whore he had for a wife." She looked apologetically at Olivia. "I'm sorry, but those were his exact words."

"How terrible for you!"

"Yes, it was," she agreed. "I decided then that there was nothing that would convince me to produce an heir for this man. He was insane. I had no doubt about that fact at all. I began taking precautions against any possibility that I could conceive his child.

"The months went by and I was terribly lonely. I think after a while the marquis began to get suspicious that I was actively working to prevent begetting a child, but he never said anything specific. He began spending more and more of his time in London, leaving me here at the Park. That's when I met my second husband."

"Mr. Nottingham," Olivia interjected.

"Yes. He was a wonderful man—so kind, so gentle. It was natural that we should fall in love. We were blissfully happy whenever we were together. Years passed and we were completely unaware of anything but our love. We kept saying over and over again how tragic it was that we couldn't have a child.

"And then I had an idea. I wouldn't have the marquis's son, but I could have Solomon's. The marquis needed an heir, and nothing would make Solomon happier than having a son. And I had one, too. John's father never suspected. At least I had thought he never suspected. Now I'm not so sure."

"What do you mean?"

"When John was about five years old, Solomon convinced me to leave my husband and run away with him to Italy. He said we could start a new life there, and no one need ever know that we weren't really married." She interrupted her narrative to look Olivia straight in the eye. "I don't want your pity, Olivia, I just want you to understand why I did what I did. John's father was a monster. It's a miracle I stayed with him as long as I did. When Solomon asked me to go away with him, I had reached the end of my tolerance for the marquis's abuse. I simply couldn't stay with him any longer.

"Solomon and I planned our departure very carefully. My husband was going to be in London for a full month. A week after he had left, I told the servants I was taking John to visit my father. Instead, the carriage took us to Dover. But the marquis found out! Somehow and in some way that only he knew, Lord Traverston found out about our plans.

"Oh, my husband was very clever. He didn't want me,

he never did. But he said that he would kill Solomon and John on the spot if I didn't turn John over to him. He said he needed an heir and that I had no right to deny John his heritage. Given the options, I had no choice. I gave him my son.

"When he had John, the marquis told us we were never to contact my son, never to tell him that I was still alive. He threatened to do all sorts of horrible things to John if I ever tried to get in touch with him. I agreed. Again, what could I do? And so, Lord Traverston put about the story of our death in a shipwreck, and that was the end of that. Until now."

Olivia sat studying her mother-in-law in amazed silence. Finally she asked, "Does John know about all this?"

Felicity leaned forward, her frustration apparent. "That's why I came here this afternoon. I tried to tell him. He wouldn't listen. He wouldn't let me explain. All he can see is that I left him. I can only imagine what his life was like with the marquis. As I said, I believe he knew John was not his son, and my poor child had no one there to act as a buffer for the abuse that horrible man probably felt obliged to dole out. It must have been terrible for a boy John's age."

"Felicity," said Olivia with sudden comprehension, "you mentioned a child born on the wrong side of the blanket." She colored slightly when she couldn't bring herself to say the word *bastard*. "Was that child David Hamilton, by any chance?"

The older woman looked suddenly wary. "Yes. Do you know him?"

"I have a passing familiarity with him," she temporized.

Felicity looked at her sharply. "Olivia," she said slowly, "I have reason to believe that any child of the last marquis would be unstable. The whole history of the

Markston family is filled with stories of ancestors with cruel and unpredictable personalities.''

"Are you sure John isn't the marquis's son?" Olivia asked, trying to steer the conversation away from her husband's brother.

"There is no question of it. It fair broke Solomon's heart to leave him behind, not to mention what it did to me. But it was a conscious decision on my part. I pleaded with Solomon, for John's sake, to leave him behind. The blame for this whole predicament lies squarely with me.''

"I think you are too hard on yourself, Felicity," she replied softly. "I don't see what other choice you could have made."

Mrs. Nottingham sighed heavily. She seemed to age before Olivia's eyes. "I wish I could absolve myself, but I cannot. I have already accepted the blame, but the burden is a heavy one to carry.''

"But this means that John is not the heir to the Traverston title and estates," said Olivia suddenly, jumping to the logical conclusion.

Again the hard look appeared in her mother-in-law's eyes. "No, he is not. But it doesn't matter." She leaned forward in her chair, gripping the arms for emphasis. "Listen to me, Olivia. There is no heir apparent to John. If his birthright is challenged, the estate will revert back to the crown. Or worse, David will think of some way to claim legitimacy by the old marquis and inherit everything. That must not happen." She said the last words slowly, forcefully. "John doesn't know about his birth. No one does, except you. I'm not even sure why I told you except that I felt somehow you needed to know.

"There is no reason for anyone to find out. I didn't suffer all these years in pain and remorse only to have the one gift I could truly give to my son taken away from him now, at the last hour. Solomon is dead now... I have nothing left. Do you understand me?''

Olivia felt numb. "Perfectly."

"Olivia," she said, softening her approach somewhat, "the Markstons were all a wicked lot. I've done the best thing possible for them. I've given them new, untainted blood with John. Surely you have to see the rightness in that."

Olivia stood up slowly, her mind clouded by a sort of numbing fog. She wandered to the mantel and placed her hand upon it, staring at her slender fingers so that she wouldn't have to look at her guest. "I don't know what to think anymore." Finally she moved her head in the direction of the dowager marchioness, but she still didn't look at her.

"That ring on your finger represents a terrible past, child. Only you can make it mean a promising future."

Her eyes grew round with surprise. She moved to look in Mrs. Nottingham's face. "This ring was yours?"

She made a soft snorting sound. "I never considered that a ring. I considered it a fetter."

Olivia dropped her eyes again, her voice quiet. "I had no idea where it came from."

Both women were silent. Finally the older woman asked, "What are you going to do now, Olivia?"

"I don't know." Her pale eyes met with her mother-in-law's light gray ones. "I do know that John has to be told, though."

"Then it will be up to you to tell him. He won't listen to me."

Olivia looked pained. "He may not listen to me now, either," she replied, remembering the way the marquis had stormed from the room.

Felicity let out another one of her heartfelt sighs and got up from her chair. She looked around aimlessly, as if trying to determine what to do next. Olivia was immediately contrite.

"If you've come all the way from Italy, then I imagine

you've had a tiring journey. How thoughtless of me to keep you here talking when I know all you really want is a hot bath. Let me ring for the housekeeper to show you to your room.''

Felicity smiled, but it was a sad smile. ''You're too kind, my child. I think we both needed the chat. But yes, I would like to be shown my room.''

They shared one last quiet, empathic moment together before the servant came in response to Olivia's summons. A few minutes later, Traverston's mother was on her way upstairs in the company of the housekeeper. Olivia sat back down in the armchair she had vacated earlier in order to think through these new developments, but she couldn't sit still. She paced up and down the rug a few times before finally resolving to go and find the earl. She wasn't sure what she would say to him about Mrs. Nottingham's appearance, or if she would say anything at all, but she felt in need of his comforting presence.

Ten minutes later, she ran into him in the music room. He wasn't playing the pianoforte, just studying some sheets of music in a distracted fashion. When he heard Olivia's footsteps approaching, he turned to her, a look of relief washing over his features.

''Olivia, thank God,'' he said with feeling.

''Alex,'' she replied, becoming even more worried than before. ''What is it?''

''Traverston is getting ready to leave!''

She wrinkled her forehead in confusion, not understanding him. ''Leave? What do you mean? Leave for where?''

''To London!''

''What?''

He waved his hands about impatiently. ''To London!'' he repeated again.

''Did he say why?''

Alex shook his head, unhappy with this whole new state of affairs. "Something about his mother."

Olivia looked away, a knot of dread growing in the pit of her stomach. "Did he say when he was coming back?"

He hesitated. "He didn't say." When Olivia remained silent, he continued. "My God, Olivia, what is this all about? Traverston's mother is dead, isn't she?"

"No." She looked at the earl, her eyes pleading for the comfort she was unable to ask for in words. "She's here, at the Park."

"Right now?"

She nodded. "I've put her in one of the guest suites. Oh, Alex," she moaned, "what am I going to do?"

He looked at her helplessly. "I don't know, Olivia. I really don't know."

Chapter Fifteen

Dinner that night was a dreary affair. Far from the cheery little repasts of previous evenings, the meal was served in state in honor of Traverston's mother. But as soon as the first course arrived on the gleaming silver plates, Olivia regretted the rash impulse that had caused her to order a formal dinner. The distance between diners, the oppressive presence of the servants and the generally constrained atmosphere made all attempts at conversation stilted and unnatural. Added to all of this, thought Olivia miserably, was the empty chair at the head of the table where Traverston should have been.

By general agreement, the young marchioness and her two guests had agreed to call it an early night. With relief, Olivia broke away from both Monquefort and her mother-in-law, heading automatically toward the warm coziness of the library. But when she reached the closed door of the room, she hesitated. If Traverston was in there now, as he almost always was after dinner, it would be unwise to disturb him. Unhappily Olivia turned away, her slippered feet making almost no sound on the marble floor of the hallway.

When she reached the safety of her own room, Olivia sighed with relief. She hadn't realized how earnestly she had been avoiding everyone until she had reached her own door. Moving more easily, she opened the door and went in, reaching behind her to undo the first hook and eye of her dress as she went. After releasing one or two more, she walked over to the bellpull to call her abigail. Moments later, Bess appeared to help her out of her clothes, and Olivia gladly gave herself over to the woman's capable hands. With a deep breath, she purposely blocked out all thought of the day's events and began going about her usual bedtime routine.

Moments before she climbed into the giant tester bed, Olivia would have sworn she was too keyed up to sleep. But the pillow was soft and the day had been long, and before she knew it, she was fast in the land of dreams.

Silence woke Olivia hours later. Not any kind of silence, but the heavy, pregnant variety that didn't permit a single sound of any kind to penetrate its totality. With a sharp intake of breath, Olivia's eyes shot open and she flew into an upright position.

Her eyes met with a man's. Olivia brought a hand to heart, gulping down the fear that had jolted her awake. Despite his brooding appearance and hooded eyes, however, her husband looked quite normal in his silk dressing gown. The heavily quilted material was tied around his middle with a sash, and in his hand was the ever-present glass of brandy.

Self-consciously, she ran a hand around the blanket of her unbound hair and pulled the glossy strands over one shoulder. "You startled me," she said as easily as she could.

He sat in a chair at the foot of the bed, staring at her with dark, inscrutable eyes. He remained silent and unmoving, his eyes hypnotizing her like those of a cobra. He gave the unsettling impression of getting ready to strike out at her. His body was tense and his muscles coiled and bunched beneath the robe. She stopped breathing, afraid to move even a fraction of an inch as she frantically tried to imagine what he wanted.

Olivia hadn't realized she had actually asked the question aloud until he replied, "I want you out of my mind."

She inhaled sharply at the intensity of his words. "What do you mean?"

Even though she had been half expecting it, when Traverston sprang out of the chair Olivia flinched backward reflexively. But he stopped short of a full pounce, lingering at the edge of the bed. Leaning toward her and using the mattress to support his weight on both hands, Traverston replied in a surprisingly mild tone, "I mean, my dear wife, I want you out of my mind."

Olivia felt like the proverbial mouse being toyed with before being devoured in one gulp by the cat. "I...I don't understand," she stuttered.

"Don't you? I find that difficult to believe, Olivia. I really do. Don't you have any idea how you eat at my senses? How you curl your fingers into my brain with your long slim hands and stay there despite my every attempt to dislodge you?" She shook her head once, her eyes unable to leave his.

"Everywhere I go, you are there. I try to keep you at a distance, but you won't let me. Your eyes plead with me, beg me to leave you alone and to love you all at the same time. I hear your voice, your laughter when I go to bed at night and when I wake up again in the morning. My dreams are solely of you. If you're not there, I'm miserable. But if you are there, I'm tormented." He leaned in further.

"I want you out of my head."

The sweet scent of brandy drifted on the heavy, warm waves of the night air. Slowly comprehension dawned on Olivia. "You're drunk," she said incredulously.

He stood upright swiftly and threw his head back, a bitter laugh escaping his lips. "Yes, you're quite right.

I've shot the cat, I'm in my cups, and downright bosky, as they would say." He looked away and added almost inaudibly, "Otherwise, madam, I definitely would not be in here with you tonight."

"My lord," said Olivia, regaining her dignity, "I really think you should return to your room now."

He turned and stared at her, all humor gone from his face. His eyes bored into her head. "Why is that, Olivia? Aren't you my wife? Don't I belong here?" He snapped his head around to look at the room in confusion, the brandy making his rapid movements jerk him off balance. With exaggerated surprise, he righted himself again and then snapped his fingers. "Oh yes, that's right! You consider this your room." His eyes narrowed. "We've never consummated our marriage, have we?" Sarcasm dripped from his words. "How silly of me to forget. That must make you terribly uncomfortable right now."

He moved to sit down on the coverlet, his body half twisted as he strove to maintain eye contact with her. "You probably haven't got the vaguest idea what I'm capable of, do you? What rights I might demand?" He lowered his voice then, and his words came out on a silken purr. "But then, you may know all about it. You may have just been playing with me all along. I really don't know what goes on behind that beautifully sculptured mask of yours, do I?"

Olivia pulled the sheet lying around her waist up to her bosom as Traverston's eyes raked over her body in its thin lawn nightgown. Her voice was a mere whisper in the dark as she strove to hold down her mounting terror. "I don't know what you're talking about. I think you've become unbalanced, my lord. You are imagining things."

"Am I?" he asked with the lift of a brow. His eyes traveled down her neck to where she clutched the sheet. He seemed to see right through the bedclothes, and he smirked appreciatively at the corporeal treasure she sought to hide from him.

Olivia blushed scarlet. As discreetly as she could, she began to edge toward the side of the bed farthest from her husband. She stopped abruptly when he laughed. The sound sent chills down her spine.

"There's no bed in the entire world big enough to allow you to escape from me if I desire your body, Olivia."

"Then you do not?" she asked with an odd mixture of hope and disappointment.

"I didn't say that," he corrected as he jumped off the end and stalked over to her side of the bed.

Olivia moved with alacrity. Traverston could say whatever he liked, tease her however he wanted, but she knew that he was too deadly an adversary in this game for her to take chances. She jumped off the side of the bed opposite her husband, taking the sheet with her. With quick, deft movements, she wrapped it around her body, concealing her figure's enticing shapeliness. Her eyes were wide and wary as she watched Traverston slowly come to a stop.

Reversing his course, he put a hand out to catch one of the bedposts, using it to swing himself around to the bottom edge of the bed. He moved gracefully, without hurry, holding Olivia's gaze as he worked his way around the bed. Olivia backed up a step, trying to keep a distance between herself and him. She bumped into a side table just as she watched her husband round the second corner of the bed. She looked over her shoulder for a fraction of a second in order to see her escape. But that small increment of time was too long, and when she looked back again, he was there, cornering her between the wall, the table and the bed. Her heart pounded in her chest when she saw the fire in his eyes.

"Is the thought of my touch so terrible, Olivia, that

you have to run away from me?'' he whispered with frightening intensity.

"What are you going to do?" Fear made her voice quiver.

His eyes devoured her exposed flesh. He grabbed the edge of the sheet and yanked it from her grasp in one deft motion. In a second, she stood in front of him dressed only in her nightgown. Its narrow band of lace around the neck did nothing to hide the white expanse of chest he was currently concentrating on.

She was frightened, but she was determined not to show it. She fought down the urge to cover herself with her hands, knowing he would only gloat at her feeble attempts to hide herself. Drawing on some strange and hitherto unknown reserve of strength, she held her head up and kept her eyes on his face. A feeling of triumph passed through her as she refrained from flinching when his hand made contact with the bare skin of her arm. But the victory was short-lived.

He moved in closer to her. The smell of brandy permeated her senses. He was just inches from her face. In this light, his eyes looked like dark pools of oil set afire. Olivia closed her eyes to escape his nearness.

"Oh, no," he said from behind his tightly clenched jaws. "You can't hide behind your wall tonight. No locking me out this time, Olivia. When I make love to you, I want it to be with a real woman with real feelings, not a china doll. Not an ice queen."

Oh, God, she thought despairingly as she felt the tears well up in her eyes. Not again, Lord. Please, don't let him make me cry again.

As if he were reading her mind, he said triumphantly, "Yes! Let them come, Olivia. Cry your heart out! Weep and wail! Anything but your damned indifference."

She opened her eyes as the first tear spilled down her cheek. "You don't want me," she whispered, tormented by her conflicting emotions. "You don't care anything about me. All you want to do is wound those around you." She closed her eyes again. "Please, just leave me alone." She tensed and waited for the onslaught to come.

The room was quiet. Five seconds passed. Then ten. After a full minute, when Olivia could still feel Traverston's hand burning the flesh of her upper arm, she cautiously opened her eyes.

The rage was gone. His face was still close, less than a foot. But he was stone cold sober. Not a trace remained of his earlier intoxicated demeanor. The lines on his face had formed themselves into an almost incredulous expression. And his eyes... Olivia could scarcely believe what she saw. The depth of feeling in them was unfathomable, and the knowledge made her gasp involuntarily. She looked harder to be sure, but she had seen them correctly. His eyes were hurt...sad, even.

Unbidden, the words came out before Traverston could stop them. She had struck too deep a chord to deny the truth. "How can you say that?" he asked softly. He was truly surprised by her accusation. "Don't you know? Can't you tell? You are my life."

Olivia's eyes widened as she heard his proclamation. The declaration was so simple, so out of keeping with his earlier tirade, there was no way she could doubt his belief in what he said. Her jaw dropped ever so slightly with surprise, and she gazed at the man before her in stunned disbelief.

The hand that reached out to stroke her face was gentle, even reverent. The furrows of his brow deepened into concern as he touched the silky smoothness of her skin. The back of his fingers caressed her cheek slowly, wonderingly, as if he meant to say with his touch all the things he couldn't possibly say with mere words. As his eyes moved from the area of his gentle ministrations back to her gaze, he realized that her shock had given way to something else. Something more pliant; something much more beautiful.

Further words were not necessary, and Traverston slowly bent his head to drink of her lips as he had been longing to do ever since their passionate embrace in the Merriweathers' garden. Her lips were soft and yielding. He brushed his mouth across hers with aching deliberation, reveling in their silky warmth.

The effect of Traverston's kiss was devastating on Olivia. She closed her eyes as his lips made contact with hers, and she felt her knees go weak with the sensations he aroused. She felt as drunk as Traverston had been, heady with strange and beguiling emotions that made her insides ache and her blood rush to her skin. Instinctively she reached out to draw him closer to her. In less than a second, he was there, his body drawn up fully against her own.

He deepened the kiss. When his tongue wrapped itself around hers, Olivia let out an involuntary moan and gripped him tighter. The warm sensation of earlier flooded all of her senses. Her breathing became difficult. His kisses grew harder and more demanding. Seeking him without conscious thought, Olivia moved her head first one way and then another, trying desperately to get more of him to invade her senses.

For a second, Olivia was shocked out of her cocoon of pleasure when Traverston slid his hand up from her waist to her breast. His palm cupped the rounded mound of flesh without hesitation, and his fingers immediately set to rubbing the nipple. She pulled her head back for a second to protest, but his mouth captured hers again before she could make a sound. Within moments, she forgot her initial fear and submitted her body to his endless demands. She became engulfed by his desire. It was at once frightening and terribly exciting. His hand on her breast and his smooth, seeking tongue seemed to stroke at an inner being she had no idea existed. It grew like a new wellspring, erupting inside and pouring throughout her body. It was larger than herself, and it demanded to be fed.

Desperate to feed this creation, Olivia splayed her hands across his back and felt for the source of this new sensation. She rubbed her hands downward, feeling the tight, corded muscles that made up his strong back. Slowly, with increasing pressure, she moved her hands upward and over his hard shoulders, then up his neck and into his hair. It was coarse and thick, and it waved over his collar like some live thing. She wrapped her hands in the strands, curling her fingers and letting the feel of his hair sink in as she flexed and unflexed her hands in restless passion. Again her hands plunged down his back. She discovered the taut muscles there anew, every discovery fueling the fire in her body.

As if her mouth was suddenly not enough for him, Traverston broke the contact and began searing the skin over her face and then down her neck with his kisses. They left hot, wet, sensuous fiery trails on her skin, and she gasped in pleasure even as she kept up her hands' determined exploration of him.

It was so sudden, so quick, Olivia couldn't help but make a startled exclamation when he took the nipple of her left breast between his lips. She looked down at her opened nightgown, noting, with a combination of wonder and fear, the limp ties dangling down her chest and his dark head bent over her. She had only vaguely begun to wonder how it had happened when she lost all ability to think as he gently applied his teeth to the rosy tip of her breast.

Her hands stopped their movement as she let the agonizing and wonderful sensation that began somewhere in her loins shoot through her to her chest and back down again. Wordless exclamations escaped her, driven from somewhere deep inside her throat, and Traverston was once again covering her mouth with his own before she could fully understand what was happening to her. Emboldened by his actions and needful of closer contact with him, Olivia felt for the lapels of his robe and daringly plunged her hands inside. The contact of her hands on the bare skin of his chest sent a shiver through her husband, and she was rewarded with a low moan from him.

His hands moved to her waist, and gently but firmly he pulled her from the wall and closer to him. Still thrusting and tangling his tongue with hers, he turned with her, then rocked her back a few steps until her legs were against the bed. Gently they fell together onto the bed, their mouths still locked together in their wild dance of passion.

He shifted to his side, leaving her lying on her back. Then his hand was once again inside her night rail, and he was fondling her breast, rubbing aching sensuality into every part of her body. She clutched at the soft material of his robe and arched her back with unknowing invitation.

His mouth once again on her throat and seeking the frantically beating pulse there, Traverston slowly slid his hand down her side. She covered his hair with her hand, reaching to once again tangle her fingers there as she felt his hand move over her stomach, across her hip and finally down her thigh.

As Traverston lifted the hem of her gown and ran his hand up her leg, he brought his head back to cover her mouth with his own. The warm, plunging sensation of his tongue in her mouth awoke a new, deeper need to get close to this man she called her husband, and Olivia welcomed the feel of his hand on her bare leg. Chills of the most pleasurable kind swept through her body as the hand stroked its way upward, finally finding that most secret place of her womanhood.

Again he used his mouth to silence her budding protest, and the sensations that swept through her body as he touched her nub of pleasure robbed her of the ability to speak or even to think. She was caught in a spiraling whirl of pleasure with every stroke of his long fingers, and she could do nothing to stop her mounting desire for a kind of satisfaction she had no idea how to achieve.

She tugged frantically at his robe, her hands gripping and tearing at the silk. As it came undone beneath her hands, she pushed against his warm skin. Every muscle, every hair under her fingers and palms was vividly outlined in her brain, even though her eyes were closed. The feel of him was exotic and intoxicating to her. She lost the rational power of thought and, like an animal, she moved her hips with untrained yearning.

When he removed his hand, Olivia almost cried out in protest. But the small, secretive part of her that she had shared with no one came to her rescue, and she held back. Instead, she opened her eyes, looking past her own desire to see his eyes gazing at her with dark passion. He had removed his robe, and tentatively, Olivia glanced downward over his body, but she could bring herself to look no further than his lean stomach and the hair growing down his chest and past his belly button. Quickly she whipped her eyes upward to lock with his again, and he moved forward to kiss her, his mouth gentle and assuring.

It took only a moment to reheat the embers of Olivia's earlier desire, and as he slipped the thin night rail over her head to reveal her slim, full-figured body in all of its pale glory, she knew only the breathless excitement of finally being as close to him as possible. He held her tightly in his arms. The nipples on her breasts were hard as they became buried in the hairs on his chest. His hands slid over her and pulled her closer. He brought her thigh up and over his, and for the first time Olivia truly became aware of the differences between men and women.

The hard shaft of his manhood pressed against her, and startled by the intimate contact, she gasped. Her eyes flew to his, looking for some kind of assurance for what was to come next.

Slowly he allowed his gaze to meet hers. His dark eyes were warm with the fullness of his arousal, echoing the desire she already knew existed by the evidence of what lay between her legs. But they were pools of satisfaction and determination, as well, as if he knew this was the right and natural course for them. But more than that, there was some other emotion there, too, an as-yet-unnamed one that Olivia knew could only be called love. He smiled lazily at her, his eyes glowing with that special emotion, and she, too, suddenly knew it was the right course for them.

Letting herself relax, she tentatively smiled back, and Traverston leaned forward and once again began his seduction of her. As they struggled and twisted to allow their mouths to come more fully together, he slipped his hand between them and once again found the mound of delight between her thighs. Within moments, Olivia's body had reached the point of heated tension, and Traverston sensed her need for release. As gently as he could, he slid his manhood into the junction between her thighs. The pain was brief. Olivia flinched and dug her fingernails into his naked back, but he had already stopped his forced entry. Then, slowly, gently, he slipped into her.

His first push over, Olivia was startled to feel him slowly backing out again. But just as she opened her mouth to protest, he was there again. Slowly, carefully, the rhythm built. He sought her mouth and plunged his tongue into hers in a wicked imitation of their lower bodies. She wrapped her arms tighter as the tension built. She nipped his tongue as it whipped around her mouth, releasing it as he slid out again. The heated volcano building inside her was begging for release, and instinctively, she grabbed his hips and moved her own in a complementary motion to his.

Traverston grimaced as she moved faster. Then suddenly, she arched her back and threw her head back as the warm waves of an exhilarating sensation cascaded over her. Her joy was wordless but not soundless. It would have been impossible for her to keep silent at the end of the hard earned, passionate journey he had led her on.

As Traverston felt her first spasms, he relaxed and let his own body join hers in the wild dance of release. He had had many women before, but he had never expected the incredible effect Olivia's explosive response would have on him and his own ability to enjoy the act of lovemaking. As his body took over and his muscles rippled involuntarily, he took on a new awareness and a new wonder for what loving a woman was all about.

Still feeling awed and a little afraid of her effect on him, Traverston slowly opened his eyes and looked down at the tired and spent face above the slim body beneath him. Her hair was spread over the pillow, and her long lashes were dark against cheeks now flushed with exertion. He waited with his breath held for her to open her eyes, wondering what she could be thinking about after all that had happened.

The transition was rapid. One moment, she had been lying with her eyes closed. The next they were wide open. She looked up at the dark face rimmed with an unruly shock of black hair hovering above her, and suddenly she smiled. She brought her hand up and caressed his cheek where the telltale blue-black shadow was just forming.

With relief, Traverston let out his breath and grabbed her hand as if it were a lifeline. He turned it over and kissed her palm, his relief at her reaction to their love-making genuine. She smiled wider and brought her other hand up to caress back his long raven hair.

When he released her hand, he gently disengaged himself from her and rolled onto his back. He breathed once deeply, as if to contemplate the enormity of what he had just done, and then looked over at the beautiful woman lying next to him. He smiled and held out his hand, and she eagerly scooted over to snuggle into his side.

Her head on his shoulder and his arm around her back, Traverston smoothed back her long hair with one hand and stared up at the ceiling. He took another deep breath and let it out slowly. His hand moved down her back, then over her arm. Finally he settled for softly stroking the skin of her upper arm as she lay curled against his side.

Olivia meant to ask questions. There were a million racing through her mind. Was this the beginning of a new relationship for them? Did this event put an end to their standoff? Did making love to her mean anything at all to him? And most importantly, did he love her? She thought he did, but she needed to hear it from him. She couldn't assume anything anymore. Her mind wouldn't allow it.

But in minutes, the tender caresses Traverston bestowed on her soothed away the need to think, and with it, the need to ask questions. Her last thought, just before she fell asleep, was to wonder what it would be like to have him with her every night, and if she could ever be so lucky.

The Olivia who came down the steps at nine o'clock the next morning was a pale shadow of the one who had made her debut in the fashionable world two months before. Her head bowed, her lovely face lined with worry, she crossed the hallway with an air of high distraction. Her morning gown of light rose-colored silk only heightened the lack of color in her cheeks. She looked drawn and unsure, very much unlike the self-possessed queen of the early London season.

Monquefort crossed to her side immediately when she entered the breakfast room, for once forgetting all about the food on his plate. The dowager marchioness also got to her feet in concern. Wearily Olivia waved them both away, looking around her with a vagueness associated with confusion. "Has Traverston already eaten?" she asked the room at large with a faint frown creasing her face.

Monquefort shared a worried look with Olivia's mother-in-law. Finally he looked at his best friend's wife and replied slowly, "He left at dawn, Olivia."

"Left?" she asked with genuine puzzlement. After their glorious union last night? Where on earth could he have gone?

In a rush, the events of yesterday afternoon flooded over her. She wavered uncertainly on her feet, and Monquefort rushed to escort her to a chair before she fell down.

He had left. After all that had gone on between them last night, he had still left, just as he had threatened to do. She couldn't believe it. She didn't want to believe. Her heart breaking, she forced herself to acknowledge the fact of his departure. "Oh, yes," she replied quietly, her face unnaturally expressive and sad. She looked as if she were going to be sick. "Thank you for reminding me, Alex. How silly of me to forget."

Monquefort pulled a chair close to the table and patted her hand with halfhearted reassurance. "I'm sure he'll be back soon. Come and have a bite to eat, Olivia," he invited. "You look as if you have had a hard night, and food will make you feel better."

Even through her pain, Olivia had enough feeling left to smile crookedly at Alex's simple solution to her problems. "I'm not hungry, thank you, my friend. I don't think I could eat anything right now." She let her gaze wander over to her mother-in-law, her brow becoming increasingly wrinkled as she held the old woman's look. Finally she spoke, her voice a quiet whisper in the parlor, "Your son visited me in my bedroom last night."

Alex looked at the dowager quickly, an embarrassed flush coloring his cheeks bright red. "I don't think you really need to go into the details, Olivia..."

"I told him he was unbalanced, Felicity," she interrupted before the earl could finish, "and now he has gone to London in order to save me from himself." As the words came out, she realized the truth in them, and her tone grew stronger. "He thinks he'll hurt me, and he doesn't want to do that. He thinks it's better this way, better to avoid me, rather than run the possibility of hurting me, just as his father hurt his mother."

For a long moment, they were all silent. Finally the earl asked, "What are you going to do?"

They were words she had asked herself not a moment earlier. What if she was wrong? What if the marquis had no feelings for her? After all, not once during their passionate night of lovemaking had he said he loved her. Not once.

The neglected, unsure part of her screamed that she was being used. Just as her father had used her emotions to abuse her, Traverston was now trying to do so as well, only with a lover's deadly accuracy. She should let him go. She should wall herself off from him. He would only destroy her in the end. She would be well and truly dead inside by the time he was done with her.

But the other part of her, the part that remembered being held in Traverston's arms refused this explanation. She had seen him look at her with affection. No, she corrected herself, with love. In his mind, her husband was doing his very best to protect her. He didn't want to see her hurt, so he was avoiding her. He would never allow himself to get near her again, lest he run the risk of engaging her affections and then turning on her in his instability.

But her affections were already engaged. Of that, she could have no further doubts. She loved him, and it was time he found out the truth about himself.

She turned her pale eyes on the earl. "I'm going after him."

The carriage bounced along the road made uneven from a recent rain, jostling its occupants against the well-padded interior. The Earl of Monquefort gripped one of the leather straps set into the coach's side, his eyes falling warily on his companion. "You're sure you're doing the right thing?" he asked.

Olivia looked at him, the tired circles under her eyes fading with her new resolve. "No, I'm not sure, Alex, but I have to do something."

His brow furrowed deeper. He brooded for a moment as he looked out the window. Then, as if he couldn't help himself from asking, he blurted, "You love him, don't you?"

She gazed into his eyes candidly. Their pale depths were the color of shallow water. But even as he looked, he could see her mind dart away from the mirrors her eyes created, and she shut herself off from him. "I don't know. I'm not sure I'm capable of loving anyone, Alex."

"I don't believe that."

"Then you are more assured than I." She held his look for a moment longer, letting him see the pain behind her eyes before she turned away.

Yesterday, she had been sure. But this morning? Hours of traveling toward her destiny had frightened her, and her mind skittered away from the looming confrontation. What if he didn't want her even after he knew the truth about his father? What would happen to her then? When Olivia's thoughts took these turns, she knew it was dangerous to admit she loved the marquis. If she failed in her quest, then he could well and truly destroy her. All of her newfound hope, all of her new courage would be gone. And how could she face life again as the living husk that she had been? Olivia was not sure that she could.

The remainder of the journey was conducted in silence. When the coach-and-four pulled up in front of Traverston's Berkeley Square home hours later, Monquefort alighted and helped Olivia disembark before the footman could come to their assistance.

The Marchioness of Traverston barely had eyes for her new town home. She glanced over the Palladian exterior and its simple, graceful architecture without really seeing it as she hurried toward the front door. She was anxious to find out if her husband was at home.

News of the marriage had already reached the ears of the London staff and they were anxious to greet their mistress properly. Olivia chaffed at the prolonged welcome, but she was too well-bred to show her impatience. Sadly the affair reminded her of the last time she had met her husband's retainers. Traverston had been absent that time as well.

Once all of the introductions had been completed, Olivia followed the housekeeper up the stairs to her husband's suite of rooms, leaving Monquefort to attend to his own affairs. Even though she had expected it, Olivia couldn't help the feeling of disappointment when she discovered the rooms were empty. Unable to stand the suspense any longer, Olivia turned and asked the plump and kindly retainer, "Is my husband in his study then, Mrs. Pool?"

The housekeeper looked at her oddly. "The staff

hasn't seen hide nor hair of the master since early this morning, my lady. Isn't he expecting you, mistress?''

Olivia recognized a bid for gossip when she saw one. Trying vainly to allay the woman's suspicions, she replied casually, "Oh, well... I wanted to surprise him. He is expecting me, of course, but not for another few days yet."

Mrs. Pool eyed the new marchioness with cautious disbelief. "Well, that's funny, my lady. He didn't mention anything to me."

Olivia smiled wanly. "Doubtless he was planning to. I'm sure he just forgot."

Mrs. Pool nodded her head, but she didn't seem convinced.

An hour later when Olivia's gowns had been unpacked by the upstairs maid and hung in the armoire, the housekeeper came back up to see her. "Lord Buxley is downstairs, my lady. I told him you wouldn't want to be disturbed after your long journey, but he wouldn't listen to me. I even told him the master was out, but he didn't seem to care."

"No, that's all right, Mrs. Pool. Tell him I'll be down in a minute." Olivia sighed with relief as the housekeeper left, the servant leaving a trail of perturbed propriety in her wake. Let her think whatever she likes, she sighed to herself sourly. She truly didn't feel like being alone with her thoughts at the moment. Trust Alex to understand her feelings and anticipate her needs. She gathered her skirts up and started out the door.

"How is it that you can look so radiant only one hour after your arrival?"

"Oh, bosh!" Olivia replied as she came down the stairs, her gown's skirts caught up in one hand. She looked into the earl's teasing eyes and found herself smiling back at him despite herself. "That is the biggest whisker I've ever heard, my lord!"

He took her free hand in his own as she descended the last step. "I can't help it if you are the most beautiful woman in England, *chérie*." His tone held a teasing note, but his eyes were warm enough to cause her to blush faintly.

As the front door banged open, Olivia looked up in horror to see her husband stride through the door. Quickly, but not quick enough to prevent Traverston from witnessing their closeness of a second before, Olivia withdrew her hand from the earl's strong clasp.

With an ease that spoke of being caught in compromising situations many times before, Monquefort turned to face his friend. "Trav! You're home I see. Olivia and I rode over here, neck or nothing, in pursuit of you."

"You seem to be doing just fine without me, Alex," he drawled as he stripped off his hat and gloves.

Monquefort laughed easily. "Don't be daft, man. If I wanted to run off with your wife, I certainly wouldn't have brought her back to your home when I was done."

Traverston quirked an eyebrow as he paused to take the earl's measure. "No?"

"John!"

The marquis's eyes shot to Olivia at her spontaneous interjection. He studied her with an enigmatic expression a second or two before turning away.

"Don't mind him, Olivia," lied Monquefort smoothly. "I've seen him in these kinds of moods before. There is nothing you can say that will make it come out all right, trust me. It's best just to leave him alone when he's like this." He put a hand out and leaned against the banister. "I came over to ask if you'd like to attend the opera with me tonight. I know we've had a hard trip, but I have a box at the Drury that will just go to waste if we don't go. Señor Firruzzi is singing the part of Tamino in *The Magic Flute*."

"Well, I... " She glanced over at her husband, who

was studiously avoiding her look. She turned back to the earl. "I don't think I should."

Monquefort's sudden impatience surprised her. "Well, I don't see why not. Traverston isn't planning on entertaining you tonight."

She looked over at her husband again. He moved his attention from the hat in his hands and his eyes locked with hers. Vainly she looked for some indication, some acknowledgment of their intimate night together just two days ago. But she searched without success. His eyes were blank, expressionless. Reluctantly she tore her gaze from him and sought the reassuring face of the earl. If this was how it was with him, anything would be better than staying at home and being ignored. She didn't think she could stand that. But she had to try one last time.

"I... I suppose. Perhaps you'll come with us, my lord?" She looked back at the marquis with a hopeful expression.

"I have other plans. But you must do as you see fit, Lady Traverston."

The hollow sound of the same words she had used on him two days ago, in conjunction with his marble features, left her cold and shivering. Olivia's shoulders drooped forward a little.

Monquefort briefly took hold of Olivia's arm and squeezed it reassuringly. He was angry with his friend, but he knew he had no right to interfere in his affairs. Instead he said, "I'll see you at eight, then, my lady." With a last warm look of farewell, he took his leave of the couple.

The entry hall was strangely quiet once the earl had left. Olivia stood uncertainly, not sure what to do next. After roaming the walls with his eyes, Traverston finally met and held her gaze. "I have some work to do. I'll be in my study."

As he started to leave, Olivia raised her arm in an

unconscious gesture to stop him. "Trav," she began, lapsing into the safe term of affection she had heard Alex use on occasion.

Slowly he turned around to face her. He was a statue again. She couldn't reach him. Still she had to try. "Are you certain you wouldn't wish to join us?"

For a moment he was tempted. As she stood there, her eyes silently pleading with him, he almost gave in. She was so vulnerable at times, despite her attempts to be otherwise. Right now she reminded him of a small child pleading for a special treat.

But he could not. To do so would be akin to murder, and he loved her too well to seal her fate with his self-ishness.

"I said, I have other plans." With that, he turned on his heel and headed for his study.

Chapter Sixteen

The conversation in the carriage on the way to the Theatre Royal was desultory and oppressive, mimicking the unusually humid night air and offering the passengers no relief. Olivia painted a polite expression onto her face as she listened with disinterest to the overly bright chatter of the woman opposite her. Her affected mannerisms left Olivia wanting, although for what she couldn't have said. She turned her head and glanced out the window.

She had known Alex would probably invite at least one other couple to attend the opera with them, but two couples seemed far more company than she could tolerate just at the moment. Fortunately, the news was not all bad. With another lady to help carry the bulk of feminine chatter this evening, her comments, or lack thereof, could go largely unnoticed.

Still it was with relief that Lady Traverston alighted from the stuffy conveyance as the coach stopped about a block away from the theater, the three tall arches gracing its entrance just barely visible. As she took Monquefort's arm, she lifted her chin a tad, steeling herself to walk straight ahead and into the incredible crush lining the street to get into the building. With a sympathetic grin,

Alex patted the hand that rested lightly on his arm. She tried to smile back encouragingly, but all she could manage was a rather tired expression.

The cacophony of chatter and laughter inside the theater was even more oppressive to Olivia than it was outside. She shifted forward in her seat to look down into the pit below. A shudder swept through her as she tried to imagine what it was like for the people jostled together in the airless opera house's lower seats. At least here in Alex's private box, she thought, she had some room to herself.

Olivia sighed with relief when the overture began with its signature triple series of impressive chords. The noise of the crowd did not die down noticeably, however, until Señor Firruzzi took the stage to open the first act with his amazing tenor voice.

With the start of the performance, Olivia now had a genuine excuse not to respond to the constant chatter of the other two couples behind her. She settled back ever so slightly in her chair, anticipating an entertaining show—or at least one that would keep her mind off her husband and abate her overwhelming sense of restlessness.

But it was not to be. The harder she tried not to think of Traverston, the more he invaded her mind. Soon the opera faded into nothing but a vague buzz in the background of her brain, and all she became aware of was the desperate need to see him.

What was he planning to do tonight? Was he out with some friends from his club, or was he gambling in some gaming hall in St. James's Square? Was he sitting alone in their house in Berkeley Square? Somehow she doubted the latter possibility.

She shifted in her seat. The heat was intolerable. Had it been this warm before? She could swear the temperature had risen at least ten degrees in the past five minutes. Olivia fanned herself as vigorously as she dared with her dainty chicken-skin fan, wondering if having an almost useless fan to cool oneself with was more or less foolish than the edicts of society that prevented using the fan for anything more strenuous than flirting.

The Earl of Monquefort's warm hand on her own brought her attention back to the occupants of the box. The women were still idly chattering away. She glanced at the ladies' husbands. The men were absorbed in ogling the opera singers on the stage, too occupied to hear what their wives had to say. But Alex was not similarly distracted.

"Aren't you feeling well, my lady?" His tone was solicitous, concerned.

She smiled as well as she could for him. He was sweet to be so considerate of her. All he had wanted was to give her a distraction by bringing her here, and she must seem terribly ungrateful to him. "Yes, of course. Perfectly well. Why should you wonder?"

He turned in his chair to grasp her other hand in his own. "Forgive me for prying, Olivia, but you don't look at all the thing."

"Dearest Alex," she replied affectionately with the tiniest hint of wistfulness in her voice, "you worry too much about me. Aren't there any other ladies for you to fawn over?"

His gaze was uncommonly serious. "None that matter."

Her own smile faded and she let her gaze fall to her lap. Her hands toyed with the tiny fan as she wondered how she could possibly distract him with a topic other than herself.

He let her be silent a minute. Then he asked tenderly,

"Won't you trust in me, my dear, and tell me what is wrong?"

She did not miss the term of endearment. This was dangerous ground. She did not want to give him the wrong impression, and yet his sympathy was too hard to ignore.

The earl studied her as she kept her eyes averted. He let go of her hands and moved back a little in his chair to give her room. A slow anger at Traverston began smoldering in him as he looked at his companion's solemn face. He knew the marquis was the cause of her blue study. She didn't have to tell him in order for him to know.

For the hundredth time in the past month, the earl's breast was moved with pity. Olivia was so beautiful, so lovely. Her pale blue sarcenet gown overlaid with the finest netting of silver made her look like some fairy-tale queen. She held her shoulders back straight and proud, further enhancing the image. Her hair, lustrous and glowing in the lamplight, wreathed the top of her head like a crown. Her skin was like alabaster, her eyes the color of the western horizon in the early morning. She was stunning…enchanting.

And she was unhappy. He knew that, despite her attempts to hide her feelings from him. If he were honest, Olivia was really more like a delicate blue flower than a queen. A queen is invulnerable, invincible. A flower is not.

Yes, he decided, Olivia was definitely a flower. A delicate wildflower whose petals could easily be crushed and wilted. She needed to be handled gently.

He gripped the arms of his chair tighter. One thing was for sure—she did not deserve to be treated the way Traverston was treating her. Olivia should be loved and cherished, her budding feelings nurtured and cared for. Instead she was being slowly smothered by her husband. Her will to survive was fast fading, and soon what few defenses she had left would crumble.

His hands flexed repeatedly on the armrests, seeking some source of outlet for the emotions pouring through him. He felt so powerless to help her.

Not quite able to keep his frustration from showing, he spoke his thoughts aloud. "It's Traverston, isn't it?"

Quickly Olivia looked up at him, her eyes beseeching. He could almost hear the words, as if he were reading her mind. *No please, Alex. Not here, not now. Don't do this to me.*

An oath escaped Monquefort's lips. Several heads around them turned in their direction. He cursed again, more quietly this time as he saw the unwanted attention he was drawing to them. But he wasn't going to give up. She needed him. He took her hands again and gripped them tightly, turning her fingers almost bloodless with his concern. "What did he do now, Olivia?" He spoke softly but with a hint of steel in his tone. He would protect her and defend her with his dying breath.

Olivia glanced around them, afraid to speak. *Dear Alex.* If she spoke now, she didn't think she could hold back the torrent of emotion threatening to break over her. Trying to look anywhere but at the earl, she let her gaze linger on the crowd around them.

And then she saw him. His raven hair and majestic bearing were unmistakable. The low light of the theater enhanced his sharply chiseled cheekbones and prominent jaw and made his entire face a playground of light and shadows. Her heart stopped beating. Traverston was here! He had come to the opera after all.

The flash of platinum blond hair distracted her for a moment. Her eyes moved a fraction to the left. There was a woman entering her husband's box! Then the head of heavenly hair moved toward Traverston. A fraction of a second later it came to rest against his shoulder. A petulantly seductive face tilted upward to reveal emerald green eyes—eyes that Traverston's wife recognized very well.

Olivia's sharp intake of breath drew Monquefort's eyes away from their close scrutiny of her face. He leaned forward in his chair, intently examining the other boxes and searching for the cause of her distress. This time his oath caused all heads around them to turn in their direction.

"Damn his black and rotten soul!" The earl stood up abruptly, the sudden movement knocking his chair backward.

"Alex, no!" she pleaded as her mind threatened to go numb with shock. She grabbed his arm, checking his movement as he started to head out of the box.

He gazed down at her, seeing her expression through a red haze. His words were strangely quiet, but there could be no mistaking the passion behind them.

"I'm going to kill him."

"No." Her voice was firmer, stronger than before. "No," she repeated more quietly. She waited until he was looking at her again before continuing. "Take me home, Alex," she commanded. Her eyes shifted silently to indicate the gawking onlookers. They came back to his face, warning him not to argue with her.

He stared at her incredulously, but her look was compelling. She cut him off before he could speak again. "Please. Alex. Take me home."

He stood motionless a moment, her hand still gripping his wrist. Behind him, on stage, the first act drew to a close. As the curtain came down, the crowd below and around them began moving like a rough and tempestuous sea, surging for the doors. He glanced back at the box across the way and watched Traverston help Lady Chisolm to her feet. Briefly he weighed his need to see Traverston's blood on his hands against Olivia's plea. With stiff, unwieldy motions, he grabbed her cloak and tossed it roughly around her shoulders as she turned to let him assist her. In a protective gesture, he wrapped an arm around her, stopping briefly once before they exited the box to cast a hostile look back at his former friend.

Outside in the hall, before they could comfortably make the short jog to the staircase, the encounter Olivia had been dreading happened. It was as if fate had taken a hand tonight and was determined that Olivia confront her husband with his perfidy.

But she would give that fate no excuse to mock her. Did Traverston seek to humiliate her with the one woman he had said meant nothing? Fine, she thought grimly. Let him try. She was made of stronger material than he seemed to be inclined to believe.

She felt the muscles in the earl's arm go rigid when he spotted the marquis with the countess. Gripping his arm tighter, she whispered to him fiercely, "This is my battle, Alex. Let me handle it." A glance at his face confirmed the fact that while he might not like it, he would say nothing too provocative to the marquis.

As Olivia could have predicted, Beatrice was the one to speak first. To the young marchioness, it appeared as though the countess could barely contain her glee at running into the wife of her paramour. "Olivia, my dear," purred the golden-haired goddess, leaning further into Traverston's arm as she raised her voice to carry to the crowds around her. "What a lovely surprise to find you here. Trav never mentioned that you were going to come." She glanced with unconcealed speculation at the earl. "But perhaps he didn't know."

Unconsciously Olivia threw back her shoulders and

stood regally straight as she gazed with unnerving coolness at the woman before her. "Countess," she responded without a trace of warmth in her voice, "your appearance, on the other hand, comes as no surprise."

Beatrice's laugh was rich and full, and it drew the attention of all those around her. "My dear simple child," she crowed, "whatever could you mean?"

Olivia could not look at her husband, so she kept her gaze trained on the blond beauty. "Simply that if I had considered you a threat, you wouldn't be here tonight."

As the countess began to sputter indignantly at the insult, Olivia calmly looked up at her companion. "I appreciate your escort, my lord. If you would be so kind as to see me home?"

Monquefort reluctantly unlocked his baleful gaze from that of the marquis's to look down at his companion. What he saw in her face caused him to immediately acquiesce to her request, and he guided her around the other couple and down the stairs without a single word.

Outside, Monquefort left Olivia's side to track down his carriage. When it arrived, he helped her inside the luxurious coach with gentle solicitude. Too gentle. Olivia couldn't mistake his regard.

The drive to Traverston's town house seemed to take hours. Olivia couldn't pass the time by talking to her companion, either. She knew neither one of them could tolerate conversation right now. He was too angry on her behalf to listen and she was too numb to offer assurances she didn't feel.

She glanced at him and saw his body turned so that he could look out the window. She followed the hard line of his jaw with her eye. She could see the seething anger in him through every rigid line of his body. But the fact meant nothing to her— nothing next to the empty desolation growing in the pit of her stomach. It was Traverston she loved, not Alex. The final acknowledgment was devastating.

"Trav," announced the widowed countess snuggled close to his side, regaining her aplomb almost immediately. "Let's leave this boring little playhouse and go back to my apartment." She glanced at him coyly through her lashes. "I'm sure we can find some better way to pass the time together than this."

He gazed down into her eyes, his own clouded by the recent exchange. Already the crowds around them were murmuring and speculating on the exchange between the marquis's two women. His stomach twisted at the thought of what such a dispassionate speech must have cost Olivia.

Abruptly the marquis drew away. Something seemed to snap in him as he turned to face his companion. He removed her clinging hands from his arm, not quite disguising the disgust he was now feeling for her. "It was a mistake to come here with you tonight, Beatrice," he replied coldly. "And it would be a bigger mistake to leave with you."

He ignored her outraged exclamation as he continued. "Doubtless Hamilton is waiting for you to report back to him in any case, and I'd hate to keep you from him."

Her stunned look was the only confirmation he needed to verify his suspicions. He had suspected all along that Beatrice and his brother had something up their sleeves. His timely reunion with his ex-mistress had followed just a little too closely on the heels of his "marriage" to be believable. That, coupled with the knowledge that Beatrice had begun seeing his brother shortly after he had removed his patronage from her, equaled one very likely candidate for intrigue.

He wouldn't have bothered with her at all tonight except that his curiosity drew him to accept her invitation to attend the opera. He wanted to know what would drive a proud woman like Beatrice to seek a man who had dismissed her repeatedly. After Olivia announced her intention to come with Monquefort tonight, he was even more driven to attend. Not from any desire to wound his wife; the truth was far from it. His jealousy of her regard for Monquefort made him want to keep an eye on her.

And it appeared as though his jealousy had been justified. He saw the protective way the earl had ushered her out of their box. And it would have been impossible to ignore the man's hostility a minute ago. Alex's solicitous attitude toward his wife and his antagonism toward himself could only have been motivated by deep feelings for her. Feelings he would undoubtedly give in to as he comforted her tonight, thought the marquis grimly.

Unconsciously his face grew darker as he looked down on Lady Chisolm. He studied the beautiful blonde before him, scrutinizing her flawless face with brutal intensity. But he didn't see any of her numerous attributes. Rather, he saw only a cold, heartless woman who was not above taking her revenge.

"Good night, Beatrice," he said firmly as he executed the tiniest of bows, and he turned to walk down the stairs to the exit.

Lady Beatrice Chisolm was looking anything but seductive at the moment, mused David Hamilton as he watched her pace the length of her boudoir. Her body was hard and taut with unvented rage. Her face was deathly pale and she kept clenching and unclenching her hands into tight little balls that she swung forcefully during her angry exercise.

Suddenly she turned on him. "You haven't said a word, David. You've just sat there and listened to me rave. This whole thing was your idea in the first place." She glared at him. "What are we going to do now?"

Hamilton looked at his fingernails with studied non-chalance. His leg swung lazily from the arm of the chair where he had placed it negligently some ten minutes earlier when Beatrice's tirade had begun. He flicked an imaginary piece of dirt out from under one of his nails before looking up at her. His eyes were surprisingly devoid of any passionate response. "We, my dear lady, are not going to do anything."

"What do you mean we're not going to do anything?" she shrieked.

He swung his leg a few more times before slowly placing it on the floor. Then he leaned back into a more comfortable position. "The operative word in that sentence was *we*. *We* are not going to do anything." He paused and let his eyes grow cold. "I am."

Beatrice took a few short strides forward. Hamilton's glittering gaze stopped her before she could continue with her initial impulse to slap him, however. More calmly than she had originally intended, she asked, "And what are you going to do? Did you find out if they had really been married all along? Can we use that to disgrace him?" Her eyes grew bright with hope as she asked the last question.

He got up from the chair and walked idly over to her silver-framed mirror. One hand moved up to twitch his cravat into place, but it was a gesture for show only. His neck cloth was perfect, as always. He didn't look at her as he replied, "What I choose to do is none of your business, Beatrice." He slid his eyes sideways to catch hers in the mirror. "I suggest you don't forget that."

"Why, you...you..." she stuttered, her rage making her incoherent. "You...beast! You filthy beast! After all I've done for you, to stand there and just dismiss me out of hand as if I were of no more import than your servant! Why I ought to..."

He spun to face her directly. "Don't be angry, my dear, you don't have the looks for it. Your eyes lose their soft seductive look and your lips become quite thin when you're angry." His eyes were positively glacial. "It's not a pretty picture."

"You...you..." Red color suffused her face as she sought strong enough words to express her feeling of outrage.

"Yes, I know," he said, looking bored. "I'm a beast. You've already mentioned that." He picked up his hat from the corner table by the bed and began to make his way across her room to the door. "Try not to get apoplectic, my dear. Traverston is hardly worth it."

"If you take one step out that door, don't ever plan on walking back through it!"

Hamilton paused and looked over his shoulder. Beatrice's face had gone completely white again. She really had the most fascinating physiology, he thought. His mouth quirked up into a small mocking expression as he moved to face her more fully. "That was well done, my dear. Have you ever thought about treading the boards? I'm sure you could rival the talented Mrs. Siddons if you so chose." At her speechlessness, he mocked, "Oh, don't stop on my account, please. This is very entertaining. You may even tempt me to stay a while longer if you keep it up."

Beatrice was not accustomed to being laughed at. She was used to laughing at others, but not being the cause for amusement. The unusual sensation was not at all to her liking. Her eyes narrowed and she said more calmly, reaching for his cutting tone, "I always knew you were cruel, David. I just didn't know how cruel."

In a flash he was by her side, gripping her arm with a

terrible force. "Do you think I'm cruel, my love? Do you think I'm a bastard? Well, I am. You haven't the slightest idea what I'm capable of.

"For years I have planned my brother's downfall... years! And just when I'm about to give him the *coup de grâce* you come into the picture, sashaying your skirts and muddling in my affairs. You've ruined everything! You and your petty schemes for revenge. I should kill you, torture you, burn you at the stake for what you've done! Don't you dare try to reproach me for anything!"

He laughed, the sound coming like bitter bile up his throat. "You think I've been cruel!" He turned to face her again, his smoke-colored eyes searing her skin with their intensity. "I'll tell you what is cruel, Beatrice. Your inflicting me with all of your vain posturing and posing—that's cruel. Listening to your vapid droning voice go on and on about how mistreated you've been—that's cruel. What I've done to you is nothing compared to that.

"My brother was right. I never used to take his table scraps. I'm amazed that I had the patience to do so now." He shook his head from side to side, not really seeing her. "I thought I could use you. I thought some information you may have gleaned from John during your tryst with him could be helpful in my plan to bring him to his knees. But your head is empty. You can't see beyond your own pert little nose. Maybe I should do the world a favor and put you out of our misery."

Beatrice watched his eyes glisten in the dim room. "You're crazy." The sudden revelation came softly from her lips. Louder, she repeated, "You're crazy, that's what you are. I never realized it before, but I see it now."

His smile was ugly. "I may have maggots in my brain, dear heart, but you're still a useless, vapid female." Abruptly he let her go. "Good night, Beatrice." He tapped his hat into place and moved toward the door. He paused in the doorway, his hand on the handle. "Same time tomorrow?"

He laughed again as she stared at him in horror.

The news article in the *Gazette* in Traverston's hand wouldn't stay in focus. It was a problem he seemed to be having more and more frequently, he thought wryly. He brought the newspaper crashing down into his lap, giving up trying to read it with a frustrated sigh. He picked up the glass of sherry at his elbow and took a long drink.

The problem was simple. He was at Brooke's while Monquefort was with Olivia, comforting her after her discovery of her husband's shocking betrayal, no doubt. The thought stuck in his craw, choking him.

If only he could be with her. If only he could explain to her that there was no other woman he would rather be with than his wife. "Why not?" he asked himself. He mentally stamped the question down. It was better if she were with the earl, he reminded himself. Her husband could only do her harm.

Traverston's mood was not improved with the appearance of his brother in the entrance to the room. The marquis's face grew two shades darker as he watched Hamilton skim the room, obviously searching for something. When his gaze landed on the marquis, Traverston knew Hamilton had found it.

With brisk, purposeful strides, Hamilton moved toward his brother.

He came to a halt a small distance from the marquis's booted feet. Without glancing to either side of him to see who might be nearby, he began without preamble, "This game has gone on for far too long, brother-mine. Let's end it now, shall we?"

Lazily Traverston reached for his glass again. He asked

with apparent disinterest, "To what game are you referring, David?"

Hamilton's single sharp bark of laughter caused heads to turn. Noting the attention, he replied more quietly, "To this." He gestured between them. "To us."

The marquis took an annoyingly long pull from his glass. Lowering the rim a few inches, he looked calmly at the man hovering over him. "The only game going on here, David, is the one in your head."

Hamilton dropped into an armchair across from his brother, his eyes sharp and knowing. He nodded his head after a moment and crossed one leg over his knee before answering. "You don't fool me, John, not for a moment. You'd like to be rid of me, you know you would."

Traverston didn't blink an eye. "Indeed, I don't deny it."

Hamilton's reaction was almost relieved. He slapped his thigh with his hand and actually smiled. "There! See? I knew it." His smile became frozen into place. "Then why don't we just have at it, eh? You call your seconds and I'll call mine. This can be over tomorrow at dawn." His voice was softly persuasive.

Traverston's grip tightened on his glass. "Don't tease me, David," he replied, the effort at restraining himself showing plainly. "I've had a bad day."

Hamilton's eyes sparkled with mischief. "And it's about to get a lot worse."

The marquis stiffened. "What do you mean?"

Laughter bubbled from Hamilton's lips. He sat back in his chair and wagged his head humorously from side to side. He pointed his finger at his brother and shook it, his mirth making the words slow to come out. Traverston had to rein in his impatience with both hands to keep from leaping out of his chair and strangling his brother.

Finally Hamilton managed to disclose the source of his amusement.

"I've got Olivia," he said, still smiling pleasantly.

Traverston's heart stopped beating. Then, with anger boiling up inside him, he slowly gripped both armrests and levered himself up out of the chair. He towered over his brother, rage visibly shaking his hands. Hamilton made no attempt to hide.

As Traverston brought one fist up in a threatening gesture, Hamilton threw up a hand, his face losing all of its earlier humor. "Tut-tut, dear brother. Let's not be hasty." He made a show of looking around the public room. "Let's not forget where we are."

"Blast your damned impertinence!" But the sanity of his words had already made their impression. The marquis dropped his fist a fraction of an inch. "What do you want?"

"Merely what I told you earlier, John." His eyes glittered like ice. "I want you to accept my offer of a duel."

"And if I don't?" he growled.

Hamilton made a show of looking at his fingernails. "You remember what happened to Alice, don't you, dear brother?" he asked with deceptive casualness. He looked up into his eyes. "It won't be quite the same for your wife, since Olivia's not a virgin, but I imagine I can make it painful for her all the same."

"Touch a hair on her head and you die."

Hamilton shrugged off the threat. "Yes, well, I'm giving you the opportunity to make sure nothing does happen to her. Just show up tomorrow at dawn."

The silence stretched on, but neither man dropped the other's gaze.

Finally Traverston said, "You didn't have to take her, you know. I would have gladly jumped at the chance to blow your brains out."

He smiled coldly. "I didn't want to take that chance, John. You've gotten so respectable over the years, I wasn't sure you'd agree to meet me on the playing field, what with a wife to think about." He shook his head, his amusement and smugness as thick around him as a shield. "And this one—" he touched the side of his nose and looked up at his brother with wicked understanding "—this one means an awful lot to you, doesn't she?" He held up his hand to ward off the marquis's denial. "No, no. Please. Let's not pretend. I already know that you have been married for a much longer time than anyone else supposes." He laughed quietly. "You really should be more careful about what you say to Beatrice, old boy. That woman would betray you for a tuppence."

Traverston's eyes would have made his brother spontaneously burst into flames had it been possible. "You shouldn't have let my honor concern you, David. You don't know me as well as you think."

He smiled again and rose from his chair. "Oh, no." He stood and faced his brother at eye level. "I know you very well. You and I are one and the same, John." Then he called out over his shoulder as he began to walk away, "Or have you forgotten who our father was?"

As the marquis watched his brother saunter way, his blood shrieked through his veins like a cry for vengeance. No, thought the marquis grimly. He had not.

"I had nothing to do with it, I swear!" Beatrice's voice rang out on a cry of pain as the marquis gripped her arm tighter. "I saw him right after I left you, it's true, but he didn't tell me what he was planning."

"Woman," growled the marquis with the threat of death in his voice, "you have lied to me once too often. I'm having a hard time believing your silver tongue now!"

"It's true!" she screamed at him, rage mixing with the tears that had started streaming down her face. "I didn't plan this with him! If he took your wife, I don't know where she is!"

The marquis stared at her with implacable fury, then abruptly let her go. "Damn you, Beatrice," he said harshly as he spun away in an attempt to control himself, "if there is one hair on her head that he has damaged..."

She hugged her sore arm to her chest and rubbed at the bruise the marquis had left. "If there is anyone here to be damned, my lord, it is you, not I," she exclaimed without heat. The marquis's attack had left her feeling used and tired, and she had no further strength for venom.

"Neither your soul nor mine is of any consequence right now, Countess. The only thing that matters is Olivia."

"Indeed?" She laughed softly. "Is that why you were in such a rush to be with me tonight?"

He turned to look at her, his black brows lowering in a scowl. "You don't have the first clue as to what is going on, Beatrice. You never did."

Her gaze fell on his face with remarkable perception. "Don't I, Trav?" she asked lightly. "Don't I at that? I think it is quite plain what is going on. You love her, that is what is happening."

He threw himself away from her. "Don't be ridiculous."

A small, knowing smile began to light her face, and she stalked toward him like the hunter toward her prey. "Am I being ridiculous? I don't think so." Her voice took on a singsong quality as she continued. "I've seen a man tormented by love before, Traverston dear, and you are the picture perfect image of one. You love her, body and soul, and it scares you to death, doesn't it?" She hovered near him, daring him to deny the truth.

Violently he spun on his heel, bringing his face to within inches of hers. Reflexively she pulled back, but then, almost immediately, she saw his fear within his anger, and she smiled in triumph. "Yes, it does," she confirmed with satisfaction. "Good. You should be frightened."

She laughed and turned away from him, confident that he could do her no harm now. "The all-powerful marquis, brought to his knees by love for a mere child. God," she muttered wondrously, "I never thought I'd see this day." Still smiling to herself, she reached out and picked up a brush. She toyed with it briefly before she glanced up at him again, her triumph lighting her eyes.

"It's amusing to think that the Ice Queen has succeeded where I have failed. But this is one success I gladly concede, for she has managed to hurt you far worse than I ever could."

"What do you mean?"

Her eyes opened wide with feigned innocence, as if his question were too simple to be believed. "But, Traverston," she mocked, "why should you need to ask? I'd have thought the answer quite easy to be perceived."

"Answer me, woman!" he demanded sharply. "I'm in no mood for your riddles."

Her eyes narrowed and she set down the brush. Straightening her shoulders, she looked him full in the face with her hate and declared, "Because she loves another, you fool. Your wife is in love with the earl! What better revenge could I ask for than that you throw down your heart for a mere chit who refuses you for another? Even I couldn't have come up with anything more satisfying than watching you play out this little drama."

Vainly the marquis attempted to dismiss her words, but he could not. With bitterness, he choked down the reply he would have flung in her teeth, and asked her once more, "Where is Olivia?"

She smiled the smile of death at him. "I haven't got the faintest idea. But I do know that she isn't safe with David."

Beatrice's mocking laughter haunted him all the way out the door.

Chapter Seventeen

The brass door knocker sounded unnaturally loud in the still night air as it pounded against the front door of the Earl of Monquefort's town home. With open curiosity, the earl looked up from his desk at the clock on the mantel. The ornate hands of the Louis XVI gold gilded timepiece indicated several minutes past two in the morning. Frowning at the early-morning interruption, the earl got up from his chair and crossed to the door of the library. He came into the hallway just in time to see one of his sleepy footmen pull open the front door.

Anger marred the handsome lines of Monquefort's face as he watched Traverston barge into his house, pushing past his retainer like a runaway wagon train. The earl was just getting ready to ring a peal over his onetime friend's head when the marquis saw him and headed off his outburst by saying, "Alex! Thank God, you are here."

"John," replied the earl, thoroughly confused, "What are you doing here, man? It's two o'clock in the morning!"

"I know," Traverston declared tiredly as he reached the earl. He put one hand out to take him by the arm and turn him back in the direction of the library. He looked over his shoulder at the retainer, who was suddenly alert and taking pains not to appear so. "I need to speak to you in private," he explained in quieter tones, pulling the earl along with him toward the hall.

When Monquefort was once again seated at his desk and the marquis had closed the mahogany door to the earl's private library, Traverston began without hesitation. "Is Olivia here with you?"

Monquefort's look was incredulous. He jumped to his feet. "What in blazes do you mean, Trav? Isn't she at home with you?"

Disappointment washed over the marquis as he passed a hand across his brow. "No, she's not. I was just there less than an hour ago. The butler said she left with Hamilton, not long after you left her." He began pacing the room agitatedly, his worry evident. After a moment he turned to face the earl again. "I believe David has kidnapped her." He waited for Monquefort's explosion. It wasn't long in coming.

"Hamilton! Why on earth would she go with him?"

Traverston's look was grim. "I doubt it was by choice." He hesitated before continuing. "A little after midnight, I went to my club. David approached me there and challenged me to a duel. He told me he has taken Olivia to ensure my attendance on the field at dawn tomorrow." He laughed bitterly. "As if I needed that kind of incentive."

Monquefort's normally lively countenance was unusually reserved. "What are you going to do?" he asked briefly.

Traverston stared at his friend as if he thought he might grow horns at any minute. "Why, I'm going to accept, of course."

"No," replied Monquefort, shaking his head. "I mean

about Olivia. You're not just going to let him keep her until then, are you?"

The marquis looked penetratingly at Monquefort. "I don't see what other options I have, Alex." Before the earl could retort, he interjected, "I don't want her in his company, either, believe me. I know what he is capable of, more so than you. And despite what appearances may seem, I care for Olivia very much. If I had a choice, I would rescue her this minute.

"But that's just it—I don't have a choice. I have about three hours or so until dawn when the duel is supposed to take place. It would be impossible to track her down between now and then. Even if I could find her readily, which, knowing David, I wouldn't be able to do, I'd still wind up having to fight him in order to get her back. He's not going to let me just waltz off with her after all the trouble he's gone through to take her, you know."

Monquefort digested this in silence. He knew Traverston was right, but it galled him to be so helpless. He looked down and fiddled with one of the papers on his desk. Quietly he asked, "You'll allow me to act as your second, of course?"

Traverston smiled grimly. "That's why I'm here."

"I thought you believed Olivia was with me."

The marquis could not miss the implied accusation in his friend's words. He waited until Monquefort looked at him before replying seriously, "I had hoped, Alex, for her sake that she was. I had wished, selfishly, for mine that she was not."

The earl turned to walk away from his friend. He fought the resentment rising in his throat, but he couldn't silence the words before they came out. "You were with Beatrice at the opera tonight."

Traverston's sigh was profound. "Yes, I was. I had hoped to learn what scheme she and David were plotting against me." He watched the earl's tightly coiled pacing with sad eyes. "I knew they were up to something. I had no idea it involved Olivia."

"Damn," muttered the earl softly. "If only I had stayed with her."

Wearily the marquis ran a hand through his hair. He fought to keep the bitterness out of his tone, but he couldn't hold back the loathing he felt at himself. "It wasn't your place to be with her." His voice was heavy with self-reproach. "It was mine."

Monquefort bit back the urge to reply that he was damn right it was his place. Remorse was easy once the damage had been done. Now it was Olivia's turn to pay for Traverston's neglect.

But Monquefort couldn't afford to feel like this now. The most important thing was Olivia. He stopped his frustrated pacing and walked back over to the marquis. "What do we do until dawn?"

Galvanized once more, Traverston replied, "Call on the doctor, Alex. Inform him of the duel. I doubt David will see to such a detail. He'd be delighted to see me bleed to death. I wouldn't mind watching him squirm on the ground without medical attention myself, but at least one of us has to play the gentleman. In the meantime, I'll call on Seinheart to act as my other second."

Immediately Monquefort began moving toward the door, glad to have some occupation until the fated time. He paused as he reached the portal. "Do you think she's all right?" he asked without looking at the marquis.

He missed the pained expression that passed across Traverston's face. "I hope so."

The fog blanketing the dew-damp grounds clung to the walls both inside and outside of the coach. Olivia shivered, a chill sweeping down her spine despite the rug across her knees and the hot brick at her feet. The fog felt as though it were inside her, crawling underneath her skin and wrapping around her internal organs. Moments later a second chill sped down her spine. She twitched the rug on her lap and inched forward in her seat, trying to peer out the misted glass window once again.

Outside, the eerie half-light of early morning mingled with the eddies and swirls of fog. She could just barely make out the figures of three men some distance from the coach. They were standing close together, their stances indicating varying degrees of tension. Hamilton, however, or so Olivia guessed by the man's general build, appeared relaxed and unconcerned. He was bearing most of his weight on one foot, his hand on his hip and his head cocked to the same side. He must be listening to what one of the other fellows had to say, she decided.

She moved her head a little to look in the other direction. But still there was nothing. The road leading away from where the coach had come from some fifteen minutes earlier was as yet deserted. With a dissatisfied sigh, Olivia scooted back in her seat and leaned her head against the squabs. Wearily she closed her eyes.

Her mind cast back to a few hours ago, the images replaying in her head. Alex was so sweet, so dear. But, as she had discovered last night, she loved Traverston, not the earl. Her sigh was heartfelt.

When the coach pulled up to the entrance of the Markstons' town home twenty minutes after they had left the theater, the Earl of Monquefort practically sprang out of the door. His tightly controlled anger was visible with every movement he made. Seconds later, he turned in one quick whipcord movement and helped Olivia alight.

The lamplight spilling onto the sidewalk in front of the house turned everything in its vicinity golden and soft.

Olivia emerged into this light, her beauty enhanced by the soft aura of the lamp's glow. In a single second, all of Monquefort's anger vanished to be replaced with stronger, more disturbing emotions of a different nature.

Olivia led the way up the stairs and into the house. The earl helped her to remove her wrap, his assistance much sweeter and gentler than it had been in the opera house. She smiled at him, only a remnant of her sadness visible to him.

"Won't you stay for a minute, Alex?" she asked. Her voice was persuasive and compelling, but without a hint of seduction. It was more wistful than anything else. "I'm sure I can get Shipley to bring us some tea."

"Thank you, my lady," he replied with a hint of his old smile, "but I think I'd prefer something a bit stronger tonight."

Olivia's eyes glowed at the reproof. "Of course. How silly of me. Claret?" She smiled as he nodded. Then she began to lead the way to one of the house's smaller salons.

The blue salon at the end of the hallway on the main floor was a tastefully decorated room. The textured wallpaper of blue fleurs-de-lis on a white background gave the room character, while the low pile rug on the floor added comfort and warmth. Gracefully Olivia indicated one of the French settees while she arranged for refreshments.

The earl's eyebrows quirked together with amusement as Olivia sat down across the low table from him. He had expected her to sit next to him on the settee. "Don't you trust your old Uncle Alex, Olivia?" he asked with a flirtatious grin. But he couldn't quite keep the pain out of his eyes.

Olivia's first impulse was to dodge his tease as she had always done, but now was the time for honesty, not playfulness. Instead she locked her gaze with his. "Did I ever tell you about the time I first saw my husband, Alex?" She watched the amusement leave his face and something inscrutable take its place. He shook his head slowly. "I was ten years old," she continued. "He came into my father's house and had a private conversation with him." She shifted in her seat, looking for the right words to express the way she felt. After a moment she went on. "I only had two brief glimpses of John, but in my mind he was the most handsome man I had ever seen. I dubbed him my pirate." She smiled fondly at the memory.

"The same day he visited my father, I saw him for the second time at Norwood Park. The house was a mess back then, although I barely remember the details. I only had eyes for John. He was so kind to me, Alex, so good. It was the last time I remembered any man being so nice to me."

She stared the earl in the eyes, trying to make him understand. "My father died two years later, but before he passed away, he made my life a living hell." She moved one hand in a frustrated gesture as she clarified, "It's not that he meant to, you see...he just...did."

"I think I understand, Olivia," interrupted the earl. "You don't have to continue."

"Yes, I do," she replied firmly. "You don't understand at all.

"You see, during that time, when my father was still alive, I dreamed a lot. I dreamed of being rescued by my pirate...by John." Her eyes were alive with new understanding. "He's all I've ever allowed myself to think about, to hope for, for the last eight years of my life. In my mind I've killed every other hope, but I can't rid myself of this one." Her eyes turned suddenly sad and remorseful. "You can't compete with that, Alex."

"I've asked you this before, Olivia, but you love him, don't you?"

She stared at him silently for a minute, trying to read his expression. It was wistful, sad, angry and hopeful, all at once. She got up from her seat and moved to one side of the room. Her hands sought a means of expressing herself as she finally replied, "It's more than just love. It's...I don't know. Need sounds too depraved, but that's almost what it is." She turned to face him again, her face beseeching. "I need John. He is my husband. It may be foolish to feel the way I do, but I can't help it. This...feeling, this whatever it is, hangs between us, all of the time. I sense it every time we are together. It's physical, psychological, mental." She dropped her hands helplessly. "I can't explain it."

Monquefort got up and came over to stand next to her. Gently he tucked behind her ear a stray strand of her hair that had fallen forward. "Even with the way he hurts you, you love him." It wasn't a question.

She looked up at him, his body close to hers but not arousing her in any way. "He doesn't mean to," she answered softly. "I'm sure of it."

Monquefort dropped his hand quickly. She sensed his frustration as he strode a few steps away from her. With his back still to her, he said, "I guess I should be leaving then."

She came up to him and put her hand on his back. Her touch was light, but she felt the shiver in him that it caused. "Please don't be angry," she begged.

Monquefort hesitated, but then turned to face her. He smiled, but it was one without his usual charm. "I could never be angry at you, Olivia." He bent and kissed her gently on her cheek. "Good night, my angel," he said quietly, and turned to leave the room.

When he had gone, Olivia dropped to the settee

Monquefort had vacated and sat staring sightlessly at the far wall. This wasn't supposed to happen, she thought. She shouldn't have fallen in love with Traverston, and Alex shouldn't have fallen in love with her. Why did things always turn out to be so complicated?

Olivia had no idea how much time had passed before a tentative knock on the door frame alerted her to the butler's presence. He came forward uncertainly saying, "I beg your pardon, my lady, but there is a gentleman here who urgently requests a word with you."

Olivia glanced up at the clock, wondering who could possibly be calling at this late hour. She hesitated a moment before the servant interjected, "He says it's an emergency."

Quickly she got up from her seat and followed the butler to one of the front parlors. She was surprised to find David Hamilton seated just inside the doorway. He jumped to his feet when he spied her and quickly crossed to her side.

"Oh, my dear Olivia," he began as he took one of her hands in his own. "How I hate to be the one to tell you this."

Bewildered, Olivia withdrew her hand from his. "Tell me what, Mr. Hamilton?" she asked with a frown between her eyes. She had not missed his familiar use of her given name, and she had not forgotten what had transpired between them the last time she had seen her brother-in-law.

"Pray, forgive me," he begged contritely. "I have been inappropriately familiar. It must be the shock." Olivia's frown deepened as he indicated one of the chairs close by. "Won't you sit down, Lady Traverston?"

Gingerly Olivia sat where he had indicated, her eyes never leaving his face. "It's your husband," he said when they were both finally seated. "I'm afraid there has been an accident."

"What do you mean? What kind of accident?"

Hamilton dropped his gaze to his lap, apparently embarrassed. "It's my fault I'm afraid. I'm the one who provoked her."

"What...what..." Olivia shook her head as if to clear the thoughts crowding her mind. "I beg you, start at the beginning, Mr. Hamilton," she said in a stronger voice.

"I apologize again, my dear." He took a deep breath. "Lady Chisolm, with whom you are familiar, developed a...uh, *tendre* for your husband, Lady Traverston, before the two of you were married. After your marriage was announced in the *Gazette*, Beatrice went sort of berserk. She vowed her revenge against the marquis, and she declared she would stop at nothing to see him dead." He paused and took another deep breath. He held it a few seconds, then expelled it slowly before continuing. "Tonight, when Traverston tried to leave the opera and go after you, Beatrice had him jumped. Two hired thugs accosted him in an alley. He is lying at my house, mortally wounded, I'm afraid."

For a moment, Olivia couldn't breathe. The air in her lungs seemed to evaporate and leave her with nothing to fill her aching chest. When she felt her heart begin to pound painfully again, she found enough strength to say incredulously, "It can't be true."

Hamilton heard her and instantly contradicted, "Yes. Yes, I'm so sorry, but it is." He watched the blood drain from her face and continued ruthlessly, "Lady Traverston, I fear there isn't much time. If you wish to see him before it is too late—"

"Yes!" Olivia jumped on the word. She came quickly to her feet. "God, yes. Is your carriage out front?"

Hamilton took her elbow and began ushering her from

the house. She was almost out the door before he asked quietly, "Shouldn't you take a cloak, Lady Traverston?"

Olivia turned in his grasp, her look somewhat befuddled. "Yes, of course," she responded absently. It was a few more minutes until they exited the house once again.

Hamilton's coach had gone several miles before Olivia had pulled enough out of her reverie to notice the distance they had traveled. When she did, she turned startled eyes on her husband's brother and asked, "Don't you live in Mayfair, too, Mr. Hamilton?"

He looked at her with unconcealed amusement. "As a matter of fact, I do."

With confusion, Olivia pulled back the curtain from the coach's window and surveyed the dimly lit part of town through which they were traveling. She dropped the curtain after watching the scenery for several seconds. She turned her face back to the carriage's only other occupant. "We are not in Mayfair now, Mr. Hamilton." Her voice was cold.

He laughed quietly, as if at some private joke. His hair became a trifle disarrayed as he shook his head several times. "No, we are not."

She waited. When no further information seemed to be forthcoming, she raised one eyebrow. In her haughtiest manner she asked, "And just where, may I inquire, are you taking me?"

Hamilton's smirk repulsed Olivia. His voice was oily as he responded, "To an inn not very far from here."

"Mr. Hamilton, are you going to explain yourself, or do I have to lower my dignity and ask you a series of questions in order to get any kind of meaningful answer from you?"

His eyes glittered in the dim light of the carriage. "I don't know. Maybe you will. Maybe a lot of things might happen. I haven't decided yet."

Resolutely she turned her face from him and clamped her lips together. To the outside, she appeared supremely indifferent to their destination. On the inside, though, she was seething.

Petulantly Hamilton relented with surprising quickness. "You've already guessed by now, I'm sure, that your husband is fine. Although it's my hope he won't stay that way for long."

She snapped her head back toward him. "What do you mean?"

He smiled humorlessly. "In a short while, my brother is graciously going to agree to meet me on the dueling field. At that time, I intend to make sure he never leaves the site of our little meeting."

She pierced him with her gaze. "You're going to kill him." Her voice was flat.

"Oh, I don't know about that," he replied with false cheerfulness. "I may just permanently maim him. That would be nearly as good as killing him. We'll just have to see."

"What do you want with me?" Her voice was sharp.

"You, my dear lady," he said, devouring her with his eyes, "are bait. Ah," he said as the coach came to a halt, "we have arrived."

After his return from challenging her husband, Olivia spent the next three hours in Hamilton's company, listening to him gloat about how clever he had been in finally trapping his brother. He ate an excessive amount of food at the inn, stuffing himself with everything from smoked salmon to duck pâté. He didn't drink any great quantity of wine, though, Olivia noticed. She had even taken a glass or two herself over the protests of her churning stomach, in the hopes he would be fooled into taking one glass too many. It was to no effect, however. Hamilton had his objective too clear in his sights to forget himself enough to drink heavily.

The thrum of horses' hooves broke into Olivia's thoughts and she quickly sat up and looked out the window again. Out of the corner of the glass she spied a coach-and-four rapidly approaching her own vehicle. Not a second after the coach came to a stop, Traverston jumped out the door and landed on the grassy earth. He walked with long, hurried strides toward the coach where Olivia sat, but as she fumbled with the handle to the door, she saw Hamilton intercept him.

She paused, her fingers frozen to the pane. She couldn't see Hamilton's face, but she could see her husband's. Their words were lost to her through the padded walls of the coach, but Traverston's face was implacable. After a minute, Hamilton stepped aside and let the marquis continue on to her coach.

Olivia was right next to the door as her husband flung it open, his worried countenance only a few feet away from her. He didn't hesitate as he reached in the vehicle to take her in his arms. She came willingly and flung herself against him. His hand moved to her hair, burrowing into her elegant coiffure and damaging it irreparably. But she didn't care. She turned her face into his neck, breathing in his masculine smell.

A moment passed before he pulled back, his eyes dark pools of concern. "Are you all right?" he asked softly.

She nodded and smiled tentatively, too choked to speak. He drank in the sight of her a few more seconds, then reached out with one hand to cup her face gently. His eyes caressed her, and her smile grew stronger in response.

"I want you to stay here, Olivia," he said, still holding her face. He interrupted her protest with stern words,

"Promise me. Promise me you'll stay in this coach no matter what happens."

She looked into his eyes, seeing the hard intractableness of his command written there. Hesitantly she nodded, then with more feeling as his eyes penetrated deeper into her skull. Finally he released her, moving back to cast one more long look her way. Then he closed the door.

Olivia immediately scooted back to the window and watched him stride away, his legs carrying him to the center of the field where six other men stood waiting. The fog had cleared a little, and the morning light was getting brighter by the minute. Soon she could make out the details fairly well.

A short discussion took place, then the men broke up into little groups. One of the men who had arrived with Hamilton walked to his curricle, pausing there to retrieve a large box. When he returned to the field, he approached Hamilton and Traverston, who were standing with two of their seconds. The man opened the box. The brothers looked into it. Traverston reached in first and drew out a pistol. A moment later, Hamilton took out another one. The man with the box then retreated to his carriage again.

Striding together, Traverston and Hamilton walked to a spot previously picked out by one of the seconds. They faced each other grimly, then turned in opposite directions. As the count started, Olivia watched her husband and his brother move off in opposite directions with rhythmic synchronization.

Time seemed to slow down for Olivia as she watched Traverston and Hamilton pace away from each other. The count was a faint sound in her ears, reaching her as if from some great distance. The swirling fog cut off from her sight everything past the dueling field, giving the whole spectacle the quality of a dream.

And then, Hamilton turned. Even as Olivia opened her mouth to scream a warning, she saw Traverston turn a split second later than his brother. Hamilton lowered his pistol. A shot split the morning air with deafening loudness. Smoke billowed from the end of his gun. Olivia watched as her husband staggered backward, the bullet taking him in the shoulder.

A determined look crossed Traverston's face. He lowered the muzzle of his pistol. A second shot rang out. A heartbeat later, Traverston and Hamilton fell simultaneously to the ground.

Chapter Eighteen

Olivia had opened the door to the carriage and jumped
down to the ground before Hamilton's coachman could
move from his seat. She stumbled initially in her haste,
going down on one knee, but she was back up again and
running almost before she was aware of her fall. Within
a matter of seconds, she was kneeling on the ground beside Traverston. The sight of the growing patch of red
just below his left shoulder caused her to gasp in shock.
But Olivia was not a female to lose her head in a crisis.
Quickly she bent over and ripped a section of her petticoat, then turned back to place the elegantly embroidered
material firmly against his chest. Tears started in her eyes
as Traverston stirred beneath her hand, his growing pain
evident.

She felt gentle hands on her shoulders. They started to
try to pull her away, but Olivia fought back violently.
She would have kept on struggling, but a familiar voice
in her ear won through to her brain.

"For God's sake, Olivia!" entreated the desperate
voice of the earl. "Let the doctor look at him!"

She looked up at Monquefort and saw him through the

haze of her tears. But it was still several seconds before she had enough composure to comply with his command.

As Olivia moved back a couple of feet, one of the men she had seen earlier in Traverston's company bent over to examine him. The doctor was a middle-aged man. His appearance was not so much of a physician as a well-to-do tradesman. Still he probed the wound with experienced hands, and Olivia was somewhat reassured that he knew what he was doing.

The doctor was several minutes in looking at Traverston's wound. Olivia unashamedly held her ground as the surgeon removed the marquis's cravat and unbuttoned his shirt. Unable to stand the suspense any longer, Monquefort finally broke the continued silence. "Is he going to be all right?"

Without looking up, the doctor replied, "I believe so. The bullet has passed through the meat beneath the collarbone. I don't think it hit bone, but I'm not completely sure." Finally he looked up at the small group huddled around the patient. "We'll have to get him up off this wet ground as soon as possible. There's a chance his wound may incur infection."

The earl immediately turned to Traverston's other second. After exchanging a meaningful look, the earl and Seinheart hoisted him up off the ground as gently as they could. As they carried the inert marquis toward the Markstons' coach, Olivia was left alone with the doctor. He studied her briefly before asking bluntly, "You're Lady Traverston?"

"Yes, I am," she replied. She faced him defiantly, daring him to tell her what to expect.

"Your ladyship is going to have her hands full in the next couple of days," he began without preamble. "I suggest you get a full-time nurse to help you take care of him."

"No." She dismissed the suggestion with a chopping motion of her hand. "I'll do it myself."

His eyes narrowed. "Have you ever taken care of a wounded man before?" he asked in hard accents.

She hesitated momentarily. "No..."

"It's not an easy task, and hardly one for a well-bred young lady like yourself. You'll have to clean his wound and rebandage it frequently. You'll have to feed him, clean him and take care of his more personal functions." His look was skeptical. "This isn't a task for the faint-hearted. You'd do better leaving it to someone more qualified."

Her eyes gleamed with the light of determination. "I'll take your words under advisement."

He snorted. "Yes, I can see that you will." He began moving away toward the other body still lying prostrate on the ground. Hamilton's seconds were standing uncertainly next to his body. "I'll come round your house as soon as I see to Mr. Hamilton's family's needs."

Olivia's eyes flew to Traverston's half brother. Even from this distance she could see his wide-open, blankly staring eyes. "Isn't he going to be all right?" she called out, uncertain for the first time since the grim outcome of the duel.

The doctor was gruff as he turned back around to face her. "You shouldn't be seeing this, my lady. Go home and take care of your husband now." He waited until Olivia looked one last time at the still form on the ground. He resumed his course when she had picked up her skirts and begun running to her husband's carriage.

For Olivia, the ride home stretched into eternity. Every time the carriage hit a bump in the road, Traverston stirred restlessly or cried out in pain. Olivia winced with him as she held his head in her lap. He was unconscious, she was sure. But his pain was obviously very great.

The Markstons' arrival at the London town house threw their well-established home into chaos. Servants flew in every direction in response to Olivia's commands as Monquefort and Seinheart carried the marquis up the stairs to the master suite. When Olivia was finally satisfied that all of her orders for Traverston's care and comfort were being carried out, she climbed the stairs to his room herself, her feet dragging wearily on the carpeted steps. She hesitated in front of the closed door to his bedroom, once again unsure of herself. Then she resolutely threw back her shoulders and tilted her chin up a fraction of an inch. She brusquely turned the handle and went in.

At the far end of the room, Monquefort stood with Traverston's valet. They were talking quietly and casting occasional worried glances toward the bed. Seinheart stood some distance away on the opposite side of the room. His complexion was ghostly white, and he looked up with relief upon Olivia's entrance. His long, lanky stride took him quickly across the room to her side before she could move. He made his apologies to her in the soft, sympathetic tones of a person uncomfortable in a sickroom. But after the first few words, it became clear to him that she was not listening to a word he said. Even as he took his awkward leave of her, Olivia's eyes were still fixed on the pale facial features of her husband lying prostrate on the bed.

Slowly she advanced into the room. Monquefort and Traverston's valet must have undressed him while she had been downstairs, for he was now lying in a nightshirt with the sheet pulled up under his arms. She reached the bed, her mind mesmerized by the sight of him lying so helpless. Tentatively she put out one hand to touch his brow. Sweat stood out visibly on his skin. As her cool hand touched his heated forehead, all of her uncertainties left her, and she knew what she had to do. She picked up a cloth she had noticed on the table next to his bed and gently wiped his face.

His eyelids fluttered. She felt rather than saw Monquefort move in to stand beside her. Suddenly Traverston's eyes were open. His gray irises were unnaturally bright as they focused on the still form of his wife. He opened his mouth once, then closed it again. He tried again. His tongue darted out and he licked his lips, seeking some moisture to make his words understood. Finally he whispered his message almost inaudibly.

"Stay away from me."

Olivia stood still with shock, her brain frozen numb as she watched Traverston close his eyes again. The earl recognized her paralysis and moved forward instinctively to comfort her. He leaned over and whispered in her ear, "He's delirious, Olivia. He doesn't know what he is saying."

Quickly Olivia regained her composure. She relaxed her stance and tried to appear unconcerned. "No, of course. You're right," she said quietly. She gave him a tentative smile and turned to tidy up the medical supplies lying near the side of the bed.

But she didn't really believe the earl. Traverston had been fully aware of what he had said. She was certain of it. She was just not completely sure why.

At that moment, the doctor walked into the room, sparing Olivia from having to make any further protestations to her friend. She gave in to the physician's request to leave the room with good grace, gliding to the door and closing it behind her quietly. Once outside, she closed her eyes and took a deep breath, acknowledging the pain

Traverston's words had caused her. He didn't want her. Not now. Not ever.

Olivia slammed her defensive wall back into place when she heard the door open behind her. The earl had followed her out of the bedroom, his services having also been dismissed by the doctor. Without a word, he took Olivia's hand in his own and led her to the sitting room adjoining the master bedroom. He escorted her to a sofa, then walked to the bellpull. The summons was answered promptly by one of the younger housemaids. In short, economical terms, he ordered brandy. When it arrived, he moved over to where Olivia sat and thrust the glass into her hand. "Here, drink this," he commanded.

Olivia was about to protest when she caught the implacable look in his eyes. Obediently she took the glass from him and took a large sip, grimacing as the fiery liquid burned its way down her throat. "Another," he ordered in an unequivocal tone. She sipped at the drink again. The liquor slid down her throat, its bite not nearly as bad as the first time.

Once he was satisfied she had imbibed enough of the alcohol, the earl dropped down onto the sofa beside her. "I'm sorry, Olivia," he began in more pliable tones, "but you needed that. You looked quite done in."

She lifted the corners of her mouth into a tiny smile, but the effect on him was less than she had intended. "It's quite all right, you know," he continued. "You've had a shock. I actually think you've held up rather famously considering what you've been through in the last twenty-four hours."

Olivia felt unequal to this fulsome praise, so she said nothing at all. Instead she looked down at the glass in her hand, momentarily forgetting how it had gotten there.

Monquefort became disconcerted at her continued silence. He, too, looked down at the brandy glass she was holding. Absentmindedly, he plucked it from her hand. He swirled it a few times before tossing the contents down his throat. Then he placed the glass on the table in front of him before he turned to his companion.

"Look," he began uneasily, "if it's about what Traverston said, I wouldn't give it another thought."

Olivia turned angry eyes on him. "Don't patronize me, Alex," she said with uncharacteristic heat. "I didn't expect that from you."

"Sorry," he said, his expression indicating how taken aback he was with her reaction. "I was only trying to help."

Immediately Olivia became contrite. Her look softened as she replied, "I know you were." She patted his hand reassuringly. "I'm just rather tense right now. It's the shock, just as you said."

They were both quiet a while longer. Monquefort fidgeted in his seat, debating on whether or not he should interfere. Normally he didn't get involved in the romantic details of other people's lives, but these weren't just other people. This was Olivia's life…and Traverston's, of course.

"I know you don't want to hear it from me, Olivia, but I don't think you should wear the willow for him."

She looked up from her study of her clasped hands, her eyes bonding with the earl's. Their pained expression was at odds with her words. "I don't know what you mean."

"Yes, you do," he responded angrily. "Look at the way you're sitting here, mourning for him. You're right, I shouldn't have patronized you earlier. I should have just come out with the truth. Traverston does not want you, all right? You heard him. I heard him."

He lowered his voice and took one of her hands in his own. "But I want you," he entreated, "with all of my heart. I'll never forget about you, or ignore you, and I'll never leave you for another woman. If you were mine, you would be the center of my life. I'd never hurt you in any way.

"You need someone to protect you, to look out for you. You need someone to shield you from the world and make everything all right again. I can do that. I can be that person for you." He pulled one hand from hers to gently place it on her face. "Won't you let me do that for you, *chérie?*"

Olivia held his gaze a moment longer before she sighed and broke the contact. Removing her hand from his grasp, she got up slowly from her seat and walked away two steps. So much had happened in the past few days. Her mind was a whirl. How could she explain to him what she felt? How could she make him understand?

Her back still to him, she began speaking quietly, "You say I need someone to shield me from the world, Alex, but I say I need someone to make me live again." She turned toward him, her face alive with her desire to make him understand. "This life I've been leading has not *been* a life. For eight years I've wandered through an existence, ignoring everything the world has to offer me. All of the joys, all of the sorrows…everything has passed right by me.

"I did this to myself, Alex. I withdrew from the world. I thought that if I went my own way, and let no one and nothing affect me, I could get through this world without pain. I could somehow manage to live my life like a dream—the substance all vague and shadowy, insubstantial and ultimately harmless.

"It wasn't a conscious choice. I think it's something I did out of self-defense when my father was still alive. People have always seemed as though they were out to hurt me. So I thought if I withdrew from them, they couldn't get to me. And it worked. Until I met John.''

She came back over and sat down next to the earl. Her body turned at an angle toward his so that their knees touched. ''John saw right through me. He knew what I was doing even before I did, and he made it his goal to shake me from my complacency. I just don't think he meant to care for me in the process.

''Alex, I can't convince you that John and I are right for each other. I think I know what is going on in his mind, but I'm not completely sure. Maybe this terrible accident, as horrible as it seems now, is what we both need. He can't run away from me right now, and I can't leave him.''

The earl moved his legs away and his eyes sought the brandy glass again. He picked up the glass and palmed it, toying with the bowl between his hands. Still looking away from her, he sighed. ''I suppose you're right.'' Then his eyes came back to her face. ''But you will think about my offer, won't you? If this thing with Traverston doesn't work out as you expect?''

The corners of her mouth drooped a little. ''I'll think about it, Alex, but I can't promise you anything.''

He got up and sighed heavily. ''Then that will have to do for now.'' He looked around the room as if searching for something he had forgotten, his gaze distracted. But he was unable to find anything else he could seize on as an excuse for staying. Finally he asked, ''Is there anything I can do for you before I leave? Anything I can get you?''

''No, the servants will see to everything,'' she replied. She remained seated as he made for the door. He looked back at her before leaving. ''I'll be in touch. Let me know how he is doing.''

She nodded. He cast one more longing look in her direction before opening the door and taking his leave.

Olivia was alone no more than a minute before the doctor knocked briefly on the connecting door and entered. "I hope I'm not disturbing you, my lady, but Lord Monquefort told me where I might find your ladyship," he apologized. When she waved away the explanation, he continued. "I've had a chance to examine your husband more thoroughly, and I'm afraid the bullet has nicked the bone."

Olivia stood up in alarm. "What does that mean?"

"It means the healing process will not be as simple as I had hoped. There is a good chance he will catch a fever." He then proceeded to reiterate at great length all of the reasons she should hire a full-time nurse.

Finally Olivia cut him off. "I appreciate your concerns, Doctor, but I am sure I can manage. Now if you have some practical medical advice you'd like to impart to me...?" She let her words trail off meaningfully.

A half hour later, the physician took his leave of the Markstons' Mayfair mansion. He gave Olivia a packet of herbs to mix with Traverston's tea, as well as some laudanum to ease his pain. Before he went, he also managed to confirm the fact of Hamilton's death to her, assuring her that no one could possibly doubt that Traverston had killed his cousin out of self-defense. Uneasy but somewhat reassured, Olivia saw the doctor off.

By the time she made her way back into Traverston's room, it was well past noon. Making her footsteps as quiet as possible, Olivia crossed to the bed. She relieved the valet who had been keeping watch on her husband and began to see to his needs herself.

Near the dinner hour, a light scratch on the bedroom door alerted Olivia to a visitor. She was getting up from her chair when to her surprise, Mrs. Nottingham, Lord Traverston's mother, walked through the door.

Quickly Olivia hurried to her side. In hushed tones Felicity said, "I've just heard. Is he all right?"

"We won't know for sure for some time. I think he's beginning to take a fever."

Traverston's mother moved over to the bed, still holding tightly to her daughter-in-law's hand. She studied her son's pale face in the darkened room. After a while, she led Olivia back to the door, hovering there as she started quizzing the younger woman. She was careful to keep her voice to a whisper. "What happened?" she asked, her gray eyes intense with concern.

Briefly Olivia related the story of the duel to the older woman. As she completed her tale with a description of Traverston's wounds and the possibility for infection, the dowager marchioness nodded grimly. "We will know shortly how he shall fare." She gripped her daughter-in-law's hand tightly. "If you are going to nurse him yourself, my child, you're going to need help."

Olivia saw the determination in Felicity's face. She hesitated only a second before she nodded. Felicity broke into the first smile Olivia had ever seen on her face. "We'll do it together, my girl," she said, squeezing her hand for emphasis. "He may not like it, but I don't think he has a choice."

Then a small frown marred Olivia's forehead as a thought occurred to her. "But how comes it that you are here, Felicity?" she asked. "I thought you had determined to stay at Norwood Park."

Her mother-in-law nodded, her smile fading. "I can't explain it. I was there, sitting in the house after you left, and suddenly I just felt that I had to be here somehow. Even if it meant being thrown out of the house again."

She glanced over at the bed, a frown adding more wrinkles to her face than usual. "It appears I was right."

In silence, both women studied the still figure on the bed, each keeping her own disturbing thoughts to herself.

That evening, Traverston did come down with a fever. Olivia sat up with him during the night, taking pains to keep a cool wet rag on his forehead at all times. She struggled to hold his head up and make him drink the herbal tea prescribed by the doctor. Once she tried to feed him broth, but he wouldn't eat it. She bathed his body numerous times in an attempt to keep his body temperature down and changed his bandages twice. When she wasn't doing any of these chores, the valet came in periodically to help her change the sweat-dampened sheets and take care of his more personal bodily functions. During the whole process, she watched him turn restlessly and endeavored to keep him from harming his shoulder. He never became conscious during the entire night.

At dawn the next morning, Felicity came in to take over the watch. She sent an exhausted Olivia to her bed and promised to wake her if there were any new developments. When Olivia woke some five hours later, there were none.

The routine Olivia and her mother-in-law established in taking care of Traverston continued without pause for two full days. Monquefort stopped in twice to see how his friend was doing, but Olivia had the servants send him away with word of no change.

On the morning of the third day the cycle broke. As Felicity entered the sickroom to take her turn nursing the marquis, Olivia glanced up from his bedside, her face wreathed in smiles. "His fever has broken," she announced in soft but triumphant tones.

Her mother-in-law came and put a hand on her son's cool forehead. She turned to share in the younger woman's smile. "We've done it," she said quietly, not quite able to keep the pride out of her voice.

The doctor's early-morning visit to the Markstons confirmed what the two women had already suspected. Traverston was well on his way to recovery. The fever had left his body, and the physician explained that his lordship would probably sleep soundly the better part of the day.

When the doctor had left, Felicity took one look at Olivia's exhausted face and urged her to take to her bed. When Olivia protested that Traverston might wake up, Felicity cajoled, "I'll wake you the moment he does, dear. I promise."

Reluctantly Olivia obeyed her mother-in-law. She wanted to stay, but she was well and truly exhausted. She had never really let herself completely go to sleep since Traverston's illness. She had always been afraid that she would be asleep when he needed her most. Now that the worst part of his illness was over, however, she gratefully climbed into her bed and fell almost immediately into a deep slumber.

Around ten o'clock that night, Traverston opened his eyes. He looked around his bedroom uncertainly, his eyes alighting on the shaded lamp by his bedside. After a moment they moved on, probing the darkness around his bed. They passed by the figure in the chair, moved on to the curtained windows, then came zeroing back in on the figure. He had not been mistaken. His mother sat five feet away from his bed, her slight form leaning comfortably against the padded upholstery of an armchair. She was studying him with curiosity.

"What..." he croaked, only to realize his throat was parched with thirst.

With unhurried movements, Felicity got up from her chair and went to get the glass of water by his bed. She held his head up and assisted him in taking a long drink. Complacently she set the glass down when he was done, and then moved to settle back down in her chair.

"What are you doing here?" he finally asked, his voice sounding stronger than before.

Her eyes glittered with amusement. "I'm helping to nurse you back to health."

His black brows drew together in consternation and he tried to lift himself higher in his bed. Immediately he desisted, the movement having caused pain to shoot through his shoulder. "You!" he murmured in amazement, then began trying to sit up again, more gingerly this time.

There was a definite sparkle in her eyes. "Your wife and I, yes."

"Damn!" exclaimed the marquis, half from the knowledge that Olivia had been nursing him and half from the pain.

"I wouldn't try sitting if I were you," cautioned his mother dryly. "You've only just begun to heal."

He stopped his movements and glared at the woman sitting across from him. "If you'd care to give me a hand, perhaps this wouldn't be such a painful exercise."

Resignedly Felicity got out of her chair. She pushed several pillows behind the marquis's back as she said, "You always were a stubborn boy." She helped him to lift himself a little higher on the bed, noticing, as she did, the sweat break out on his forehead from the effort.

"I'm surprised you remember, ma'am," he replied spitefully. "It was such a brief period in history for you."

"Oh, I remember all right," she responded, unperturbed. She settled herself comfortably in her chair once again.

He glared heatedly away from her. "Isn't there anyone

else you can bother right now, or am I the only one sick enough to be caught in your talons?''

She smiled humorlessly. "You can't fool me, you know," she said in response. "I know what you are trying to do."

He shot a malevolent look at her. "And what, pray tell, am I trying to do?" he asked sarcastically.

Again she failed to be ruffled by his anger. "You're trying to pick a fight with me."

"And why would I want to do that?"

"Because you're angry with me, as you have every right to be. But I won't fight with you, John."

He tore his gaze away from her again, focusing his eyes on the pool of light cast by the oil lamp on his bedside table.

"I am going to take advantage of this opportunity, however."

His eyes riveted on her again. "What do you mean?" he asked sharply.

"I mean, my dear boy," she said, leaning forward onto her lap, "I'm going to take advantage of your helplessness to tell you what you wouldn't listen to when I came to Norwood Park."

"You don't have anything to say that I care to hear," he replied sulkily.

"Well then, by all means, glare at the lamp! I don't care!" Her voice took on an unnaturally hard edge as she said, "But at least I know I have done my duty by informing you of your true parentage." She sat back in her chair and waited for her words to take effect.

Slowly Traverston's lips clamped together with anger. Then, flatly he inquired, "Are you trying to tell me I'm not your son?"

She laughed, the full-throated sound out of keeping in

the sickroom. His eyes turned dark as he growled, "I hardly think the question a source of amusement!"

She bit down her laughter, bringing a hand to her chest with the effort. "I'm sorry," she choked as she wiped a tear from her eye. "You may wish I was not your mother, but I'm afraid that isn't it. I definitely was the one who bore you."

His eyes narrowed. "Then what, woman? What are you trying to say?"

"I'm telling you that you are not the fourth Marquis of Traverston," she replied soberly.

Stunned, the marquis sank back into his pillows. It was a moment before he found his voice. "Then who is my father?"

"Your father was Solomon Nottingham, my second husband."

"Was?"

She nodded sadly. "He's dead now, God rest his soul."

Abruptly Traverston's face changed, his lines turning hard with anger. "Very clever, ma'am," he said angrily. "But it won't work."

Felicity frowned, genuinely confused. "What do you mean?"

"I mean," he said angrily, "that your attempt to take advantage of my illness to confuse me and regain entrance into my life won't work!"

Traverston's mother slapped the arm of her chair in outrage. "Of all the pigheaded, obstinate…why on earth would I try and do that? Do you really think I would sink so low as to lie to you…" She stopped, amazed. "But of course you do," she said almost to herself. "You just told me as much." She stared at him as he gloated smugly. Finally she mused aloud, "And to think I actually felt sorry for you. I thought, here he is, believing himself to be the only offspring of an insane man, married to a beautiful, lovely woman he probably feels incapable of loving for fear of what harm he may do to her. When really, he's been thinking of no one but himself all along." She slapped her thigh in self-mockery, shaking her head as she stood up from the chair.

"What do you know of Olivia?" he asked, his tone still vicious, but he was much less sure of himself now.

She turned to look back at him, her glare scathing. "I know she is a sensitive young woman who is wasting her feelings on someone incapable of returning them." She swung her body to face him across the full length of the bed. "Do you know, John? I thought you would have been able to weather your upbringing with the marquis better than you have for the simple reason that you were made of sterner stuff than he. You had better building material—a sound mind. But it appears he has wreaked his revenge on me by turning you into a spoiled, self-centered man. I feel very sorry for Olivia. Very sorry indeed that she has you to look forward to for the rest of her life."

Felicity had almost made it to the door before Traverston found the ability to swallow his pride. "Wait!" he called, his voice coming faintly across the chamber, reminding his mother that he still was not well. She turned and waited for him to continue. "I…apologize," he stated baldly. "I've acted very poorly. I'm…interested in what you have to say." He hesitated. "Won't you come back and tell me a little about my father?" he requested. "Please."

The last word was so soft, Felicity was almost unsure he had said it. Still it was enough for now. She let him hang a little longer, then she came striding back purposefully toward the bed. "Well," she began, "it all started when I was just a slip of a girl…"

* * *

Through the haze of sleep, Olivia heard the sound of curtains being pulled back from her bedroom windows. She turned over in her bed, burying her face into the pillow. Soft footsteps padded across the carpet. The muted sound of clinking dishes drifted over from the far side of the room. The seconds ticked by. Five, then ten. After fifteen seconds, Olivia bolted upright in her bed. The brightness of the room caught her off guard, however, and she sat blinking her eyes for a few moments before she was able to focus them on the intruder.

Just as her eyes adjusted to the light, Felicity walked forward to stand at the end of her bed. Her smile was kind as she asked, "How are you doing this morning, my dear?"

"Felicity!" responded Olivia, still somewhat dazed. She glanced around the room, realizing for the first time it was morning. Hurriedly she started to climb out of bed as she cried, "I must go and see John!"

Traverston's mother moved quickly to forestall the younger woman's rush. "He's fine, Olivia," she responded soothingly. "He's sleeping. If you go in now, you may disturb him."

Olivia paused in the act of throwing back the covers. "Oh." Again she looked vaguely at her surroundings, then back at her mother-in-law. "How long have I been asleep?" she asked with a frown.

"Over twenty-four hours," Felicity answered with a humorous smile. "I knew you were exhausted."

Olivia smiled a little ruefully. "It appears you were right." Then her frown returned as she had a new thought. "Did he wake up?"

Felicity sat down on the bed beside her daughter-in-law. She looked fondly at her. "He did. Around ten o'clock last night."

Olivia was unable to keep the hurt from her eyes as she asked, "Why didn't you wake me?"

"He asked me not to."

"Oh," she replied again.

At Olivia's crestfallen look, Felicity patted her hand. "I'm sure he was only thinking of your health, my dear. I told him how exhausted you were from looking after him."

Olivia nodded, but she didn't meet her mother-in-law's eyes.

Refraining with difficulty from giving her any more encouraging news, Felicity got off the bed and moved toward one of the windows. She made a pretense of looking out before turning around to face the younger woman, a gentle smile hugging her face. "It's a beautiful day, child. Why don't you find some excuse to go outside for an hour or two? Maybe that nice earl will take you for a drive in the park."

"I'd really rather not leave John," she replied slowly.

"Oh, I'm sure a few minutes won't matter. Besides, you've been cooped up in the house for days on end. You've hardly seen any of London since you've been here."

Olivia gave her a humorous smile. "I've lived here for the past eight years of my life, Felicity. I can't imagine that there is anything out there I haven't seen." She looked thoughtful. "But you haven't been here in an age. Why don't you spend a few hours going about town today? After all this rest I've had, I'm sure I can manage alone."

Felicity smiled warmly. "I might just do that." She moved to the bed again. "Now come and eat your breakfast. It's getting cold as we sit here and chat."

Obediently Olivia got up and threw the wrapper at the end of her bed around her nightgown. She moved to the small table where the maid had left her breakfast tray and sat down. Felicity sat across from her as she began to remove the lids from the dishes.

After declining Olivia's offer to share her food, Felicity spoke again. "I had a small talk with John last night," she began. Olivia stopped chewing her toast and looked with concern at her mother-in-law. Felicity smiled and shook her head slightly. "No," she answered in response to the unvoiced question in her eyes, "he did not kick me out, although I thought at first he might. Actually, he said that he would like to go back to Norwood Park as soon as possible, unless you might wish otherwise."

"No," she replied hastily. "Leaving is fine with me." Small wrinkles marred her brow as she asked, "Is he fit to travel?"

"Undoubtedly not, but we shall see what the doctor has to say." She paused before adding meaningfully, "He thought you might want to ask your grandmother to come for a visit."

She stared at Felicity in surprise. "He said that?"

The older woman nodded, her eyes laughing at Olivia's reaction. Olivia thoughtfully chewed her toast. After a moment, Felicity stood up. "Well, I have a few things I would like to take care of this morning. I think I'll leave you to your toilette now."

Olivia got up from the table, dropping the toast back onto her plate as she did so. She hurriedly wiped her hands on a napkin, then moved to accompany her mother-in-law to the door. She paused as she opened the door, looking meaningfully into the aged face that was still somehow full of life and exuberance. "Thank you for everything, Felicity," she said softly. "You've been a tremendous help." She bent forward and kissed her gently on the cheek.

Felicity smiled warmly at her, bringing her hand to

touch the girl's face in a feathery-light caress of affection. But there was a hint of sadness and sympathy in her expression as she replied, ''Sometimes, child, we have to experience the worst in life before we can appreciate the good things.'' She held her hand against the other's cheek for a moment longer, then dropped it and turned to go through the door.

Chapter Nineteen

The warm gentle breeze caressed Olivia's skin as she made her way through the meadow, her long skirts trailing over the tall grass. A butterfly landed briefly on her short-brimmed hat before merrily taking flight again, its colorful body joining the riotous clash of several fluttering fellows hovering in front of her. Involuntarily a smile broke out on her face as she closed the gap between herself and her husband where he sat beneath a maple tree. His black scowl caused her to chuckle.

As Olivia's laughter reached him, Traverston looked up and met her sparkling eyes with a responding twinkle in his own. Ruefully he looked back down at the chessboard before him and tried to regain his concentration, but gave up with a roll of his eyes as Olivia's laugh rang out again.

"How can I concentrate on my next move if you keep disturbing my peace?" he asked in mock frustration.

"Oh, posh!" she responded playfully. "You're going to be trounced soundly again no matter how much time I give you, so stop pretending otherwise."

Traverston snorted in disgust. "Females!" he said with disparagement, but his eyes were still glowing.

Olivia sat down in the chair opposite him, her smile lingering softly about her mouth as she watched the marquis's brow furrow in concentration. A soft giggle escaped her as he reached out to move his queen, and he glanced up at her in question. She shook her head slowly, then laughed again as a look of determination crossed his face. With more force than was necessary, he slapped down his queen on the board, several squares from its original position. Immediately Olivia picked up her rook and took the marquis's queen.

With impish delight she said, "Checkmate," and proceeded to deposit the queen with her hoard of other captured pieces.

"Argh!" cried Traverston in disgust, and he slapped his thigh with his unslung arm. He tried to look at Olivia with anger and frustration, but he couldn't refrain from appearing amused instead.

As they stared at each other, Olivia's smile slowly began to fade. Traverston's look had turned from amusement to hunger, and she felt her heart thump loudly in her chest. Uncomfortably she broke the eye contact and began replacing the chess pieces on the board.

"Olivia," began the marquis, unwilling to let the moment pass, "I wanted to thank you for spending so much time with me while I have been incapacitated. These past three weeks cannot have been very much fun for you, and I wanted to let you know that I have appreciated your company."

She glanced up unwillingly from the board, her smile tentative. "Nonsense, my lord. I enjoy beating you at chess."

He reached out across the table and took one of her hands in his own good one, stilling their task of resetting the board. He waited until she was looking at him again, her eyes meeting his with the skittishness of a doe. "I mean it," he said quietly, and his voice conveyed an intensity she had never heard from him.

She smiled tentatively again and removed her hand from his. With as much grace as she could muster when she felt as awkward and graceless as a schoolgirl, Olivia got up from her chair and gathered her skirts in one hand. "Perhaps we should go in to lunch now, my lord. In any case, the doctor should be here soon to look at your shoulder."

"Damn doctors," he grumbled darkly, but he got up from the table anyway.

As Olivia made her way through the tall and waving grass, he paused for a minute to let her move a little ahead in order to facilitate his contemplation of her graceful body. He watched her for a long moment, his own steps slower than hers, and she rapidly got ahead of him. Then she halted and cast a playful look at him over her shoulder.

"Coming, my lord?" she called with wicked gleefulness, and as she turned her head to continue on again, he knew with the certainty born of long years of pain, that tonight would bring an end to their suffering.

After lunch, the doctor came to Norwood Park and immediately went up to Traverston's room to examine his patient. Olivia joined Felicity and Lady Raleigh in the blue salon, but quickly decided to leave because the old women's reminiscing made her feel *de trop*. She met with the doctor as she came into the hall.

"Ah, Lady Traverston," began the country physician congenially. "I've just seen your husband."

"And?" she prompted.

"As far as I'm concerned," he replied, placing his hand on her arm, "he can take off the sling today."

She clapped her hands together. "That's wonderful!"

He nodded and began moving toward the door, his hand on her arm guiding her with him. "Yes, your husband is a very fit man, Lady Traverston." He smiled kindly. "And you've done a very fine job nursing him back to health."

Olivia blushed prettily. "You're too kind, Doctor."

He smiled again and removed his hand. "I'll be back to see him next Tuesday, but I expect the visit will be very routine. He's coming along just fine."

Olivia thanked the physician and watched him walk down the front steps and mount his horse. As Olivia turned back into the house, a footman approached her bearing a silver salver. "A note for you, my lady," he intoned solemnly, and waited as she took the proffered letter.

With curiosity, Olivia turned the note over and recognized her husband's seal. She broke the wafer as she climbed the main staircase, her steps slowing as she read the single written line, the script bold and masculine:

Olivia,
    I would be honored if you would dine alone with me in our suite tonight.

                                                    T

On the first landing, just below the ancient tapestry adorning the back wall, she came to a full halt. Why would he wish to dine alone with her, she thought, when they had eaten dinner with his mother and her grandmother every night since he was considered well enough to come downstairs? Even as hope leapt in her breast, she crushed it ruthlessly. She had chosen to stay with him, she reminded herself, but that didn't mean she had to go out of her way to get hurt. She would expect nothing from this intimate dinner with her husband. He would explain his motives to her in his own good time.

At seven o'clock that evening, a light rapping noise on the connecting door to her bedroom sent Olivia's heart racing. She moved her hand up to her throat, uncomfortably aware of how low-cut her new gown was and belatedly wishing she had chosen another dress for the occasion. But a few seconds were all she needed to remind herself that nothing would come of this evening, and in a clear voice she gave permission to enter.

Traverston was ruthlessly handsome in a coat of blue superfine and buff breeches. A feeling of pride crept over Olivia as she realized that her husband could compete with any of the *ton* in good looks and regal bearing tonight. His snowy cravat, absent of any adornment except a single diamond stud buried in the depths of its intricate folds, perfectly complemented his plain yellow waistcoat.

Unable to stop herself, Olivia smiled warmly up at him as he advanced into the room. "Good evening, my lord. No sling, I see."

Traverston's eyes devoured his wife, lingering over her décolletage in the process of taking in her appearance from head to toe. When they came back up to meet with her own, they had a warm, delicious glow in them. "You look stunning, Olivia."

A blush began creeping up Olivia's neck and face, but she was able to hold his gaze as she replied breathlessly, "You are too kind, my lord."

Deciding it was best not to rush things, Traverston turned to indicate the connecting door. "After you," he said, and held his hand out to show that she should precede him.

Olivia gave the marquis a confused look, but she moved obediently toward the door. Once on the other side of the door, Traverston's purpose became clear. In his bedroom was an intimate dinner set for two. Olivia's blush became even deeper as she asked, "Are we going to eat in here?"

Traverston's smile was amused. "Something wrong?"

Again Olivia's hand flew to her chest. She opened her mouth to say something, but one look at her husband's face made her forget her protests. Her pulse racing in her veins, she replied softly, "No."

"Good." He held out a chair for her and helped her into it. Once seated, he uncovered the silver platters and explained, "I thought we could dispense with the servants for tonight, but if there is anything you want that isn't here…"

"No," she interrupted, her haste causing him to lift an eyebrow in amusement. She blushed again. "Everything's fine."

The dinner proceeded smoothly with Traverston exerting every effort to make sure Olivia felt at ease the entire time. They laughed and exchanged stories. He had included champagne with the evening's arrangements, and the wine helped to facilitate the conversation. By the time they had finished eating the strawberries and cream the cook had arranged for dessert, there was a comfortable, relaxed air between them.

Therefore, it seemed natural when Traverston got up from his chair and came around to Olivia's side. He assisted her in getting up, and then escorted her to a sofa in front of the fireplace. The warm weather precluded a fire, but the setting was romantic all the same. Olivia's heart began beating fiercely again as Traverston refused to relinquish her hand once they were seated.

For a long moment, he didn't say anything. He just held her gaze with his own. She wasn't sure if he was simply gathering his thoughts, or was unable to say anything. She knew the latter definitely applied to her. Finally he spoke.

"Olivia, I don't know where to begin. I have so much to say to you I get tongue-tied just thinking about all of it. I hope you'll be patient with me."

She dropped her eyes. "You don't have to say anything at all, my lord."

"John," he replied. "My name is John."

She looked up quickly, her expression puzzled. Then he continued. "You tried to use it once before, and I wouldn't let you. Please do so now."

She tested the word out tentatively. He smiled encouragingly and squeezed her hand. "It sounds remarkably pleasant coming from you." His voice was a deep rumble in his chest. She dropped her eyes again and waited for him to continue.

"Olivia, I want to tell you a story. It's about a young boy who was abandoned by his mother." Here she made eye contact with him again. "Only he didn't know she had abandoned him. He thought she had died. His father told him she was a wicked woman who had tried to run off with another man, and whom God punished by sinking the ship she was traveling in. He filled the boy's head with terrible tales of his mother. Tales that don't bear detailing but that the boy was too young to refute.

"As the boy grew older, he saw that his father was a mean, cruel man. But rather than try and confront his father, he avoided him. He went away to public school. First Eton, then Oxford. The boy had to come back for holidays, of course, but he usually managed to spend those with his grandfather on his mother's side. Still, in all, the boy was rather isolated from human companionship. That's why when the boy met Alice, he fell head over heels in love.

"Alice was a dear, sweet, adorable child. She was the

product of an impoverished daughter of a peeress and a penniless minister. She was trusting and kind. She never had a harsh word for anyone, and she was terribly innocent. The boy, now a young man, met Alice in his last year at Oxford and asked her to marry him. To his delight and surprise, Alice agreed.

"After his graduation, the young man brought Alice to his family's home. The young man's father was against the marriage. He railed violently against the match. But the young man stood his ground.

"Rather than put Alice up in his father's house where she would be subjected to his temper, the young man put her up at a local inn. She was properly chaperoned by a maid, so all was seemingly in the eyes of the community. The young man didn't give her well-being there a second thought.

"That evening, the young man's cousin, at the direction of his father, stole into Alice's room at the inn." Traverston paused. He glanced away from the searching eyes of his wife and fought back the anger and bitterness that rose up in him every time he remembered Alice. But it was only a moment before he turned back to her, his dark eyes inscrutable. "The cousin brutalized and raped her. The next morning, the young man found her a shattered husk of the person she once was. Unable to live with what had happened to her, Alice killed herself the next day."

Olivia stared at Traverston in horror. "I'm so sorry, John. That must have been terrible for you."

The muscles in his jaw flexed and his look grew grimmer. "After she died, my father told me to my face that he had engineered the whole plot. He laughed about it. Told me that David was his true son, the one after his own heart and to whom he would leave his money. He was very proud of his success," he ended bitterly.

She squeezed his hand. "What did you do?"

"I?" He laughed harshly. "I did nothing. That was the worst part of the whole story. My father obligingly died of a heart attack a short time later. He couldn't alter the succession in David's favor, so I inherited everything, what little was left. My brother, as I have thought of him for so long, ran off to the Continent for several years. When he came back, I had already burned the anger out of me. Only desperation was left."

"What do you mean?"

Traverston looked at her a moment and then took her other hand in his own. He held both tightly as he explained. "You have to know, Olivia, that the history of my family is an ugly one. There has been no shortage of madmen in my ancestry."

"Yes," she replied. "Your mother told me."

"Then you must understand that I thought I was one of them." He took away one of his hands and ran it through his hair. "It wasn't just this one act of violence, Olivia. My father enacted repeated atrocities, some of which I only found out about after his death. The only future I could see for myself and my heirs was more of the same. It had to stop.

"I ran through the last of the family fortune in about five years. It went that fast. I had mortgaged the Park twice. My pockets were to let. On top of that, I had one of the worst reputations as a rakehell in the county. Don't get me wrong, it's not something I am proud of, it's just that my chosen method for wiping out the Markston line took me in that direction."

Olivia waited until he was ready to go on, and she prompted softly, "Then what happened?"

"My grandfather, my mother's father, died. He left me a fortune. At the time, I thought the old man had seen to curse me. He hardly knew me at all, but he wrote his will in such a way that I would inherit his fortune only if I got married. If I chose not to find a wife, however, the entire fortune would go to David. With those as my alternatives, you can see I had no choice."

Olivia looked down at her lap. Her voice was barely audible as she replied, "Yes, I can see that."

"No," he said in a different tone, "you don't see at all, Olivia." He put his hand under her chin and tilted her face back toward him. "I was cursed because I wound up with the most beautiful, wonderful wife a man could have. A wife who needed a husband who could love her and tell her all the things she needed to hear to believe in herself again. Because until recently, you hadn't believed in yourself for years, Olivia.

"When I saw you at the Eddingtons' ball—the tall, cool regal queen of society—all I could remember was the lovely, trusting, bright-eyed child you had been, and I wondered what had happened to that sweet innocent girl. That night you looked as though you could take on the entire world and not bat an eyelash in the process.

"But then I saw it. That sweet child was still there, still in you, but she was locked away from the rest of the world where no one but I could see her. You were determined not to let anyone close to you, Olivia, and the pain in your heart spoke to the pain in mine."

He held her face, forcing her to meet his gaze when she would have pulled back. "I've loved you since the moment I saw you gliding across that ballroom, Olivia, and every moment since then has been pure anguish for me. I've wanted nothing more than to hold you in my arms, to give you everything you've ever wanted from life and more, but I could not.

"How could I—a man whose future was fated to be filled with cruel insanity and hate—try to love a woman who needed someone who would always be there for her,

who would always love her? I could not do that to you.
I could not love you only to destroy you with my cruelty,
my family heritage.

"In the beginning, I had meant to avoid you, to keep
my distance. But that became impossible. I was torn with
the desire to be with you and to make you react to my
presence. You were so cool and distant. I couldn't stand
the thought of your being that way with me. I wanted to
make you hate me, despise me, loathe me...for your own
good, but also because I could handle anything but your
damned indifference.

"But don't you see, Olivia? I've failed in all aspects
of my task. Instead of wiping out the Markston line, here
I am with a fortune to make most men green with envy.
And instead of making you hate me, here you are, in my
bedroom, alone with me." He paused, searching her eyes.
"And you don't hate me, do you?"

She shook her head, causing a tear to slip down her
cheek with the motion. Gently he reached forward and
wiped it away. His own eyes were tormented as he asked
softly, "Then why do you cry now, beloved? I've inflicted so much harm on you already, I can't bear to bring
you more pain. Tell me what you want from me and it
is yours." He paused again, the ache in his chest unbearable. "Is it Alex? Are you in love with him?"

"No." The word came bursting from her lips followed
with a sob. Traverston gathered her in his arms, relishing
the soft feel of her body against his even as his heart was
torn with concern. He kissed her hair, rubbing his lips
over the silky strands and caressing her with his hands.
"Then what is it? Tell me," he entreated.

Olivia took a few minutes to compose herself. Traverston's arms were so strong and comforting, she was
reluctant to break away. But his question deserved an
answer. She pulled back enough to look him in the eyes,

her own eyes two pools of suffering. "If you feel this way, if you really love me, then why did you tell me to go away when you were wounded? I feared I had died that day."

Traverston sighed in relief, a gentle smile curling his lips upward as he caressed her cheek. His eyes roved over her entire face, drinking in the wisps of hair that had escaped her coiffure and had fallen across her brow, the tearstained eyes and soft skin of her cheeks. His thumb found the almost invisible dimple in her chin. Then his eyes smiled sweetly into hers. "I didn't know I was not the third Marquis of Traverston's son then. I know it now. I didn't want you falling in love with a wounded man, or even feeling sympathy for one. Not if that man could turn around and hurt you in the end."

"But I knew you were not his son," she replied angrily. "It's what your mother came to Norwood Park to tell you."

He laughed, the sound genuinely joyful. "Yes, well, I can be pigheaded sometimes." Then his eyes grew serious and his voice hesitant. "It doesn't bother you to know I am not the legitimate marquis? There is no heir apparent. Legally, the estate should revert back to the crown."

Olivia gazed lovingly up at him, her eyes full of trust and confidence. "Most men merely inherit their titles, my lord. You have earned yours. I can't think of anyone who deserves it more."

Traverston looked at her a moment longer as if unable to comprehend the good fortune that was finally his after so much time. Then, no longer able to resist the temptation her soft lips posed, his mouth came crashing down on hers.

* * * * *

Heartbreak RANCH

Four generations of independent women...
Four heartwarming, romantic stories of the West...
Four incredible authors...

Fern Michaels
Jill Marie Landis
Dorsey Kelley
Chelley Kitzmiller

Saddle up with Heartbreak Ranch, an outstanding
Western collection that will take you on a whirlwind
trip through four generations and the exciting,
romantic adventures of four strong women who
have inherited the ranch from Bella Duprey,
famed Barbary Coast madam.

Available in March,
wherever Harlequin books are sold.

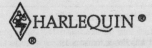

HARLEQUIN ®

HTBK

Free Gift Offer

With a Free Gift proof-of-purchase
from any Harlequin® book, you can receive
a beautiful cubic zirconia pendant.

This stunning marquise-shaped stone is a genuine cubic
zirconia—accented by an 18" gold tone necklace.
(Approximate retail value $19.95)

Send for yours today...
compliments of ◈HARLEQUIN®

To receive your free gift, a cubic zirconia pendant, send us one original proof-of-purchase, photocopies not accepted, from the back of any Harlequin Romance®, Harlequin Presents®, Harlequin Temptation®, Harlequin Superromance®, Harlequin Intrigue®, Harlequin American Romance®, or Harlequin Historicals® title available in February, March or April at your favorite retail outlet, together with the Free Gift Certificate, plus a check or money order for $1.65 U.S./$2.15 CAN. (do not send cash) to cover postage and handling, payable to Harlequin Free Gift Offer. We will send you the specified gift. Allow 6 to 8 weeks for delivery. Offer good until April 30, 1997, or while quantities last. Offer valid in the U.S. and Canada only.

Free Gift Certificate

Name: _____

Address: _____

City: _____ State/Province: _____ Zip/Postal Code: _____

Mail this certificate, one proof-of-purchase and a check or money order for postage and handling to: HARLEQUIN FREE GIFT OFFER 1997. In the U.S.: 3010 Walden Avenue, P.O. Box 9071, Buffalo NY 14269-9057. In Canada: P.O. Box 604, Fort Erie, Ontario L2Z 5X3.

FREE GIFT OFFER   084-KEZ
ONE PROOF-OF-PURCHASE
To collect your fabulous FREE GIFT, a cubic zirconia pendant, you must include this
original proof-of-purchase for each gift with the properly completed Free Gift Certificate.

084-KEZ

Happy Birthday to

It's party time....
This year is our
40th anniversary!

Forty years of
bringing you the best
in romance fiction—and
the best just keeps
getting better!

To celebrate, we're planning
three months of fun, and prizes.

Not to mention, of course,
some fabulous books...

The party starts in **April** with:

Betty Neels
Emma Richmond
Kate Denton
Barbara McMahon

Come join the party!

You're About to Become a *Privileged Woman*

Reap the rewards of fabulous free gifts and benefits with proofs-of-purchase from Harlequin and Silhouette books

Pages & Privileges™

It's our way of thanking you for buying our books at your favorite retail stores.

Harlequin and Silhouette— the most privileged readers in the world!

For more information about Harlequin and Silhouette's PAGES & PRIVILEGES program call the Pages & Privileges Benefits Desk: 1-503-794-2499

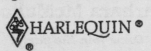